CHARLESTON'S DAUGHTER

Sabra Waldfogel

Cover Design: James Egan of BookFly Designs
Author Photograph: Megan Dobratz

978-0-9913964-2-9—ebook
978-0-9913964-7-4—print book

Sabra Waldfogel, Publisher
www.sabrawaldfogel.com

Published in Minneapolis, Minnesota

Table of Contents

Part 1: Widows and Orphans – 1858   1

   Chapter 1: A Father's Love 3

   Chapter 2: A Matter of Conscience 24

   Chapter 3: Goods and Chattels 53

   Chapter 4: The Basket Name 74

Part 2: A Fragile Freedom – 1859   107

   Chapter 5: Hearth and Home. 108

   Chapter 6: Free Persons of Color 144

   Chapter 7: A Southern Voice 177

   Chapter 8: Love Is Sweet 198

   Chapter 9: Sumter County 222

   Chapter 10: Freedom Is Sweeter 238

   Chapter 11: The Abolitionist 273

   Chapter 12: The Badge of Servitude 296

   Chapter 13: The Purloined Letter 321

Part 3: Confederates in Slavery – 1860   343

   Chapter 14: Slaves Have No Mothers 344

   Chapter 15: You Must Be Mad 374

   Chapter 16: We Are All Slaves Now 394

   Chapter 17: The Northern Star 432

Historical Note 458

Further Reading 463

If You Enjoyed This Book 464

Author Biography 466

PART 1

Widows and Orphans

1858

Chapter 1: A Father's Love

CARO LINGERED IN THE DOORWAY of her mother's room to watch as Bel brushed her mother's gleaming dark hair.

"Don't pull so, Bel," her mother said.

Bel was sixteen. She was as brown as a pecan and spoke with the thick accent of her home in the Low Country. She had just arrived at the Jarvie house on St. Helena Island, an hour's ferry ride south of Charleston. Caro's father, softhearted about all his servants, had asked her mother to take her on as a lady's maid, even though Bel had been a kitchen maid all her life.

"I'm sorry, ma'am," Bel murmured.

"It's all right. Give me the brush."

Bel extended the brush as though it were a stirring spoon. Her mother pulled it from Bel's hand with a sigh of exasperation. "I'll do it."

When Caro was very small, she loved to watch her mother at her dressing table as she brushed her hair. Caro had loved the hairbrush, too, a shining tortoiseshell with a gleaming silver inlay. Her father had given her a similar brush on her last birthday, and as a further extravagance, he'd had it engraved with her initials, *CJ*, for Caroline Jarvie.

Bel hunched a little as she waited. She muttered, "Ma'am, do you still need me?"

"No. Go downstairs and see if you can help Dulcie." Dulcie was the cook.

Bel ducked her head. "Yes, ma'am." Her footsteps echoed heavily on the back stairs.

Kitty sighed. "She acts like she's fresh from the rice field," she said. It was unfair. She brushed her own hair and asked Caro, "Do I look all right?"

Caro put her hands on her mother's shoulders and regarded the dual reflection in the dressing table mirror. "You look lovely, Mama," she said. Twice Caro's age, her mother was as beautiful as ever and as proud of praise.

Kitty turned to kiss her on the cheek. "You, too," she said.

"We look just alike," Caro said, teasing her.

She ignored it. "Is the dress all right?"

Their similar looks were enhanced by their similar dresses, pretty and made from lightweight cotton, suitable for a warm summer evening at home. Her father liked to see his ladies well-dressed, even if they didn't go out. "As pretty as mine."

Kitty shook her head. "Hand me my earbobs. The diamonds."

The diamond earrings had been a gift from her father when Caro was born. When her mother tossed her head, the diamonds flashed, and the gold gleamed. They dazzled, like the slender, dark-eyed woman whose figure showed no evidence of having borne a daughter eighteen years ago or of having conceived and lost two children since.

Kitty regarded herself in the mirror again and nodded in satisfaction. She held out her arm. "Shall we? Your father is waiting."

She walked with a sprightly step as they descended the mahogany staircase, which was gleaming from its weekly polish. She glanced at the portraits on the staircase wall. "Dusty," she said. "Someone isn't doing her duty."

Caro peeked at the portraits, which were glossy enough to show the dust. They were pictures of her father as a young man and the wife he had married when he was young. Caro didn't mind seeing a coat of dust on Eliza Herriot's flawless face. Eliza had been an heiress as well as a beauty, bringing her own holdings in Colleton County to add to her new husband's, giving him a thousand acres and five hundred slaves, making him a wealthy planter as well as a successful Charleston lawyer.

She had disappointed him in only one thing: no child had ever survived, and the last one had killed her. After Eliza's death, James Jarvie bought the house on St. Helena Island as a retreat, not a plantation, and he had buried himself here in grief.

Caro and her mother paused at the foot of the stairs.

From the dining room came the soft sound of the table being set. And a voice, not at all soft.

"She tell me I pull her hair like I ain't suited to be a lady's maid," Bel said.

"Talk low," said Dulcie.

Aggrieved, Bel did not. "Missus Kitty! Missus High and Mighty, and her daughter, too."

"Bel," Dulcie said, a tone very like a growl.

"Why shouldn't I say it? Don't care how light-skinned they are. How fine they dress. Diamond earbobs!" She snorted. "They slaves, the same as you and me."

Dulcie said, "Hush."

They walked into the dining room, Kitty's step light, her head high. She said, "I heard that."

Both slaves looked up in surprise.

She continued, "But Mr. Jarvie considers me the mistress of the house. Bel, if you don't care to obey me, I can send you to the kitchen. Or back to Colleton County to the field. Would you prefer that?"

Bel dropped her eyes. She whispered, "No, ma'am."

"Go. I need to talk to Dulcie."

When Bel was gone, Dulcie said, "She full of herself, Miss Catherine."

Twenty years ago, Dulcie and Kitty had been servants together, housemaid and kitchen maid. Now Kitty acted as the mistress of the house, and Dulcie obeyed her. Her mother had treated Dulcie with kindness. She had persuaded Caro's father to employ Dulcie's whole family as house servants, and Dulcie had the satisfaction of seeing her husband serve as the Jarvie coachman and her children as her assistants in the kitchen.

Now Kitty said, "Teach her. And if you can't, speak to me."

"I'll do that, Miss Catherine."

Caro tightened her arm around her mother's. "Papa is waiting," she reminded Kitty.

Her mother shook her head as though to clear it. "We won't disappoint him," she said, smiling. Arm in arm, they sauntered into her father's study as though nothing had ever troubled either of them.

Caro loved her father's study. It was full of the books he had bought as a student at Princeton, the tomes he had acquired when he read the law, and all the books since that he read for his own pleasure. Their leather bindings had a living smell, more so on a warm day, and she never minded that their covers gave up their reddish color to stain her hands.

Her father preferred the ancients, in particular Cicero and Cato, and he had taught Caro Latin so she could read them for herself. But he also read history, telling her that it gave an educated person a better perception for the present. He didn't disdain novels. He was glad that she liked Sir Walter Scott and Charles Dickens, and he bought the newer authors for her, too, like Nathaniel Hawthorne and Herman Melville. It was an unusual education for a girl, more so for a girl of color. And it was an even better gift than the hairbrush.

SABRA WALDFOGEL

He sat in his favorite armchair, the red velvet shiny from years of use, and put down his book. "Macaulay," he said to Caro. "Since I asked you to read it and give me your opinion."

He looked older than the man in the portrait. The gold of his hair had dulled a little, and his face no longer had a boy's smoothness. But his blue eyes were as lively as they had been in his youth, and now they were full of affection.

He rose and put his arm around Kitty's waist. "You look beautiful, my dearest," he said, smiling, and he kissed her cheek with more passion than was usually shown in a downstairs room. He hugged Caro with his free arm. "You look lovely, too," he said. "My darling girls, both of you."

"Is Mr. Pereira here yet?" Kitty asked.

"He's waiting in the parlor."

"Is he here on legal business?"

Benjamin Pereira, who lived in Charleston, was her father's lawyer, but he was a friend as well. He was the only Charleston man who regularly came to visit.

"It's good to sit at the table with Mr. Pereira," Caro said, too bitterly.

"Caro!" Her mother's voice held a warning.

"Papa, I wish—how I wish—that we could sit at the table whenever your guests come."

He shook his head. "Don't wish for such a thing," he said, very softly. "You know how it pains me to say no to you." He squeezed Kitty's hand as he spoke to Caro, and they left the room together.

She hadn't forgotten the dinner her father gave for the families of the island, even though it had been months ago. He had put it off and put it off until her mother was the one to say, "James, you have to invite them." Her mother had seen to the dinner and directed the servants to ready the house. But before the guests arrived, she took Caro upstairs, retreating to her room to stay in the limbo between family and servant.

Dulcie's daughter Peggy, who served as kitchen maid, brought up their meal. Peggy set the tray down on the piecrust table. She asked Kitty, "Ma'am, is there anything else you need?" Peggy, like Dulcie, had a strong Low Country accent. She said, "Is dere anyt'ing else?"

"No, Peggy. You go on."

On the tray was the dinner put before the guests—the oysters, the shrimp remoulade, and the roast, accompanied by rice and greens—but Caro pushed it away.

As the gentlemen arrived, their voices floated up the stairs, and as they settled into the dining room, their conversation came to Caro and her mother in bursts. The claret they drank made them louder. "Still no Mrs. Jarvie?" someone asked, and the others laughed.

Even now, her father was considered a catch, and all the families of Charleston and the Low Country hoped against hope that he would marry again. Caro hated it, but she knew that the world would never admit that he was already married to her mother.

She was old enough to understand how it had happened, even though no one had explained it to her.

How did a pretty, light-skinned housemaid catch the eye of the widowed planter who owned her? However it had begun, it blossomed into a genuine affection, and once her mother was certain of her father, she allowed herself to feel something besides obligation. After Caro was born, her father gave up any pretense of trying to marry again. He had found the woman he loved, and he loved Caro as his child with equal tenderness.

He had gone to the countryside to bury himself in grief. He stayed there to protect Kitty and Caro and to keep them a secret.

❧

Today, Pereira rose from his chair in the parlor in greeting. "James," he said, shaking his friend's hand. "Miss Catherine," he said, clasping Kitty's fingers, as he would for any lady. And in a teasing tone, since he had watched her grow up, he added, "And young Miss Caroline. You get prettier every day. Married in no time."

Caro blushed. "I get smarter every day, too," she retorted. Pereira knew that her father had educated her.

Kitty said, "And saucier as well."

That made Pereira laugh. Benjamin Pereira wasn't a planter. He was the son of a Portuguese Jew from London who had made his money as a merchant. Like her father, Pereira had read the law, but he practiced it and made a living by it, handling the affairs of men many times richer than himself. He was clever, diligent, and discreet. He kept all the family secrets of the men he served, the debts incurred by bad harvests and extravagance at the gaming table, and the surprises and the embarrassments written into the wills. He was younger than James was, with curly black hair and a swarthy complexion that would have cast a shadow over his life in Charleston if he and his family were not so well-known. But his eyes were a blue startling in a man descended from Portuguese Jews.

In the dining room, where the windows had been closed and the curtains drawn against the day's heat, both were now open to catch the afternoon breeze. The August sunlight slanted over the table, giving the gold-edged English china a greater gilding and turning the claret in the crystal glasses a fiery ruby color. At the long table, big enough for a party of a dozen, they clustered together at one end en famille.

Pereira asked, "What are you reading these days, Miss Caroline?"

She threw a glance at her father. "Thomas Macaulay," she said. "When I'm not translating Cicero."

Pereira said, "James, you're giving the girl a young man's education. A lawyer's education. Whatever will she do with it?"

Her father smiled. "She'll comfort her father in his old age."

"Why shouldn't I go to college, as you did?" Caro teased them both.

Her father teased her in return. "As soon as Princeton College will allow it," he said.

Caro knew as well as he did that the thought of a colored girl at Princeton College was a folly they could all laugh about together. But she knew something else. "There is a college that would admit a young woman of color," she said.

"Is there?" Pereira asked.

"It's called Oberlin College, and it's in Ohio."

Laughing, Pereira said, "Oberlin College! A nest of vipers, from what I hear. Mad against slavery."

Kitty said, "Stop it, both of you. Don't lead her on so." Her mother's glance said, *Don't disappoint her so.*

Caro sighed and fell silent. After the plates were cleared away, when the men retired to the study, Caro followed her mother to sit in the back parlor.

Unlike the front parlor, heavy with mahogany and velvet from an earlier generation and where portraits of previous Jarvies stared disapprovingly from the walls, the back parlor was Kitty's room, a lady's room, bright with new chintz and dainty in its furnishings. Her mother lit the candles against the coming dusk. Outside, the crickets had begun to rasp and the nighttime mosquitoes to whine. The air that came through the open windows smelled of magnolia and the faint odor of the midden from the kitchen, unavoidable in the heat.

Kitty arranged herself on the settee, laying the most recent copy of *Godey's Lady's Book* on her lap, and gestured to Caro to sit next to her. She laid a light hand on Caro's arm. "Caro, don't sulk. Come look at what's newest. Shall we show it to our dressmaker to be in the latest fashion?"

Her father indulged both of them in the matter of finery. He had their dresses made by a modiste in Charleston.

Caro didn't reply. Kitty coaxed her. "You'll need a new dress or two."

"For the season?" Caro was sharp. "As though we have one!"

"Oh, Caro," her mother said, a tone of sorrow. "You know why we don't."

The conversation at the table still bothered her. "I wish I had some reason to wear it besides showing it to Papa." She knew better, but she pressed the point. "Like going to a maroon or a ball. As the free people of color in Charleston do."

The free colored families had a "season," just as the planter families did. Her mother's half brother and half sister, residents in Charleston, were free, but Kitty was estranged from them, and Caro had never met them. Their freedom was a sore point with her mother. Caro had never learned the particulars of why they were free and her mother was not, and the estrangement between Kitty and her Bennett relatives had never been explained, either.

Kitty said, "Don't worry, Caro. We'll get you married somehow."

"How? If we have no society, neither white nor colored?"

Kitty didn't reply. Caro said, "Papa doesn't know what we'll do about it." She needled her mother. "And neither do you."

With unusual severity, her mother said, "Caro, it won't be settled tonight. There's plenty of time to consider it. It isn't seemly for you to pick at me or your father. Stop it."

Caro rose.

Kitty asked, "Where are you going?"

"Upstairs to use the necessary. Is that all right?"

Kitty shook her head. "You're as impertinent as that girl Bel," she said.

"I'm the daughter of the house, and I can be as impertinent as I like," Caro said, and she slipped into the hallway to stand in the spot where she could overhear everything that was said in the study.

Her father's voice was audible through the closed door. "Ben, I need your advice about Caro."

Pereira sighed. "You can't free her, Jim."

"I know. Not if the petition for manumission has to go to the Assembly."

"That damnable law. They've never approved one."

"They have. Just one. They freed the slave who unmasked Denmark Vesey's plot for a slave uprising."

"You can write it into your will, but you can't enforce it," Pereira reminded him.

In a brooding tone, her father said, "She's eighteen, and she's old enough to be married. Who will she marry?"

So he was worried about it, as much as she and her mother were.

Pereira said, "You've educated her beyond a marriage to a man who's a slave."

"There are educated men of color," her father said.

Pereira drew in his breath in a hiss so loud that Caro could hear it in the hallway. His older brother Jacob, now dead, had remained a bachelor all his life. But he had been faithful to a free woman of color and had provided for all four children they had together. Caro knew the story well, because the woman was her mother's estranged half sister, Maria.

Her father said, "Like Maria's boys. How old are they now?"

Pereira said, "They're kin to Miss Catherine, too. Certainly you could make an inquiry...send her to call on them...ask them to help."

"Kitty is bitter against them. She won't say why."

Caro heard a chair creaking. Pereira must have risen. He said, "Her own notion isn't a bad one. To go north to Ohio. If you sent her to Oberlin, she would be safe there, and she would have the society of others like herself."

"Send her away?" her father asked.

Pereira said, "She could live as if she were free."

Her father hesitated, and when he spoke there was a catch in his voice. "I want to keep her close just a while longer," he said. "No wedding, and no thought of Ohio."

⁎⁎

THE NEXT DAY DAWNED AS HOT as the one before. In the dining room, on the sideboard, eggs and biscuits stayed warm in the chafing dishes, and beside them last night's shrimp remoulade made a reappearance, having spent the night chilled in a block of ice from the ice house.

It was so hot that Caro had little appetite. She nibbled at a biscuit, buttering each bite before she ate it in the genteel manner her mother had taught her.

"James?" her mother asked, noticing that her father hadn't eaten much, either. "Are you feeling all right?"

He smiled. He looked pale, and there were dark circles under his eyes. "Just a little headache," he said. "It's nothing."

"Shall I get you a draught of laudanum?"

"No, don't trouble yourself," he said. "It's nothing. The heat." He smiled at her as he spooned eggs and shrimp onto his plate. "Don't worry," he assured her. "I'm all right."

But he ate nothing, and by the end of the meal, he looked paler than before. He touched his fingers to his temple. "I believe I'll rest for a while," he said.

Kitty said, "I'll make up a draught of laudanum. You go back upstairs and lie down."

A headache might be a trifle that laudanum and a nap could treat, and it might be the first symptom of fever. Summer fever was serious. Black people usually recovered, but white people sickened and often died. Caro began to worry. She sat in the study and tried to read, but Macaulay didn't hold her attention. Everything in the study reminded her of her father, and it increased her worry. She moved to the back parlor and tried to hem a handkerchief. Her hands shook, and she stabbed herself with the needle and soiled the cloth with a drop of blood.

Her mother found her sucking the blood from her finger. Kitty said, "Caro, don't do that. It's unseemly. Ask Bel to bring you a sticking plaster, and use the thimble next time."

"How is he, Mama?"

"He's sleeping. I hope he's better when he wakes."

"What if he isn't?"

"Caro, stop it. People get headaches all the time in the heat. Don't fret."

"You're worried. I can see it."

Kitty shook her head. She had seen fever, too. "Don't make it worse," she said.

Despite their admonitions to each other, they worried. Every hour, Kitty ran upstairs, and every hour she reported, "He's still asleep." They ate a makeshift midday dinner that neither of them had an appetite for. Afterward, Kitty visited James again. She came down the stairs with an anxious expression on her face. "Tell Dulcie to make up some lavender water," she said. "Tell her to use the ice."

"So it is fever," Caro said, her voice rising in alarm.

"There are all kinds of fever," Kitty said.

"Summer fever."

"Most recover. Both of us had it, and we recovered."

"Fever!" Caro cried. "Why don't we go to the pines in the sickly season? Why do we stay in the Low Country, where people get fever?"

"As though we could stay in Sumter County or in a hotel in Aiken! Lavender water," Kitty repeated. "Tell Dulcie, and tell her not to dawdle with it."

Caro brought a cloth and the bowl of water, icy to the touch and faintly fragrant of lavender, up the stairs, where her mother sat at her father's bedside. The room had begun to smell of the sweat of fever. Caro handed her mother the cloth and held the bowl as Kitty dipped it into the water to bathe James's forehead, which was greasy with sweat.

He tried to smile at the cool touch of the cloth. He said softly, "That helps me."

"Hush," her mother said. "Don't tax yourself."

He lay back on the pillows, and she draped the cloth over his forehead. "Caro?" he asked. "Will you sit with me, my love?"

"Yes, Papa."

"Give me your hand." He squeezed her hand with his, which seemed hot, as though his fingers were fevered, too. "It's only a little fever. You had it. Do you remember?"

She remembered very well. She had been sick for days, her head pounding, her body burning. The doctor had come to purge her, and she was so nauseated that she needed no encouragement. She had slipped into a delirium, and through it, she had heard her mother weep and her irreligious father say, "It's in God's hands now, Kitty."

"I nearly died of it!" she cried.

He winced, and she was immediately repentant. He said faintly, "Thank God you did not."

Kitty said sharply, "Caro, that's enough. If you can't speak in a low voice and talk about something more cheering, I'll send you downstairs."

"No, let her stay," James whispered. "It does me good, knowing that both of you are here." He touched her cheek. "Oh, Caro," he said. "Cara." He had taught her a little Italian, too, and even now, the endearment stirred her.

The next morning, he was no better, and her worried mother sent for the doctor, who told them what they already knew. He recommended bleeding and an emetic. James said weakly, "Just let me rest." Kitty sent the doctor away.

Caro rose and beckoned to her mother. In the hallway, she whispered, "He's worse."

"Fever is like that," Kitty said stubbornly. "Worse before it's better."

ℰᴑℭℜ

KITTY SPENT THE NIGHT AT James's bedside, refusing any help. Caro lay sleepless across the hall. She woke every hour, yanked from sleep in a sweat of fear.

At daybreak, she threw back the covers and put on her dressing gown. The door to her father's room was ajar. Her mother had fallen asleep in the bedside chair. In sleep, she had released her grip on James's hand, and her fingers trailed against the skirt of her dress. Her father lay under the covers, his hair damp and his long, lanky body diminished.

Caro tapped on the door, and her mother's eyes flew open. Startled, confused, she said, "What is it?"

"How is he?" Caro whispered.

He stirred and spoke through cracked lips. "Caro? Is that you?"

"Yes, Papa." She slipped into the room.

With effort, he opened his eyes. His eye whites had turned yellow, the telltale sign of yellow fever. "Sit with me, Caro," he said, his voice as cracked as his lips.

Her mother saw the yellowed eyes, and she rose, pressing her hand to her mouth to stifle a cry.

Caro said softly, "Mama, rest for a little. I'll stay with him."

"You'll fetch me—"

"Yes. Mama, rest."

As Kitty left, her father whispered, "What is it, Caro? What's happened to make her weep so?"

"She sat with you all night. She slept in this chair. She's tired, Papa. You rest too. Do you want anything?"

He shook his head. She reached for his hand and cradled it in her own. She thought, *Not everyone dies of yellow fever. Perhaps Mama is right, and he'll recover.*

But his skin also began to yellow, another telltale that he was worse. They gave up all pretense of doing anything else and both of them stayed with him all the time, each of them holding a hand, getting up only to bathe his forehead or to run downstairs to ask Dulcie to replenish the warmed water with water newly chilled. Whenever he opened his eyes, Caro felt a stab of fear.

They were the ungodly yellow of the yolk of a hardboiled egg.

When her mother descended the stairs with the water basin, Caro whispered, "Papa? Can you hear me?"

"Of course."

"Can you forgive me for the trouble I've caused you?"

"You've never caused me trouble," he said. "None at all."

"For the time I argued with you about the season." She had raged and cried about being denied a season last winter, even though she knew the reason perfectly well. He had sent her to the dressmaker for an extravagant new dress that no one would ever see besides her mother and himself.

He said, "You were so pretty in that dress." He opened his yellowed eyes again. She bent her head and bit her lips.

ဢၑ

HE REFUSED FOOD, SAYING THAT he was too sick to his stomach to eat. Kitty ignored him and brought in a bowl of broth. He choked at the smell, and Caro brought the basin just in time, the pretty Meissen slop basin that ordinarily held the pitcher for his shaving water. Caro put her hand to her mouth in horror at the sight. The vomit was black with blood.

It was the worst sign, the last sign. Caro's eyes met her mother's, and Kitty looked away but not before the tears leaked from her eyes.

Caro removed the basin and wiped her father's mouth. He tried to smile. "Thank you," he whispered. He lay back on the pillow. "Stay with me, both of you." He took their hands, one in each of his own, as he often did at the dinner table instead of saying grace. They sat by his bedside, each of them clasping the weak, paper hand. He opened his eyes, yellow swallowing up the familiar blue. He said, "I'm dying."

In a voice thick with tears, Kitty said, "James, no."

"Oh, beloved," he said. He lay back on the pillows, gathering strength. He pressed their hands with a shadow of his former strength. Unable to raise his voice, he said, "I've tried to take care of you."

"Yes," Kitty said, her eyes full. "You always have."

"To make provision for you," he said, his voice slender as a thread.

Kitty squeezed one hand and Caro the other. Kitty nodded and let the tears slip down her face. Caro, worried for them both, stifled a sob.

They sat with him, bathing his forehead and holding his weakening hands until the fever closed his eyes and stilled his voice. They watched until his breath became shallow and listened as it turned into a rale. When it stopped, early in the morning, the room was lovely with sunlight, and the air was very still. The scent of magnolia and rot came through the open window, and the smell of fever and lavender water lingered in the room.

Still holding his hand, her mother bent over his body to kiss his lips. Her tears fell on his cheeks.

Her father, who wanted to keep her close forever, who wanted to take care of her forever, was gone. Caro took his hand, still warm, and pressed it to her cheek. "Caro," she whispered, her own name and the word for a man beloved.

Chapter 2: A Matter of Conscience

EMILY JARVIE; HER FATHER, Lawrence; and her step-mother, Susan, sat at breakfast in the dining room of the house in Sumter County that Susan's money had improved from a modest four-up-and-down structure into a house befitting a well-to-do planter. Her father shielded himself behind the newspaper sent from Charleston. He planned to run for election to the South Carolina Assembly in the fall, and his lawyer's gaze never wavered from politics in Charleston, even in the quiet of their summer's retreat.

She watched the curtains billow with the breeze that made the summer air of Sumter County so much cooler than Charleston's. As she buttered a biscuit, the butler hurried into the room with a letter on a tray, a worried look on his usually placid face.

"What is it, Marcus?" Lawrence asked.

"Sorry to disturb you, suh." Marcus had the accent of the Low Country, cleaned up for the big house. "Letter just come for you."

Her father took it from the tray. Susan asked, "Who is it from?"

"Benjamin Pereira. I know him but not well. He's a lawyer in Charleston."

And so was her father himself. Emily knew that the lawyers of Charleston clustered together on Broad Street, as the turkey buzzards clustered at the Charleston Market.

Susan drew her brows together. "Why is he writing to you?"

Her father opened the envelope and unfolded the letter. At the sight of the black border, Emily's heart sank.

Her father read it and said slowly, "My brother James died yesterday."

Emily had met her Uncle James, her father's elder brother, only once, when she was very small. She had a shadowy memory of a tall, slender, smiling man with a cap of golden hair. He had knelt and spoken to her with affection, as though he were used to talking to a little girl.

"We didn't even know he was ill!" Susan exclaimed.

Lawrence shook his head. "It was sudden," he said. "Yellow fever."

"When is the funeral?"

Her father gazed at a spot beyond his wife's head. His face, usually so taut and composed, seemed to sag. "Mr. Pereira asks us to go there to arrange it," he said.

Susan shook her head. "Is there no one else?"

Now her father shook his head. "It will fall to us. How soon can we go there?"

"Must we hurry?" Susan asked. "You were estranged!"

Her father's eyes clouded. "Yes, we were," he said.

Emily knew that her uncle had left Charleston after his wife died, abandoning his law practice and a career that was expected to lead to a judge's seat. He had remained on St. Helena Island since, refusing invitations to the season in Charleston or to the healthier summer air of the hills and the pines. He had always remembered her, the niece he had rarely seen, by sending her a book on her birthday. The most recent gift had been a peculiar one for an unmarried girl. He had sent her a copy of *Moby-Dick*.

Emily looked absently out the window. The conversation between her father and stepmother was familiar yet far away, like the sound of the quarrelsome jays that lived in the woods beyond the house. She stared at her hands, which were very pale in her lap against the black of her dress. Emily had been in mourning for more than a year. Her betrothed, Robert Herriot, had died two months before the wedding, and she had mourned Robert as though they had already married. Her hand went to her throat, where she still wore the brooch made of a lock of his hair.

At nineteen, Emily was well practiced in mourning. When she was twelve her mother died in childbed, and she had put on black for the first time. Her father, not knowing what to do with her, had sent her to Madame Devereaux's Charleston academy for young ladies. Even though her father lived in Charleston as well, she became a boarder who went home only twice a year. When she returned for her second summer, her father had remarried. Susan was kind to her and didn't pretend to be her mother. She didn't mind that Emily liked to read or that she spent so much time writing in her diary. When Lawrence complained that Emily preferred the company of books to society, whether in the house in Charleston or the pines of Sumter, Susan would say, "Poor chick. She still misses her mother. Don't press her, Lawrence."

She sighed.

Susan touched her arm in affection and asked, "What is it, my dear?"

"Another funeral to attend."

Susan said, "Not a great grief, though. Only a duty." She stroked the black sleeve of Emily's dress. "Only a few days on St. Helena to put things in order."

Emily's eyes filled with tears. She thought of Robert's death and his funeral, as she had every day since he was buried, and again she touched the brooch at her throat.

෫)෬

HER FATHER SEEMED DIMINISHED, shorter, quieter. In the depot of Stateburg, he bought their train tickets in silence, and once on the train, he left Emily and Susan in the first-class carriage and decamped for the smoking car, where men spat and drank in a fug of tobacco.

"Goodness," her stepmother said. "I've never seen him so quiet."

Emily smoothed the heavy black silk of her skirt and turned to gaze out the window at the familiar landscape. They never traveled from Stateburg to Charleston in the summer. That was the autumn journey, once the heat had broken and Charleston was safe from fever. It was peculiar to watch the pines disappear and to feel the summer's heat come through the windows. She shook her head but didn't reply, and her stepmother, who didn't feel right unless she was talking to someone, struck up a conversation with a lady across the aisle.

Her father didn't reappear until the train stopped in Charleston. He found a carriage to take them to the wharf for the last leg of the journey on the ferry to Beaufort. When Emily was a little girl—when her mother was still alive—it had been fashionable to spend summers on the Sea Islands in the belief that they were more healthful than Charleston. As they boarded the ferry—just like the river steamer she recalled from childhood—she had a vivid memory of standing at the railing beside her mother. Her mother's lavender scent had wafted toward her, softening the salty, marshy smell of the inlets that marked this part of the coast. Her mother had put her arm around Emily's shoulders and drawn her close. In her soft voice, she had said, "Do you recall how much pleasure we had last year? You'll see all your friends again."

Now, on the boat, Susan found a spot in the saloon and insisted that Lawrence sit with them at the little iron table. She waved away the slave who offered them refreshment. She said, "Lawrence, sit still. There are arrangements to be made."

Her father shifted in his chair. "Once we get there," he said.

"There's so much to do. A funeral to plan and then the estate to settle." Despite her father's air of command, Emily knew full well that her stepmother was the real manager in the Jarvie household. Her father would write the bank drafts, but her stepmother would arrange for the funeral service and the funeral breakfast.

Her father nodded but didn't speak.

"And the houses to look after. That big place in Colleton County, and the grand house in Charleston. The Herriot house! It's yours now." Her father didn't reply, and Susan said happily, "I wouldn't mind living in Charleston in a house like that."

"Not yet, Susan."

She leaned forward. "We can plan, can we not? What we'll do once you become the head of the family?"

Her father raised his head. There was a spot of red on his pale cheeks. "Not yet. Not now."

"Grieving or not, there is so much to take care of—"

Her father pressed his hands against the edge of the table with such force that his knuckles showed white. "Stop it!" he said, raising his voice. "It's not seemly!" He rose and strode to the railing. He stared out at the water with a rigid posture that recalled his youthful days at the military academy where he had studied as a cadet.

Susan said to Emily, "There was no love lost with James. I don't know what's gotten into him."

Emily thought, *I believe I do*, and she rose to follow him. She leaned against the railing without speaking.

He spoke so softly that she had to lean close to hear

him. "I always hoped that we might speak again, James and I," he said. "That we might reconcile someday."

She turned her head. To her surprise, her father covered her hand with his own, and she let it rest there. Even more softly, he said, "And now we never will."

She didn't reply, and they looked over the water together.

ဢာ

AT THE PIER IN BEAUFORT, they were met by a servant who introduced himself as the Jarvie coachman. He was a short man with bowed legs, his face weathered and seamed.

"What is your name?" her father asked.

"Henry, suh."

"Have you been with the family long?"

"All my life, suh. My wife, Dulcie, too. She the cook."

"Lawrence, let him load our trunks," Susan said. "You don't have to flatter him. He can't vote for you."

Emily was startled. Her stepmother was usually a staunch support to her father's ambition to the Assembly and to the family ambition, the judge's seat beyond it. She had told Emily that she would enjoy being the wife of a Charleston judge. James's death, which opened the prospect of a new standing in Charleston, had stirred new ambitions in her.

Her father's cheeks flamed red again, that spot like a dab of badly applied paint. "It never hurts to act the gentleman," he reminded his wife.

Emily felt a flash of irritation, but she laid her hand on Susan's arm. "You know that Papa will flatter anyone," she said. "It's in his nature." She tried to smile.

"That's enough," Susan said, shaking herself free and giving Henry a sharp look.

Henry said softly, "Missus, things in disorder with Marse James's passing. We all love him, and we upset. We try to do our best for you now."

Emily glanced at Henry, whose face was set in a perfect expression of contrition, and thought, *Who is the better flatterer?*

Even though her memory was old and faded, Emily recognized the houses along the road to her uncle's place. The plantations on St. Helena Island dated from the early years of the century before ostentation had overtaken country houses, and they were gracious two-story affairs, with porches on each story to catch the sea breezes, and were painted white to deflect the heat of summer. She had never visited her uncle's house, but when the coach pulled up, she felt at home. It was just like the houses where they had stayed when she was a child, and as she took it in, she imagined that she smelled lavender beneath the perfume of jessamine and the flowers the slaves called heshaberry.

When Lawrence helped them out, her stepmother rustled her skirts in her impatience. She admonished the coachman. "You take good care of those trunks."

Henry nodded and bent his head in deference. "Yes, Missus."

The door opened as they mounted the stairs. A light-skinned servant, his temples frosted with gray, stood in the doorway.

He said softly, "I'm so sorry, ma'am. We out of sorts here since Marse James passed on."

"I've come to do what I can," Susan announced. She swept past him, and Emily reluctantly followed.

The curtains had been drawn, and the house was hushed. Someone had covered the mirror in the entry-way, and the grandfather clock in the corner had been stopped so it did not tick or strike the hour while the inhabitants grieved. In a house without a wife, Emily wondered who had thought to prepare the house for mourning like that.

"Where is Mr. Jarvie?" Susan asked the butler.

"Upstairs, ma'am. They laying him out."

"Take me up there."

The butler said, "Let me settle you for a moment in the parlor...bring you something."

Susan pulled off her gloves. "Show us upstairs."

Reluctantly, he led them up the wide staircase to the second floor and tapped on the bedroom door, which was ajar. A distracted voice called, "What is it, Ambrose?"

"Mrs. Lawrence Jarvie and her daughter, ma'am."

"Why did you bring them up? We aren't ready for them." From the room drifted the smell of rubbing alcohol and lavender.

Susan pushed past Ambrose and said, "We've come to make ourselves useful, if we can."

The deceased, clad in his nightshirt, lay on the coverlet, his body carefully straightened, his eyes closed. A dark-skinned servant in a neat gray dress and a clean apron held a basin of water. Another servant wrung a cloth into it. A tall, slender woman, dressed in deep mourning, bent over the dead man. Beside her stood a girl, also in the deepest mourning, her hand on the older woman's arm.

They were so fair of skin that at first, Emily didn't realize they were colored.

Susan addressed the older of the aproned women. "What's your name?" she demanded.

"Dulcie, ma'am." She dropped her eyes. Susan turned to the younger. "And you?"

"Bel, ma'am," she whispered.

Susan turned to the slender ivory-skinned woman in the dress of a widow. "And you?" she asked.

"I'm Mrs. Jarvie," she said, in a low tone.

As Susan's face registered surprise, she said, "Mrs. Catherine Bennett Jarvie." She gestured toward the girl. Her skin was lighter than the older woman's, but her expression was the same, all too familiar to Emily, the sheen of sleeplessness over the daze of grief. "This is my daughter, Miss Caroline Jarvie."

❧❧

SUSAN GRABBED EMILY'S HAND. She pulled Emily down the stairs and marched through the house, looking for the room where the butler had settled her husband. She found Lawrence in the study, sitting in a wing chair worn with use. *My uncle must have loved that chair*, Emily thought. A decanter sat on the table by her father's elbow, and the room smelled of warmed whiskey.

Susan flung her wadded gloves onto the table, next to the decanter. Lawrence looked up. "What is it?" he asked. "How bad is the disorder?" He sipped the whiskey. "They warned you."

Her stepmother dropped into a nearby chair, struggling for words. She said, "There's a slave woman in the house who calls herself Mrs. Jarvie."

"I beg your pardon?" her father asked.

Susan cried, "She thinks of herself as his wife!"

Her father's voice took on the lawyer's tone, the sound of a man who asked distraught people questions to get at the truth. "Are there children?"

"A daughter. Almost grown."

"And what does the girl call herself?"

Susan sent Emily an imploring glance. *Help me*, it said. *Be outraged along with me.* "Miss Jarvie," she said.

Emily spoke. "Her name is Caroline," she said.

Susan asked, "What possessed him?"

Emily thought, *Didn't you see it? How beautiful they are, both of them?* She recalled the look of dazed pain on both of those lovely, light-skinned faces. *And how stricken?*

Her father drained his glass. "So that's what he was hiding, living down here."

Susan said, "There's no thought of a funeral in Charleston. I can't imagine burying him at St. Michael's."

Her father shook his head.

"Lawrence, I don't care what they call themselves. They can't stay in the house!"

Emily, who had remained standing, could not forget the look of grief on Caroline's lovely face. She was louder and sharper than she intended. "Mother, leave them be! Let them grieve! Wait until after the funeral."

Susan turned to her and spoke with a fury Emily had never felt from her stepmother before. "Who asked you?"

೫಄

SUSAN'S INSISTENCE ON A HUSHED funeral meant that she declined to hold the service in Beaufort, which had a well-established Episcopal church. She went to the tiny church on St. Helena itself, called the "White Church" because it had no provision for slaves to worship there. The minister told Susan that he would make an exception for the servants at the funeral. "Let the people grieve for their master," he said. "He was a kindly man, and they loved him."

Emily saw Susan bristle. Did the minister know the truth?

Susan said, "If you can't accommodate them..."

"They can sit in the back pews, by the door," the minister said.

Her father said decisively, "Yes, we'll allow it."

"Lawrence—"

"Until after the funeral, Susan."

ℰℭℛ

WITH A NOISELESS STEP, EMILY entered the church flanked by her father and stepmother. It was melancholy to attend another funeral, since it reminded her so vividly of Robert's, when she had been so afflicted that she had buried her face in her handkerchief. Today, as at Robert's service, the air was hot and still, heavy with the lingering smell of Sunday's incense, the silence broken by the murmur of people greeting each other as they slid into the pews.

Emily lingered near the door, where the Jarvie slaves had been accommodated. The men were in black suits, the women in dresses hastily dyed black, all of them clustered together in a phalanx of mourning for their master. In their midst sat Catherine and Caroline Jarvie, who were clad in sumptuous black dresses. But they hadn't dared to wear the lady's mourning bonnet. They had wrapped their heads in the scarves of slaves and tied them in the manner of the Low Country, with the black silk ends resting on their heads like a butterfly's wings.

In the pew just ahead—also close to the door—sat a stranger, a slender man with a swarthy complexion. He wore black, as men usually did, but his face was drawn and pale, as though he had reason to grieve.

Susan pulled on Emily's hand to guide her where she belonged: in the front row, as one of the chief mourners.

℘)⊂℞

THE HURRIED FUNERAL HAD BEEN badly attended, and few people returned to the house to pay their respects. The black Jarvies had gone upstairs. The house was quiet, not the pleasant quiet of an afternoon nap, but the painful quiet of loss—talk silenced, laughter stilled, hope extinguished.

The white Jarvies sat in the study, awaiting James's lawyer. Susan asked, "When is he coming?"

Her father closed the paper, making it rustle, and said, "I told you. At two. Soon."

Susan said irritably, "Lawrence, don't rustle the pages so."

Emily knotted her hands in her lap and said nothing.

Susan said, "Pereira, you said his name was? Who are his people? I don't remember anyone with a Low Country place named Pereira."

Emily said, "I knew a girl named Mimi Pereira at Madame Devereaux's. Her father was a merchant. They're Israelites."

Lawrence said, "Mordecai Cohen is an Israelite, and he has a thousand acres and six hundred hands on the coast."

"But this man? I thought you said he was a Charleston lawyer, not a planter."

"I've seen him on Queen Street. We have professional acquaintance in common. I didn't say I knew him well. I will say that I'm not sure I can trust a man who doesn't set foot in a church."

"I shudder to think of what's in that will," Susan said.

Her father sat upright and winced as though his back hurt him. "We'll know soon enough."

At the sound of the knock on the door, they heard footsteps on the stairs. Before Ambrose could open the door, Catherine Jarvie's voice drifted from the foyer. "Let me greet him," she said, as though she were still mistress of the house.

They heard a low-pitched voice say, "Kitty. Caro. I am so sorry—"

Ambrose interrupted. "Mr. Pereira, suh, let me show you into the parlor."

Ambrose showed them in, and without asking, the two colored women entered, still in their black funeral dresses. They had removed the scarves; their heads were bare, their dark hair silky around their ears. Catherine Jarvie said, "Thank you, Ambrose." She extended her hand to Lawrence. "Mr. Jarvie," she said.

Her father stared at the hand, so graciously proffered. He said gruffly, "Surely you don't expect me to shake your hand."

The girl Caroline plucked at her mother's sleeve. "Mama," she said softly.

The room was so quiet that Emily could hear herself breathing. She shifted in her chair. She looked down at her hands. She was too uncomfortable to raise her head and look at the woman James had called his wife and the girl who was his daughter.

"Mr. Jarvie? We've met," Pereira said.

"There was no need for you to trouble yourself," her father said. "I'm capable of reading a will you know."

"Of course," Pereira said gently. "But you know, as well as I do, that no man should lawyer himself, especially in such melancholy circumstances."

Lawrence gestured toward the two colored women. "Why are they here?"

Pereira said, "They were close to your brother. He would have wished them to hear the provisions of the will."

When Pereira extended his hand to her, Emily recognized the stranger from the church. Her classmate Mimi Pereira had been blessed with bright-blue eyes, and the trait ran in the family because Benjamin Pereira had keen blue eyes in his swarthy face. *If I didn't know he was an Israelite,* Emily thought, *I might think he was colored.* Pereira was older than her father—he was probably close to James in age—but he carried himself with a surprising grace, the light and easy step of a man who might like to dance.

Emily wondered what kind of will her uncle and this nimble man had devised together.

Pereira said to no one in particular, "May I sit at the desk?" He opened the portfolio he carried and laid the will on the desk.

Seated, he began to read in a low, sonorous voice. "I, James Durand Jarvie, of the parish of St. Helena Island in the state of South Carolina, being of good health and sound mind and memory, declare that this is my last will and testament. I hereby direct that all my just debts, both funeral and testamentary expenses, be fully paid and satisfied as soon as possible after my death." He paused, as though reminding them, and continued. "I devise and bequeath to my brother Henry Lawrence Jarvie and his heirs and assigns all my lands at Colleton County in the state of South Carolina, the plantation and tract of land bequeathed to me by my father, John Jarvie, as well as the house, its contents, and the slaves upon it, as well as the house and lands on St. Helena Island. I also devise and bequeath to my brother Henry Lawrence Jarvie and his heirs and assigns my house in King Street in Charleston with all its contents. Item, I devise and bequeath to my niece, Emily Caroline Jarvie, a dozen books from my library, the particulars to be left to her discretion."

Startled, Emily thought, *To him I was still the little girl who liked to read.*

Pereira read, "I also devise and bequeath my aforementioned brother the following Negro slaves, who are employed as servants in my house." He paused, and Catherine and Caroline sat motionless. Emily would swear they had stopped breathing.

Pereira continued, "Ambrose; Henry; his wife, Dulcie; their daughters Peggy and Mattie; and their son, Hank; also Lydia and Bel."

All of them waited to hear what James Jarvie had devised for the other two.

Pereira read, "For my servant Catherine, also called Kitty, who has been so faithful to me, forsaking all others, and her daughter Caroline, also called Caro, beloved to me, I appoint my brother Henry Lawrence Jarvie to be their guardian and to treat them with kindness, as he would members of the family, and that he free them as soon as it becomes possible."

Pereira settled his gaze on Lawrence and read, "I do hereby nominate, constitute, and appoint my brother Henry Lawrence Jarvie executor of this, my will."

In the silence, Pereira added, "He added a list of the slaves on his plantation in Colleton County, as well as the livestock, and also an inventory of the contents of this house, including his carriage and horses. I won't read it, but you can examine it at your leisure, and let me know if you find any confusion or discrepancy."

Her father said, "Treat them as members of the family." The lawyer's tone, confirming his understanding.

"He felt that way about all his servants. That they were to be treated with kindness, as members of the family."

Her father's eyes swept over Catherine and Caro, who sat unmoving, their black dresses severe against the red velvet of the side chairs in which they sat. "He meant more than that."

Pereira said, "He meant for you to take care of them."

"How?"

"To make provision for them and to maintain them."

Her father's voice rose, as if he were making a point in the courtroom. "Did my brother leave anything for their maintenance? Did he set aside any money for it?"

"There's enough in the estate for that, as for the other servants."

"Did he really want me to free them?"

Both Catherine and Caroline flinched as though they had been slapped.

"In that, he trusted you to follow your conscience," Pereira said quietly.

Emily swallowed. She glanced at Caroline, a sidelong glance, and saw how she knotted her hands in her lap. She was so fair of skin that her knuckles showed white against the black dress.

To the look of exhaustion and grief on Caroline's face was added the pallor of shock. Emily dared to let her eyes linger on them both, the widow and the orphan, and felt their grief sing along her nerves and reverberate in her heart.

§∞C3

HER STEPMOTHER DISMISSED THE two women, and her father offered Mr. Pereira refreshment, which he declined, saying that the press of business summoned him back to Charleston. As soon as Ambrose closed the door behind him, Susan turned to Lawrence. She wrung her handkerchief in her hands as though she wanted to tear it asunder. She said, "We'll have to sell them."

Her father sat up with the straight spine of the military man that his father had wanted him to be. "I can't," he answered.

"Why not?"

"James has made his wishes clear."

Susan's eyes blazed, anger turning their blue dark and murky. "You never spoke to him when he was alive," she said. "You never considered him, not for a moment. Why do you let him order you now that he's in his grave?"

Her father flushed a feverish red. "I won't defy the provision of his will."

"Oh, nonsense! No one knows what the will says, except for us."

"And Pereira," her father said. He gestured toward the second floor. "And them."

"Lawyers don't tell secrets. Not if they want to do business." She gestured toward the second floor, too, the ragged handkerchief waving in the air. "And no one will listen to anything they say."

Her father leaned forward, but Susan interrupted his unspoken words. "When we get back to Charleston, we'll arrange it."

Her father leaned farther forward. Emily had never seen him look like that, his mouth so tight, his eyes so narrow. "The moment they go onto the auction block, everyone will know. It will no longer be a secret. Or a private shame. It will come into the full light of day. Do you want that?"

Her stepmother stared at her father as though he were a fool. "Not if you sell them in Mississippi or in New Orleans."

"As though slave dealers are discreet!"

Her stepmother continued to glare at the man she had married. "I won't have them in my house," she said. "I won't stand for that!"

Her father glared back at the woman he had promised to cherish. "We'll make some arrangement," he said.

☙☼❧

THE NEXT MORNING, AS EMILY read in the back parlor, her stepmother marched into the room, a bundle of cloth in her arms. "Emily, come with me."

Emily looked up from her book. "What is it, Mother?"

"I need you to help me." Two grim lines showed on either side of her stepmother's mouth.

Emily sighed and closed the book. She followed her stepmother up the stairs to the room that had been Kitty's. The door was closed, but her mother threw it open without knocking.

Kitty and Caro sat side by side on the bed, still dressed in their mourning finery. They held hands. Both raised their heads at the sight of Susan, but neither spoke.

Susan said, "Get up, both of you."

Wordlessly, still holding hands, they rose.

Susan said, "You can't stay in the house. You'll leave today."

"Where will we go?" Kitty asked.

"You'll call me ma'am," Susan said, her voice cold.

Kitty raised her eyes to Susan's. "Where will we go, ma'am?"

"There's a cabin for you on the nigger street."

Kitty drew in her breath in surprise. "The nigger street?"

"Don't talk back to me," Susan snapped.

"Wherever we go, we'll need some time to gather our things," Kitty said. "Ma'am."

Her stepmother's eyes flashed. "You won't take anything that's in the house." She added, "Not your dresses or your jewelry."

Kitty let her eyes linger on her new mistress's face. "James gave those things to me."

Susan said, "Your master's gifts don't belong to you. Nothing in this house belongs to you."

Caro clutched her mother's hand. "My books! Let me take my books."

"Books! Nothing leaves the house. None of it is yours," Susan repeated.

Emily spoke. "Mother, at least let her have a Bible."

"Bible! She shouldn't be able to read a book." Susan glowered at Emily. "And don't you think of giving her one!"

Susan had often been curt with her servants, but Emily had never heard her speak so hatefully to a slave. Susan snapped, "You'll leave those dresses."

Kitty stared at Susan, but Caro cried out, "Will we go away naked?"

Susan lifted the bundle she carried in her arms. "I've brought you clothes." She undid the bundle and handed it to Kitty. "Take off your clothes and put these on," she said.

Kitty shook out the bundle. It contained a brown dress in the roughest kind of cotton, a coarse white apron, and a headscarf of the same material. There was a cotton chemise to go under the dress, and it had been washed so many times that it was thin and grayish. The shoes were heavy and stiff, the kind the cobblers called nigger shoes. They were the clothes of slaves who labored in the rice fields.

Susan said, "Put them on."

Caro said, "I can't wear this! At least let me put on my muslin."

Susan grabbed Caro's free arm. "You'll do as I say, and you'll keep your mouth shut."

Kitty's eyes blazed. "Don't touch her," she said.

"Who are you to order me?"

Kitty's eyes blazed. "I was James's wife," she said.

Susan grabbed Kitty's wrist. "I'm not as soft as my husband," she said. "You'll do as I say, or you'll feel the lash. I'll do it myself." She tightened her grip on Kitty's wrist until Kitty winced in pain.

"Let her go!" Caro cried. "You're hurting her!"

Susan released Kitty's wrist and turned her attention to Caro. "That goes for you, too," she hissed. "I'll beat you and I'll relish it."

"You will not."

Susan slapped Caro on the face so hard that her hand left a red mark. Caro touched her face as though no one had ever slapped her before.

"Let her be," Kitty said.

Susan growled, "Undress, or I'll give her ten lashes, here and now."

Kitty stared at Susan. In a soft voice, full of contempt, she said, "You won't touch my daughter." Her hands went to the buttons on the front of her mourning dress. As Susan watched, she began to undo them.

"Mama," Caro said, her voice a plea. "Let me help you." She reached for Kitty's buttons.

Susan said, "Shall I slap you again?"

Kitty unbuttoned her dress.

In extreme discomfort, Emily said, "Mother, please. Leave them alone. Let them do this in privacy."

"Why should I? And why should you care if they strip down to the skin? They aren't ladies. They're slaves."

"I won't stay here to watch," Emily said thickly.

"Yes, you will. I need your eyes, too. I don't trust either of them."

Emily averted her eyes, but she could hear the sounds of undressing, as familiar as her own ritual before bedtime or a bath. The rustle of silk as it was unbuttoned. The swish of a crinoline as the wearer stepped out of it.

Kitty stood before her new mistress in her corset and her underthings.

"Didn't you hear me?" Susan snapped. "Everything comes off. Everything."

"My corset?"

"A slave doesn't need a corset!" Susan shouted.

Kitty stared at Susan as though her new mistress had gone mad. "Whatever do you want with my corset?"

Susan reached again for Caro's arm. "Ten lashes," she said.

Kitty's voice was thick with contempt. She said to Caro, "Unlace me."

"Mama!" Caro cried.

"Do it."

When the corset was on the floor at Kitty's feet, Susan said, "The rest."

Kitty unbuttoned her chemise and let it fall to the floor. Her face was stony. She unbuttoned her pantalettes, and they, too, slipped to the floor. She stepped out of them and stood naked before Susan.

Susan caught Emily by the hand. "Look at her. Not so proud now, is she?"

Emily caught a glimpse of round bosom, flat belly, gleaming thigh, dark fleece. The flash of Kitty's beauty brought a stain of shame to her face. It was a concubine's beauty, the nightmare of every planter's wife.

Kitty said, "Are you satisfied now, ma'am?"

Susan glanced at the earbobs that sparkled on Kitty's lobes. "The earbobs, too."

Kitty's voice faltered. "They were a gift from James."

"Which isn't yours to keep."

Kitty's hands rose protectively to her ears. "My memory of him."

Susan shouted, "Why should I care that you have a memory of the man who kept you? Take them off!"

Caro darted forward. "How dare you!" she cried.

Susan grabbed Caro by the wrist. "I'll call Ambrose to bring my husband's belt," she said. "The one with the heavy buckle."

A tear trickled down Kitty's face. She bit her lips as she took off one earbob, then the other.

"Give them to me," Susan said. The slender hand deposited the sparkling, gleaming jewelry in her step-mother's upturned palm. Susan's hand closed over the earbobs. "Get dressed," she ordered.

Emily turned away again, her ears alert to the scratch of the rough cloth being drawn over the skin and the sound of feet struggling into ill-fitting shoes.

Susan said, "The headscarf, too. Cover your hair. All of it."

Emily looked up. With unsteady fingers, Kitty wrapped the scarf around her head and tied it as she had tied her mourning scarf.

"Now you," Susan said, nodding at Caro.

Before Caro could speak, before she could get herself another threat of punishment, Emily said, "Mother, stop it. Go away. I'll stay with them."

"What's gotten into you, Emily?" Susan said.

Emily ground her teeth as she said, "Kindness."

"If they take anything—"

Emily cried, "Then you can give me ten lashes too!" She shoved her stepmother toward the door.

"Emily," Susan warned her, as she walked stiff-legged from the room.

Shaking, Emily said to Caro, "I won't watch. I'll turn my back." She felt as though she might faint. "Tell me when you're ready." She turned away, staring at the clothes press, listening to Kitty's voice, a soft murmur, as she helped Caro with her buttons, her crinoline, and her corset laces and as Caro donned the dress and the shoes.

In the same soft voice, Kitty said, "Miss Emily."

Emily turned. They were unrecognizable, their beauty and dignity gone. With the shapeless dresses, the head-scarves that obscured their faces, and the heavy shoes, they looked like the poorest kind of slaves just up from the rice fields, who spoke Gullah so thick that educated people couldn't understand them. For a wild moment, Emily wondered if their cultivated speech would disappear along with their silk dresses and their ladies' underthings.

"Emily?" Susan called from the landing. "Are they ready?"

"Yes," Emily said.

"Send them down. The back stairs!"

Caro's face was dark with grief and anger. Emily turned away, unable to look or watch them go.

€↾

EMILY WANTED THE RETREAT OF her own room, but on the landing, she hesitated. The door to the room that had been Caro's was ajar. She slipped inside.

Like everything in the house, the room had been neglected. The bed was messily made inside its cage of mosquito netting, and clothes lay heaped on the bedside chair. Beneath the disorder, it was unmistakably a girl's room. The bed, a four-poster on a small scale, had been painted white, and the coverlet, also white, was embroidered with roses and lilies. The dressing table was covered with girlish trinkets: a rosewood box, a lace collar, and a hairbrush, tortoiseshell like her own. It was finer than her own, inlaid with silver, the initials too ornate to read.

She reached for a discarded dress and shook it out. It smelled of cedar to deter moths, and it was whole and soft in her hands. She stood before the dressing table mirror and held the dress against herself. She leaned forward, startled by the sight of herself in a color other than black.

As she handled the dress, it released another scent, a faint fragrance of lilies of the valley and an even fainter tang of sweat, Caroline's odor. The smell was too intimate. It was like a touch on the cheek.

Shaken, she thrust the dress away and let it drop back on the chair.

In the corner of the room stood a mahogany writing desk, and on the desk sat a crystal inkwell. On the well-used blotter lay a blank sheet of cream-colored rag paper, the same as Emily used to write her letters. Beside it was a volume bound in leather. A familiar tome. *Moby-Dick*, by Herman Melville, the same book that her uncle had sent on her birthday.

Emily fell into the desk chair. She felt dizzy. This room was exactly like her own in every house that her father owned. It was the room of a planter's daughter.

Chapter 3: Goods and Chattels

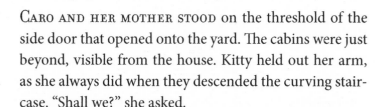

CARO AND HER MOTHER STOOD on the threshold of the side door that opened onto the yard. The cabins were just beyond, visible from the house. Kitty held out her arm, as she always did when they descended the curving staircase. "Shall we?" she asked.

Caro couldn't speak. She nodded.

Kitty stepped into the yard. She grimaced. "My shoes are too small," she said.

"Mine are too big." Caro bent down to slip them off. "You take them."

Kitty slipped off her shoes and rested her hand on Caro's shoulder as she forced her feet into Caro's shoes instead. She steadied herself. "Now you," she said to Caro.

Caro bent down to pull on the shoes. When she rose, Kitty put her arm around Caro's shoulder to pull her close. "Better?"

Caro couldn't reply.

The cabin intended for them was easy to find because the door had been left ajar. Her mother gently tugged on her arm. "Let's see," she said.

Caro viewed the room through the open door. The dirt floor had been recently swept, and the hearth had been cleaned of ashes. The cabin was empty. Not even a blanket for a makeshift sleeping pallet lay on the floor.

Caro turned at the sound of a quiet step and the rustle of a cotton dress. It was Dulcie, her face sweaty from the kitchen, her apron dirtied. She took in the ragged dresses and the coarse shoes, and her eyes traveled to Kitty's naked earlobes. Her voice full of sorrow, she said, "Oh, Kitty."

ഇരു

As MISTRESS OF THE HOUSEHOLD, Kitty had rarely sought Dulcie in the kitchen. Dulcie had come to her.

It was different now.

As a little girl, Caro had liked to spend time in the kitchen, sitting at the great pine table while Dulcie and her daughters kneaded bread, shucked oysters, peeled shrimp, or plucked chickens. In the winter, when the air was chill, the great hearth gave off a pleasant warmth, and the smell of boiling rice, along with whatever savory dishes would be served with it, filled the room.

Today this kitchen was stifling. When they stepped inside, the rest of the servants awaited the midday meal at the big pine table. Ambrose said, "Sit with us."

Kitty sat, carefully arranging her skirt. She patted the bench beside her. "Caro, join me." Kitty sniffed the air. "Peas and rice?" she asked, as though she were still the mistress of the house. "They feed you peas and rice now? James was more generous than that."

Ambrose gestured toward the house as though Lawrence and Susan might be able to hear. "Talk low," he said.

Caro thought, *He's schooling us, as the slaves say among themselves.* She remembered her father's notion of schooling, Cicero and Thomas Macaulay, and she had to bend her head and blink hard. She picked up her spoon, but Ambrose said, "Wait until I say grace."

Caro opened her mouth to protest, but Kitty said, "Caro, it's only polite."

As though it matters, Caro thought. But she put down her spoon and let Ambrose linger over a prayer for the food and for the new massa and missus. Hank, Dulcie's youngest, shifted uncomfortably on the bench beside his mother. "I'm hungry," he whispered.

"Hush," Dulcie said.

So the lengthy prayer was an admonition for all of them. When Ambrose finished, he picked up his spoon, but the only person hungry enough to eat was little Hank.

Dulcie said to Kitty, "Ambrose tell us about the will."

"Really? What did he say?" Kitty shot Ambrose her own look of reprimand.

"That Marse Lawrence inherit everything. The place in Colleton County, the house in Charleston, and this place. And all of us."

"That's true," Kitty said. "Ambrose, how did you find out?"

Ambrose chewed a mouthful of food with deliberation. "Marse Lawrence like me," he said. "He tell me."

"And I suppose that you overheard the rest," Kitty said.

Ambrose chuckled. "Don't have to eavesdrop," he said. "I serve at dinner, and they talk like I ain't there. Or can't hear."

"What else does Mr. Jarvie tell you?" Kitty asked.

Ambrose gave his former mistress a level gaze. "Can't say," he told her.

Caro thought, *That's what slaves say when they mean they know but shouldn't tell.*

"Oh, Kitty!" Dulcie cried. "What happen to us? Will they sell us?" She grabbed her husband's arm. "Split us up and sell us?"

"I don't know," Kitty said. "I believe you should ask Ambrose."

Bel stared at Caro. Through her worry shone a new expression, a ghostly malice. "What about you? Will they sell you?"

෫ඏ

CARO HAD BEEN TOO UPSET to eat. Without offering to clear the table or to wash the dishes, she ran from the kitchen to the cabin and slammed the door behind her. She fell heavily onto the dirt floor and buried her face in her hands. Her cheek ached where Susan had slapped her. She began to sob.

The door opened, and her mother knelt beside her. "Caro," she said softly.

"He never wanted this for us! He wanted to free us!"

Kitty put her arms around Caro and pressed her cheek to Caro's hair. She rocked Caro back and forth as though she were small again. "Oh, Caro," she said. "He loved us."

Caro raised her head to sob. "This is how he loved us!"

Her mother pulled her close, embracing Caro so tightly that the embrace hurt, whispering as though Caro were small again, or ill. "Hush, Caro. Hush."

Caro struggled free of her mother's grip. "They hate us. And they can do whatever they please with us."

Her mother stroked her hair. She whispered, "We don't know what will happen."

"I'm not a child," Caro said, wiping her tears away with her hand. "Don't lie to me." She shook her mother off.

She meandered into the side yard, gazing at the house that used to be hers. She burned with anger, wanting to run up the front steps, to enter through the front door, to sit in the library and read any book from the shelf, to shut the door to her room and lie on her bed with the white coverlet. *They stole it from us*, she thought. *They stole us, too.*

The side door opened to reveal a slight figure clad in black. It was Emily, gazing back at her.

She started at the sight. Emily approached her, calling softly, "Caroline."

Caro turned away, bitterness scalding her lips. *Do you like my room?* she thought. *Does it suit you? Does it cheer you any, in that black dress you wear?*

Ambrose wouldn't remind her to talk low. He would probably slap her for disobedience.

Emily came to stand awkwardly before her in the dirt of the yard. Caro couldn't look up. She was too angry.

Emily reached out her black-gloved hand to gently touch Caro's wrist, the spot that Missus Susan had grasped and bruised. In a soft, clear voice, Emily said, "I'm sorry."

As though she meant it! Caro thought, the taste of bile in her mouth.

"Please, look at me," Emily said, her voice still soft.

Caro bit her lips. She raised her eyes to Emily's and saw afresh the look of grief that accompanied the black dress, like the hair brooch at her throat.

෨෪

THAT NIGHT, CARO LAY ON THE coarse blanket that Dulcie had brought her, which offered little comfort on a packed dirt floor. The other slaves had rope beds, but Lawrence and Susan Jarvie wanted no such comfort for James Jarvie's beloved housekeeper and her daughter.

Beside her, Kitty shifted on her own blanket. Her breath came ragged.

Caro sat up. "Mama, are you crying?"

Her mother's voice was thick with tears. "I thought you were asleep."

"Oh, Mama," Caro said, and in apology for her out-burst earlier in the day, she crept close to nestle with her mother. Kitty put her arms around Caro, and even though it was too hot for an embrace, they wept softly in each other's arms until they fell asleep.

Several hours later, Caro woke in a sweat of fear. The room was so dark that she could see nothing. She had been dreaming, and the dream clung to her, worse than the night's dense heat or the whine of the mosquitoes that crept through the chinks in the boards.

She sat up, shaking. It woke her mother. "Caro? What is it?"

In the hot fug of a Carolina summer, she shuddered as though she had the ague.

"Caro." A cool hand on her brow.

It was too dark to see her mother's face. She said, "A dream—a terrible dream." She shook anew. "I dreamed you were on the block and I was watching the auction." She let terror overtake her and sobbed wildly. "I can't bear it. He never meant this for us! I know he didn't!"

Her mother took her hand away. All Caro had of her was her disembodied voice. "No, he did not." Tearless, her mother said, "Tomorrow we will call on Mr. Lawrence Jarvie and appeal to his conscience."

∞∞

IN THE MORNING, HER MOTHER smoothed her skirt and retied her headscarf. She forced her face into a pleasant expression. "How do I look?" she asked. She tossed her

head as she had when the diamonds flashed in her earlobes. There were dark circles under her eyes, and she
had become gaunt in her figure as well as in her face.

Caro said, "Awful."

Her mother laughed. "A lady stays a lady, even if she's
dressed in rags," she said.

"And nigger shoes?"

"And hasn't washed in days." Kitty held out her arm.
"Shall we?"

Caro took her mother's proffered arm. "We shall," she
said, with a pluck she didn't really feel.

When they opened the side door, Ambrose was
immediately upon them. "What do you want?"

"I want you to cajole an audience with Marse
Lawrence."

"You know he don't want to see you," Ambrose
said.

"I'm not asking him. I'm asking you. If you ask him
properly, he'll say yes."

"What do it concern?"

"It's for him to hear, not you," Kitty said impatiently.
"Although I know you will, since you listen at the door,
like Caro does."

Ambrose shook his head. "Oh, I shouldn't let you, but
you can still get round me," he said ruefully, and he left
to entreat the man who trusted him enough to talk as
though Ambrose wasn't in the room.

Kitty walked a few steps into the house. Susan didn't
appear, and they advanced into the foyer. Caro glanced

up the stairs, and her mother's eyes followed hers. The portraits of her father and his first wife were gone. In their stead, the wall was shadowed where the paint had stayed fresh.

Ambrose returned. "Come with me."

In the study, Caro hated the memory that came to her, the look of pleasure on her father's face on the day that she first translated a page from the Latin. It had been Aesop's *Fables*. She could recall the illustrations on the pages as vividly as she could remember the pride in her father's smile. "Cara," he had said.

Now the familiar desk was heaped with papers, and atop them, the ledger lay open. Lawrence slapped it shut. He didn't ask them to sit. "What is it?"

Kitty stood before Lawrence. She held herself as a lady and spoke as one. "Mr. Jarvie, sir, we are yours to dispose of, as you wish. But I beg you to think of your brother and what he wanted for us."

Lawrence flushed. He said, "That isn't your concern."

"Your consideration for your brother? No, it isn't. But I believe he would have wanted you to grant us the kindness of letting us know what our fate will be."

Lawrence's eyes rested on the marks of meanness that his wife had inflicted on Kitty Bennett Jarvie. Distressed, he said, "James was the soul of kindness."

"Yes, sir, he was."

Lawrence didn't reply, and Kitty pressed on. "He regretted that you were estranged. He always hoped it would be different between the two of you."

Pain sparked on Lawrence's face. "How would you know of that?"

Kitty said quietly, "Because he told me. He trusted me with these things."

As a husband tells a wife.

She added, "If you would honor his memory, treat us with consideration. Let us know what you intend for us."

Caro saw the grief on Lawrence's face, which was so much like his daughter Emily's. He said, "I'm selling the house."

At the word *selling*, Caro's stomach lurched.

"We're going back to Charleston, and we'll take everything with us."

"Everything?" Kitty asked.

"The plates, the china, the paintings, and the servants. All of it."

"Us, too?"

"The servants," he repeated. He paused. "All of you."

Kitty waited, but he was finished.

Caro closed her eyes. The gold-edged china. The crystal glasses that threw rainbows in the midday sunlight. The silver coffee service that Ambrose had brought to her father every morning. She thought of the paintings, already removed from the walls, and hoped that they wouldn't find their way to the midden.

She and her mother, huddled in the wagon, the chattels to go along with the goods, just as the will described them.

Lawrence said, "Go, both of you," and he looked down at the desk at the papers before him, dismissing them.

Ambrose was instantly in the room. Caro thought, *He heard everything*, and suddenly she hated the man who had always been kind to her when she was a young miss.

⁊⁃

A WEEK LATER, THE JARVIE GOODS and chattels were loaded on the ferry that docked at the Beaufort pier. Caro had visited Beaufort before, but she had never taken the ferry to Charleston, only an hour away. When her father was alive, it would have been an embarrassment to decide where she and her mother would sit on the ferry, which was big enough to have a ladies' parlor as well as a spot for gentlemen. Now there was no question.

She crowded with the slaves and the cargo below decks. The upper decks were well-guarded with railings for ladies to lean against as they gazed over the water. Below, without such an amenity, Caro and her mother sat on the floor, leaning against a trunk, hoping for a sea breeze to counteract the thick, oily smoke from the boiler. Her mother no longer smelled sweetly of lavender but of sweat and stale cloth. *I smell just as bad*, Caro thought.

She was still heartsick, and she was still in terror that she and her mother would be sold as soon as the Jarvies unpacked their trunks. But she was full of curiosity and also fired by an unreasonable hope for life in Charleston. Her mother's free relatives lived there. She might meet them and find out why they were free.

The boat hadn't gone far out to sea. The coast was still in sight. But Caro rose and turned to gaze at the open water of the ocean.

§○⅋

ONCE IN CHARLESTON, CARO watched as the drayman, assisted by Henry and Ambrose, loaded the boxes and trunks into his wagon. He was a short, sturdy man, the same color as his brawny brown horse. He wore a working man's clothes—a coarse cotton shirt and twill trousers—but they were new and fit him well. He moved with ease, and he sang as he lifted the trunks, grunting as he set them in the wagon bed. Caro recognized the song because the slaves sang it, too: "Poor Rosy."

He noticed her watching and smiled at her in a fatherly way. He said, "You has big eyes, little miss. Just up from the country?"

"St. Helena Island."

"Good cotton land," he said. "First time in Charleston?"

"Yes," she said, feeling a rush of eagerness.

"One of them Jarvie servants?"

She nodded. "Is Mr. Jarvie your master, too?" She hoped so. He had a friendly face and she hungered for friendliness.

He laughed, a rich, deep sound, like his singing voice. "Got no master," he said. "I'm a free man." He set his hand on the edge of the wagon. "Own this cart and own my horse, too." He called out to the horse, "Good boy, Mose!"

He looked at Caro, taking in her pretty face and ragged dress. "What bring you to Charleston?"

Caro's eyes stung with tears. She told the half-truth for the first time. "My old master died, and Mr. Jarvie brought me here."

Caro and Kitty, along with the rest of the servants, piled into the wagon. As the wagon jostled its way through the crowded streets, Caro craned her neck to look. Carriages filled the streets, but black people crowded the sidewalks—women carrying baskets, men with tools in their hands. Some of them wore the livery of slavery, but others were dressed in the plain clothes of working people. Caro thought of the drayman and wondered if they were free. She had never lived in a place where black skin signified anything but slavery.

Narrow houses sat on Charleston's streets. The Jarvie house on Orange Street was like that, set sideways on the lot. The front door was an afterthought. The gate to the side led to the house's true front, which looked inward to the walkway beside it. Anyone who entered could be watched from the piazzas on either story.

The gate was open, and they jounced on the gravel path to stop at the side door meant for tradesmen and servants. As the drayman helped them out, a tall, thin, light-complected woman, dressed in the neat gray cotton of a house servant, called to them, "Into the kitchen!" as though she were used to being obeyed.

The kitchen was no different from the substantial

brick building on the place on St. Helena Island. It even smelled the same, like peas and rice with bacon. Two women stood at the pine table, kneading bread in silence. They glanced at the newcomers and resumed their work.

The woman didn't invite them to sit. She let them stand in a bedraggled cluster, and she announced, "My name Cressy. Missus Susan's housekeeper. She tell me all about you, and I get you settled, even though I tell her we don't need another hand in this house. You nothing but trouble, and I ain't glad of trouble. Which of you is Ambrose?"

"I am, Miss Cressy."

"Missus Susan tell me that you Marse Lawrence's new manservant."

Ambrose nodded. "What happen to the man before me?"

Cressy gave him a dark look. "Ain't for you to care, but he go back to Colleton County." She regarded him with a fierce eye. "He drink. I hope you don't."

Ambrose made a big show of being shocked. "No, ma'am, I do not!"

Dulcie said loyally, "Mr. Ambrose a sober man, in every way."

"I didn't ask you," Cressy says. "Who is you, anyway?"

"Dulcie, ma'am, and these are my girls who help me in the kitchen, Peggy and Mattie."

"You stay here. The cook decide what to do with you." One of the silent women looked up.

Dulcie nodded. "My man, Henry, and my boy, Hank, they take care of the horses."

Cressy said, "The stable out back. You go there." She let her eyes rest on Lydia. "Lady's maid?"

"Yes, ma'am," Lydia said shyly.

"I take you in the house." And at Bel. "You, too."

She turned her attention to Kitty and Caro. She sniffed and said, "Good Lord! You two stink! And them dresses! Did you come from the rice fields?"

Kitty said, "I was James Jarvie's housekeeper, and he held me in high regard."

Cressy snorted. "I'm the housekeeper here." She peered at Caro. "I hear about you, both of you. Missus Susan don't want you in the house. Don't know what we're going to do about you."

Kitty took Caro's hand and clasped it in her own.

Cressy surveyed all her new charges and said, "I take you were you belong." She waved at Kitty and Caro. "Except for you. You don't go anywhere. Don't wander into the yard, and don't bother them in the kitchen."

"What will we do?" Caro asked.

Cressy glared at her. "Miss Susan let me punish anyone who talk back or don't act right. Keep a switch in here, close to hand. Don't make me use it."

Caro's hand stole to her cheek, where the memory of Susan's slap still lingered.

ℰℭ

THEY ATE IN THE KITCHEN, CRESSY presiding and dishing out the meager meal of peas and rice. The servants were quiet, their eyes shifting uncomfortably toward the newcomers. Caro thought of the manservant who had been dismissed. The rest of them must be wondering about their fate as well.

Ambrose, who had always presided over the table at the St. Helena place, broke the silence. He addressed the housekeeper. "Ma'am, have you been here long?"

Cressy said, "Did I speak to you?"

"Just trying to be pleasant, Miss Cressy."

"Disobedient, more like." Her gaze swept from one newcomer to another. "You all act obedient, or Marse Lawrence send you to the Work House."

"The Work House, ma'am?" Ambrose would not be cowed.

"Disobedient and ignorant, too. You ain't never heard of the Work House?" Without waiting for an answer, she said, "You go to the Work House, they punish you proper. Got the lash, got the cat-o'-nine-tails, got the paddles. And no one idle at the Work House. You work the treadmill, and if you don't step quick, it grind up your foot along with the corn. That's where you go, if you disobey."

※※※

AFTER DINNER, CRESSY TOOK Kitty and Caro to the floor above the kitchen, where the heat from the oven and the hearth rose and lingered. Doors lined both sides of a narrow corridor. Cressy unlocked a door and ushered them in.

The room was tiny and sparsely furnished with a narrow rope bed, a rickety chair, and a dresser with drawers that didn't close right. The window was shut, and the room was so hot that the air was hard to breathe. Caro could feel the heat of the oven beneath her feet.

"You stay here," Cressy said.

Kitty said, "Can we come down into the kitchen?"

"Missus Susan come into the kitchen. She don't want to see you. You stay right here, and you don't trouble anyone." Cressy fingered the key.

Kitty said, "Miss Cressy, I promise we won't stir. Please don't lock us in."

"You don't order me," Cressy said, and she shut the door and let them hear the key turn in the lock.

∞∾

THEIR IDLENESS WAS WORSE than hard labor because it was so fraught with worry. What use was an idle slave?

They gleaned what they could in the kitchen, since they were let out of their prison for meals. They learned that Cressy had been with Missus Susan since they were both small, and she was fiercely loyal to her mistress, who had made her missus over all the female slaves. The rest of James Jarvie's servants adjusted to her as well as they could. Dulcie, who had her own troubles in the kitchen, in conflict with the cook who was already there, stayed out of her way. Lydia, who was biddable, did whatever Cressy asked of her, even though it included the wash she hated. Bel sidled up to her and tried to flatter her.

Like her mistress, Cressy hated idleness, and even though she carried out her mistress's bidding in keeping

Kitty and Caro from any useful task, she loathed Kitty and Caro, who spent their days sitting in their airless room. They had been in the house only for a few days when Cressy announced after breakfast, "Now I know why Missus hate you." She gestured to Bel. "She tell me. Go on, let them know what you say."

Bel pointed to Kitty. "She Marse James's doxy." And at Caro. "And she his get."

Caro rose from the table to tower over Bel. Her cheeks flamed with anger. "My father treated my mother as his wife," she said, her gaze red-hot on Cressy. "And I am my father's daughter—I still am, even though he's gone."

Cressy turned to speak to Caro directly. "Oh, that's fine," she said. "That will do you fine, when you stand on the auction block to be some man's fancy girl." She addressed Kitty. "Like your mama before you."

They became more sure that Lawrence would ignore the plea of the will and sell them. Caro's bad dreams returned, and Kitty woke nightly to comfort her. They tried to reassure each other, but it grew harder to speak words of reassurance. Both knew that the reassurances might be lies.

Caro began to think that if she stayed here much longer, with nothing to do, nothing to read, and no hope of learning her fate, she would go mad. Being sold might be preferable, she thought. Anyone who bought her would put her to work, although she didn't like to think of what the duties might be.

They had been in their makeshift prison for two weeks when Cressy knocked on their door to say gruffly, "They want you in the house."

"Who?" Kitty asked.

"Marse Lawrence."

Her mother turned pale and clutched Caro's hand. Caro clutched back.

"Go on with you," Cressy chided.

They followed Cressy down the stairs, into the kitchen, and for the first time since they had arrived at the house, into the yard.

The yard smelled of the midden heap in the corner, but the fragrance of magnolia and camellia drifted from the garden on the other side of the fence. Caro breathed in the scent of flowers, but her chest was so tight with fear that she could barely smell it.

Cressy opened the side door and took them to the study. Caro was too distraught to look at the house or the furniture. It was a blur of white paint and wood floor, where her eyes were fixed.

Cressy said, "Don't you touch anything with them dirty hands of yours."

The study smelled of books, leather, and paper, but it also smelled of the flowers that grew in the garden outside the study window. The fragrance was strong in this room. Magnolia was suddenly the smell of fear.

Lawrence Jarvie looked up from the papers on his desk. When he spoke, his voice was clipped and curt, as though talking to them was distasteful and he wanted to finish the task as swiftly as possible. He said, "You can't stay here."

He will sell us.

"We've decided what to do with you."

The slave auction. Slave Mart.

"You'll leave today."

The auction block.

"My sister, Mary, owns a property on Tradd Street. She spends little time in Charleston, and her housekeeper looks after the place. There's a little house in the yard," he said. "She built it for one of her servants. We've decided that you can live there."

It began to dawn on Caro. Not to be sold. But to be sent away, not far, to be out of sight.

Her mother, who looked as though she might faint, said weakly, "How will we manage, sir?"

"That's not my concern," he said.

"Where is it?"

"Cressy will take you there."

Cressy fetched them, but at the side door, Ambrose stopped her. He said, "Let me wish them well."

"Marse Lawrence tell me to take them now."

"Just a moment."

"You don't order me."

Ambrose humbled himself. "I know, Miss Cressy. I beg you."

Cressy said to Kitty and Caro, "I wait for you at the gate. Don't linger."

Ambrose made no effort to press their hands. He leaned close. He whispered, "They watch." In the same low tone, he added, "Take care."

They walked down the driveway, where Cressy waited. She opened the gate and shoved them into the street. Behind them, the gate clanked shut.

Chapter 4: The Basket Name

CARO HAD NEVER WALKED FAR in her rough shoes. Now she learned that they chafed her feet.

"Why you walk so slow?" Cressy demanded, as Kitty and Caro limped behind her.

The street was full of people of color, all better dressed than they were. Caro felt sick with shame. She dreaded the thought that someone would guess, with sympathy or with scorn, what had happened to them.

But no one looked at them. It was as though no one saw them. The field hand's dress was a disguise that took away everything that made her Caroline Jarvie, James Jarvie's daughter. She was a slave without a face and without a name. She might as well have been a ghost.

Blisters began to rise on Caro's feet, and she ignored them as she followed Cressy. Every step caused more and more pain, and by the time they reached the house, Caro bit her lip against the pain in her feet.

Like the Orange Street house, this one was set sideways and made of brick that had turned dingy with age. The windows that faced the street were dim, as though no one had washed them for weeks, and the foliage around the gate had been left to overgrow.

Caro and Kitty stood at the gate with Cressy, wondering who would greet them. Cressy lifted the knocker and rapped. They waited. No one answered. Cressy rapped again. And they waited.

Someone unlocked the gate from within, and it swung open.

She was a head shorter than any of them, and shades browner. She wore a plain brown dress, darker than her skin, and her head was covered with a clean white scarf.

Cressy greeted her by saying, "You take your time."

The stranger said, "Busy in the kitchen." She had the thick accent of the Low Country.

"Empty house! Busy doing what?"

"Ain't your business," the stranger said curtly.

"Well, they here," Cressy said, gesturing at them.

The stranger appraised Kitty and Caro as though she were buying two chickens at the market. "Marse Lawrence let me know."

"They yours now." Cressy turned to go.

"Why don't you say goodbye proper?" the stranger taunted.

As she walked away, Cressy's voice floated back to them. "Don't owe you one!"

The stranger said, "She rile me, the way she full of herself."

Whoever she was, she disliked Cressy. Caro felt a prickle of hope. She asked, "Who are you?"

"Who am I, Miss Sass? My name Sophy." She looked from Caro to her mother. "What do you call yourself?"

Kitty said, "I'm Catherine Bennett Jarvie. And this is my daughter, Caroline."

"Hah! Fine names, like a dress for Sunday best. What do they call you the rest of the week?"

Caro found her voice. "My intimates call me Caro."

"Intimates! Maybe I just call you Sass. Or do you have a basket name?"

Kitty said, "I'm from Charleston. Born and bred in Charleston. I don't believe in that Low Country superstition."

Sophy shrugged. "Sass," she said. "Come with me, both of you."

They followed her along the brick walkway into the yard. At the end of the walkway stood the carriage house, built of wood, smaller and more dilapidated than the one on Orange Street. *Room for only one carriage*, Caro thought, astonished that she would care when her feet and her pride hurt so much.

Next to it was the kitchen house, also built of wood, with a great chimney in the middle. The second story held a row of small windows, lined up like the windows at the prison. Slave quarters, when the house was open.

But Sophy led them past the kitchen into the yard, where garbage had been heaped into a midden. The smell of rotting shrimp shells rose from it. Caro wondered who made so much garbage in an empty house and how a slave got her hands on enough shrimp to cause such a stink.

"Your house here," Sophy said.

It was also wooden, the size of a shed, built so hastily that no one had bothered with glass windows. Oiled paper sufficed.

Sophy said, "This is the house Betsey live in, when she get so bad with the cough no one sleep well in the kitchen house. Her daughter stay with her and take care of her."

Caro asked, "What happened to her?"

"She old," Sophy said. "She die." She turned the doorknob—this building had no lock—and pushed open the door.

They stepped inside. The air was still and damp, so dense that it was hard to take a breath. The smell of the midden seeped through the oiled paper, and the light was like the smell, decayed and oily. The floor was packed dirt.

Against the far wall stood two little rope beds, bare of any sheet, coverlet, or pillow. In the middle of the room was a small pine table, clearly a cast-off from the kitchen because the top was scarred and burned. Two rickety chairs of the roughest pine were arranged around it, and on it sat two dented tin plates, two worn tin cups, and a battered tin pitcher.

It was a house to match the dresses and the shoes: a slave's house.

Caro turned to her mother. She gazed around the room, and she fought off the urge to sob. She said, "Papa would turn in his grave to see this."

"Hush," her mother said. Her face was ashen, but she said lightly, "So this is now our home."

"Better than some," Sophy replied. "Is you hungry?"

Since her arrival in Charleston, Caro had been too wrought up to eat. Suddenly she was enormously hungry. "Yes," she said fiercely.

Kitty put a hand on Caro's arm. "We'd be glad of something to eat," she said, her tone polite.

Sophy snorted. "Ain't no ladies here," she said. "You hungry. Come eat."

They walked through the yard.

The air outside was hot and still, and they walked past the midden toward the kitchen house, where the fragrance of the garden wafted into the yard. Caro couldn't see the garden, which was separated from the yard by a wooden fence, but she was glad for its mingled perfume of roses and azalea. The garden's fence had no gate, since no one in the yard was meant to spend time in the garden. The yardman, if the place ever saw one, would be admitted to the garden through the entrance meant for servants.

Near the kitchen house, a flock of chickens pecked at the ground, eating the bran from unpolished rice.

"Unhusked rice?" Kitty asked, as though she were the mistress here.

Sophy shrugged. "Save Marse Lawrence some money."

Kitty frowned. "It puts you to the trouble of unhusking it."

"Marse Lawrence help out Miss Mary and they both appreciate that I act frugal."

Kitty's eyebrows rose. "Is he"—she used the genteel phrase—"embarrassed?"

"My, you talk fancy," Sophy said. "He always been careful with his money. Since he expect to run for the Assembly, and that cost money."

Something woke in Caro, the connection to the bigger world that her father had instilled in her. "He's in politics?" Caro asked.

"Why would you care, Miss Sass?"

"My father insisted that I read about history. And politics."

Sophy looked at her as though she were addled, but she explained, "Oh, he have ambition, and so do Missus Susan. He want to be a judge someday, like his daddy was, and the Assembly help him get there. Now he mad, I hear. Can't run this time because the estate take up his time and attention. Don't know about debt, you busybodies, but I hear that Marse James leave behind a proper mess on the Colleton place." She gave Kitty a knowing look. "Thought you might know about it."

Kitty blazed, "And why would you?"

"Oh, I hear things," Sophy said.

"Then you should keep them to yourself."

"Things good to know," Sophy said, unfazed.

Near the kitchen steps, a calico cat watched the birds eat their breakfast. Caro bent to extend her hand to the cat, which was sleek and plump, and it sniffed her hand as though hoping for something good to eat.

They paused before the kitchen, which still struck

Caro as shabby after the substantial brick building at her father's house. At the thought of her father's house—no longer his, no longer hers—her eyes stung. They walked slowly up the wooden steps, which creaked under their shoes, and pushed open the wooden door that could be secured at night with a bolt.

The kitchen was surprisingly bright, with windows on three sides—glass here because the kitchen mattered more than old Betsey's hut—but it was even hotter than in the yard. In the middle of the room, at the hearth with its big chimney, a pot simmered on the old-fashioned trivet that served as a burner in a modern wood stove. A savory smell rose from the pot, rice and peas and greens and bacon together, a richer meal than those Cressy dished out.

On the big table, its top marked by kitchen use but its construction solid, Sophy had laid three places. The white plates were green-rimmed and thick—common china but china. The tumblers were heavy, but they were glass. Beside each dish lay a cloth napkin and a spoon that that glinted where the silver plating had worn off.

Sophy told them to sit, then dished the food into bowls and handed them out. "Mind, it's hot," she said. She served herself. Caro picked up her spoon, and Sophy shot her an admonitory look. "Wait," she said. "We bless it first." She said, "Thank you, Lord, for this food," and picked up her spoon. She looked at Kitty, still sharp. "Didn't you raise your girl to say grace?"

My papa raised me to read Latin and Greek, Caro thought.

Kitty said gently, "She's very hungry, Miss Sophy."

Caro interjected. "Mama! We were never pious at home."

Sophy shook her head. "No church! Don't know what to do with you." She sighed, the sympathy surprising Caro. "Eat. Both of you. You so pale you look like ghosts."

Caro had been raised to eat like a lady, but she was much too hungry. She finished her bowl and asked, "May I have some more?"

Sophy gestured toward the pot. "You take all you want," she said.

As Caro helped herself from a pot that held enough for a dozen people, Kitty asked Sophy, "That's a lot of food for one person. Does someone else stay here?"

Sophy said, "Cook once, eat more than once. That all."

"Do you live here all alone?"

"Not that it's your business, but I do. Miss Mary don't care for Charleston since her husband die, and she spend her time with her people in the countryside. I stay here to look after the place."

"She trusts you?"

"Marse Lawrence do. I keep his house in Colleton County, and he trust me with all of it. The claret, the silver, the china. When Miss Mary need someone to watch over her house, he send me to Charleston."

So Sophy owed her unusual position to Lawrence Jarvie, just as Cressy owed her power in the house to Missus Susan. He had decided to like Sophy, as he liked Ambrose. Caro asked, "Why does he hate us so?"

Sophy said, "What do you think, Miss Sass? That he happy his brother treat a slave like a wife and give him blood kin like you? Of course he don't like you."

Her mother blanched. "Is that one of those things that's good to know?" Kitty asked.

Sophy nodded.

"How? Who told you?"

Sophy laughed, and her merry face gave her the look of a much younger woman. "People do talk," she said. "Every week at the meetinghouse. Although you wouldn't know, would you? Living godless like you used to."

Caro didn't care to be needled for not being well-brought enough for a slave from the Low Country. She remembered her manners and asked, "May I be excused?"

"Was you brought up too genteel to help with the dishes?" Sophy asked.

Caro looked from Sophy's knowing face to her mother's pale, drawn one. "Mama, was I?" she asked.

"Sass," Sophy said.

☙❧

KITTY AND CARO RETURNED TO the shack and stared into its dark, shabby interior. They had been freed from Cressy's heavy hand in Lawrence Jarvie's house, but this place was a different kind of slavery. The air inside the little window-less house was chokingly hot. Caro breathed in the stink from the kitchen midden and felt too restless to go inside.

Her mother laid a hand on her arm. She looked pale and ill. Full of consternation, Caro followed her inside.

Her mother sat heavily in the rickety chair. "I believe I'll rest for a bit," she said.

"Should I ask Sophy for a blanket? Or a pillow?"

Her mother smiled a little. "Ask her for a silk coverlet," she said. "And a lace pillowcase."

Caro crossed her arms over her chest. "Mama, how can you talk like that? Look at this! Look at us!"

Her mother raised tired, shadowed eyes to Caro's. "I know where we are, and I know what we are," she said.

"What are we going to do?"

Tears slipped down her mother's cheeks. "That I don't know," she said.

$$\mathcal{SOCR}$$

CARO COULDN'T BEAR TO watch her mother weep. She stumbled into the yard, where the smell of garbage was stronger. *Oh, Mama,* Caro thought. *Oh, Papa.* Her eyes smarted with tears. She stood in the sunshine, as her mother had warned her all her life not to do, and she rubbed her face with her hands. The tears came in full force, and she sobbed without caring who heard her.

There was a tap on her shoulder, and then came the sound of Sophy's voice. She said, "I know you grieve for your daddy, but crying don't bring him back."

Caro continued to sob.

Not unkindly, Sophy said, "It do you good to make yourself useful." She reached for Caro's hand. "Come with me. We find something for you to do. Do you know how to boil rice?"

Of course she knew. Every girl in Charleston, slave's daughter or planter's daughter, knew how to boil rice. She followed Sophy into the kitchen, where Sophy handed her a cloth. "Wipe your face. Then we get to work."

She did as Sophy bid her, stirring the rice and watching the fire beneath it. When she tired of playing house in the heat of the kitchen, she sat on the steps and petted the kitchen cat. "What's her name?" she asked Sophy.

"Chloe," Sophy said.

"Is that her basket name?" Caro teased.

"Sass," Sophy said. Her face shadowed. "Chloe my daughter name."

"Where is she? Your daughter?"

"She stay on the Low Country place," Sophy said. "They all down there, my two girls and my two boys, with their children."

"What about your husband?"

"He dead many a year."

Caro let her hand rest on the cat's soft back. She looked up. "Do you ever see them?"

"Not since I stay in Charleston." Her voice dropped. "That's why Marse Lawrence trust me. He know I can't go. If I run, I never see anyone I love, not ever again."

§⦂⦂

AS THE WEEK WORE ON, CARO watched as Sophy lived as though she were untouched by slavery. She did no work in the main house. She came and went as she pleased. Despite her economies for Lawrence Jarvie and his sister, she brought home something savory for dinner every day. They ate well: rice full of ham along with the peas, gumbo thick with shrimp and sausage, and one day, even a roast chicken.

Caro asked, "Where does the money come from, Sophy? If Mr. Jarvie is so frugal?"

Sophy looked sly. "I earn it," she said.

"How? You're a slave. Slaves don't earn money."

Sophy laughed, as she always did before telling Caro she was raised wrong. She wiped her hands on her apron. "Come with me. I show you something. We go upstairs."

Caro had yet to ascend to the second story, where the slaves slept when the house was full of them. Sophy led her up the ladderlike stair into a narrow hallway with three closed doors on either side. She walked to the end and pushed the door open.

Sophy had given herself the best room on the corridor, the one farthest from the house. It had a window on each wall and would admit a breeze at night. Someone had painted the walls of this room a regal red. The room was full of furniture, better than anything Caro had seen elsewhere in the kitchen or the yard. Sophy had a small four-poster bed draped with netting to keep the mosquitoes away and decked with two pillows and a quilted coverlet. She had a dresser, old and a little battered, but made of mahogany and inlaid with satinwood. She had a comfortable rocking chair with gryphons carved on the arms, and beside it, a little piecrust table adorned with a

Staffordshire figurine of a shepherdess bending over her lamb. On a peg on the door hung two dresses, one good black silk, evidently Sophy's Sunday best, and the other a pretty, well-made calico in a red print.

Caro asked, "How did you get all this?"

"Oh, Marse Lawrence give me the bed and the dresser because he don't need it anymore. But everything else"— her gesture took it in—"I buy with my own hand."

"How, Sophy?"

Sophy's eyes gleamed in complicity. "Tomorrow morning, you help me gather up all them eggs we've been saving. You come along with me, and I show you."

§⊃⊂র

Sophy's destination was the Central Market. As they approached, the smell, the savor of food combined with the reek of garbage, overpowered Caro. Outside the building stood a throng of market women, baskets on their heads. They were singing out their wares. "Oysters, oysters, oysters!" "Porgy walk, porgy talk, porgy eat with a knife and fork!" "Strawberry, blackberry, every kind of berry. The darker the berry, the sweeter the juice!"

Around the market, drawn by the refuse it created, roosted birds with sleek black bodies and long curved beaks set into red, mottled, featherless heads. The flock that perched on the roof regarded the flock that skulked and pecked below. Caro asked, "What are those birds?"

Sophy said, "Turkey vulture. Some folks call them Charleston eagles."

Caro watched them swoop from the rooftops to the ground. They were graceful in flight. "Goodness, they're ugly."

"Turkey vulture got to eat, too. Just looking for his dinner." She took a cloth from her pocket, laid it on the sidewalk, and set her basket atop it. She said, "Now we ready."

In a powerful voice, she began to sing: "Eggs so good, eggs so fine, come to buy these eggs of mine. Eggs, eggs, eggs, eggs!" Her voice joined the others in a threnody of commerce as the crowd swelled past.

Caro was suddenly embarrassed. Ashamed. What was she doing on the street, in the company of a Low Country market woman shrilling about eggs? The sun felt hot on her face.

"Maum Sophy!" a woman called. "Stop that racket you make. I want to buy some eggs from you!" She wore plain gray muslin and a white apron, like the Jarvie slaves.

Sophy laughed. "Miss Cissy, it is good to see you. How many eggs you need?"

"Give me a dozen. The biggest you got."

"Hold out your basket." Sophy chose the eggs carefully and set them into Cissy's basket with equal care.

Cissy regarded Caro. "Don't recall you before. Is you just up from the coast?"

"Yes," Caro said. "From St. Helena." As though she were listening to someone on the stage, she heard her own diction, so different from the speech of the Low Country.

Cissy said to Sophy, "She talk just like a lady. A white lady."

Before Caro could explain, Sophy jumped in. "She brought up in a grand house," she said. "Her massa just die, and his brother take over the house. He don't want her, so he send her to me, her and her mama."

Caro thought, *Every word of that is true.* She added, "Sophy takes good care of us."

"How much you ask for them eggs?" Cissy asked Sophy.

"Same as always. A quarter for a dozen."

Cissy dug in her pocket for the money and carefully counted it into Sophy's palm.

"I thank you, Miss Cissy," Sophy said. "You keep well."

"You too, Maum Sophy. And you too. What your name?" she asked Caro.

"Caroline."

"Young Miss Caroline." Cissy chortled. "Just like a lady!"

When Cissy was gone, Caro said irritably to Sophy, "Why would she care how I talk?"

"Because you look like you from the rice field, but you talk like you went to Madame Devereaux's."

"I can't help it," she said.

"Well, hush and help me. Still have plenty of eggs to sell. Can you sing?"

Caro thought that being able to sing a Schubert *lied* would be an unlikely way to sell an egg on the street in Charleston. "Not like you."

Sophy shrugged. "Eggs so fresh, eggs so fine, come to buy these eggs of mine!" she sang.

All her life Caro had heard the rhythm of the Low Country, the rhythm of Africa, in the speech of the slaves of St. Helena. She had always thought of it as a sign of ignorance. Today she heard it afresh. She thought, *It's just like a foreign tongue. Like French.* She could learn to speak it if she wanted to.

As the sun rose higher in the sky, as the air turned too hot for the ocean to cool it, as the smell of garbage began to overpower the smell of fresh food, people stopped to interrupt Sophy's song and buy her eggs. Unlike Cissy, a cook who needed eggs by the dozen, other customers were black people buying for themselves, an egg or two at a time, enough for a batch of biscuits or cornbread. Sophy knew them all. She asked after husbands, brothers, sisters, and children; after funerals and weddings; after parties and maroons. *No wonder she hears everything,* Caro thought.

Many people asked after Caro—it surprised her, that in this crowd was no one she knew—and she let Sophy explain for her. More than one woman glanced at Caro's face and said, "She mighty pretty. When the men find her, she get married right away!"

She recalled her mother's worry, and her father's. Too educated for a slave man, and a slave to anyone who was colored and free. The pain of it was muted now, swallowed up by the greater pain of her father's death.

The woman who bought the last of Sophy's eggs asked after Caro, and Caro herself spoke to her. She had been listening hard to the Low Country speech all day. She said, "My name Caro, and I grow up in de Jarvie house. Stay with Maum Sophy now. She take good care of me."

Sophy wished the customer well and in surprise, said to Caro, "What you say?"

Caro said, "I tried to sound like I'm from the Low Country. Did I do all right?"

"You rattle me," Sophy said. She picked up her empty basket and felt for the coins in her pocket. "We do all right. A dollar and a quarter." She counted out a few coins. "Open your hand. This for you."

"Sophy, you shouldn't," Caro said, suddenly embarrassed.

"Your pretty face made us some money today." She gave Caro the money, a quarter in silver coins. She said, "I buy us some shrimps for dinner tonight."

The money felt sweaty in Caro's palm, but its weight was pleasing. This was money she had earned by her own hand, as Sophy said. She said, "I long for oysters. Could I buy oysters with this?"

Sophy laughed. "Twenty-five cents buy you a whole gallon of oysters. They spoil before we eat them. Get a scoop for a nickel, two for a dime, and have money left over."

ഔൠ

WHEN THEY RETURNED TO Tradd Street, Caro ran to the shack, calling, "Mama! Mama!"

Kitty opened the door. "Caro, don't shout. What is it?"

Sophy said, "She come to the market with me, help me."

"Sophy and I sold eggs at the market today. I made a quarter, and I bought some oysters for us with my own money."

Kitty regarded Caro with an unhappy look. "And you got yourself a sunburn too, I see."

Caro reached for Kitty's hands. "Mama, aren't you happy? About the money and the oysters?"

Sophy spat. "Sunburn! Is that what you care about?"

"She's a planter's daughter. Who will she marry if she's burned black by standing on the street at the market?"

"She a slave! Who do you think she going to marry?"

Kitty glared at Sophy, unable to reply. She put her hand to her chest and began to cough, a dry, rasping sound.

Sophy asked, "How long you cough like that?"

Kitty was still furious. "I've had a cough before. It's nothing. I'm all right."

Sophy shrugged off Kitty's denial. "Don't help your daughter if you take ill," she said. "I make you a tea for that cough."

ဢၪ

WHEN CARO OPENED THE KITCHEN door, Sophy ignored her crestfallen face. Sophy said, "My man Sunday come tonight." She smiled. "Sunday Desmond. You meet him tonight when we all have dinner together. Your mama, too."

"If she'll eat with us."

Sophy shook her head. "She foolish to miss a fine dish of shrimps." She shooed away the cat, which had jumped on the table and was sniffing hopefully at the shrimp bucket. "Chloe, go on! You get yours later."

Several hours later, when the oyster stew simmered on the trivet next to the shrimps in tomato sauce, when the chicken was nearly roasted on the spit and the biscuits cooled in their serving dish, Sophy set the kitchen table. Kitty, drawn by the shrimp, had deigned to join them.

Sunday Desmond greeted Sophy with a big squeeze of an embrace and a kiss on the lips that left her breathless. "Sunday!" she gasped, pleased and embarrassed as a girl.

"Brought this for you, too, sugar," he said, handing her the bottle. The wine shimmered, pale yellow in the afternoon sun. "Good with a dinner of shrimps," he said.

He had a dark, seamed face and intelligent eyes, dark brown flecked with a golden color like the wine. He had the thick forearms of a workman but the sculpted hands of a craftsman. His fierce appearance was softened by his gentle tone of voice.

Sophy said, "Did you finish that job of work you had? The house on Montagu Street?"

"All done. My time my own for a few days."

"Sunday work as a carpenter," Sophy explained. "His master let him hire out."

"You're a slave?" Caro asked.

"My master don't mind because he get half of what I earn. And I'm all right, as long as I carry this." He pulled his slave's badge from his pocket. "A carpenter license cost him seven dollar a year!"

Caro asked Sophy, "Do you have a badge, too?" She had never seen it.

"Keep it in my pocket when I go out. Don't really need it. Everyone know me, and as long as I mind my own business, the Guard don't bother me."

"Why would they?" Caro asked.

Sophy said, "They keep a sharp eye on anyone black. So mind yourself when you go out." She asked Kitty, "Did Marse Lawrence buy badges for you and your girl?"

Kitty tossed her head. "No, he did not," she said.

Sunday sniffed the air appreciatively. "A fine dinner," he said affably. "Oysters, too!"

"Caro buy them for us."

Sunday laughed, a rich sound, dark like coffee and chocolate. "So this is Miss Sass that I been hearing all about."

"Does everyone in Charleston know me as Miss Sass now?" Caro asked, but she knew she was being teased, and it gave her pleasure, even as she blushed.

Sophy laughed. "Now you have a basket name," she said. "Miss Sass, that your basket name!"

ഇരുജ

LATER, AFTER KITTY AND CARO returned to the shack, Kitty settled herself on the bed. Sophy had given them a candle and some matches, and Caro lit the candle against the darkness.

Her mother's face deeply shadowed in the light of the single candle. It added to her look of strain and fatigue. She coughed again and tapped her chest, trying to make it stop. She said, "Sophy means well, but she isn't a fit companion for you. Neither she nor that man she's befriended."

Caro didn't like the sound of the cough. It softened her. She said, "They're kind to us. And they're happy together."

Kitty said, "Two slaves in a makeshift connection. Don't think of such a thing for yourself."

Caro flared, "And what kind of a connection will I have?"

∞∞

THE NEXT MORNING, AS ALL OF them sat in the kitchen together, Sophy invited Kitty and Caro to accompany them to church.

"No, thank you," Kitty said coolly.

"Do you good to go to church."

Kitty said, "Who do you think you are? Not my missus and not my mother. I'll raise my daughter as I see fit. I don't need you to drag her any deeper into slavery."

"Drag her! When you have a head full of foolishness. Act like a lady!"

Sunday cleared his throat, but both women ignored him. Kitty said, "I was the mistress of James Jarvie's house, and I'm still a lady."

94

Sophy said, "No, you a slave. You a fool to think you a lady."

Caro intervened. She grabbed her mother's hand. "Mama, stop." She reached for Sophy's hand. "You stop, too."

The two women, a fallen lady and a half-free slave, glared at each other like two cats in an alley.

"Don't fight," Caro pleaded.

Sunday said, "Not on the Lord's day, Sophy."

Sophy glared at Sunday, too. But she took a deep breath and said to Kitty, "You her mama. You want to cherish her and protect her. Won't take that from you. But you don't know Charleston like I do. I help her. I help you, too, if you let me."

"Please, Mama. Let her apologize to you."

Kitty said stiffly, "All right, Miss Sophy."

"Then you come to church with me? Even though you both godless?"

"It's the Lord's day," Caro said.

"What is your meetinghouse?" Kitty asked, her gentility returning.

Sunday said, "We go to Zion Presbyterian. The Reverend Girardeau treat us right. Black folks sit in the pews, not up in the balcony."

At the church, Sophy was an important parishioner. The Reverend Girardeau himself greeted her, giving her the dignity of her surname—a name that Caro hadn't realized she possessed. When he was introduced to Caro, he called her "Miss Jarvie," an unexpected courtesy. He greeted her mother as "Mrs. Jarvie" and pressed her hand in politeness, welcoming them both and hoping that they would return on every holy day. As in the market, Sophy's many acquaintances crowded her. They asked after Caro and requested to be introduced to Kitty.

Caro recognized Maum Cissy from the Market. She was resplendent today in a silk dress that must be a cast-off from her missus.

In the pew, her mother to her left, Sophy to her right, Caro sat. She looked around the church full of the dark faces of the enslaved, and her mother's words rang in her ears. She bowed her head, not in prayer but in tears, thinking of her father and his love for her, which was too selfish to let her go. She was a lady among slaves and a slave among ladies, and there seemed to be no place in Charleston that would have her.

℃ℂ

WHEN HER MOTHER WEARIED OF the shack, she sat in the kitchen while Sophy and Caro made themselves useful. Sophy had yet to admonish Kitty to make herself useful.

As Kitty watched Caro help Sophy string beans, the bell on the gate jangled, once and then again—the sound of someone itching with impatience. "Stay put," Sophy said. "I see who it is."

She returned with an uneasy look on her face. "Gal named Bel from Marse Lawrence. She want you."

Caro looked at her mother, and they had the same thought. Kitty rose. "I'll go with you." Sophy followed.

Bel stood at the end of the driveway, shifting from foot to foot. She was plumper than she had been, more self-important. When she saw Caro, her face worked like someone who wanted to sneer and knew she shouldn't. She said, "Marse Lawrence want to see you. Now."

"Why?"

"Didn't say. Just said to hurry."

"You ran here to drag me there, and you don't know why?"

Bel's face turned sullen. "I ain't like you. When Marse Lawrence tell me to do something, I do it. And no fancy words to ask why." Caro pulled herself up straight. Bel said, "You ain't a bit better than me. His slave, just like I am. He said to hurry."

"I'm going with her," Kitty said.

"No, you ain't. He say just Carrie."

Caro glared at Bel. "My name is Caroline," she said.

Enjoying her new power, Bel said, "If you don't shut up, I tell Marse Lawrence, and he send the Guard for you to take you to the Work House."

Sophy said, "No one need to go to the Work House. Kitty, you hush. Caro, you go."

Caro thought, *She knows something. What is it?* There was a peculiar expression on Sophy's face, the facial version of *can't say.* "Mama, I'll be right back," she said.

"If you aren't, I'll go after you, and I don't care if I end up in the Work House."

Bel grabbed her arm. "Come on," she said. "I don't care who else go to the Work House, but I don't want to."

Caro followed Bel into the street, where Bel set a swift pace. Caro's shoes still bothered her. Cross, Bel said, "Can't you walk any better than that?"

Her feet hurt, and her heart beat fast in fear.

At the Orange Street house, Bel yanked on her arm. "The side door," she said.

Caro followed Bel down the driveway, through the servant door, and through the back hallway. Bel ventured into the main hallway and moved with less surety. She stopped outside the study and tapped on the door. "Marse?" she called.

Lawrence's irritated voice floated into the hall. "Yes?"

"I bring her like you ask me."

"Well, show her in."

Bel shoved her, rather than showed her, into the room. Lawrence said, "You can go, Bel."

"Yes, Massa," Bel said, backing out the door.

He didn't invite her to sit. He said, "Your mistress and I have been discussing what to do with you."

It was as she feared. They had been talking about selling her.

The room swam before her eyes.

The auction block. A pretty, light-skinned girl for a man's fancy. A man crueler than her father who bought a girl to keep, use for pleasure, and cast away.

Now she was doubly sorry that she hadn't been invited

to sit because she would disgrace herself by falling to the floor in a faint.

Lawrence said, "We've made a decision."

Torn from her mother to be sold as a fancy girl. The room seemed to go black.

"We have decided to give you the laundry."

Caro blinked. Laundry? In her surprise, she said the first thing that came into her head. "Doesn't Lydia do the laundry?" As soon as the words left her mouth, she imagined Sophy's voice: "Sass."

His cheeks colored, as they had when the will was read. This was an embarrassment for him. It would be his wife's task if she didn't loathe Caro so much. He said, "The weekly wash. Bel will instruct you on the particulars."

She stammered, "Come here to do the wash?"

"No, not here," he said.

It's Missus Susan, she thought. *She doesn't even want me in the yard, where she can't see me.*

"Take it to Tradd Street. Do it there."

She tried to still her racing heart and her trembling legs. The wash. The weekly wash. In the yard of the house on Tradd Street. Out of sight, with Sophy.

"Go," he said, and turned his attention to a paper on the desk.

She turned to go.

He said, "Don't turn your back on me."

She halted and turned again. "What do you want of me?"

SABRA WALDFOGEL

"Back out of the room. And you'll address me as Master."

Caro took a deep breath and dropped her eyes as demurely as she could. In a tone that would have done credit to a girl at Madame Devereaux's, she said, "Yes, Master." Despite her trembling legs, she backed from the room.

Bel was waiting. She didn't speak. She grabbed Caro by the arm and dragged her out the side door, through the yard, and into the kitchen that doubled as the wash house. On the table lay a big bundle, wrapped in a sheet. Bel said, "You take this. You bring it back next week. And you do it right."

❧❧

WHEN CARO STAGGERED INTO THE yard at Tradd Street, the bundle in her arms, her mother flew to her. "Are you all right?"

She dropped the bundle on the steps and rubbed her arms. She shook all over but not from carrying a heavy load.

Sophy asked, "What have you got there?"

"What does it look like? Wash," Caro snapped.

"Why you tote it in your arms?"

"How else would I carry it?"

Sophy hefted the bundle, and with an easy motion, she positioned it on her head, steadying it with her hand. "Like this," she said, her voice muffled.

"How do you manage it?"

Sophy's laughter struggled through the dirty cloth. "Every Low Country woman learn it," she said. "This weigh less than a sheaf of rice, and I carry a sheaf of rice many a time when I was a girl." She put the bundle on the ground. She was still laughing. "Uh-hm, you the most ignorant girl I ever saw," she said. "Did your mama forget to teach you how to do the wash, too?"

Caro was suddenly very angry. She kicked the bundle with all her might. She thought of everything she knew, everything that was now so useless to her, and she began to sob noisily. The fear of the morning returned to her. She wailed, "I thought he was going to sell me! Put me on the block to be a fancy girl!"

Kitty embraced her and sobbed with her.

Sophy let them both cry. When they broke apart, she said to Caro, "I school you. We do the wash together. We add it to mine, when I do it."

ഔ

CARO HAD OBSERVED LYDIA DOING the wash in the yard of the King Street house, but she had never touched the washtub herself. Under Sophy's eye, she heated the water for the tub and added the soap and the bluing. When she slipped the clothes into the water, Sophy added her wash, too. Sophy gave her a wooden pole. "You stir them around, get them good and full of soap," she said. Caro obeyed her.

Kitty opened the door of the shack and walked across the yard. Sophy was still angry with her. She called, "Don't you want to make yourself useful today?"

"No, I do not," Kitty said, and she walked into the kitchen, where she knew she would find coffee on the hob of the stove.

Caro and Sophy worked all morning to wash and wring the clothes, and by the time they hung them to dry, Caro was sorry that she had ever had a harsh word for Lydia. Sophy said, "They take a while to dry in this damp heat. Hang overnight." She looked up at the cloudless sky. "Pray it don't rain. Because then we wash them all over again."

Once the clothes were dry, Sophy taught her how to iron, and that was even worse than washing. Sophy showed her how to heat the iron on the trivet on the hearth, and she burned herself more than once to test it. Sophy let her learn on a tea towel, but she watched carefully, and more than once she snatched the iron away, scolding, "Don't scorch!"

Caro rubbed the newest burn on her hand and thought, *If Mr. Jarvie wanted to torment me on purpose, he couldn't have found a better way to do it.*

When the clothes were ironed, she helped Sophy fold them neatly and tie them into a bundle to take back to the house on Orange Street.

When she arrived, Bel came to meet her in the kitchen. She untied the bundle. She shook out the topmost shirt, inspected it, and to Caro's disgust, sniffed it, even though all it smelled of was soap and bleach. Taking the shirt, Bel left for the house, and Caro stood uneasily at the table while Dulcie worked at the stove without speaking to her.

Bel returned with another bundle. *Another week's torment,* Caro thought. Bel said, "This for you."

Caro nodded.

Bel held out her fist. "This for you, too."

"What is it?"

Bel opened her hand. In it sat five silver dimes.

In surprise, Caro said, "Why would he pay me?"

"I don't know. He say to give it to you. Go on, and come back next week."

In the driveway, Caro tried to balance the bundle on her head and steady it with her hand. It was too heavy and too ungainly. Her head ached beneath it. She wrapped her arms around it and lugged it back to Tradd Street, where she heaved it onto the kitchen table.

Sophy looked up from the cornbread she stirred and said, "Next time I do less, and you do more."

Caro said, "He paid me."

"Really? How much do he pay you?"

Her arms aching, Caro pulled the money from her pocket to show Sophy.

Sophy said, "That ain't right. For a load like he give you, a washwoman get two, three dollar."

"Why would he pay me at all, Sophy? He hates me."

"Someone in that house feel bad about turning you out," Sophy said. "They persuade him, and he pay you. But not much."

෨)෬

SEVERAL DAYS LATER, AS CARO labored over the next load, Sophy announced another visitor. Caro stood upright and pressed her hands to her sore back. "Not Bel again!"

"No," Sophy said. "Miss Emily."

Caro wiped her soapy hands on her apron.

Emily came into the yard with a gentle step, as though she were worried about intruding. She wore a black dress—she must have many, but it looked just like the others—and her face was hidden inside a black bonnet. Over her arm she carried a basket covered with a cotton cloth.

At the sight of Emily Jarvie, before her in the flesh and not a shadow or the flicker of a silk skirt, Caro felt her anger return. She dropped her eyes, not in servility but in rage.

Emily said, "Caroline. Is your mother here?"

As Sophy fetched Kitty, Emily said, "I'm sorry to disturb you at your work."

Caro tried to say, "It's all right," but she was too angry to do more than mumble.

When Kitty arrived, Emily greeted her, too. "Catherine."

"Miss Emily," her mother said politely.

Emily unfolded the cloth and lifted the basket. "I had some shawls that my mother gave me," she said. "They never suited me, and I thought they would look better on you, both of you."

Caro could see the folded shawls. They were pretty paisleys of the quality a lady would wear. Perhaps she wasn't lying, and they were a gift instead of charity.

Emily said, "It will be cold when winter comes. I'd be glad to know that you're warm enough."

Kitty said, "That's kind of you, Miss Emily."

Emily shook out the topmost shawl, a paisley in a dark-red pattern. "This is for you, Catherine," she said gravely.

Kitty shook it out with a practiced gesture and draped it over her shoulders.

Emily smiled. "It does suit you," she said.

Caro thought, *This is quite a show to pretend it isn't charity.* She felt less angry. She wondered what color Emily thought would suit her.

Emily took out the second shawl. "And this is yours, Caroline," she said, the faintest smile on her face.

It was blue, and it was the softest wool she had ever touched. She put it on, forgetting her field hand's dress and her soapy apron, and she thought, *If this is charity, she is the slyest girl I've ever met.*

Caro pressed the shawl to her cheek. And it came to her. Before she guarded her tongue, she blurted it out. "It was your idea, wasn't it? The washing?"

Emily flushed bright red. She nodded. "I can ask my

mother's friends if they need a laundress, if it would help you," she said.

Kitty, unhappy about the laundry but astute about making an ally, said firmly, "We appreciate what you do for us, Miss Emily. We both thank you."

Emily reached for Caro, touching her gently on the wrist, the spot where Missus Susan had once bruised her.

As Emily walked down the driveway to the gate, Caro followed the sight of that slender, black-clad figure until it disappeared.

PART 2

A Fragile Freedom

1859

Chapter 5: Hearth and Home

AT HER STEPMOTHER'S INSISTENCE, Emily had inherited Caro's furniture from St. Helena Island. Now she slept in Caro's bed, brushed her hair before Caro's dressing table, and stored her clothes in Caro's clothes press. Susan had brought Caro's dresses to Charleston as well. They were so fine that Susan had said, "When you put off your mourning, we'll have them made over for you."

Her stepmother had taken nothing of Kitty's, save for her jewelry. She had gotten rid of Kitty's dresses. She had stripped the good cotton sheets from Kitty's bed and given the pillows and the coverlet to Dulcie. She had removed all the ornaments and knickknacks that had belonged to Kitty and was about to pack them away when Emily had said, "Let me have the portrait of Uncle James."

It was a miniature painted on ivory set in a gilded frame, and the sight of it was as distasteful to her stepmother as Kitty's chemises and crinolines. "Do you really want it?"

The artist had caught her uncle in the sunny expression that Emily remembered from her visit to him as a little girl. Emily could understand why Kitty had wanted to see that image every day when she woke and just before she slept.

Emily said, "I'd like to have something to remember him by."

"It was hers," Susan said, her hand curling over the little oval of ivory.

Emily said, "Now it's ours," and she held out her hand for it.

Her stepmother shook her head. "Emily, I don't know what's gotten into you since your uncle died." She gave the portrait to Emily.

Now, back in Charleston, Emily gazed at the portrait of James, his smile still alive in its framework of ivory and gold, and she thought of Kitty. "Nothing in this house is yours," her stepmother had said to Kitty, but she had been wrong. Emily owned a portrait of Robert, which she had kept with her since his death. She had difficulty remembering his living face, and the portrait was now her memory. Emily thought of the widow's mask of grief, which she herself knew so well, and her hand closed over the portrait.

She should bring Caro something she would treasure, too. She thought of the Bible she had pleaded to give to Caro. She was ready to put her own Bible, with its gilt-edged pages, into her basket, but suddenly she had a better idea. She smoothed the skirt of her black dress, put on the bonnet draped with black crape, and picked up a basket.

At the foot of the stairs, Ambrose asked her, "Are you wanting to go out, Miss Emily?"

"I am, Ambrose. Can you unlock the gate for me?"

"Miss Susan take the carriage. Don't you want to wait?"

"I'm only going to the market. It isn't far."

"I can ask one of them little girls to carry that basket for you, Miss Emily."

She smiled. It was easy to keep an even temper with the new servants. She liked Ambrose, even when he was being a busybody and a fusspot. "It's all right, Ambrose. I can manage by myself."

He opened the gate for her, and she left the fragrant shade of the garden for the bright sun and the reek of the street. She blinked against the sun and adjusted her bonnet to shade her eyes better. She balanced the basket on her arm, and for the second time, sought the house on Tradd Street.

At the gate, Emily rang the bell. Now she knew to wait, but it seemed a long moment in the sun until she heard the footsteps that were not in a hurry and saw the familiar dark face.

"Oh, Miss Emily!" Sophy said. "You come back."

"I've come again to see Catherine and Caroline to find out how they're faring."

Sophy regarded her with mistrust. "Did your mama send you this time?"

"No. She doesn't know I'm here."

Sophy gave her a bright, beady look. "You wait a moment." She bustled off. Now she was in a hurry.

Emily thought, *Does she think I don't know? She's going to warn them I've come.* Emily knew, as her step-mother did not, that the servants called Susan "the Old Jay" behind her back, and they whistled a jay's call to let anyone who was dawdling or sleeping to straighten up and look bright for the missus.

Emily waited. Under her bonnet, an unladylike drop of sweat trickled down her face. She wondered how care-ful their response would be, when Sophy finally admitted her into the shade of the driveway.

Sophy returned. "Now you come with me."

Sophy guided her into the overgrown yard, where the smell of garbage was still strong. As they walked past the kitchen, the cat jumped off the steps to brush against her dress. "Shoo!" Sophy said.

Emily bent to pet the cat, and it rubbed against her hand, purring.

"They in their little house today," Sophy said, and she stopped before Betsey's old shack.

Emily, who had been fond of Betsey, had a vague memory of visiting her before she died, but she had no memory of this building, smaller than a slave's cabin on the Low Country place, with peeling boards, a splintered door, and oiled paper over the windows.

Sophy knocked on the door and pushed it open. Emily had no recollection of a dirt floor, or shabby rope beds, or rickety furniture.

Inside, Catherine and Caroline stood, awaiting her. She murmured, "How are you?"

Kitty murmured back, "We're all right, Miss Emily."

"Did the shawls suit you?"

"Very much, Miss Emily," Kitty said. "We'll welcome them when the weather turns cold."

Emily took in the shack. She said, "This doesn't suit you."

Caro started forward, but Kitty said, "We're grateful for it, Miss Emily."

Emily sighed. Kitty was haggard. Grief had blurred her beauty, and she looked older than the beautiful widow that Emily had first seen tending to James Jarvie's body. Her eyes were shadowed. Looking at her, Emily felt a stab of pain. She remembered the months after Robert's death, when she had been in such a daze that she scarcely knew whether she was awake or asleep.

Emily said to Kitty, "I've brought something for you." She took the portrait from the basket and presented it to Kitty.

Kitty bent her head over the portrait as though she were unable to believe that it had come back to her. She reached for the picture and cradled it in her hands. She gently stroked the surface, as though she were touching her husband's beloved face. She looked up. "Miss Emily, I can't accept this from you," she said, handing it back. "I can't have anyone thinking I stole it."

Emily didn't reach for it. "If anyone asks, I'll tell the truth. That I gave it to you."

Kitty weakened.

Emily said, "But no one will know because I'll keep it a secret."

"Miss Emily—"

"I want you to have it."

"Is that a command, Miss Emily?"

What a peculiar thing for a slave to say. Emily thought of her stepmother and answered with a soft voice and a sweet smile to belie the words. "Yes, it is."

"I have something for you too, Caroline," Emily said, and she drew the book from her basket.

Caroline received the book with hands practiced in handling a volume. When she realized what it was, her face suffused with surprise. She raised her eyes to Emily's. "How did you know?"

"I saw it in your room at St. Helena."

"I hadn't finished it. I have yearned for this book."

Emily gazed at the girl who wore a Low Country kerchief, a field hand's dress, and a pair of coarse shoes but who spoke with the diction of a boarder at Madame Devereaux's. Emily knew that many slaves could read. She had found Ambrose reading the envelopes of her father's correspondence before he brought the letters on a silver tray. She had kept Ambrose's secret.

But this seemed different. Uncle James had given Emily a copy of the Melville book, too, and expected her to read it with understanding. She intruded to ask, "How were you educated?"

Caro said quietly, "My father taught me."

"Why?"

Caro stared at Emily, an insolence softened by the tears that brimmed in her eyes. "Because he loved me," she said.

Emily thought of her own father, who had given her anything she required but nothing that she treasured. She turned away, unable to watch Caro weep. She couldn't bear to see the orphan, but she was equally disturbed by the slave who liked books as she herself did.

"I must go," she said, and she left them to walk unsteadily to the kitchen. The cat followed her up the steps, mewing for her attention, but she ignored it. She pushed the door open and sat heavily at the kitchen table.

"Miss Emily?" Sophy asked. "You look mighty pale. Are you all right?"

"A cup of water, please."

"What's the matter?"

"I never met a slave girl who speaks like that."

"Did she sass you?"

Emily said, "She talked about books."

"She talk a lot of foolishness," Sophy said, handing Emily the glass and watching as she drank. "Is you hungry, Miss Emily? I have fresh biscuit."

Emily shook her head. She rose and picked up her basket. "Sophy, will you unlock the gate for me?"

At the gate, Sophy said, "If Caro act disrespectful to you, I chastise her, Miss Emily. I punish her, if you like."

Emily thought of the cultivated voice, alight at the

thought of Melville, and the dark eyes awash in tears. "No, Sophy. Don't do that."

"You do right, coming to see them. Do your Christian duty."

Emily nodded. She stepped into the heat and stink of the street. She walked back to Orange Street in a daze at their audacity, hers and Caro's. It would take more Christian charity than she could muster to accept that a book could stir a slave girl's soul.

℘℘℘

EMILY LAID DOWN HER PEN AND closed her diary. She picked up the portrait of Robert, which she always kept by her as she wrote, and touched the face forever smiling on the ivory surface. She tried to recall the living man, the sound of his voice, the glint of sunlight on his hair, the smell of his skin as he leaned close enough to kiss her, the touch of his lips on her face. He was fading, just as the flowers he had given her for a keepsake had faded. She pressed the portrait against her cheek, the spot that he had always kissed, and murmured, "I am so sorry, beloved."

Susan Jarvie tapped on the door to Emily's room. "Emily," she said, as softly as she ever pitched her voice, and entered.

Emily set the portrait on her writing desk, next to the diary. "What is it, Mother?"

Susan picked up Robert's portrait. "I thought you wanted to look at Uncle James for a while," she said.

"It saddened me too much. I put that away." Emily prayed that her stepmother would never ask to see where it had gone.

Holding Robert's portrait, Susan asked, "Isn't it time to put this away, too?"

Emily's hand went to the brooch at her throat. "Mother, please," she said.

"It's been nearly two years. It would be different if you had married him, or if you had been a widow."

Emily whispered, "I loved him as though I married him."

"Oh, Emily. You didn't marry him. It's time. You don't have to wear full mourning for Uncle James since you weren't close to him. Would you consider it? Wearing gray, at least, and leaving off the mourning bonnet?"

"I can't forget him."

"No one is asking you to forget him." She set down the portrait and came to stand behind Emily, letting her hands rest affectionately on Emily's shoulders. "You should be married, Emily."

"Not yet," Emily said. "Not just yet."

Susan stroked her shoulders. "Are you tired of Charleston? Would you like to go back to Sumter County?"

Emily sighed. "I don't know," she said.

"You could stay with your sister." Emily's half sister, Nancy, ten years her senior, had married an upcountry cotton planter and lived in Sumter County year-round. "You could see the new baby." The baby was nine months old, able to smile at a doting aunt. "And the Aiken girls are still there. They can keep you company."

The Aiken girls, Jane and Camilla, distant kin to Nancy's husband Charles, were a little younger than Emily. They chattered like a flock of Carolina wrens, chirping about bonnets and dresses and young men who might be beaux and young men who had been captured as husbands. Emily doubted that they had read a book between the two of them since they had been liberated from Madame Togno's, an even more exclusive and restrictive place to be finished than Madame Devereaux's.

"Do you want me to go?" Emily asked.

Susan bent to kiss the part of Emily's hair. "Not at all," she said. "Only to do what might cheer you."

Into Emily's mind flashed the memory of Caroline, whose face lit with joy as she spied the cover of *Moby-Dick*. She sighed and closed the diary. She said, "I'll go to Sumter County until the frost."

"When you return, will you consider the other? Putting off your mourning?"

"Ask me again when I return, Mother."

⋇

WHEN THE COACHMAN HANDED HER out, Emily took the first deep breath in weeks. She let the cool, pine-scented air flow into her and over her. In relief, she undid the strings of her mourning bonnet and let it slip down her back.

Her sister waited for her on the first-floor piazza. Nancy held out her arms, and Emily dutifully went into Nancy's embrace. Nancy released her. "Still in that black dress," she said.

Stung, Emily asked, "Were you ever in mourning?"

"Of course," Nancy said. "For two months. Isn't that enough for an uncle you barely knew?"

"I still remember Robert," Emily said, clenching her skirt in her hand.

"Oh, Emily," Nancy said, in the motherly tone that she had always used with her half sister.

"Not you, too," Emily said. "Mother has already chided me."

Nancy said, "This is no way to start your visit, Emily. Come in. Charles has been making improvements again. I'll show you." She gestured toward the Doric columns. "Those are new. Aren't they fine?"

They were a replica of the columns on the much more imposing house of one of Charles's cousins, whose wealth was anchored by a Low Country plantation. They only summered here. Nancy had married into the upcountry branch of the sprawling Aiken family, younger sons who had turned to cotton and had made their fortunes in the cotton boom of the last fifteen years.

"Very fine," Emily murmured. Emily could remember when Stateburg was a small and rustic place. Now it was doubly full of money from the profit in cotton and the profit that came when a rich upcountry man married a Low Country heiress.

"Come inside and see," Nancy said. "I've been making improvements, too."

She led Emily into the front parlor, which had been wallpapered in a lustrous pattern of brocade. The furniture was in the newest style: dark, carved, and ornate. "What happened to all the furniture you inherited from the Aikens?" Emily asked.

"It's in the back parlor." Nancy grinned. "Charles's mama is very angry with me for putting the family heirlooms out of sight. I was so tired of them! I wanted something new."

"It dazzles," Emily murmured.

"I can tell you don't like it. Have you seen the house on King Street?" Without waiting for an answer, Nancy said, "The Herriot house! Imagine us living in the Herriot house!"

Emily said quietly, "It was James Jarvie's house, and we don't live in it yet. The Herriot cousins are still renting it."

"Mother wrote me that she visited them. It's grand, and everything is a hundred years old. She hated the furniture, too." Nancy laughed. "When you move in, there's no one to stop her from throwing it out!"

She had accompanied her mother on that visit. She thought of the Sheraton settee in the parlor, with its lovely curved legs, and the matching chairs, so daintily made, given to the servants as castoffs, or worse, cut up to be burned like kindling. Poor furniture, cast out.

"Emily, are you listening at all? You're worse than ever, woolgathering. I saw you with a book in your hand as you got out of the coach." It was true. Thinking of Caroline, she had brought the Melville. "How many books did you bring in your trunk?"

"Just a few. I thought I'd have a quiet visit."

Nancy shook her head. "The summer season is almost over, and you're still in mourning," she said. "A man will look at a girl if she's wearing a pretty dress. Not many men will look at a girl who decks herself out like a widow."

Emily had met many widowers whose black suits were the dress of business as well as that of mourning, and she had seen how greedy they were to remarry. "A man will look at any woman who catches his eye," she said, still sharp with her sister.

Nancy sighed and put her arm around Emily's shoulders. "All right. For your sake, we'll have a quiet visit."

☙ℭ☙

"Quiet" meant that the calls began at eleven, just after the breakfast dishes had been cleared away. Nancy excused herself—"I have things to look after"—and sent Emily into the back parlor, where the Sheraton furniture had been exiled. Camilla Aiken, who was the first to arrive, bounded into the house. Cicero, the dignified butler, trailed behind her, saying, "Miss, I can't announce you if you run like that!"

Camilla, who was younger than Jane, liked to boast that she was taller. Her hair was blonder and more lustrous than her sister's, and even though her mother dressed her in girlish white, her muslin dress was adorned with the draped and tiered "pagoda" sleeves that *Godey's* liked so much and girdled with a deep pink ribbon. "Emily!" she said, grinning. "I heard you arrived yesterday!"

"Where is Jane?"

Camilla plumped down on the nearest chair too vigorously for its fragile lines and didn't bother to smooth her skirt. "Such news, Emily!"

"Is she all right?"

"Better than all right. She's in a tizzy!"

"Stop it, Camilla. You're making my head ache. What's happened?"

"Her best beau, that planter from Mississippi, just asked for her. Just yesterday! And she said yes."

"I didn't know he was her best beau."

"Did being in Charleston addle you? He's been here all summer, sitting by her at every picnic, walking with her in the evenings, and dancing with her at every party. I knew he'd ask for her. I saw them together under the live oak in our front yard last week. He kissed her!"

The news came to Emily like a letter from a foreign country. It was of mild interest, but it had nothing to do with her. "How nice," she said. "I'm glad for her."

Camilla leaned forward. If they had been sitting side by side, she would have poked Emily in the ribs with her elbow. "Nice! Is that all you can say? It's grand! He has nearly a thousand acres and three hundred hands. He's the richest planter in the county. A Carolina man who went there ten years ago with nothing, and he's made a fortune there."

Emily tried to recall the man, since she had surely met him more than once, and could not. "What is he like?"

"He's a gentleman, even though he thinks about cotton all the time. Handsome, too. He wears white linen, even in Sumter County. He says that Mississippi has thinned his blood so much that he feels the heat all the time."

"I hope he isn't ailing."

"Oh no. Jane tells me that he dances with considerable vigor!"

Emily blinked at Camilla, who was supposed to be too innocent to think about a man's vigor. "When will the wedding be?"

"Not for months. There's the trousseau to think of, and the church, and the wedding breakfast, and the wedding journey. Both Mama and Jane will be in a tizzy together, arranging everything." Camilla laughed. "Jane is in such a state that I think she's forgotten there will be a husband at the end of it."

A vigorous man to greet her in the marriage bed. Emily shook her head. What was wrong with her? These were thoughts that belonged in a barnyard. Why did they come to her? Robert's caresses had been chaste and delicate. She asked, "Does she love him?"

"I suppose so. Whenever she mentions him, she blushes. It's an even chance whether she'll laugh or cry."

"Tell her that I wish the best for her," Emily said, smoothing the black silk of her skirt.

"Oh, you can do better than that. We're having a party in a week to celebrate the engagement. Dancing, and music, and cards for the gentlemen, and such a supper. Our poor cook is in a tizzy, too."

Emily nodded politely. Camilla leaned forward again, and Emily wondered what confidence she'd impart. She said, "Now that Jane's taken care of, I can get married!"

Emily sighed and hoped that Camilla would keep her thoughts about manly vigor to herself.

"Emily, what's wrong with you? Don't you care? Getting married is important!"

"Yes, it is," Emily said. Distant news from a place far away.

"I'm not going to bother with any of these upcountry men," Camilla said. "All they care about is drinking and hunting, hunting and drinking. And all they talk about is cotton and politics, when it isn't politics and cotton! I want to marry a Low Country man. Someone refined and grand. Someone who has a big place on the coast and a fine summer house—I don't mind the pines, for the summer—and a house in Charleston, too, for the races and the season. A house like your uncle's. That's what I want!"

"You're supposed to want it, Camilla, but you aren't supposed to say so."

Camilla smiled, and her teeth gleamed a predatory white. "A girl can have ambitions, too," she said.

Only to snare a rich man and bring him down with

the efficiency of a cottonmouth snake. Emily looked at her hands.

"Emily, cheer up. There's the engagement party to look forward to. Why don't you put off your mourning? You could dance."

This was a message louder and closer to home. Emily raised her head. "Not yet," she said.

Camilla leaned close enough to grasp her hands. "Oh, Emily. We all know you loved Robert Herriot, and that his death was a blow to you. But it's been almost two years. Isn't it time? Time to give the men hope? Even a widow can get married again, and you aren't a widow."

"I'm not ready," she said, her hand stealing to the ornament at her throat.

"I wish you'd set aside that thing. Even jet would be better. There's something so morbid about a hair brooch."

Emily was suddenly very angry. She said to Camilla, "I hope that you marry a Low Country man who's as rich as Croesus and twice your age. He'll die well before you do, and make you a rich widow. Then we'll see how you like it."

Camilla burst into laughter. "Wouldn't that be a thing!" she said. "Then I'd have a thousand acres and six hundred slaves and three grand houses. All for myself!" Still laughing, she rose. "We'll send out proper invitations for the engagement party. Don't stay home, Emily. Mother will want to see you, even if you're dressed like a crow."

Her laughter echoed in the hall as dignified Cicero asked, "Miss, shall I call for your carriage?"

∞⁂

NANCY'S DEFINITION OF "QUIET" included a guest for midday dinner later that day. "Don't fuss, Emily," she said. "It's our neighbor, Mr. John Ellison. Hardly a crowd."

She knew Ellison only slightly. He was a local man from a poor farming family, and her father had never taken notice of him. Ellison had risen to wealth only within the past few years, as his cotton plantation had prospered and expanded. She had never met his wife. "Will Mrs. Ellison join us?"

"Emily, sometimes I wonder if you have peanuts stuck in your ears. Don't you recall? She died two years ago."

Just when I had lost Robert, she thought. "Did you invite him here?"

"I won't stand for any more foolishness from you. He's a friend to Charles. They hunt together, and they'll talk about horses. He won't even take notice of you."

He was a sturdy man, with the ruddy complexion and the crow's-feet of someone who spent a great deal of time outdoors. *Weather-beaten*, she thought, comparing him to Robert, who had been slight and pale. He took her hand with too much strength for politeness. Camilla would call him vigorous.

Nancy was proven right. Ellison addressed all his conversation to Charles. She thought of Camilla again.

Hunting and drinking and politics and cotton. He had a good appetite. He got up twice to refill his plate at the sideboard, and he let Charles refill his glass twice.

Nancy was the one to say, in good humor, "Can't politics wait until you've retired to the library after dinner? We ladies don't read the papers and don't follow it as you do."

Ellison's ruddy face flushed. "Beg your pardon, Miss Nancy. I don't often converse with ladies, and I don't know what interests them."

"Well, there is the news of the day about Miss Jane Aiken's engagement."

Ellison, so eloquent on the subject of horses and cotton, stared at his plate and mumbled, "It's a fine thing. He's a good man."

"It's a grand thing! We'll all have the chance to celebrate with her."

Ellison said, "I don't have much society since my wife died."

"Oh, pshaw, Mr. Ellison. You should. The ladies would be as glad of it as the gentlemen!"

He looked dutifully at Emily. As though he had been prompted, he said, "Miss Emily, your sister told me about your loss. I'm sorry to hear about it."

Emily flushed. She said, "Did she tell you that she thinks it's wrong that I'm still in mourning?"

Ellison looked puzzled. "Why would it be wrong? He was close to you."

She felt her color and her temper rise. "Of course he was! I nearly married him!" She rose and threw her napkin on the table. Nancy had managed this, Emily was sure of it. "I'm tired of it, Nancy! Tired of it!" She cast a baleful glance at Ellison. "Lying to me, when all you wanted was to put the widower in the way of the girl who dresses like a widow!"

She ran from the room, discovering that if she breathed too deeply, she would start to sob. She leaned against the wall in the hallway, her eyes blurred with anger.

Nancy's tread resounded on the wood floor. Nancy didn't pull her aside. She raised her voice in the hall, where it was perfectly audible in the dining room. "How dare you," she said. "I won't have such rudeness at my table! You'll go back into the dining room and apologize to our guest."

"I will not," Emily said. "I'll go upstairs to pack my things, and I'll go back to Charleston." She was breathing hard, as though she'd been running through the woods.

There was a tap on the doorframe. "Excuse me," said Ellison.

"Leave us alone," Nancy said, in a tone just as rude as Emily's.

"Mrs. Aiken, if she ain't ready to marry again—or even to think about marrying again—it was wrong to press her."

Emily looked up in surprise.

"Miss Emily?" he inquired, a soft tone for so rough-looking a man. "My wife was barely cold in her grave when the ladies of the county started to bring their girls around to get me married again. I weren't ready, either."

Emily swallowed hard.

He gestured toward her black dress. "I meant to say I was sorry about your uncle, but I'm sorry about your young man, too. I'm sorry for your losses, both of them."

Emily stared at him.

"Will you accept an apology, Miss Emily? Would you come back to the table with me? Finish your dinner?"

He was kinder and wiser than she had given him credit for. He offered her his arm, and she accepted that, too.

𝕊𝕆ℚℝ

CAMILLA CALLED DAILY, TELLING her more about wedding preparations and maidenly modesty than she wanted to hear. She said to Emily, "So Mr. Ellison came to dine with you."

Emily shook her head. "Just a friendly visit over dinner."

"I heard differently. That he was invited here to be put in your way, and he in yours."

"Camilla, if you don't *shut up*"—she spat out the vulgar words—"I'll pull your hair and slap you."

Camilla said, "Would you feel any better knowing that he was put in my way, too? And in the way of every girl in Sumter County."

"I thought he wasn't ready to marry again."

"Is that what he said?"

Puzzled, Emily said, "He's a little rough and plain-spoken, but he seems like a decent man. Why won't any of the girls have him?"

Camilla gave an unladylike snort. "Visit his place. Go to the stables with him. You'll see it."

"What?"

"He loves his horses better than he ever loved his wife," Camilla said.

&)C&

MR. ELLISON'S HOUSE WAS NO different from any other in the county—four rooms on each of its two stories—but his carriage house, which included his stable, was large enough to accommodate a carriage as well as the buggy and had room enough for a dozen horses. He insisted on giving Emily the tour of his place before the meal was served. Charles accompanied them, and Emily had no worry in Ellison's company. "I hope you don't mind," he said to Emily. "I'm proud of it, and I like to show it off."

She obliged him. He took them past the pleasant gardens that surrounded the house and escorted them to see the cotton fields. Grinning, he said, "It's a fine place, Miss Emily. Five hundred acres in cotton and corn, a place to give those Mississippi men a run for their money. And over a hundred hands to work it!" He watched as the slaves stooped to reach for the bolls.

"How many horses do you keep, Mr. Ellison?"

"I have a dozen. Come see. You too, Aiken. I've just

bought a new hunter. A black beauty!" He took Emily to the stable, large enough for a dozen horses, every stall occupied. He stopped to show her the black mare, stroking the animal's neck. "Ain't she fine?" he said, his face full of admiration.

"Very fine."

"You like your horses," Emily observed softly.

"Horses don't disappoint," Ellison said. His plain face darkened for a moment.

They walked back to the house. In the side yard, a slave woman sat in a chair, watching as her charges—a boy of four and a child of indeterminate sex, still of an age to crawl and dressed in a long white gown—played.

Ellison ran to scoop up the little boy. "Johnny!" he said, holding the child high as he cried out in fear and glee. He lowered the child and rubbed his face against the boy's cheek.

"Daddy!" the little boy cried. He set the boy down. "And Amelia!" He bent low to pet the golden head of the crawler, as though she were a puppy, and bent even lower, to kiss the curls.

He stood up and asked the nurse, "Polly, how do my young'uns get on today?"

The nurse was very young, Caroline's age, Emily thought, and her face was dark brown and smoothed of emotion under her white scarf. "They get on fine, Marse John," she said.

Against her bosom, which strained against her bodice, she held another child, a suckling infant only a few months old. It was heavily swaddled, but Emily caught a glimpse of the little face. The baby had the milky complexion that spoke of racial mixture.

ΩΩ

EMILY REGARDED HER REFLECTION in the dressing table mirror and sighed. She had made no end of trouble about wearing mourning. She had bickered with her sister, insulted Camilla, and mortified herself before John Ellison for this dress. Now, as her sister's maid readied her for the party at the Aikens', she saw herself through Camilla's eyes: a girl in crow's feathers whose only jewel was a lock of a dead man's hair. *Robert,* she thought, *beloved.* But he was too far away, and even his memory now slipped through her hands like a wisp of smoke, a wraith too insubstantial to grasp.

"Miss?" the maid asked. "Is you ready?"

Her sister's servant was so quiet and self-effacing that Emily had trouble remembering her name. "Yes, thank you," she said. She rose to attend a party where dancing was the chief celebration, even though she had denied herself the pleasure of it.

The Aiken house blazed with candlelight in the fall dusk. The great chandelier in the ballroom shone like the sun at midday. The room was as loud as the crowd at the races, the chatter of the women drowned out by the laughter of the men. The house smelled of the cut roses and gardenias from the front garden and the odor of cigar smoke from the card-players in the parlor behind the ballroom.

The bride-to-be, anticipating her future, wore a dress festooned with roses in red silk and made with a draped white satin even whiter than the flesh of her arms and neck. She also wore a spray of rosebuds in her hair, which gleamed golden in the candlelight. Beside her stood her future husband, dressed in his habitual white suit, his hair also golden and worn long, his expression pleased and a little dazed, whether from champagne or the prospect of matrimony, Emily couldn't guess. With difficulty, Emily took Jane's hands and wished her every happiness. Her fiancé pressed Emily's hand with such vigor that Emily was glad when he released it.

The more she told herself not to recall it, the more she thought of her own engagement and its celebration. She would find a chair set against the wall, where she would sit with the married women, the true widows, and the dowagers who had outlived marriage. And she would not cry, not in public, not at a joyous celebration.

As she made her way past the punchbowl, Camilla grasped her hand. "There you are," she said. Her color was very high. She held a young man by the other hand. Under thick brows, his eyes were dark and keen, and his beard surrounded a mouth set in the faintest smile. Beneath his frock coat, where an old-fashioned Carolina man would wear a neckcloth and a fashionable one would tie a slender cravat, he wore a loose and flowing scarf in an astonishingly bright red.

"Emily!" cried Camilla, in such an unrestrained voice that Emily wondered how much champagne she had sipped. "This is my naughty cousin Joshua, who ran away to study at Harvard College in Boston and stayed north to live in Ohio."

Emily barely had time to say, "Pleased to make your acquaintance," before Camilla interrupted her. "But I'm going to dance with him first, and after that, he can flirt with whoever he wants to!"

Emily thought, *I can't bear it. I can't breathe in here.* She didn't hasten, but she made her way to the door and down the great staircase to the front door. The first-floor piazza was still crowded with arrivals as she slipped onto the grounds. She had been at the Aiken house in daylight, and she knew what she sought. In the side garden, under the live oak tree, was a wrought iron bench, where she collapsed gratefully. She rested her hand on the metal, which was pleasantly cool to the touch in the fall night. She breathed in the air, scented with pine and the gardenia in its last moment of bloom. This late in the season, the crickets had quieted, but the swallows were out, swooping against the indigo sky, and the owls called, their cry eerie and reassuring at the same time. The waxing moon cast a silvery light on the gray bark of the live oak, turning its leaves to silver as well.

She sat long enough to cool her face and calm the desire to sob. She promised herself she would go back soon. It wasn't seemly to attend a dance and sit alone in the garden. That was worse than sitting by the wall.

In the faint light, she could see a frock coat but not a face. The voice was a surprise. "Pardon me," he said. "I didn't think that anyone else would be here. I didn't mean to disturb you."

It was Camilla's cousin Joshua.

"I needed a breath of air. And a moment of quiet, too," Emily said.

"It's quite a press in there."

Emily said, "The whole county knows Miss Aiken and rejoices with her."

"Shall we make a proper introduction?" he asked.

She rose and held out her hand. "Miss Emily Jarvie," she said.

He pressed her hand with dry, confident fingers. "Mr. Joshua Aiken."

She smoothed her skirt, readying herself to sit, and invited him to join her. The bench was wide enough for decorum. He didn't press her in any way. She asked, "How are you connected with the Aiken family?"

"Oh, a dog-and-cat kind of cousin. We're Sumter County people from way back. My father has a place near the Kershaw County border. Three hundred acres, cotton and corn."

"What keeps you in Ohio, Mr. Aiken? Since no one grows cotton there."

He laughed. "There are corn farmers but not in Cincinnati, where I live. I'm the editor of a ladies' magazine called *Hearth and Home*."

"I don't know it."

"Ah, that's our trouble. We model ourselves on *Godey's*, and as my publisher is fond of reminding me, they *goad* us to our efforts for greater circulation every month." He laughed. "We publish news of the latest in fashion and aids to household management, but we also try to publish literature. Stories and sketches. That's my purview, since I studied literature at Harvard College."

"What do you read, Mr. Aiken?"

"I keep my eye on the newest books. That tells me what our readers prefer. We can't pay the best-known writers as much as *Godey's* or *Harper's*, so I strive to find writers who will interest our readers but cost us less."

She said, "I love books, but I never thought of them as a business."

"Ah, shame on me for talking about business at an engagement party. I'm always delighted to find someone who loves books. What do you prefer to read, Miss Jarvie?"

"I like novels best, even though some people think they're trifling," she said. "I read history, too." She thought again of Caroline, her face alight as she held a book in her hands.

"Do you write, Miss Jarvie?"

"I keep a diary," she said, blushing.

"What do you write in your diary?"

She met his eyes, which were very dark in the moon's faint light. "Whatever I see. Whatever I think. And whatever I feel." She admitted, "I have no one to tell. So I write it instead."

He said gently, "It's often lonely to see keenly. And to feel keenly. As many writers do."

If she let him go on, he'd start to flirt with her. She asked, "Why did you leave South Carolina, Mr. Aiken?"

"My father keeps control of the place, and my brothers are waiting for him to let it go so they'll have something to do. I watched them fall into idleness and dissipation, and I didn't want that for myself. I wanted to be occupied. And that occupation turned out to be literature and *Hearth and Home* in Cincinnati."

This was easier, asking him about himself, deflecting from her own desire to confide. "How do you find Cincinnati?"

Even in the faint light, she saw him smile. It was a broad, sunny smile, showing strong, white teeth. "It's an impatient kind of place, Miss Jarvie. Not just the weather, although I'm glad of a wool coat in the winter. They're northerners, and they do everything quickly. The way they walk and their speech. They have business to transact, and they hurry to do it. Even the married women are brisk in the streets and the shops. And there are many unmarried women who work for a living, and they take their business as seriously as the men do."

She thought of a cold place, full of wool-clad people bent on commerce. She asked, "Are there Negroes in Cincinnati?"

"Of course. My barber is a man of color. He's intelligent and jolly with his customers. And brisk!" He laughed, softening his words. "He can't make any money shaving me, so he's concocted an unguent for my hair and my beard and profits by selling me that." He stroked his beard, which was well-groomed and a little bristly, despite the unguent.

She felt a little uneasy to hear about a free black man who prospered. But weren't there barbers in Charleston who were free persons of color? She deflected again. "Mr. Aiken, I believe you're becoming a northerner, to talk so bluntly about your barber and your beard with a lady."

"Or a man without manners, perhaps. It's such a pleasure to talk to a lady who likes to read and write that I may have forgotten myself. I hope I haven't offended you."

It was impossible to be offended by this cheerful, businesslike Carolina transplant who loved literature and made a living selling it. "No, Mr. Aiken, you haven't."

"You look a little chilled, Miss Jarvie. Would you like to go inside?"

"I would, even though I can't dance since I'm still in mourning."

He said, "The Aikens told me about your uncle. I didn't want to be blunt about that. It was recent, I hear."

"In August." She met his eyes and said, "Did they tell you about the other loss? My betrothed?"

He returned her gaze. "Even less reason to be blunt," he said softly. "What a terrible loss, Miss Jarvie, and how difficult to come here with your heart still heavy."

"You're very kind," she said, meaning it.

He rose and offered her his arm. "I could do with a spot of supper," he said. "Could you?"

She rose and laced her arm through his. "I could," she said. "What do people eat in Cincinnati? Are they brisk about their food, too?"

He laughed. "The Aikens feed me much better than my landlady at the boarding house in Cincinnati," he said. "I take full advantage of it while I'm here."

As they made their way back to the light and the noise and the smoky perfume of the house, she asked him, "How much longer will you stay in Sumter County?"

"For a few more days," he said. "My mother says she sees me too little and always wants me to linger."

As they mounted the steps, Camilla, who stood in the doorway, called out to them. "Cousin Joshua! Where have you been hiding? Have you been flirting with my friend Emily?"

He laughed, a good, full, rich laugh. "Cousin Camilla, you're like a force of nature! You're like a hurricane in the Sea Islands!" He stepped lightly across the threshold into the house, and with the lightest step she had managed in a long time, Emily came with him.

∞⌘

SEVERAL DAYS LATER, EMILY WOKE to find the maid-servant lighting a fire in the bedroom fireplace. "Cold last night, miss," she said. "Frost come."

Emily rose to look out the window. Frost coated the lawn. Fall was over, and so was the fever. She could go back to Charleston, if she wanted to.

By midmorning the frost had burned away, and it

was pleasant enough to sit on the first-floor piazza if she wrapped a shawl around her shoulders. She took *Moby-Dick* with her—she had read less than usual on this visit—and she had just found her place when Joshua Aiken, buttoned in a wool coat against the cold, bounded up the steps and greeted her with a broad smile.

"Mr. Aiken!" she said. "It's brisk today. You must feel comfortable."

"Oh, I do, Miss Jarvie. What about you? Are you warm enough?"

"It's kind of you to ask. I am."

It was strange to see him in daylight. He looked younger without the flicker of candlelight or the glimmer of moonlight. His eyes were a lighter brown than she remembered, and his lips were rosier. He unbuttoned his coat, and today, he wore an ordinary black cravat.

She gestured to a chair and he sat. He said, "I'm glad to see you again, Miss Jarvie."

"Likewise, Mr. Aiken."

"I hope your sister doesn't mind that I call on you like this. On the piazza."

Emily said, "If she does, I'll tell her that you've become a Yankee and lost your manners in Cincinnati."

"No," he said, smiling. "Just tell her that my manners have become very *brisk*." He said, "I'm returning to Cincinnati tomorrow, and I wanted to see you before I left."

Oh, no, she thought. *Not to ask to write to me. Not to ask to court me. Not after his kindness at the engagement party.* "Mr. Aiken, I am still in mourning."

"I hadn't forgotten," he said gently. "No, today my purpose is quite different. I'm here in my northerner's guise. I'm here on a matter of business."

She stared at him in surprise. "Business? What possible business could you have with me?"

"Miss Jarvie, I'm wondering if you might see to writing something for *Hearth and Home*."

She stammered, "I never thought of such a thing. I've never set my hand to it."

"Might you be persuaded to try?"

"I don't know."

"Just a sketch, Miss Jarvie. Something about Charleston or South Carolina. Something you have observed and thought about."

"I wouldn't know where to start or what subject to take up."

"Most of our readers are northern ladies," he said. "The South is a foreign place to them, and an exotic one. Think of something you might show a northern visitor to give her the flavor of Carolina."

She was too surprised even to stammer.

He said, "Nothing inflammatory, please. We're like *Godey's* in that we avoid the topics of the day. We don't want to offend. But there are many subjects that would interest a lady. I would trust you to find one, and I leave that to your discretion."

Emily stared at the book in her lap.

He broke the silence. "If I've overstepped my bounds, or if I've offended you…"

She swiftly raised her head. "No. It's such a surprise. No one has ever asked me for such a thing before."

"Surely you wrote for your teachers at school?"

She thought of Madame Devereaux's forbidding face. "At Madame Devereaux's, we were taught never to put ourselves forward," she said. "To efface ourselves."

He leaned forward, his expression earnest. "Madame Devereaux sounds like a tyrant to discourage her scholars so. You're no longer under her instruction. It might be time to throw off her tyranny."

Startled, Emily said, "You make it sound like an insurrection!"

He shook his head. "I should never forget that I'm in South Carolina," he said. "Let me start afresh. I have faith in you as a writer, Miss Jarvie. I would welcome a thousand words, three closely written pages, from you, on the subject of the charms of Charleston, suitable for a lady's eye. Is that easier to take?"

"Very brisk," she said, but the joke was weak since she was still so startled.

He took a silver case from his pocket and snapped it open. "This my card," he said. "With my address at *Hearth and Home.*"

She took the card and scrutinized the address as though it held an answer. Trembling, she said, "I can only promise to try, Mr. Aiken."

The broad smile appeared again. "I look forward to seeing your effort, Miss Jarvie." He rose, as did she. She held out her hand, and to her surprise, he didn't press it as a gentleman pressed a lady's fingers. He shook it, as he would to seal an agreement.

She watched him walk away and turned the card in her hands. She shook her head in astonishment as she put the card in her pocket.

Nancy opened the door. Standing in the doorway, she said, "Who was that?"

"Mr. Joshua Aiken. Jane and Camilla's cousin. Didn't you meet him the other night?"

"I don't recall. Why did he come to see you? Do I dare hope for a thaw?"

Emily laughed outright. Her secret warmed her. "He hasn't a dime," she said.

"Well, at least you entertained him. Why did he leave so swiftly? You didn't send him packing?"

Emily put her hand in her pocket and curled it around the card. She said, "Of course not. He lives up in Cincinnati, and he's learned how to be a Yankee. He was in a hurry."

₨ℓℂℜ

EMILY RETURNED TO CHARLESTON a few days later. Escaping her stepmother's scrutiny, she excused herself, saying that she wanted to lie down in her room. Upstairs, she waved away Lydia, who wanted to unpack and undress her and fuss over her hair. "It can wait," she said. "Leave me be for a while."

She sat in the chair before the dressing table to look at herself. She looked better than she had when she left

Charleston. Livelier, with a better color in her cheeks. The black dress was too severe next to her face, which was made rosier by the air of the pines.

She stared at herself, trying to see herself as a stranger might. As Joshua Aiken had. The hair brooch, which had become so familiar, was suddenly obvious to her. The hair had lost its living sheen a long time ago, and its silky texture felt like dust under her fingers. She unpinned it and let it rest in her hand. With a resolute motion, she unlocked her jewelry box and laid Robert's hair inside. She closed the box and locked the brooch away.

Chapter 6: Free Persons of Color

KITTY WRAPPED THE PORTRAIT of James in black silk
and hid it under her bed. She had not lost her fear that
someone would accuse her of having stolen it. Caro, who
couldn't bear to put a book on the dirt floor, left the Melville volume in plain sight on the pine table, where she
saw it all the time. It no longer gave her pleasure. It was
a reproach, reminding her of a life that she was likely to
never have again.

Her father's portrait made her mother melancholy.
Caro knew that her mother took it out at night to press
her cheek against before she fell asleep. The Melville book
made Caro irritable, an anger like a heat rash, hidden and
miserable and unresponsive to any cure. Her discomfort
made her sharp with her mother.

Sophy had told her, "Don't talk like that to your
mama," and Sophy's reprimand made her itch with anger
at Sophy, too.

Early one morning, after breakfast and before the
chores of the day, Caro stood in the shack as her mother
sat on the rope bed as though it were a settee, arranging

her meager skirt as though she still wore a crinoline and hoops. Her mother's façade of being a lady in their reduced circumstances grated on Caro. They were not ladies playacting at being slaves. They were truly slaves.

Sophy tapped on the door and called, "Miss Caroline! The wash water all ready, all hot. You come to help me?"

Caro had come to hate the task of the wash. She hated the feeling of scalding water on her hands. She hated the sting of the soap as it rose in the steam. She hated the weight of the wet cloth, and she hated the task of ironing even more. After a day of wash, her arms and back ached. She thought of the five thin dimes she would receive, a quarter of what she was due, and she hated that, too.

No, she thought. But she called back, "Yes, Sophy."

Her mother, who had never touched a dirty petticoat or held the stirring pole, said to her, "You don't have to do that, you know."

Caro snapped, "Yes, I do."

"Sophy will do it."

Caro turned to stare at her mother. Through her irritation, she saw the haggard face, the hollows in the cheekbones, the deep shadows under the lovely eyes. Their new life had leached the rosy color from her mother's lips, turning them dry and pale. It had made her thinner and had worsened her cough. Caro asked, "Who will earn our fifty cents if I don't?"

"As though I wanted the task! Or the money!"

Caro forced herself to stay angry. Otherwise she feared she would start to cry. "As though I do!"

Her mother said, "We won't live like this forever."

"How? What will we do? When will it be different?"

Her mother's eyes grew wide, and they glistened with tears. "I don't know," she said.

At a better time, Caro would have knelt at her mother's feet to touch her cheek and try to console her. Now she said, "Why don't we find your relations in Charleston? The Bennetts? Why don't we go to see them?"

Now anger enlivened her mother's face. "We will not," she said.

∽◌∼

ONCE THE CLOTHES WERE HUNG to dry, she sat with Sophy in the kitchen to eat a biscuit smeared with jam. She wiped the crumbs from her mouth with the napkin and asked, "Sophy, do you know of a free man named Thomas Bennett?"

Sophy set down her coffee cup. "Mr. Thomas Bennett? Free man of color? Run a tailoring business on Queen Street, serve all the best families in Charleston? Everyone know of him. Why you ask?"

"He's my mother's half brother."

"Why don't you go to see him?"

"My mother won't hear of it."

"Why not?"

"She won't tell me. All I know is that they're estranged." She said, "I never thought much of it. My father was estranged from his family, too." Caro asked, "Why is my uncle free and my mother not?"

"Why do a white man free one slave and not another? Don't know. He still your flesh and blood. You go to him, he help you."

"I wish I could make my mother see it."

Sophy put her gnarled hand over Caro's. "I know you love your mama, and she love you," she said. "But she act like she lost in the woods in Charleston. Many a way for a Charleston slave to make a life and earn a living." She clasped Caro's fingers. "By your own hand. She can't see that."

Five dimes, when she was owed three dollars. Caro returned Sophy's handclasp. "But I do."

"You wise to think of going to your uncle. Whatever happen between him and your mama, he still your flesh and blood. You go."

"My mother doesn't want us to beg," Caro said.

"Can you sew?" Sophy asked.

"Of course I can."

"Fine sewing?"

Caro snorted. "I made myself a trousseau," she said.

"He a tailor," Sophy said. "His wife, her family all dressmakers, and if he don't have something, they will. You don't go to beg. You go to ask him about work."

Caro looked down at her miserable dress. "Not like this," she said.

"We neaten you up a bit, but it help that you go to him looking poor," Sophy said. "That way, he pity you, and he more likely to help you."

"Sophy, I never met anyone better at getting round someone than you."

Sophy chuckled. "Why do you think Marse Lawrence trust me so much?" she asked.

⁂

HER APRON WASHED AND PRESSED, her headscarf neatly tied, her shoes cleaned, Caro walked resolutely toward Thomas Bennett's shop on Queen Street. *Not to ask for charity*, she reminded herself, *but for work.*

Amid the commercial splendor of Queen Street, Thomas Bennett's shop stood out. The glass of his storefront flashed brilliantly in the sun, and the bell jangled cheerfully as she pushed open the door. Just inside the door was a little sitting area with a pair of good chairs in the Sheraton style and a little marble-topped table between so customers could be served refreshments.

Thomas Bennett himself stood behind the mahogany counter. He was a light-brown man in a white shirt fierce with starch and a beautifully cut, beautifully made wool suit that advertised his business as a tailor. His expression was smooth, as though he starched and pressed it as well. A customer, a young man in an extravagant top hat and long-tailed coat, leaned against the counter. "I'm particular about my shirt fronts," he explained to Thomas. "Mind the tucks when you make them up."

Next to Thomas stood a young man, making a note as the customer ordered his shirts. He had the palest of brown skin, dark curly hair, and arresting hazel eyes, an oddity in a colored face. Caro tried hard not to stare at him. He was beautiful as her father had been beautiful.

Caro was miserably conscious of how wretchedly she was dressed. She reminded herself that she was kin to these elegant people. She forced herself to stand up straight.

When the young man was satisfied, he turned to go. At the sight of Caro, he sniffed and raised his eyebrows. "The back door," he said, unkindly.

Thomas said affably, "It's all right, Mr. Herriot."

"Hah!" said the young fop, and the bell jangled as the door shut.

Thomas inclined his head. "You should have come in the back," he said. "Who are you?"

She approached the gleaming wooden counter. Many merchants were satisfied with oak or even pine, but Thomas's counter was mahogany. She didn't lean against it. "Caroline Jarvie, sir," she said. "Kitty Bennett is my mother."

Thomas Bennett's smooth commercial expression faltered. He said, "Kitty's girl. You're Kitty's girl." He shook his head. "You have the look of her, when she was young." He righted himself. "I was very sorry to hear about Mr. Jarvie." His expression was smooth again.

She was taken aback that he was so cool. But she was relieved that he hadn't thrown her out. "Thank you, sir."

The young man stared at her. She thought, *I look even worse than I realized.*

Thomas explained to him, "Caroline is my half sister's

girl. Kitty left Charleston some years ago. I don't believe you've ever met her."

The young man continued to gape at her, an expression at odds with his polished appearance, as his uncle said, "This is Danny. My nephew. Maria's eldest boy." Thomas looked askance at Caro. "You know of Maria?"

"Yes, sir, I do," Caro said. "Even though we've never met, either."

Danny remembered his manners and extended his hand. "I'm pleased to meet you," he said.

His fingers were pricked and callused from wielding the needle. She said, "I'm pleased to meet you." She met the hazel eyes. "Are you a Bennett, too?"

Danny let go her hand. "Since my father died, we're called Pereira," he said. Did the faintest shadow of sadness pass over his face?

Now she remembered. He was kin to her father's friend, the lawyer Benjamin Pereira.

"How is your mother?" Thomas asked, sympathy warming his tone.

Caro looked up. "She misses him greatly."

He nodded, the slightest incline of his chin toward the snowy shirtfront. "How are you faring, the two of you?"

As though he didn't know, since the story had undoubtedly made its way from the mouths of the gossips that Sophy knew at Zion Presbyterian to their friends, among them free people of color, like the Bennetts.

"We're taking in a little money," she said. "Doing

some laundry." She forced a light tone, as though she were talking about the newest mode for trimming a bonnet. "But it would be good to bring in more." She smiled. "That's why I came to you, Uncle Thomas. I don't want to trouble you. I wouldn't ask for charity. But I hoped…" she faltered, and thought of the five dimes in her palm. Her payment. Her underpayment. "Sir, I hoped that you might have some work for me." The rest of the words came in a rush. "I can do fine sewing."

He asked, "Does Mr. Jarvie know that you hire out?"

"He sends us the laundry himself," she said, still light. "And he pays us. I don't think he would mind if I hired myself out."

"It would be different if I employed you," Thomas said.

"Why? If he doesn't know and doesn't care?"

Thomas sighed. "It would make difficulties for me," he said. "I have too much custom among his friends. If I hired you, he might hear of it."

So he had heard, and he knew the whole story—the anger and the turning out. He probably knew the terms of the will.

He continued, "If you would speak to him and make some arrangement with him, I might consider it."

Caro's heart sank. And he must know perfectly well that Lawrence Jarvie would never agree to her employment with Thomas Bennett.

Seeing her disappointment, he softened again. "You're welcome to join us at our Sunday service," he said.

She held out her hand. "Thank you, Uncle Thomas," she said. As the door closed behind her, the cheerful bell mocked her.

Her mother had been right, and now she had to trudge back to Tradd Street in the coarse shoes that still gave her blisters. Tears stung behind her eyes, and she blinked against them. A lady didn't go barefoot in the street, and she didn't weep, either.

The door opened and the bell jangled again. It was her cousin, Danny Pereira. If it was a disgrace to cry in public, it was worse to cry before her well-dressed cousin.

Danny said, "Miss Caroline." His eyes glowed in the morning sun. He bent close, and she wondered why. In the softest of voices, he said, "I am very sorry about your father."

ഗാരു

WHEN SHE RETURNED TO TRADD Street, she opened the kitchen door to find Sophy at the kitchen table. Sophy asked, "How do it go?"

Caro shook her head. She fought the tears that started in her eyes.

Her mother entered the kitchen and saw Caro's stricken face. "What is it, Caro?" she asked, her tone softer than it had been in days. "What's wrong?"

"I went to see my uncle," Caro said, falling heavily into a chair.

"Is that what you call Lawrence Jarvie these days?"

"Your brother," she said. "Uncle Thomas Bennett."

Kitty seemed to swell with anger. "You went to Thomas?"

"Yes," Caro said.

"You went begging to Thomas?"

"Not to beg," Caro said. "To ask for work."

Kitty turned on Sophy. "You put her up to it."

Sophy, who had been peeling a potato, put down her knife. "No, it were her notion. But I didn't discourage her."

Kitty raged at Sophy. "What did you say to me? That I am her mother, and you would respect that? Is that how you show it?"

Sophy said, "Just want to help."

Two spots of color blazed on Kitty's cheeks. "When I want your help, you meddling old woman, I'll ask for it." She reached for Caro's hand. "Come with me," she ordered.

Caro felt wretched. She had made trouble and everything was worse than before. Tears welled in her eyes as she followed her mother, her head down. She thought, *Why doesn't anyone ask me what I want?*

⁐⁖

A FEW DAYS LATER, SOPHY'S MAN, Sunday, came to visit. Sunday kissed Caro on the cheek and asked, "Where is your pretty mama?"

Caro was silent. Sophy said, "She mad at me, so she sit in that little shack and sulk. Won't eat with us."

Sunday said to Sophy, "What happen?"

"I encourage Caro to take matters into her own hands, and she do." Sophy explained Caro's family connections and her fruitless effort.

"Thomas Bennett? He watch himself, all the time," Sunday said. "If he anger one rich white man, he tell everyone he know. And it ruin his custom. He a free man, but he in debt to every one of them for a living."

Caro had never realized that a free man of color might be so constrained.

"Well, we have a pleasant dinner tonight," Sophy said. "You bring us hock!"

He lifted the bottle in his hand. "We savor this because it the last bottle for a while," he said.

Sophy asked, "No new job of work, now that you finish the last one?"

"Not yet." Worry had added creases to his face.

Sophy put a consoling hand on his arm. "You find something. You the best carpenter in Charleston!"

He laughed, a bitter sound. "Could be the best carpenter since Jesus, and I still have trouble!"

Caro asked, "Why? I thought your master didn't mind that you hired out."

"Oh, he don't. He never do. It's them white workmen who stir things up. They mad that black men hire out."

Caro asked, "Why would they care?"

"Say we take the work away. That we take the bread from their mouths." He sighed. "They even go to the city council—that were earlier this year—and ask them to consider a law to forbid slaves hiring out. The city council say no. Everyone on the council a master, and many of them profit by hiring their people out."

"Like your master."

Sunday nodded. "Now they mad again, the white workmen, and they say they go the Assembly to ask for the same thing."

Caro said, "But everyone in the Assembly is a master. They'd never agree to it."

Sunday said, "You a sharp one."

Sophy said, "Her daddy crazy to make her read all them books, but he didn't raise her to be a fool."

"Well, they cause a lot of trouble, even if they never get the Assembly to do a thing."

Sophy said, "The last time it happen, you say, 'It blow over. It be all right.' And it were. Be all right this time, too."

Sunday said, "So it hard all of a sudden to hire out. Men who hire me, they wait to see how it go. Wait to see how much trouble the white workmen cause."

Caro thought of her uncle, whose smooth face hid his worry. "Are they angry about tailors and seamstresses, too?" she asked.

"I expect so. Upset about anyone who hire out."

Caro nodded. It gave her an odd kind of reassurance. As a free man of color, as a success in his business, as a man who might hire out slaves, Uncle Thomas had more difficulty than his feelings for a niece who looked like the half sister he had put aside.

⊰⊱

Several days later, as Caro ate a midmorning biscuit in the kitchen, the door opened and her mother came in. She looked tired, as though anger wore her out. She sniffed the air. "Is there coffee?"

"You know there is."

Kitty poured herself a cup and sat to drink it.

Caro said, "Sophy will be back before you're finished."

"I won't let Sophy order me," Kitty said, as though her petulance over the last week had been a careful decision and not a pout.

Caro sighed.

Kitty had just drained the heavy china cup when Sophy returned, ushering in a visitor.

Danny Pereira carried a bundle wrapped in brown paper and tied with string, and Caro hoped for a moment that Thomas had changed his mind, despite all the difficulty of hiring out, and sent her sewing. Today he was composed, his smooth expression a replica of his uncle's.

"Who is this, Caro?" Kitty asked.

Caro introduced Danny to her mother, who sat up very straight, her lips pressed together in anger, as Danny said politely, "How do you do, Miss Catherine."

"What brings you here?" Kitty asked.

Danny set the bundle on the table, taking care to put it in a dry spot. He said, "Miss Catherine, your daughter called on my uncle a few days ago, and he regrets that he was rude to her." Caro thought, *He's learned Thomas's tone of cajolery. Perhaps Thomas educates him in tactfulness as he teaches him tailoring.*

Kitty said, "What did she expect, going to him like a beggar?"

"Oh, Miss Catherine, it was nothing like that. She asked him most politely for work. And he had to say no, since he has his hands full with all of us—three tailors and two apprentices." Caro was grateful for this fib.

"What does he want now?" Kitty asked.

Danny said, "He would like to invite your daughter to attend church with us a week from Sunday. And to join us for dinner afterward." He added, "He would be glad to extend the invitation to you, as well."

"Tell him no," Kitty said.

Caro cried, "Mama!"

He rested his hand on the bundle. "Perhaps this would help," he said.

"What is it?" Caro asked.

As Danny undid the string, Caro noticed that the skin of his hand was several shades lighter than the wrapping paper. He peeled away the paper and shook the contents out.

It was a dress, very fine cotton, printed in a yellow windowpane plaid with an edging of gray, each square in the pattern filled with a yellow rosebud. The skirt was full, designed for a crinoline underneath, and the sleeves flared at the elbow in the style that *Godey's* called "the pagoda."

"This is for you," Danny said to Caro, smiling. Caro put out her hand to touch it. Fabric made from Sea Island cotton, as sleek and light as silk.

Kitty was angrier than ever. "We don't take charity," she said.

Danny flushed. "We wouldn't think of such a thing," he said. "Thomas's daughter Charlotte is a seamstress. A customer ordered this dress and never paid for it. She's taken it as a loss. Uncle Thomas thought of a use for it."

Caro stroked the fabric as she stroked the cat. "Mama," she said, as though they were at the dressmaker's again. "Look at how fine this is."

"His castoffs!" Kitty said.

Caro took her hand away. Her mother's bitterness seemed to burn her skin. As much as she felt delight at this dress, she knew the real reason for it. It wasn't charity.

Thomas had sent Caro this dress to spare himself shame. She couldn't come to church as part of his family dressed like a field hand.

Caro looked up to see that Danny watched as she touched the dress. He must have seen many people, men and women, white and black, free and slave, yearn so for a piece of cloth.

With the tact of a tailor, he addressed Kitty. "I'm sorry that I've troubled you, Miss Catherine. I can take the dress away and make your apologies to my uncle."

Kitty looked at Caro, whose hand still rested on the dress, her touch light but full of longing. "Mama," Caro said softly. "It's so pretty. It would make me so happy…"

The unspoken words hung in the air: for the first time since Papa died.

Kitty looked from the dress to Danny, whose expression was as polite as an undertaker's. She looked at Caro, who made no effort to hide her happiness. With some difficulty, Kitty said, "It would be mean of spirit to say no." She looked at Caro. "To the dress or to the invitation. Not for myself but for my daughter." She glanced at Danny. "Please give your uncle my thanks."

Delighted, Caro rose to hug her mother, and Kitty allowed it but without any pleasure.

The dress took very little alteration, a nip in the waist and the hem to let down, and Caro showed the result to Sophy, twirling around to make the skirt bell out. Sophy said, "It look better with a crinoline, but you still pretty in it."

Caro looked down at her shoes, which looked worse than ever.

"Them shoes is dreadful," Sophy said.

"I know."

Sophy grinned. "Maybe these suit you better," and she ran upstairs, returning with a pair of brown leather boots suitable for walking, with little heels, pointed toes, and a row of buttons up the side. A lady's shoes to go with the lady's dress.

"Where did you get these?" Caro asked in amazement.

"Bought them. Some grand lady give them up, and someone else sell them."

Sophy was obviously lying; the boots were new. "Sophy, you fooler. You had them made for me."

Sophy said gruffly, "Put them on, and we see if they fit."

They did. In her new dress, in her new boots, Caro filled with joy. This was different from her uncle's charity. It was a pure gift. She hugged Sophy and exclaimed with a girl's delight, "Thank you, Sophy. Oh, thank you!"

😐∂ℛ

TRINITY METHODIST SAT ON MEETING Street like the other toney churches of Charleston and shared its tall white columns with buildings like the courthouse and the Work House. At Trinity Methodist, Sophy had told her, a free man of color like Thomas Bennett could rent a pew, even if it was the farthest from God's altar, instead of sitting in the balcony with the dark-skinned and the enslaved.

Caro approached the church with a light step. She scanned the crowd on the sidewalk for the Bennetts. She quickened her pace when she saw a familiar face, one lighter than a piece of brown butcher paper.

He knew the dress, but when he saw her, his cheeks flushed. He stammered, "You look so different!"

"It's a good thing, I hope," she said, smiling. She arched her neck and widened her eyes. She preened.

Danny, who had oiled her way into owning this dress by calming her mother's fury about it, choked on his words. "I didn't recognize you," he said.

A woman in a beautifully made black dress—she must be a Bennett to be so well tailored—swept up to them. "Danny, who is this?" she demanded.

Caro had once seen a portrait of her mother's father, Samuel Bennett. This woman, whoever she was, had the elegant long nose and high cheekbones of the planter Bennetts. She was a handsome woman, but her Bennett looks didn't add to beauty. She wasn't stout, but even though she was properly corseted, she had the form of a woman who had borne a number of children.

Still flushed, still tongue-tied, Danny faltered. He said to Caro, "May I introduce my mother, Mrs. Maria Pereira?"

Caro held herself tall. She said, "I'm pleased to meet you, ma'am."

Maria Pereira said curtly to her son, "Who is this, Danny?"

"Mama, it's Caroline, Kitty's daughter."

Maria gave her a terrible gaze. Not like Sophy's, considering a chicken at the market. Like a slave dealer's, deciding if she were worth a bid or not. With no kindness, she said, "How is your mother?"

Caro smiled. All her lady's training came back to her—how to put poison into the sugar. She replied, "She grieves for my father. As you can well imagine."

Maria said, "Danny, come with me."

"Mama, she's here to worship with us."

"She can sit with Thomas and his girls." She held out her arm. "Danny, now."

Danny's expression lost its luster. "Yes, Mama." To Caro, he said, "Excuse me," and he let his mother bear him away.

ഇൽൽ

After the service, the Bennetts and the Pereiras gathered at Thomas's house on Queen Street, not far from his shop. The Bennett house was a single house, like grander houses in Charleston, two stories tall and graced with a piazza on the second floor, but it was made of wood rather than brick or stone. It was an ambitious house for a man of color. It had recently been painted a bright white, and the gate was in better condition than the gate of the house on Tradd Street.

They crowded inside: Thomas and his wife; their four daughters, two of them married with families; and their two sons, also with their wives and children. The Pereiras followed, Maria and Danny and his two younger brothers, Ben and Thomas. They arranged themselves in the parlor, the girls crushed onto the sofas, the men standing, the little ones on the floor before the hearth. The women hurried to the back to help Thomas's wife in the kitchen to set out the dinner.

Thomas's dining room, just to the right of the parlor, was big enough for a long mahogany table in the Sheraton style and was ringed with mahogany chairs to match.

Caro wondered if Thomas had inherited them or whether he had bought them "with his own hand," as Sophy put it. The table was laid with a brilliantly white cloth, and each place was set with porcelain dishes, white with blue borders, and silverware. The glasses were crystal, which sparkled when the sun hit them. The water pitcher was silver, too.

The walls, where a richer man would have displayed his ancestral portraits, were graced with some very pretty depictions of castles in England. They were prints that had been hand-colored. Caro, who had grown up with the oils that her father called "pictures," knew the difference.

As paterfamilias, Thomas took the head of the table, with his wife and eldest son to his right. Maria held another place of honor, to his left, with Danny at her elbow. Thomas's younger daughters, Charlotte and Anna, who had crowded Caro in the pew and on the sofa, now pulled her to sit next to them at the foot of the table. Danny was so far away that she would have to send him a note to converse with him.

As it came, the meal delighted her. Oysters in butter. Turtle soup with sherry and cream. Shrimp in sauce, finer than Sophy's. A roasted duck, its skin crackled and fat. A roast of beef. Biscuits made by a practiced hand. Corn cooked into a relish. Summer greens and tomatoes. She had eaten like this every day of her life before her father died, and she had taken it for granted. Now she savored it.

Around her, Charlotte and Anna chattered like starlings, not caring if she listened or not and not caring if she joined in or not.

Charlotte said, "Anna, did you hear? Miss DeReef is entertaining suitors."

Anna snorted. "You mean that every free colored man in Charleston is calling on her, hoping for her father's blessing," she said.

Miss DeReef's father was the richest free man of color in Charleston. He had made a fortune in real estate; he owned so much land in the Neck that DeReef's Court was named after him. He had a dozen slaves. The DeReefs, who were very light of complexion, claimed that they were an amalgam of Spanish and Indian blood. Every person of color knew it was a fib. The DeReefs were African, however far removed.

Charlotte asked, "Who has the advantage?"

"We should lay wagers, like at the races," Anna said, laughing.

"Well, Eslanda Weston is getting married. No one will have to wager on it. It's to be at Zion Presbyterian, but the party will be small."

"For shame?"

"Anna!" Charlotte said. "Of course not. For privacy. Not everyone likes that the Reverend Girardeau marries people of color."

"But she's free! And so is her fiancé. What is his name? McKinley?" Anna laughed. "Christopher Columbus McKinley. He's from the upcountry."

Charlotte said, "The last marriage the reverend performed was between slaves. And that was mobbed. Don't laugh so, Anna."

"Don't preach so, Charlotte. There's no debating society for young ladies." She leaned backward and called to the head of the table. "Danny! Will you speak again at the Society?"

Charlotte laughed. "I'd go to the Clionian Debating Society if Danny were to speak again. He's as eloquent as a minister."

"Or a politician!" Anna said.

"Anna! As though a colored man could rise in politics in South Carolina!"

At their giddy talk, Caro felt dizzy. This was the world she had missed, the round of flirtations, engagements, marriages, lectures, and amusements of the free people of color in Charleston. They were as merry as the idle children of the richest planters. Listening to them, no one would ever know that all week long, they toughened their hands with the labor of the needle.

Charlotte addressed Caro, who divided her attention between a slice of cake and a scoop of watermelon ice. She said, "That dress suits you beautifully."

Caught unawares, Caro chewed and swallowed. "Thank you."

"Did you alter it yourself?"

"Yes, I did."

"I'll tell Papa. He'll be glad to know that you can sew."

"Yes, I can," Caro said quietly.

Charlotte addressed Anna again. She said, "Did you hear that Papa's best tailor is leaving Charleston?"

"Mr. Johnson?" Anna asked.

"He's going to Canada. He says he's lost faith in Charleston. It's no place for a man of color anymore. He has family there already. They left after the Fugitive Slave Act, don't you remember?"

"Oh yes. They wrote to us last winter, didn't they, Charlotte?"

Charlotte chuckled. "They said that they were free to be colder than they'd ever been in their lives. And that the tailoring business in Toronto is dreadful. No one in Canada will patronize a colored tailor."

"And Mr. Johnson is set on going? To freeze and starve in Toronto?"

Charlotte said, "Yes, all for freedom in Toronto."

Caro set down her fork. She had eaten too much, and suddenly she felt ill. If it was cold in Oberlin, Ohio, she wouldn't mind it. To be free in Oberlin, Ohio! She wished she could excuse herself. She needed a breath of air, even if it were Charleston's air, hot and humid and saturated with slavery.

When the Bennetts finally let her go, she escaped to the sidewalk and took a deep breath, savoring the smell of azalea and not minding the smell of rot. Her head was still swimming. As she steadied herself, Danny ran down the steps to tug gently on her sleeve.

She thought that his eyes were a light brown, but they were changeable. Now they were green.

He said, "I wanted to apologize for the way my mother spoke to you."

She nodded.

"She's very hopeful of my future and fierce in protecting me." He let his hand rest on her pagoda sleeve. "She expects great things of me."

"Perhaps you'll be the first colored politician in South Carolina," she teased.

He said, "Before my father died, he wanted to make provision for me to attend college. But he could not, and now all I have is the money I save from my wages and my mother's encouragement."

"College?" she asked. "Did he want you to go up North?"

"He hoped to send me abroad. To London or Edinburgh. He said that Scotland had so few people of color that no one would show any prejudice against me."

"Scotland!" she said, laughing. "Not someplace like Oberlin in Ohio?"

Now he laughed, too. He had very white teeth, pearlescent in his pale-brown face, and a full, rosy mouth. "Oberlin!" he said. "No South Carolinian should go to Oberlin, even a person of color. They eat abolitionism for breakfast, spread on their toast like jam!"

He leaned toward her and let his hand slip down her arm to touch the wrist that the pagoda sleeve left bare. He dropped his voice. "I can talk to Uncle Thomas about giving you work," he said.

"The business about hiring out—"

He leaned closer. "Let me talk to him," he repeated.

The door flew open, and Anna, the worst chatterer among the Bennett girls, called out, "Danny! Your mother says that you're to stop flirting with Caro and come inside!"

He let go of her arm, but he smiled before he ran up the stairs.

ℵℴℤ

THE NEXT DAY, SOPHY TOLD HER that someone wanted her at the gate. "You get more visitors than Marse Lawrence and Missus Susan," she grumbled.

"Who is it?"

"A boy."

Kitty looked up. "I'll see who it is," she said.

Caro trembled. Was it Danny? She flew to the gate, letting her mother lag behind her.

But it was someone else.

Kitty asked, "Who are you, and what do you want?" It was her haughty tone. Caro had never known until today how much her mother could sound like her estranged half sister.

Caro thought the messenger was white until she recalled that it was a younger Pereira whose skin glowed even lighter than his fair-skinned brothers and cousins. She said, "Mama, it's Danny's little brother, Ben."

He said to Caro, "My mother, Mrs. Pereira, wants to see you. She'll be at home this afternoon."

"Did she say why?"

Ben Pereira regarded her with the supercilious expression that all the Pereiras could summon. "We live on Montagu Court," he said. "This afternoon, at three o'clock."

Kitty said, "You can tell her that her sister, Kitty Bennett Jarvie, will be there as well."

Ben's face registered surprise. Kitty repeated, "Her sister. Catherine Bennett. She'll know who I am, even if you don't."

Puzzled, even a little deflated, Ben said, "Yes, ma'am," as he left.

Kitty turned to Caro. "I'll be paying a call this afternoon," she said.

"You'd go with me? To see her?"

"I won't abandon you to her," her mother said.

"Like that?" Caro gestured at the ragged dress.

Her mother's hands went to her earlobes. She fingered the spot where the earbobs had once dazzled, and she drew herself up very straight. "As I am," she said. "Without charity from anyone. You put on the pretty dress they gave you. You'll have to do for both of us."

⁎)(⁎

HER MOTHER STOPPED ON THE sidewalk to observe the house on Montagu Court. Like the Bennett house, it was a two-story wooden single with fresh paint and well-tended shrubbery in front. She said, "She's done very well for herself, if she owns it."

At the front door, her mother hesitated. Caro asked, "What is it, Mama?"

"I never thought I'd do this," she said, unable to raise her hand to the knocker.

"I will." Caro rapped on the front door.

Maria herself answered it. She lost her composure. "What are you doing here?" she demanded of Kitty.

Caro watched as Kitty took in Maria's substance and comfort, and Maria took in Kitty's ill fortune.

Her mother smiled. "Is that the best you can do, Maria? After not seeing me for twenty years?"

With ill grace, Maria said, "Come inside."

She ushered them into the parlor, which was austerely furnished in the Georgian style of the late eighteenth century still so prevalent in Charleston decades later. A dainty sofa stood against the far wall, and a Sheraton chair upholstered in brocade—a little faded but still good—stood before each window, a nest of little tables next to one and a piecrust table next to the other.

"It's lovely, Maria," her mother said, as though she had been made welcome.

Maria inclined her head but didn't reply.

A round mirror, its frame ornate and gilded, hung on the far wall, and Caro saw herself reflected in it, her face a little drawn above the cheerful print of her dress.

Maria didn't offer them refreshment, but she said curtly, "Sit down." Kitty took the settee, the best piece of furniture in the room, where she could spread her narrow skirt and command a good view of her sister. Caro perched on a side chair. She felt like an unwelcome cat and was ready to leap up and run.

Maria spoke to Kitty as though Caro weren't there, slighting them both. "She has a pretty face. Your face, when you were younger."

"She takes after her father, too."

"As though that helps her!"

"Don't speak against my father," Caro said.

Maria ignored her. She spoke to Kitty again. "I don't want her angling after my son."

"Why would she do that?" Kitty asked, as though Caro were an heiress the young men yearned after.

"If she thinks that her pretty face will make her fortune—if that's something you encouraged her to think—she's a fool."

Her mother bristled. Caro wondered if these sisters had always been like this. The canny one and the pretty one. They must have been.

Maria said, "You always were a fool, Kitty. All those years in James Jarvie's house, and what did you have to show for it?"

Her mother's hand stole to her earlobe.

"I heard that Mrs. Susan Jarvie stripped you of the dress on your back." She stared at her half sister. "Now I know it."

"Aunt Maria!" Caro pleaded.

"Don't call me that," Maria snapped. "What did he leave you besides a daughter with a pretty face?"

Her mother raised her dark, expressive eyes to her half sister's. She held herself in a lady's posture, despite the ruin of her dress. "His love," she said firmly. "James loved me."

"Love!" Maria snorted. "There's no profit in love. By the time Mr. Pereira died, I had this house and everything in it." She gestured around the room. "I had two rental properties in my name that give me income, even now. I had two slaves that I hire out, who bring me a living. And what do you have, Kitty?" She looked as though she would spit. "Did he free you? Either of you?"

Her mother smiled. How could she remain so calm? When she spoke, she had found the poison to put in the sugar. "Has it ever occurred to you, Maria, that your father freed you because he loved your mother as he never loved mine?" She dropped her eyes and her voice. "Was that worth so little?"

Maria's face darkened. "I don't know why he freed me. He never told me why. But I know that he sold you a week after your mother died."

"Wasn't I worthy?" Kitty asked, her voice still soft. "An orphan of twelve?"

As though Maria had received rather than given the hurt, she said to her half sister, "I don't want to see you." She turned her attention to Caro. "Nor you, anywhere near my son. Now go." She extended her hands in a gesture to sweep them away.

The door shut very firmly behind them as they departed.

On the sidewalk again, her mother said to her, "Now you know why we're estranged."

"Oh, Mama," Caro said miserably, thinking of her

mother, orphaned and sold away to James Jarvie. "Why didn't you tell me?"

"I never speak of it." Her tone locked it away again. She gazed at the neat house with its sparkling windows. "And in case you're wondering, I don't want you angling for that boy, either."

⁊ʕʘ

A FEW DAYS LATER, WHEN THE BELL at the gate jangled, Sophy went to answer it. She came back, smiling broadly. "Another visitor," she said. "That handsome young man who bring you the dress. Name of Danny."

Caro flew to the gate. Danny stood just inside, shaded by the crape myrtles. He smiled broadly, too. "Uncle Thomas sent me," he said. "He wants you to come to the shop right away."

"Is it about the sewing? The hiring out?"

His smile told her that it was.

"What happened to change his mind?" Caro asked.

"I don't know. But I do know that he and my mother had quite a fight about it." He laughed. "I didn't have to stand at the keyhole listening. You could hear it all over the house!"

So he knew that trick, too. "What was the fight about?"

"Uncle Thomas told my mother that how he ran his business was none of hers, and she said it was, if he was going to hire a slave's daughter to flirt with her son. And he put his foot down, telling her that he could assure her that it was a matter of business and only a matter of business, if that would satisfy her. I never heard him raise his voice like that. She got very sulky and told him that it had better remain a matter of business, or he'd hear from her. He reminded her that he was the head of the family, and she owed him more respect than that. Oh, she didn't like it! She was sulky with all of us afterward." He reached for her hands. "Come now. Come with me."

At the shop, Thomas spoke to her with a tailor's tact. He said, "We're very pressed now that Mr. Johnson is gone. The rest of my men can handle the tailoring, but it would be a great help to send out the shirts. Can you do finish work?"

"Oh yes. Plain sewing, fine sewing, and buttonholes, too."

"Could you show me? Sew a sample?"

"Of course." She asked, "The hiring out. I thought it was a difficulty."

"I made some inquiries."

She felt a stab of fear. "Did you talk to Mr. Jarvie?"

"It wasn't necessary. I'm satisfied that he's indifferent to how you manage. As long as you're discreet, it won't be a problem."

"Thank you, Uncle Thomas," she said. She was pleased. Why did tears rise to her eyes?

"Come in back."

The workroom had none of the elegance of the shopfront. Thomas's workers and apprentices, needles in hand, sat elbow-to-elbow at a large table. Cloth crowded every unused space, and the tickle of cottony lint and the scratch of wool filled the air.

Thomas said to Danny, "Give her some scraps to test her sewing."

He rummaged among the bits of cloth. Thomas found her a chair to perch on and gave her the scraps and a threaded needle. "A plain seam and a felled one," Thomas said to Caro. "Danny, I need to be in front. Let me know when she's finished."

As Danny watched her, she made her best effort to make the tiniest and firmest stitches and fell the seam so that it would lie flat and not be felt against the skin, as her mother had taught her. She sewed more carefully than she had ever sewed, and finally she said to Danny, "I'm done."

"I'll fetch Uncle Thomas."

Thomas bent over the cloth to see how straight the seams were. He pulled the fabric apart, testing the strength of the stitching. He ran his finger over the felling, as Caro had thought he would, satisfied at how flat it was. "It will do," he said to Caro, in a professional rather than a familial tone. "Danny, how many shirts have we pieced and not yet sewn?"

"Half a dozen, I think."

"Bundle them up for Miss Caroline to work on."

As Danny wrapped the shirts, Thomas said, "I'll give you fifty cents for a shirt. The seams and the finishing." Was that a glimmer of familial feeling?

"Thank you, Uncle Thomas," she said.

He handed her the bundle, and his face softened. "Give your mother my best regards," he said. Much more than a glimmer. What an odd family the Bennetts were. "And my deepest condolences."

Chapter 7: A Southern Voice

"EMILY, WHERE ARE YOU GOING?" Susan asked as she descended the stairs.

Emily fastened her cloak. "Out for a bit of air."

"Don't you want to take the carriage?"

Emily laughed. "That would defeat the purpose of taking the air," she said. "Just to the market and back."

Susan took Emily's hands. "You're livelier since you came back from the pines," she said.

"The cold air does me good. It makes me feel brisk!" She smiled at the memory of Joshua Aiken.

"Well, go on, then. But don't take a chill!"

"I won't," Emily said, pleased that her stepmother was pleased. She ran down the great marble staircase with a nimble stride.

Since she accepted Mr. Aiken's offer, Emily traveled through Charleston with new eyes. She studied the places and the sights she knew so well, wondering what might interest a northern lady, deliberating how she might turn the familiar into the exotic for her hypothetical visitor. She now took her sketchbook with her—she had learned to draw at Madame Devereaux's, too—hoping that some-thing might strike her and spark her thoughts for the sketch in words to accompany the drawing.

At the market, she lingered and looked. She listened, too. Did the street sellers in northern cities sing like the porgy man and the oyster women of Charleston? Above the rest, a familiar voice rose: "Eggs so fresh, eggs so fine..." It was Sophy, extolling the eggs in the basket at her feet, and beside her stood Caroline.

Caro wore a plain gray cotton dress, but it was whole and new, and above it, she had tied a scarf bright with flowers that enlivened her face. She spoke to a stout wom-an with a basket over her arm whose badge proclaimed her as a servant. Emily overheard her with surprise. She spoke the dialect of the Low Country, the speech drenched in the rhythms of Africa, as though she'd been born to it.

"Miss Emily!" Sophy called. She held up a fragile orb. "This the last of them. Do you need an egg?"

Emily laughed. "Ask Dulcie," she said. "She is the general of the kitchen, and of eggs!" She turned to Caro. "Caroline," she said.

"Yes, Miss Emily?" The Low Country accent was gone. The planter's daughter spoke in her place.

"You look better," Emily said, touching her head to indicate the scarf.

"Thank you, Miss Emily."

"Did my inquiries help? About the washing?"

Caro inclined her head. Evidently not, but she replied

with tact, "I thank you for it, Miss Emily." She gestured toward Sophy. "Sophy employs me in the market, and that helps us, too."

"How is your mother?"

Her distress was too much for her to mask.

Emily asked, "Is she ill?"

"No, Miss Emily. Not ill. But not right, either."

Emily recalled the weeks after Robert's death, when all food tasted like sand, the days were the weight of iron, and the nights were a torment of waking every hour in a sweat to remember that he was gone and she was still here. She said softly, "She grieves for your father."

"Oh yes," Caro said, and she blinked, pretending that the sun bothered her eyes.

"Can I help?" Emily asked.

Caro blinked again. "She wears your shawl," she said.

"And the portrait?"

"She cherishes it."

"The other gift?"

Caro's eyes widened in surprise.

Emily thought, *I've transgressed, even to mention it here.*

But Caro said, very softly, "I cherish it."

Sophy called to Caro. "What are you whispering about with Miss Emily?"

Sophy observed, too, Emily realized. And saw closely. She pulled the sketchbook from her pocket. "Sophy, would you oblige me?"

"How, Miss Emily?"

"Would you let me sketch you?"

Sophy glanced at the sketchbook and the pencil. "Take my portrait?"

"Just a quick sketch."

"All right. What you want me to do?"

"Whatever you were doing before I interrupted you."

"Singing out my wares?"

"Yes."

She sketched—it was rough and quick—and showed it to Sophy. Sophy said, "Caro, look." She laughed. "It look just like me!"

Emily was pleased. She had captured Sophy's energy and her dignity and had even caught the intrepid look in her eye. Emily tore the page from the sketchbook. "Keep it, Sophy," she said.

"Thank you, Miss Emily." She gathered up her empty basket and put the sketch into it. "Caro, we go home," she said, her voice a warning.

Emily left the market trembling, as though she had done wrong.

At home, she sat at her desk, thinking of Mr. Aiken's words, that a writer's life—an observer's life, as he had offered to her—was a lonely one. The other girls of her acquaintance were like Camilla Aiken, intent on marriage and disdainful of books. Now she had met a kindred spirit. And she was her father's slave, one he disliked so much that he had banished her from his sight.

It wasn't unusual to feel affection for a slave. Emily liked her maid, Lydia, whose voice was soft and whose hands were gentle with her laces and her hair. She liked their cook, Dulcie, who fussed over her in the kitchen and always offered her a biscuit or a cookie to eat. She liked her father's manservant, Ambrose, whose sense of decorum made him protective of her. But this was different. It went beneath the surface of the neat gray dress and the servant's mask, the guise of a slave. It flew to the heart, which yearned for books, and to the soul, which hungered to speak of them.

You shouldn't even be able to read, her stepmother had said to Caro.

She thought of Caro's eyes, so dark at the thought of her mother's grief, so bright with pleasure as she held a book in her hands.

Yes, she thought.

～○◯◯～

EMILY LEFT FOR TRADD STREET wrapped in a shawl against the chill of late fall, a basket over her arm as a ruse. Her sketchbook, hidden deep in her pocket, bumped against her leg as she walked. She had lied to her stepmother about where she was going. She had lied to Ambrose, too. Her stepmother had believed her. Ambrose had pretended to.

She shivered as she stood at the gate, waiting for Sophy. She told herself, *I don't have to do this.* She could perform another act of charity. She could see Catherine and inquire after her health. She could make another sketch of Sophy.

What did she yearn for? How much did she yearn for it?

Her heart pounded as Sophy opened the gate to her. "You here for Caroline, I reckon," she said, as though she knew. "You go on, she in the kitchen." She smiled. "I go out. You two can whisper all you like."

Caro sat alone in the kitchen, stringing beans for midday dinner. She looked up, set down the beans, and rose. "Miss Emily? Do you want some coffee?"

Too nervous to accept, Emily shook her head. She sat and so did Caro.

Caro said, "My mother is resting, but I can bring her to see you."

Emily found her voice. "No, I came to talk to you."

Caro sat very still. She asked, "What is it, Miss Emily?"

Was she afraid? Emily thought of her stepmother's cruelty and her father's threats. She had to force her words out. She stammered, "The book. The Melville book."

Caroline's eyes opened wide. "The book?"

"Yes. I wanted," she stammered. "I wanted to know if you'd finished it."

"The book?"

"I wanted to ask what you thought of it."

Relief flooded Caro's face. "Miss Emily, it's not right to ask me. You must have friends. Others you can talk to about what you read."

Emily hadn't realized how tightly she had knotted her hands. She said, "Not one like you."

Caro reflected. "What do you want from me, Miss Emily?"

Emily thought of Joshua Aiken urging her to overthrow the tyranny of Madame Devereaux, who had taught her to keep her opinions to herself. She took a deep breath. "To tell me what you really thought of Mr. Melville's book."

She had spoken as though they were friends. But friendship didn't grow in slavery's soil. It was a fragile seedling nurtured by kindness. She thought of Lydia's gentleness, Dulcie's solicitude, and Ambrose's concern— all the result of command.

Caro deliberated. And when she spoke, she spoke as the girl whose father had taught her Latin and Greek. "Such a fierce book," she said. "Full of so much longing."

"Longing?"

Caro talked to her, but she addressed something beyond her as well. "Captain Ahab. A man full of desire. Maddened by it. In pursuit of something he can never capture, and that destroys him."

"There's great danger in that kind of hunger, I think," Emily said, feeling it roil within her.

"Oh yes. But a great inspiration, too."

What did Caro long for? Emily ached to ask. But she did not. She said, "It was an unsettling book, as well as a difficult one."

"Books don't always cheer us," Caro said.

"That's true," Emily said. "Although I'm gladder when they do."

"My father always said that books help us reflect on ourselves and understand ourselves better. Sometimes there's great pain in reflection. And in understanding."

Why did Emily think again of Joshua Aiken, who knew that she wrote because her soul was so hungry? "You would rather understand," she said to Caro. "And feel the pain along with it."

"Yes, I would," Caro said.

She was a slave, but she had been raised as a planter's daughter. Their connection was fraught with danger. And with inspiration. Emily asked, "Is there anything else you would like to read?"

Caro smiled. It transformed her face. She said, "Whatever you bring to me, I'll read it with pleasure."

☙❧

ONCE EMILY HAD FOUND THE subject for her sketch, she struggled with it. She wrote out her thousand words over and over, wanting them to speak clearly to the Yankee strangers who knew nothing of Charleston. She was writing a tale of adventure for the ladies of the North, and if she twined philosophy around it, she wanted it to be light enough for them to digest easily.

She still kept Robert's portrait on her desk, but as she wrote, she recalled the face of Joshua Aiken, his eyes lit with humor, his mouth mobile in the midst of that dark, bristling beard, his South Carolina voice made brisk by tenure in the North. And as she struggled with the words, crossed them out, and wrote again, she thought of Caro saying, *Whatever you bring to me, I'll read it with pleasure.*

On a dull winter day, when the light had failed so much that she would need a candle to write any more, she put down her pen and shook out the cramp in her hand. She had made a fair copy, good enough for someone to read. She worried again about the words she had written because she was still afraid to send them to Mr. Aiken. He had encouraged her, but he had a cold, businesslike eye for literature, too. He would want more than something he could praise. He would want something he could sell.

She heard a voice, torn between a slave's decorum and the fierce desire of an agile mind to talk about what it treasured. *It's not right...surely you have a friend you could show it to.*

She murmured, "Not like you."

She tucked her thousand words, her three sheets of paper, into her sketchbook and put everything into her pocket. She slipped from the house, avoiding the eyes and the questions of her servants and her stepmother.

She found Caroline and Sophy in the yard, at work at the washtub. She said, "I'm sorry to interrupt you."

Caroline straightened up and put her hand to her back. "I'm happy to be interrupted," she said.

"Sophy, may I purloin Caroline from you for a moment?"

Sophy looked darkly at Emily. "Is that a big word that mean take her away from her work?"

"Just for a moment."

They settled in the kitchen, where the hearth gave off a warmth that made sweat prickle along her spine.

Caro said, "What is it, Miss Emily?"

This time she didn't stammer. "I've brought you something new to read."

Caroline's eyes gleamed. "Another book?"

"It's something I wrote." She began to stammer again as she explained about meeting Mr. Aiken and about his request for a piece of writing for *Hearth and Home*.

Caroline listened intently. When Emily had finished, she said, "You're asking me to read something you've written. And to tell you what I think of it."

"Yes," Emily said.

"Is that a command, Miss Emily?"

"No," Emily said softly. "Will you try?"

"I'll do my best."

Caro read it slowly, taking care, and the time she spent was the longest half hour that Emily had ever suffered. When she looked up, Emily felt short of breath. She asked, "What do you think?"

There was a long, terrible silence, and Emily broke it with a rush of words. "Don't fox me. Don't flatter me, either."

Caro put the manuscript on the table, laying her hand on it as though it were a pet. She smiled. She said, "I like it very much, Miss Emily."

Emily had not realized that she was shaking. "You do?"

"Yes. It's clever. It's subtle. You write about our eagles, the ugly birds we're so proud of, but you speak of us. The little drawings—are those yours?"

"Don't you remember that I drew Sophy at the market?"

"Yes, I do. You drew the turkey vultures at Sophy's feet!"

Emily breathed out in relief. "Now I can only hope that Mr. Aiken will like it, too."

"I trust that he will," Caro replied.

"You read so keenly. You understand."

Caro laid her hands flat on the table. Her fingers were shriveled with being in the wash's hot water, but the fingers were long and tapered, shaped to hold a pen. "As my father taught me," she said, her voice very low.

ℰℭ

DULCIE'S LITTLE BOY RAN TO THE post office to retrieve the day's letters, but Ambrose brought them to Susan on a silver tray as she and Emily sat in the back parlor. Susan flipped through them, taking the letters addressed to herself. She picked up an envelope and looked at it in puzzlement. "Emily, what is this? Why is a Mr. Aiken of *Hearth and Home* writing to you?"

Emily's heart pounded so hard that she had to cough. She said brightly, "Oh, Mr. Aiken! I met him when I was in Sumter County. He's a cousin to Jane and Camilla. He works for a ladies' magazine up North. I believe he wants me to take out a subscription."

Susan turned the envelope over. "That's quite rude of him," she said. "Soliciting you for his business because you're a friend to the Aikens. We take *Godey's*, and we certainly don't want it. Write to him and tell him so."

Emily held out her hand. "Give me the envelope so I have the address, and I will."

She put the envelope in her pocket and restrained the impulse to bolt up the stairs to the privacy of her room. She waited until her stepmother had sifted through all the letters and complained about how many she would need to reply to, then excused herself.

She sat heavily in her desk chair—it was Caro's old chair, a pretty thing made of mahogany and too fragile for strong emotion—and opened the envelope with clumsy, trembling fingers.

"My Dear Miss Jarvie," she read, and the words swam before her eyes. What if he had hated the piece? What if he never wanted to hear from her again?

I was delighted to receive your thousand words. The story of the eagles of Charleston strikes just the right exotic note for our readers. And your touch of satire will reach the cleverest among them. I didn't know that you could draw. The drawings are delightful, too.

We usually pay two dollars for a thousand words, but because of the drawings, I have increased your payment to three dollars. I have enclosed a bank draft for that amount.

I understand how southern families feel about a daughter's name in print and have taken the liberty of giving you a nom de plume. In our pages, you will be "A Southern Voice." I hope that will be agreeable to you.

I am even more delighted to tell you that I would be glad to publish your sketches regularly. We can accommodate one a month, and if all goes well, even more.

I close with the most cordial of regards—

Mr. Joshua Aiken, Editor

She reread the letter. She held up the bank drafts. She shook her head in wonderment and secreted everything in her pocket.

As soon as she could slip past her stepmother and servants, she had someone to see.

She found Caro in the kitchen, stirring a pot of rice. Sophy, who escorted her from the gate, said to her, "You got that purloining look on your face, Miss Emily. Go on, take her away from her work. You can go upstairs to talk. Warmer than the yard."

"Upstairs?"

"Follow me," Caro said, putting down the spoon. She led her up the staircase, which was more like a ladder, to the second floor. She was uneasy on it. Caro grasped her hand. "Careful," she said. "I had to get used to it, too."

"Where are you taking me?"

Caro led her into the narrow hall and pushed open the first door they came to. "It was a servant's room when

the house was open," she said. The room was meagerly furnished, with a little rope bed bare of blanket or sheet and a chair. The walls had been painted white, but they were now cracked and peeling.

"Does anyone stay here now?" Emily asked.

"No. But it's quiet. Take the chair, Miss Emily, it's a nicer place to sit than the bed."

As Emily sat, Caro said, "Have you brought me something new to read?"

"I have," she said. She pulled the letter from her pocket. "Tell me I'm not dreaming."

She waited as Caro read the letter, swiftly, since the letter was so much shorter than the sketch had been. "Not a dream at all," she said, smiling. "Not when there's a bank draft with it."

"I never received a bank draft before. What shall I do with it?"

"I never had a bank draft, either," Caro said.

For a moment, Emily saw the pampered daughter of a rich planter who never touched a coin or worried about money.

"But if you went to a lawyer, I'm sure he could help you. Like Mr. Pereira."

Emily frowned. "He handles some of my father's affairs," she said. "I don't want my father to know that I'm writing or that I'm being paid for it."

"Tell Mr. Pereira so. He's very discreet. He always was with my father's affairs." Caro handed her the letter.

Emily said, "My stepmother received the letter, and it would have been the worse for me if she'd opened it."

"She shouldn't know that you write, either."

"She would hate it, even more than my father," Emily said.

"Have the letters sent to me," Caro said.

"To you?"

"I go to the post office to retrieve the mail, and no one would think anything of it. Hah!" she said. "They can think I'm retrieving letters for Miss Mary."

"Why would you do that?" Emily asked.

"To help you," she said, and Emily heard the rest. "To spite them."

Emily said, "Is it right, Caroline? To bring you into an intrigue?"

"Who would suspect me of an intrigue?" she asked, folding her hands and dropping her eyes to the floor.

She hides in plain sight, Emily thought. *The lady or the slave, depending on who looks or who does not.* "Don't you open the letters," Emily said. But it was not quite the tease she intended.

Caro looked up. "I wouldn't dream of it," she said, a tease to match Emily's intention. "How should I let you know that I have a letter for you?"

ഇൗൽ

WHENEVER SHE WENT OUT, Emily looked for subjects. She took her sketchbook, which let her see more keenly.

It gave her an occupation and a determination on the street. It made her brisk, like the far-off citizens of Cincinnati who surrounded Mr. Aiken himself.

She halted on the sidewalk before the house on King Street, the splendid house that Uncle James had willed to them. The Jarvies had yet to move, since the Herriot relations he had rented to were loath to leave. Her stepmother was impatient, but her father said, "I won't press them. I need their goodwill." He had turned his thoughts to running for the Assembly again. He would need their support.

A heavy wrought iron fence fronted the house. She had walked past this house many times, but today she saw the twisted iron spikes, sharp enough to wound anyone who tried to surmount them, that fortified the fence.

Emily pulled out her sketchbook.

The front door opened, and Mr. Herriot ran jauntily down the stairs. He was young, not yet thirty, and dressed like a man of fashion in a tall beaver hat and a tight-fitting frock coat. "Miss Jarvie!" he greeted her. "What are you doing here?"

She lifted the sketchbook. "Just making a sketch," she said. "The house is so handsome. I wanted to draw it."

He laughed. His teeth were white, and the canines were sharp. "Oh, it will be yours soon enough," he said.

"Sir, what are those fearsome spikes on the fence?"

"You don't know the story? My father put them there after the slave uprising. The Vesey rebellion." He added, "They're called chevaux-de-frise. They were used in wartime to deter an assault."

Charlestonians had a long memory. The ghost of Denmark Vesey, who was successful in rousing the slaves of Charleston nearly four decades ago, still haunted them. And those who came originally from San Domingo, where the slaves' rebellion was bloody and successful, still recalled its terror in their nightmares, and they had passed on these stories to their children.

Emily said, "Surely they aren't needed anymore. Isn't the fence deterrent enough?"

Mr. Herriot lost his smile. "We hear more of rebellion from the North every day," he said. "They would delight in driving our slaves to insurrection. We may have need of those spikes yet."

"I hope not," Emily murmured, and she raised her eyes to the fence again. She wondered if the iron spikes would interest a northern lady or if she would recoil from them. It was peculiar to look at everything familiar as though she had never seen it before.

Several days later, she walked briskly toward the office of Mr. Pereira. In her pocket was an encouraging letter from Mr. Aiken. He had written to tell her that *Hearth and Home*'s readers had enjoyed the work of "A Southern Voice," and he had enclosed their letters so that she could read them herself. Emily had never realized that writing for publication, unlike writing in a diary, was a kind of conversation.

Mr. Pereira greeted her, settled her comfortably in his office, and bade his servant to bring her a cup of coffee. He asked, "How can I help you, Miss Jarvie?"

She said, "Caroline told me that you would be discreet."

"How is she?" he asked.

"She's well, sir."

His swarthy face grew grave. "Are you in a scrape, Miss Jarvie?"

"Oh no," she said. She drew the bank drafts from her pocket to show him. "It's a little matter of money. Just a trifle. I want to keep it safe, but I don't want to trouble my father about it."

He took the bank drafts from her, examining them closely, turning them over to read the back as well as the front. He said, "As long as there's no irregularity in the way you came by them, Miss Jarvie, there shouldn't be a difficulty."

"Irregularity?" She wrinkled her brow, pretending to a deeper naivete than she truly had.

"I shouldn't press you so. Three dollars is too little for a debt of honor or an embarrassment at the dressmaker's. But I'm curious why a bank in Ohio has sent you any sum, even one as small as three dollars."

She blushed and was glad of it because she knew it would discomfit him. "I met the editor of an Ohio magazine in Sumter County," she said. "He's distant kin to the Aikens. He asked me to write a squib for his magazine, and when I did, he paid me for it." She looked archly at Mr. Pereira. "Is that irregular, sir?"

He said, "Not in the legal meaning. But I know your

father, and I can see that it might disquiet him to see his daughter's name in print."

She leaned forward. "He won't," she said. "I use a nom de plume."

Holding the notes between his fingers, he asked, "What would you like to do with your earnings, Miss Jarvie?"

"I'd like to save them. I don't know how. I hoped you could help me with that, sir."

He set the notes on his desk and regarded them as though they represented a much greater sum than three dollars. "It's no trouble to open a bank account in your name," he said. "I can make the arrangement with the Bank of Charleston."

"Do I need to visit the bank?"

"Not at all. They can send me the papers, and you can come here to sign them."

"Thank you, sir." She asked, "Do I owe you a consideration?"

He smiled. "Don't trouble yourself," he said. "I would do it for James's memory, even if your father hadn't retained me to settle the estate. I consider it my duty to the Jarvie family."

She said softly, "You were a good friend to my Uncle James, were you not?"

A faint shadow of grief crossed his face. "I was."

"You must miss him a great deal."

The shadow deepened. "I do."

"Please, sir, don't let my father know that I've asked you to help me."

"I'll keep it in confidence. He won't know unless you tell him yourself, Miss Jarvie."

ဢႠ

When she returned to the house on Orange Street, her stepmother called to her from the parlor. "Emily, is that you?"

"Yes, Mother."

"Ambrose told me you'd gone out for a walk. In this weather!"

She laughed. "It suits me, Mother."

Susan said, "Well, you are sprightlier these days since you came back from Sumter County. Is it more than exercise, Emily? Did you meet someone in Sumter County to make your eyes sparkle?"

Emily was suddenly wary. "What did Nancy write to you?"

"She said that after insulting their nearest neighbor, a Mr. John Ellison, you went out of your way to be cordial to him."

"He invited us to dine, and he showed me his place. Charles accompanied us. He has a stable of very fine horses, and Charles and I both admired them," she said, unable to suppress a blush.

Susan smiled. "When we return to Sumter County in the summer, will you be cordial to him again?"

"Of course, Mother."

"Did you write to that forward man at the magazine? The one who pressed a subscription on you?"

"I did," Emily said. "There won't be any more trouble about a subscription."

Her stepmother rose and laid her hand on Emily's cheek. "You're a good girl, Emily," she said. "I couldn't have asked for a better daughter."

"Thank you, Mother," she said.

As she ran up the stairs to her room, she thought, *I have become such a deceiver.*

She closed the door, and with her newly widened eyes, she looked at herself. The dressing table mirror revealed the sparkle that her stepmother had seen in her eyes and a flush of pink in her cheeks. The black dress was at odds with the lively expression on her face. She picked up Robert's portrait and waited for it to speak to her. Instead, she saw the animated face of Joshua Aiken and heard his voice, as though he had read his letters aloud to her.

But in her palm, the portrait was nothing more than a scrap of painted ivory. Robert had gone. She opened the drawer of the dressing table and gently laid the portrait in its farthest corner, where she would never see it.

She was free of Robert's ghost, and her freedom dizzied her.

Chapter 8: Love Is Sweet

As Caro sat at breakfast with Sophy and her mother, Sophy asked, "What do you and Miss Emily whisper about the last time she visit?"

Kitty asked, "What are you talking about, Sophy?"

Caro thought of her promise to help Emily deceive her father and blushed. She said, "Miss Emily wanted me to read something she wrote."

"Why she ask you?" Sophy sounded surprised.

"Sophy, she knows I can read. That's no secret. She wanted my opinion of it."

Kitty regarded Caro with surprise. Sophy said, "That's the oddest thing I ever hear."

Caro's opinion of herself had risen since she had begun to work for her uncle Thomas and earn decent money for it. "Why shouldn't she ask me? I'm educated, just like she is."

Her mother said thoughtfully, "It's not a bad thing to have an ally in the Jarvie house."

Sophy snorted. "Ally! She have a kinder heart than

her daddy, that's certain. But she only your friend as long as it suit her, Miss Sass. When it don't, she forget all about you. Don't fool yourself because she bring a shawl and a book."

Sophy's words stung. Sophy was usually right, an authority derived from experience. As Caro left the table to go to the post office, she allowed herself a moment of doubt as to why she was abetting Emily Jarvie in lying to her father.

But Caro kept her promise to Emily. Every week, she hastened to the post office on East Bay Street to ask for letters addressed to Lawrence's sister. Whenever a letter came from Ohio, Caro relished her part in Emily's deception.

Today, as she turned empty-handed from the window, she very nearly ran into Danny Pereira, who blushed as he greeted her. "Miss Caroline!" he said. "I didn't expect to see you here."

She had her fib ready. "Letters come to Miss Mary on Tradd Street," she said. "I collect them and take them to Ambrose to send to her." She felt a pang, remembering the days when Ambrose brought the day's mail into the parlor on a silver tray. She had never known if Ambrose could read. She tossed her head and said lightly, "What about you? Don't you have a little messenger boy to fetch your letters?"

He laughed as though she had said something clever. "Of course we do. But Uncle Thomas asked me to write out the bills this month, and I decided to mail them, too."

"He must trust you a great deal." It was a pleasure to take a teasing, flattering tone. A belle's tone.

"I believe he does. But he also knows that I write a better hand than the other men who work for him."

She looked at the sheaf of bills that attested to the health of Uncle Thomas's business. "Your hand must ache."

He laughed again. "No worse than if I cut out a suit."

"A tailor's woes," she said, smiling. If she had a letter in her hand, she could hold it like a fan.

"After I give these to the postmaster, may I walk with you?" he asked.

Now she smiled, not coquetting but in earnest. "Yes."

Even though she joined the Bennetts at church and Sunday dinner, and she had gone to the shop, Uncle Thomas and Aunt Maria both made an effort to keep Danny at arm's length from her. It was mischievous of her to see him and speak to him without the hovering interference of the Bennetts. So she was doubly glad of it.

He asked, "Where are you bound?"

"Back to Tradd Street. I have shirts to sew! Three dollars to earn!"

He said, "I'm very glad that Uncle Thomas was persuaded to employ you."

"So am I," she said, meeting those changeable eyes.

They were brown today and luminous, as though a light glowed behind them.

He said, "I wish we had the opportunity for conversation."

"So do I."

"I know I'm not welcome on Tradd Street."

She halted. "Sophy would welcome you."

"But your mother would not!" he said, sobered by the thought.

She put her hand on his arm. Even though the day was warm, he wore a wool suit. Always the tailor, always thinking of his uncle's business. "There must be a way," she said, encouraging him. Was that angling?

He blushed again. "Oh, there is," he said.

She let her hand rest on his arm. "How?"

"Come to the shop at our quiet hour," he said. "Uncle Thomas takes his dinner at two, as his custom does."

෩൝

WHEN CARO MADE HER NEXT visit, finished shirts in hand, she arrived at two in the afternoon. As Danny had promised, the shop was empty, save for himself, and his businesslike look dissolved into a look of pleasure when she opened the door.

She laid her bundle on the counter. "Has Uncle Thomas left you in his stead?" she asked, teasing.

"Yes," he teased back, "since this is the hour we're least likely to do any business."

"I thought he trusted you to write out the bills."

"But not to flatter the grandees of Charleston. Not yet." He said, "I need more practice in flattery. I want to call on your mother."

Caro said, "Oh, she can be flattered. But she can be steely, too. She's more like your mother than she would ever admit."

"And yet they hate each other so much."

Caro sighed. "Do you know the story?"

"No, only that they're bitter. It seems strange that they would feel it and keep it alive after twenty years."

"Your mother told me." She relayed it to him: Samuel Bennett's preference and his decision to free one daughter and not the other.

"How wrong," he said. "How unfair."

"Fairness doesn't enter into it," she said, trying to keep the family bitterness from her voice.

"It's their quarrel, not ours," he said. He put his hands on the counter, close to her own.

"Do you think so?" she asked.

"I believe so with all my heart," he said, his eyes shining.

"Then we'll start afresh, the two of us."

He touched her hand with his fingertip. It felt as gentle as a butterfly alighting. "We will." He said, "Let me take the finished work. I have the new batch in back."

He returned with the next week's work and laid it on the counter. He had no knotted scrap in his hand. She asked, "The wage?"

He said, "Hold out your hands."

Puzzled, she did so, and he pulled the coins from his pocket. He counted them out, twelve silver quarters, and when she curled her hands over them, to keep them safe, he curled his hands over hers. He blushed, and as she met his eyes, she blushed too. He asked, "Will you come again? At this quiet hour?"

"Yes," she said, happiness singing in her ears.

ℰℭℜ

Caro spent the week sewing with eagerness in her heart. She hadn't realized she was smiling as she worked in the kitchen. As she bundled the finished shirts to take to the shop, her mother and Sophy had noticed it. Her mother said, "You've been smiling as you work. Singing, too. It's that boy, Danny."

Caro tried to hide her emotion. "No, it's the money. So glad to earn a living!" She thought of Danny pressing the money into her hands and blushed.

Kitty was sharp. "I don't like that you work for Thomas," she said.

It was a jab, as they both knew. Her mother wore a pretty new dress, which fit her and suited her because Caro had spent some of her hard-earned money on a length of cloth for her mother. Her mother had been listless and tired—she was sick over the winter, and her cough had lingered—but she brightened at the sight of the cloth. As Caro sewed to make a living, Kitty busied herself with cutting out a dress for herself and sewing it together.

Her mother's mood irritated her. She resented that Kitty had made no effort to help her. *If we both sewed,* she thought, *we might make six dollars a week.* The resentment festered now and spilled over when her mother nagged her working for her uncle.

Caro was equally sharp with her mother. "Should I stop? Do you want to lose the three dollars a week?"

Sophy tried to make peace. "She a good girl," she said to Kitty. "She work hard and help you. She help all of us."

But Kitty wouldn't let it go. "I didn't like it when you went to Thomas," she said. "I didn't like it when he employed you—it's charity, no matter what he says. I don't like that you see Maria's boy every week at the dinner table, and I know you see him at the shop, too." She gave her daughter a scathing look. "What do you think Danny Pereira wants from you?"

Caro picked up the bundle of finished shirts. "He wants me to sew half a dozen shirts for his uncle," she said, with irritation.

"What do you think he will do for you?"

"Give me my wages and another half a dozen shirts," Caro said, hugging the bundle to her chest.

Kitty said, "You know he can't marry you."

"Marry me! All he's done is pay me the money his uncle owes me." Suddenly overcome with annoyance, Caro said, "As though I have suitors lined up, and I could say yes or no to any of them as I please! Perhaps I should find a rich planter to see if I can *catch his fancy.*"

As she clutched the bundle and fled the kitchen, she heard her mother cough.

☙❧

As before, the shop was quiet. At the sight of her, Danny said softly, "You came back," in a tone not at all suited for a matter of business.

She thought of all the opposition to her interest in him, and his in her, and said lightly, "I came for my wages!"

He grinned. "But there's no hurry. Uncle Thomas won't be back for an hour."

She set the bundle on the counter. "Does your mother still bedevil you about me?"

"Of course. And yours?"

"Yes. As though I'll take it to heart if she repeats it often enough."

Danny said, "We do nothing wrong." He gestured around the shop as a reminder.

Caro laughed. She said, "Oh, we do. But we do it in plain sight, so we can pretend otherwise."

He leaned forward. She could smell the pomade he used to restrain the curls in his hair. "Would you defy your mother for me?"

She leaned forward, too, close enough to tease. "I will," she said.

He started and stood back. Blushing, he said, "I thought I heard a hand on the door."

He hadn't. The bell would jangle if anyone turned the knob. She thought, *I startled him. Or he startled himself.*

She stood upright, her hands resting lightly on the counter, as any customer's might. She asked, "Does your work for Uncle Thomas leave you time to read?"

"A little. When the debating society met, I had the opportunity to read more. They had a fine library."

"The Clionian Debating Society?"

"You remembered that."

"Of course I did. It's no more? Why is that?"

He sighed. "The climate of Charleston makes it difficult," he said.

"For free men to meet and debate?"

"For free men of color to gather, no matter how innocent their purpose."

"I hadn't thought that free people of color would feel so," she said, even as she remembered the conversation at the Sunday dinner table about the flight to Canada.

He said, "Oh, we do." His face suddenly somber, he said, "Every day, I rue my father's death and the loss of the opportunity to leave Charleston to live and study elsewhere."

She wished that she could reach for his hand. "Your father, what was he like?"

His expression flickered.

"I'm sorry. I didn't mean to grieve you."

"It's sad to remember," he said. "But it's sadder still that no one asks, and I have no one to tell."

She nodded.

"He loved us. He took care of us, but it was more than

that. He cherished us. He never married, and we were his family. He felt so, and we knew it."

"My father cherished me, too," she said.

"And yet…" Danny's expression hardened. "He loved us well, but it was all in private. He could never admit to us in public."

"Ah, I know," she said. "Why do you think my father kept us on St. Helena Island, far from the eyes and tongues of Charleston? We were his secret."

Danny sighed. "I know it couldn't be otherwise. But it hurt me. I let it hurt me. His funeral was held in the synagogue, and none of us were welcome there."

She nodded. "And now you miss him. You miss the hope he offered you."

He looked away. Did tears web his lashes? "My father believed in me," he said. "He thought I was anyone's equal in intelligence and that I should be able to exercise it freely. That was his dream for me."

Very softly, she said, "My father didn't know what to dream for me when he educated me. I dreamed for myself."

"Oberlin College," he said.

"You remembered."

"Of course." He raised his eyes to hers. His lashes were wet. "Why not? You're anyone's equal in intelligence, too."

His words, meant to be kind, gave her pain. "And now I might as well want to fly or walk on the face of the moon."

"Oh no," he said, his expression determined. "But there must be a way." He reached for her hand, and she let it rest in his. "Edinburgh. Oberlin. The two of us, here and now."

He didn't smile, but the clasp of his hand was a promise.

෩෬

AT THE SUNDAY SERVICE, CARO continued to find herself squeezed between Anna and Charlotte. Danny gave her the smallest nod of greeting, but it warmed her as though he'd taken her hand.

At dinner, she listened to her cousins gossip. Anna said, "Caro, did you hear? Miss DeReef finally made up her mind. She's engaged!"

The good fortune of the richest heiress of color in Charleston was remote enough to cause Caro no pain. She nodded.

Charlotte added, "And such a fuss! Her family is giving a party to celebrate her engagement."

"When?" Caro asked.

"Two weeks hence," Anna said.

"Mama," Charlotte called to the end of the table. "Can we bring Caro along when we go?"

Charlotte's mother frowned. "To Miss DeReef's party?"

"Why not? There's time for her to make a new dress."

Thomas said to his daughter, "It's not a matter of a dress, and you know it."

His wife cast a disapproving look at Charlotte. "It's cruel to talk of these things to Caro," she said.

Charlotte looked perplexed. "Of an amusement?"

Thomas said, "Of our social obligations, which she does not share."

Caro drew in her breath. Suddenly she saw herself as her mother had described her. The poor relation. The charity case. The recipient of a cast-off dress. Good enough to tuck away at the family dinner table but not to take to the celebrations of Charleston's free persons of color, where marriages were hatched.

Anna laid her hand on Caro's arm. "There are so many amusements in the summer," she said. "Are you going to the German Festival?"

Caro said dully, "I don't know. What is it?"

Charlotte cried out, "It's such fun. All kinds of entertainments! Shooting matches, acrobatics, and music. And after the sun sets, a spectacular display of fireworks!"

Anna tried to repair the damage her mother had wrought. "Papa, why don't we take Caro to the German Festival this year? It's no obligation. Everyone goes there."

Even slaves, Caro thought.

Her mother said sharply, "Anna, don't raise your voice to your father, and take your elbows off the table!"

"Will you hire a carriage again this year? To take us there in style?"

"Anna!" her mother called back, her voice close to a shout. "You're a young lady, not a market woman! Lower your voice, or your father will let you walk there!"

Maria shot Caro a look of reproach. Her voice was low, but it carried to the foot of the table. "Thomas, we'll discuss it later," she said.

Thomas said, "Now is not the time to decide, Anna."

It would never be. Caro was too sick of charity to finish her dinner. She longed to leave the table and wished never to return.

⁂

The Bennett snub ate at her all week. It bothered her as she sewed, every seam and buttonhole reminding of her servitude to her uncle Thomas. It was all the bitterer because she could not refuse it. How would she and her mother manage without the charity of the Bennetts?

She folded her work into a bundle and set out for the shop. Once there, she laid the bundle on the counter. Despite Danny's pleased smile, she said sharply, "Will you join your cousins to go to the German Festival?"

"Oh, Caro," he said, his expression rueful.

"Will you go in the carriage?" she prodded.

He leaned forward. "I pleaded for you after you left."

"Why did you bother?"

"Caro, I am so sorry."

She stepped back from the counter. "Now you know what they think I'm good for. Pity. Charity. I'm not good enough to mingle with the DeReefs, and I'm not good enough for you."

"They think so. I don't." He reached for her, but she

stepped farther away. He pleaded with her. "You know
what I think of you, and how I feel about you."

"Do I?"

He was too upset for his usual flattery. "Caro, you are
so lovely. So clever. We are so much alike."

"Oh, we are not," she said, letting the tears rise to her
eyes. "You're free and I am not." She turned to go, not
wanting him to see her cry.

ಬಾಡ

BACK AT TRADD STREET, SHE ignored Sophy's greeting
and went upstairs to the room where she and Emily had
exchanged confidences. She lay on the rope bed and
sobbed. She had been a fool to think that she and Danny
could overcome the difference between slave and free.
She thought of the light in his eyes and the hope in his
voice as he talked about the future, and she sobbed afresh,
overwhelmed with despair.

The tap on the door disturbed her. Sophy sat down on
the bed and put a gentle hand on Caro's shoulder. "Did
that boy break your heart?" she said.

Caro sat up. She wiped her face with her sleeve, a gesture her mother would have chastised her for. She said,
"Sophy, it's all wrong, and I can't make it right."

"You quarrel?"

"His family. My mother."

Sophy reached to stroke Caro's hair. "I don't know
about them Bennetts, but I understand your mama. She

bother you and hurt you, but she afraid for you. That why she so harsh on you about young Danny."

"Sophy, who will I marry? Who will have me?"

"Is this about getting married? Or do something else start it?"

"They snubbed me," Caro said.

"Snub you! You cry your heart out because they rude to you?"

"I'm not good enough to go to the German Festival with them. The German Festival, where anyone can go, black or white, slave or free!"

Sophy said, "You break your heart over the German Festival?"

"Don't laugh at me."

"So them Bennetts go, and take young Danny along, and hurt your feelings because they don't take you?"

Caro sat up. "Yes," she said.

Now Sophy laughed in earnest. "Sunday and I go every year. We take you, if you want. Might cheer you."

"It won't fix a thing."

"It always so crowded that no one notice if a boy and a girl find a spot to meet and talk," Sophy said. She squeezed Caro's hand. "You wear that pretty dress of yours when we go."

∞∞

SUNDAY DIDN'T HIRE A CARRIAGE, but he told them that his neighbor, a drayman, owed him a favor. Caro recognized the horse before she recognized the driver. "Mose!"

she cried, throwing her arm over the animal's dark-brown neck.

Sunday's neighbor was the drayman who had brought her to the Jarvie house from the docks. His name was Lewis. Sunday asked, "Where your wife today? Miss Celia?"

"She work," Lewis said. "And so do I. Make a lot of money ferrying people to the festival."

Sunday joined Lewis up front, but Sophy and Caro settled into the bed of the wagon, which was made more comfortable today with a lining of blankets.

As they got underway, Caro gazed around with interest. Driving, even in a cart, was a lost pleasure that she had once taken for granted. Vehicles jammed the street, smart little broughams as well as large, ornate private coaches owned by well-to-do families. Carriages shared the road with carts and wagons, doing a brisk business taking passengers to the festival. Lewis maneuvered swiftly in the thick of the traffic, urging the horse, "Get along, Mose! Get a move on!" And suddenly they stopped with such a jolt that Caro fell against Sophy, who cried, "What the matter?"

Caro righted herself. Just ahead, a hired hansom carriage had stopped inches from someone's coach. It was someone grand, to judge from the shining paint and the glossy matching bay horses. The carriage door flew open, and the passenger leaped out. He wore the towering top hat favored by Charleston's fops. He yelled at the hired coachman, "What in God's name have you done?"

The coachman hopped from his seat. "What's the matter?"

"You nearly ran into me!" the man cried. He took in the hired carriage and saw who stared out the windows at him. He said to the coachman, "This is what happens when *niggers dressed in finery* hire carriages to cavort around town." He addressed the coachman. "You should be ashamed of yourself. A white man, transporting *these people!*"

The coachman raised his voice. "I drive this coach for hire," he said, aggrieved. "I drive whoever pays me to hire it. I don't inquire who they are, and I don't turn them away."

The man's coachman, dressed in livery, approached his irate master. He said softly, "Massa, it's all right. Ain't no damage done here. Set down quiet in your own carriage, and I steady the horses. We go on our way."

"Niggers dressed in finery!" the man repeated, and jumped into his own carriage, slamming the door shut.

As traffic began to move again, their wagon pulled alongside the hired coach. The occupants were visible through the open windows, and Caro recognized them. Her unease dissolved, replaced by anticipation. The people who had been insulted were her Bennett cousins.

❧☙

CARO THOUGHT SHE HAD BECOME used to crowds in the streets of Charleston, but the push and the swirl of the festival throng created a dust that made her eyes water. Black and white, families and couples, all mingled together, the brown of skin careful not to jostle the white. Caro delighted in the sight of so many people so fashionably dressed, black as well as white, the men in frock coats and tall beaver hats, the women in great swaying hoops and ruffled bonnets. The air smelled of sweat, perfume, horses, and frying sausages.

Sunday wanted to see the riflemen, whose marksmanship was the centerpiece of the festival. They found a spot in the crowd and watched. The sharpshooters' tan suits were reminiscent of uniforms, and while most of them sported bowler hats against the sun, a few had donned metal helmets that looked as though they were remnants from the Napoleonic Wars.

The sound of gunshots made Sophy uneasy. She said to Caro, "They put me too much in mind of the militia and the Guard."

Sunday said, "Sophy, honey, we go to watch the acrobats instead, if that please you." His hand stole around Sophy's, as though they were courting.

The acrobats, a group of trim young men in tight-fitting cotton outfits, were captivating. Even Caro's attention was held by the way they leaped and tumbled and contorted themselves and built an impossibly high human pyramid. Sophy smiled as she watched.

After the acrobats, they were spectators at a bowling match, a sedate sport invigorated by the enthusiasm of

the bowlers. They also watched a footrace, where com-
petition enlivened the activity, and cheered the runners,
even though they were German strangers.

Sunday remarked, "Them Germans do like their
exercise."

Caro shifted from one foot to another. She forced
herself not to crane her neck as she scanned the crowd.
Truly, all of Charleston was here today. How would she
find Danny in this throng?

The brass band began to play, the drum punctuating
the cheerful sound of the horns. Caro asked, "Will there
be dancing later?" She thought of dancing with Danny
and had to stifle a smile.

"They have a dance hall," Sophy said, "but we ain't
welcome there."

Caro now tried to stifle her disappointment.

"It's all right," Sunday said. "Plenty of other amusements here."

Sophy exclaimed over the carousel, where children,
black as well as white, rode the painted horses. Sunday stopped before the organ grinder, captivated by the
capers of his monkey. They made their way to halt again
in the crowd that gathered around a tall pole.

"What's that?" Caro asked.

"That the greased pole," Sunday said. "Whoever
climb it win a prize." They lingered as a white man made
the attempt—probably a German, but who knew—but
slipped before he was halfway to the top. A black man,

dressed in patched clothes, was the next to try. The crowd cheered as he inched his way upward. But he failed, too, despite their encouragement.

Caro thought that it was a countrified, vulgar kind of amusement. She said nothing, since Sunday's pleasure was so obvious, and Sophy was happy along with him. Caro glanced around the crowd again. She knew why she felt so listless. She had come here for Danny, and without him, all the pleasures of the festival were flat and dull.

Sunday turned to them and asked, "Ladies, is you hungry?"

"I am," Sophy said.

"Miss Sass?" It was his affectionate, cajoling tone. He wanted her to enjoy herself.

She remembered her manners. "Oh yes," she said, trying to sound eager.

They followed the smell of sausages to find the carts where food was sold. The festival vendors didn't sing. They were gruff Germans, intent on the food they prepared.

Sunday said, "German food for a German Festival."

When the food came, Caro looked surprised. Sophy said, "It's sausage like them Germans eat it."

"On a bread roll? And what is the garnish?"

Sunday chewed and swallowed. "Pickled cabbage!" he said.

Caro shook her head and tasted it. *Remember your manners*, she thought. "It's not bad," she said.

Sunday laughed. "Can tell by your face that you like oysters better. We get some later."

After they ate, they strolled, finding their acquaintances among the crowd where black and white, slave and free, mingled together. As in the market, Sophy stopped frequently to greet someone she knew. Caro let her chatter. She wanted very badly to crane her neck to look for Danny. But she pretended that Sophy's friends and acquaintances interested her and spoke politely as they asked after her.

She would never find Danny. She struggled not to sigh. She would remember her manners and pretend that everything at the festival interested and amused her.

And suddenly, there he was, arm in arm with Anna and Charlotte, who were chattering to each other as though he wasn't there. His expression was determined. Seeing him, she wanted to laugh. He was pretending, just as she was.

Charlotte stopped so abruptly that several people bumped into her. She ignored them and said, "Caro! What a surprise to see you here!"

Caro said sweetly, "So it's true! Everyone comes to the German Festival!"

Anna nodded in her direction but seemed to have difficulty speaking.

Danny unlaced himself from his cousins. Caro introduced Sophy and Sunday. Charlotte smiled, but Anna only inclined her head.

Danny said, "Anna, Charlotte, go on ahead. I'll catch up to you soon. At the rifle range."

"Danny." Anna's voice was a warning. Her father's warning.

Sophy said, "We look after him for you. Keep an eye on him for you."

"A few minutes," Danny said firmly.

Charlotte took Anna's arm, and with an ill grace, Anna allowed herself to be led away.

Danny said, "It's such a press here. Shall we go into the park? It's cooler there." He led them from the rifle range into the park, which had been prettily arranged with paths that snaked around the trees. He found them a bench in the shade.

Sophy said, "Sunday, let's sit, and the young folks can walk a bit, if they will."

"Just for a moment," Danny said gravely to Sophy.

Sophy nodded.

His face alight, he held out his arm to Caro, and her spirits rose as she took it.

He whispered, "If we leave the path, there's a spot in the trees."

"Who else have you taken there?" she teased.

He grinned. "My brother and I used to hide there when we were small."

They left the path for the trees, which were as private as a wilderness. The roar of the festival came to them faintly in the cool afternoon shadows.

They stood face to face. He reached for her hand. "Caro, I am so sorry," he said. "I've been miserable to think that you're angry with me."

"The fault was mine," she said, her anger gone as though she had never felt it. "I was wrong to quarrel with you."

"You'll forgive me?"

"I've already forgiven you."

She trembled to see the joy on his face. He raised his hand to her cheek and stroked it with his gentle fingers. "Caro," he said, his voice full of tenderness.

She had forgotten the sound of her name spoken with tenderness.

He drew her close and leaned toward her. He kissed her, his lips as gentle as his touch, and joy spread through her. He moved his hands to embrace her, and the joy was followed by warmth throughout her body. He clasped her around the waist, and she twined her arms around his neck. They were the same height, and the kiss was easy for both of them.

They kissed for so long that she had to pull away. "Let me draw breath," she said, laughing.

"I've made you breathless," he said, teasing.

"You've made me happy," she said. Suddenly her eyes welled with tears.

"Caro? What is it, my dearest Caro?"

Caro. Cara. The sob escaped despite her best efforts to quell it. "Is it wrong to be so happy so soon after my father's passing?"

Danny asked, "Would he be pleased to know that you're happy?"

The tears spilled out, and she raised her hand to her face. "My happiness was always a joy to him."

Danny touched her skin where the tears left their trail. "Then it isn't wrong at all." He leaned close again. "I love you," he whispered, and let his mouth travel from the salty, silvery glint of sorrow to her lips.

Chapter 9: Sumter County

It was too easy to get used to deception, Emily marveled as she slipped her sketchbook into her pocket. She felt a momentary twinge at deceiving her stepmother, who trusted her. It would be worse if she were making an assignation. But she was not. She had a book in her pocket, and she would trade it for a letter.

She was bound for Tradd Street.

Just before she left, Susan smiled. "You look so much prettier now that you've put off your mourning," she said. Her stepmother touched her cheek. "And happier, too."

She found Caro alone in the kitchen at her sewing. She rose, a gesture of respect, but her smile was quick and sunny. Caro said, "Miss Emily, I scarcely recognized you."

"I've put off my mourning." The dress was a gray plaid much enlivened by a purple stripe, with sweeping sleeves and a billowing skirt. She said, "I didn't intend to wear a dress so bright. But when I saw the length, I was captivated by it."

Caro laughed. "I think like a seamstress now," she said. "Turn around. Let me see the back."

Emily turned, letting Caro look at the pleats in the skirt, and then she twirled, letting the skirt bell and the hoops sway.

They laughed together, two serious young women with reason for happiness. Emily sat and Caro followed suit. Emily leaned forward. "You look so bright," she said.

Caro leaned forward, too. "I have reason to," she said, and blushed.

Emily laughed, a purely happy sound. She said to Caro, "So you have a beau."

"Stop it," Caro said, blushing harder.

Emily laid a hand on her arm. She was smiling. "Oh, it's wicked to tease, I know, but the more you contradict and the more you blush, the surer I am."

"You can't tell anyone."

Emily asked, "Who is it? Do I know him?"

"Danny Pereira. My aunt Maria's son."

"What does your mother say?"

"She doesn't know." Caro's voice dropped to a whisper. "She can't."

Emily thought of all her own deceptions. It would be easy to add this to it. She said, "I brought you something." She pulled the book from her pocket.

Caro reached for it eagerly. At the sight of the title on the spine, she smiled as happily as she had at Emily's tease. "Macaulay! How did you know I wanted this so?"

Emily felt delighted too. "I asked Mr. Pereira what you might want to read, and he told me."

Caro asked, "Do you see him often?"

"Only about the bank drafts. He keeps them a secret for me."

Caro didn't reply. Her cheeks were still pink. She said, "I have a letter for you."

"I hoped so."

She handed Emily the letter from Mr. Aiken, which Emily tore open to read. She looked up, smiling. She said, "Mr. Aiken will be visiting Sumter County in a few weeks. When I go there, I'll see him again."

Caro said, "You have a beau, too."

"Mr. Aiken is my editor. And my friend."

"I hear a contradiction," Caro said. "I see a blush."

Emily laughed. "Now I'll have to tell you to stop it."

"I will if you will, Miss Emily."

Their shared happiness made it easier to speak freely to one another. Emily said, "My friends call me Emily."

Surprise shadowed Caro's face. She said softly, "Do you mean it? Do you dare it?"

"Yes," Emily said.

∞∞

As EMILY LEFT TRADD STREET, she was smiling again. So Caro had a secret, too. *I wonder if I will meet him,* Emily thought, surprised at the idea that she would hope to make the acquaintance of a person of color.

Her mind was elsewhere at midday, when she sat down with her father and stepmother for dinner. It was too hot to stay in Charleston, but she knew why her father

CHARLESTON'S DAUGHTER

lingered in the heat. As a young unmarried woman, she wasn't supposed to know, but every planter's daughter knew the rhythm of the rice crop and could discern whether the season had been kind to rice or not. It didn't hurt that her stepmother fretted loudly over her father's affairs and that her distress was like a barometer that anyone—the innocent and the slave alike—could hear and make sense of.

It had been a bad year for rice, and the rice crop on her father's place in Colleton County had been a disappointment. Her uncle's place, which had given Susan so much hope, had been neglected and mismanaged for years. Her father had visited and had returned with pain on his face. The affairs were in a tangle. The overseer was a drunk who never raised his hand to anyone. The slaves took advantage; they were indolent. Emily had stood in the foyer, and the voices in the study were perfectly audible. Her father had said, "It will take months to set things right. Years, perhaps."

Susan asked, "How did he manage?"

"I don't know. It will be up to me to straighten it out."

Buoyed by the hope of James Jarvie's fortune, her father had arranged to expand the upland plantations that Susan had brought to their union. As a cotton planter, her father was further in debt, and unless cotton did well this year, he would stay in debt. Her stepmother had begun to plan for the refurbishment of the house on King Street, even though the Herriots were still living there. Emily lingered in the foyer on the day that Susan

225

pressed her husband about money for new furnishings and repairs, and she heard her father groan.

Her father had renewed his effort to run for an Assembly seat, and he needed to entertain the well-to-do of Charleston all summer in the pines and throughout the round of parties that began when Charleston woke up again in the fall and stretched throughout the winter until the season ended.

Today, at the table, Susan said, "I know business keeps you in town, Lawrence, but Emily and I will go to Sumter County soon."

"Don't let me keep you," her father said.

"We won't." She glanced at Emily, who was rosy in her new dress. "Now that Emily is out of mourning, she'll find herself a husband in no time."

Her father turned pale and compressed his lips, a sure sign that he was about to lose his temper. He said, "I shudder at the expense of a wedding."

He had beaten her to it. Emily had been ready to make a protest herself: "Mother, don't even mention it. I'm not ready yet."

෪෬

As their coachman, Henry, handed them from the carriage, Susan said to Emily, "The house looks so small after King Street."

Her stepmother was angling—there was no other word—for that house.

Emily breathed in the pine-scented air of Sumter County, which was so much easier on the lungs than Charleston's. She looked fondly at the plain white house where she had spent every summer of her childhood. She said, "It's comfortable here. Even though it's plain."

Susan dismissed Henry with a wave of her hand. "Can you imagine asking the Aikens to dine with us?"

"When I was a little girl coming here, the Aikens used to have a little pine cottage as their summer place. I don't think they'd mind our house."

Susan reached for Emily's hand. "I'm so glad you put off your mourning," she said.

Emily wondered what Mr. Aiken would say, and the color rose in her cheeks. Her stepmother misunderstood her, seeing a belle's eagerness. "Jane Aiken did very well last year," Susan said. "Perhaps we can be hopeful for you, too."

The next day, Emily surprised her stepmother by asking if she could take the carriage to call on the Aikens. "Camilla and I got on just fine the last time I visited," she said.

Susan said, "Camilla Aiken hasn't read a book since she left school. What do you two talk about?"

"She makes me laugh."

Susan regarded Emily, who had a lively expression and a dress brightened with purple, and said, "Then it's all right. Go to see her and give my regards to her mother and sister."

Emily found Camilla sitting alone in the front parlor of the house that had been built to replace the pine cabin. Like the grand houses of Charleston—like the house on King Street, where they would live sooner rather than later, if her stepmother had her way—it was austere and elegant, furnished with the Sheraton pieces that the family had preserved and still cherished. Camilla sat on a pretty sofa that framed her white dress. Despite her fashionable muslin and her fashionable curls, Camilla looked tired and cross. When Emily asked after the family, Camilla said, "Jane's still in a tizzy and Mama's still in a tizzy and for all they know, I'm at the bottom of the backyard well."

Emily laughed. "It can't be as bad as that!"

Camilla pouted. "Jane got someone grand and handsome, and all I get is Mr. Ellison. And my poky old cousin Joshua, who won't even live in South Carolina."

Slowly, as though she didn't know and didn't much care, Emily asked, "Is Mr. Aiken in Sumter County?"

"He's come for a few weeks." Camilla looked sly. "You seemed to like him when you were here last fall."

"He's a pleasant man," Emily said. She was worse than a deceiver. She had come to delight in deception. "But I can't imagine that my papa would want me to marry a man who lives in Ohio."

"Oh, you'd be surprised what can happen when a Carolina man falls in love with a girl whose family has property in Colleton County. And enough hands to work all of it. Wouldn't your father make you a good settlement?"

She recalled her father's worries about his estate and her uncle's. About his campaign and her wedding, even though it was only a figment of her stepmother's imagination. "I never thought of it," Emily said.

"What a goose you are. How do penniless men get on in the world? Ask your papa what he's planned for you."

Emily felt cold and uneasy. She asked, "Do you expect to see Mr. Aiken?"

"We'll see everyone. We're having a barbecue in a few days, with music and dancing, and the whole county's invited. Now that you're out of mourning, you can dance again."

Emily considered this.

Camilla began to laugh. "Penniless men. I've been warned against them, and now I'm warning you."

☙❧

THE DAY OF THE BARBECUE dawned sunny and pleasant. Susan said, "The Aikens are lucky in everything. Even in the weather."

Lawrence looked up from his newspaper, frowning.

Emily asked, "What is it, Papa? Does the news trouble you?"

"Emily, the news is none of your concern. Don't bother your father."

Emily, who read the *Sumter Watchman* in secret, after her father finished with it, had an inkling of the reason for her father's disquiet. The *Watchman* was on guard against the enemies of slavery, and as the price of cotton rose ever higher, the planters of Sumter County grew more and more outspoken in defense of the institution that made their fortunes. But she was not supposed to know, any more than their slaves were, about the anger that roiled through the South.

Susan rose. "Emily, let your father read the news in peace. Come upstairs. It's time to dress." She smiled fondly. "In one of your pretty new dresses."

Emily thought, *I'll see Mr. Aiken today.* It was like the fizz of the champagne she had drunk at Jane Aiken's engagement party. "Yes, Mother," she said obediently, as she prepared to meet a penniless man she knew her parents would disapprove of and that she hoped they would overlook.

Lydia helped her into her dress, which was a cream-colored cotton with an ornate lozenge-shaped border in light purple—reminiscent of light mourning—and pagoda sleeves that extended only to the elbow. The undersleeves were a voile so delicate that it was translucent and exposed the shape of her forearm. Lydia said, "You look pretty, Miss Emily." Emily looked at the cheval mirror, where she could see herself from bonnet to boots. Lydia was a flatterer, but today she was right. The anticipation of seeing Mr. Aiken brought the color to her cheeks.

It was like the engagement party but in daylight. The second-floor piazza had been arranged like a parlor, with chairs and settees, and in the side yard, on the lawn next to the garden, long dining tables had been set up under a canopy. The smell of roasting shoat drifted from the pit behind the house. It would be country food, barbecued shoat and cornbread, fried chicken, and new vegetables. The sound of conversation and laughter drifted from the piazzas and the gardens.

"What a press!" Susan said. "Where are Mr. and Mrs. Aiken? We should pay our respects."

As they worked their way through the crowd, Lawrence and Susan ahead, Emily demurely behind, a familiar, sturdy, vigorous figure hailed them. "Mr. Ellison!" Susan said. "Are you acquainted with Miss Emily?"

"I surely am, Mrs. Jarvie. Met her last fall when she visited her sister."

Nancy had stayed home today. She was expecting again, and she said that the smell of food made her ill.

Emily held out her hand. She said to Susan, "Mr. Ellison was very kind to me when I stayed with Nancy."

Susan's eyebrows rose. "I had no idea you were so well acquainted," she said.

John Ellison shot Emily a knowing look. He said, "I'm glad Miss Emily's out of her mourning, but you shouldn't press her."

Emily laughed. Susan said, "Mr. Ellison, excuse us, we need to find Mr. and Mrs. Aiken."

Susan took Emily aside. She said, "You didn't tell me you flirted with Mr. Ellison last fall."

"I didn't. He dined with Nancy and her husband. He's their nearest neighbor. We were courteous to each other." The half-truths caught in her throat. She was impatient for her real purpose here today: Joshua Aiken.

Susan gave her a searching look. "You're out of mourning," she said, "but you need to be careful who you pay attention to and who pays attention to you."

Mother, I'm here to see a penniless younger son, and I don't care if he wants my dowry or not. Unmarried girls, like slaves, knew how to act obedient. She said, "I know."

They pressed on, but they made no progress toward their hosts, since they halted every few steps to greet the people of the county they knew. Emily's dress was exclaimed on. "You're out of mourning!" The women told her that her dress was lovely, and the men, bolder, told Emily that she was pretty.

They came upon Camilla, bright and rosy and impetuous, who greeted Susan and Lawrence with politesse and said to Emily, "Your dress!"

Emily nodded.

Camilla grasped the hand of the young man who stood at her shoulder. "Cousin Joshua, Miss Emily is no longer in mourning!"

He gazed at her with his keen dark eyes and smiled at her with the rosy mouth surrounded by the dark whiskers. He removed his hat, and the breeze stirred his thick dark hair. "Miss Jarvie," he said. He looked as she remembered him. He looked as she had imagined him.

Her breath caught in her throat. "Mr. Aiken," she said, hoping that she sounded demure rather than eager.

Susan said, "Miss Camilla, please introduce us."

Camilla, unusually polite, introduced Mr. Aiken as her cousin, whom she had known since they were children. Mr. Aiken, smiling, added that their families were distantly connected, and it was kind of Miss Camilla to think so well of him. Camilla, still restrained, further explained that Mr. Aiken and his family had attended her sister's engagement party and that she had made him an introduction to Emily. Demurely—Camilla was better at this than Emily herself—she said to Susan, "I hope I didn't blunder, Mrs. Jarvie."

"Oh no," Susan said, taking in the northern frock coat and the ready-made hat and disapproving of both. "It's kind of you to remember your childhood companion."

She makes him sound like a faithful dog, Emily thought.

When they finally made their way to the piazza and mounted its steps, they paid their respects to the reigning family of Sumter County. It was like greeting the members of royalty. A quick word, a press of the hand, and an obeisance, and it was over.

Emily said, "Mother, I'm feeling a little faint with the sun. Will you excuse me? I want to sit in the shade."

Her stepmother gave her that searching look again. That warning look.

She wasn't faint. She was giddy. She moved with a swift step, looking for the northern frock coat and hat that Susan disapproved of.

She found him near the dining table, just as a man-servant approached with glasses of iced and sweetened tea. The servant was an Aiken slave, and Emily had never seen him before. He didn't speak, but he offered the tray.

Mr. Aiken took a glass and waited as the servant held the tray for Emily. The slave slipped away, as silent and as insubstantial as a shadow.

Mr. Aiken said, "We take our ease today, and they work so hard."

She was too startled to raise her glass to her lips. She curled her hand around the cold, sweating surface, and before she spoke, she remembered Caro, whom she had always found at work, either with her hands plunged into the washtub or with her head bent over her sewing. She said, "Do you consider the servants, Mr. Aiken?"

He met her eyes, and the brown gaze was as warm as a caress. "I try to consider everyone, Miss Jarvie," he said.

She wished that she could invite him to sit beneath the great live oak, but today it was probably occupied by a couple who could court in plain sight. She would conduct her business in plain sight, too. "It's good to see you again, Mr. Aiken," she said.

He smiled like a man given a gift. "It's been a great pleasure to get your letters, Miss Jarvie. Not only for the sketches. But to hear from you and know that you're flourishing."

"I am," she said. "I have an occupation now, and it suits me. I look at Charleston as my readers would, to see it as they might. I see everything from two sides now: theirs as well as my own."

"You're truly becoming a writer, Miss Jarvie."

"That's high praise, coming from you."

"It's meant to be." He smiled and gestured toward the

dress. "You look very different. More than the dress. Your face is livelier. Your step is quicker. Is your heart lighter, too?"

She met his eyes without a trace of coquetry. "Yes, it is."

He didn't flinch, but he retreated to a safer subject. "What have you been reading, Miss Jarvie?"

"I've taken your recommendation. I'm reading Mr. Henry David Thoreau."

"Did you have any trouble finding it in Charleston?"

"The bookseller gave me a very odd look when I asked for it. But he ordered it for me."

"What did you think of it?"

She said, "Such a strange way to live—all in solitude, bound only by one's own conscience, in defiance of the things that society believes in, which he thinks are wrong."

The sound of fiddle music drifted from the back garden along with the smell of roasting shoat. The conversation buzzed and hummed, as the bees and flies did, and the occasional shout of laughter was like the cry of a jay.

The man who had left South Carolina said fiercely, "But there is such freedom in it!"

She, who lived in South Carolina in its heart in Charleston, said softly, "And such disorder. And such terror!"

He put a gentle hand on her arm. "I've overstepped, as I'm so likely to do," he said. "I've disturbed you."

She looked into his eyes, not flinching. She said, "When you look keenly and feel deeply, many things are disturbing. Should we shy from them? Or should we face them?"

"You're brave to say so," he said. "Braver than I am, since you remain here."

She had never considered leaving, but she had a sudden vision of herself warmly dressed in wool, striding briskly down the streets of Cincinnati, Ohio, free to write about anything that she saw and felt. She said, "I must never forget that I'm in South Carolina."

"Write to me," he said, his tone soft and urgent. "Tell me."

Confide in me, he meant, as she once confided in her diary. Her girl's secrets seemed small and tame. He would encourage her to tell secrets that were full of danger. "I will," she said, her voice trembling a little. "Mr. Aiken, I promise I will."

His voice dropped very low. "When you write to me, will you address me as Joshua?" he asked.

"Yes," she whispered. "And you must call me Emily, as my friends do."

As she had asked Caro to do.

The music floated through the air, the cry of the fiddles and the sadder, slower call of the banjo. He said, "I shouldn't keep you any longer." His smile was wistful. "Now that you're a belle again, you should dance with the men of Sumter County."

She nodded. She drank the rest of her tea, bracing herself to take up the smile of the belle. She walked away swiftly, not looking back, leaving her glass on the tray of a servant whose face she didn't see to take her place with the unmarried girls who looked for partners among the unmarried men.

In the back garden, the dancers were assembling. The Aikens held to the old ways for their summer picnics, and the dances were the old-fashioned kind, the reels and jigs where the dancers faced each other and nothing touched save their hands.

John Ellison came up to her, his ruddy face flushed a little with drinking in the sun. His eyes were a fierce blue. He asked, "May I have this dance, Miss Emily?"

She said, "My pleasure, sir." Her spirit hovered elsewhere, yearning for Joshua, but in the world's sight, she smiled brightly and held out her hand to dance the reel with John Ellison.

Chapter 10: Freedom Is Sweeter

CARO LET HER SEWING FALL into her lap. Days later, she could still feel the ghost of Danny's kiss. She raised her fingers to her lips, as though she could capture it.

Sophy stood at the table, kneading biscuit dough. "Since you come back from the festival, you act moonstruck."

"It's nothing, Sophy," she fibbed, hastily picking up the shirt.

"Is it that boy Danny?"

Before she could deny it, the bell on the gate jangled. Sophy said, "For you, since you have as many callers as any lady."

Sophy brought Danny into the kitchen. He blushed when he saw her and stammered, "I was at the post office, and it's so close that I stopped along the way."

Caro recalled the warmth she had felt when he held her at the festival, and the color rose in her face, too. Sophy said to him, "Set down. I got coffee, if you want some."

He sat so slowly and so awkwardly that Sophy said,

"You moonstruck, too. Hah!" He blushed an even deeper red as she handed him the cup.

Caro wanted to reach for his hand. She wanted to put her arms around his neck and tangle her fingers in the curls that grew there. She wanted to pull him close and kiss him again. Instead she sat in silence, blushing, as he did. Dumbstruck.

He drank a few dutiful sips, and said, "Miss Sophy, I'm making some deliveries for my uncle. May Caro walk with me?"

"I don't mind. Her mama, that a different story."

Caro said, "I don't want to bother her. She's not feeling well."

Sophy asked, "Her cough bad again?"

"She says she's too tired to get out of bed." Her mother had been sick like this before. When she lost her last baby, she had stayed in bed for weeks. Caro pushed the thought of her mother's health from her mind.

Sophy said, "You leave Caro time to do her work. She walk through the city on your uncle's business, that don't earn her keep."

Danny said gravely, "I won't keep her long, Miss Sophy. I promise." He rose and reached for her hand. Caro smiled at the feeling of his fingers curled around hers.

☙❧

AS THEY LEFT THE HOUSE AND turned into the street, Danny said, "I fibbed a little."

"Only a little?" she teased.

"I have to make a delivery in the Neck."

The Neck was a long walk away and they took their time traveling north on King Street. Caro had never strayed so far from the narrow confines of the well-to-do parts of Charleston that hugged the harbor. She felt an internal heat of her own, and the fragrance of late-blooming summer flowers mingled with the scent of pomade from Danny's hair, which sprang from his head in the heat. He didn't touch her, but his presence was warmth enough.

"Who is your customer in the Neck? Is it one of the DeReefs?" She was surprised that her uncle did business with the people who lived in the Neck. The DeReefs lived there, but so did many people with little money. And slaves who lived out, as Sunday Desmond did.

"Hah!" Danny said. "The DeReefs patronize the Westons because they're family."

"I'm surprised you sell to anyone in the Neck."

Danny asked her, "Why would you begrudge a man in the Neck a good suit?"

"Even a slave?"

He said, "We ask to see their money, not their badges or their papers. If they pay us, we're satisfied."

"Money is the great leveler," she said.

He laughed. "You learned Latin and Greek and read Cicero and Macaulay, and you never realized that?"

"I've learned many things since I came to Charleston."

"That there is freedom in money. And what else?"

She laughed. Happiness surged through her. "How handsome the men of Charleston are."

He blushed.

"And what flirts they can be!"

After the Neck, he had another delivery to a mansion just west of the Battery, where they were admitted to the side door to transact their business in the kitchen. In this house, they were doubly unwelcome, as people of trade and of color. The maid took the bundle from Danny with a sniff.

As they left, Danny said, "Her master hasn't paid his bill for months."

"For shame!"

"The richer they are, the worse they are," Danny said. "And we can't insist because they'll think we're insolent, and they might take away their custom altogether."

"So your living is fragile," Caro said.

He sighed. "It's a fragile business to be a free person of color in Charleston," he said.

His arms were now unburdened, and she reached for his hand. "Let's talk of happier things," she said lightly, her tone just like her mother's.

He said, "I would dearly love an ice. May I buy you one?"

The ice seller was a market woman who had bought eggs from Sophy. She spooned the ices into paper cups, her dark face gleaming with the sweat of the summer. She said to Caro, "You keep that pretty young man close, Miss Caro. You tell him to marry you!"

Danny laughed. He asked Caro, "I like the watermelon. What flavor do you want?"

"Oh, the lemon. I like the tart and the sweet together."

They were only a block from the Battery, and he led her there. They couldn't stand on the Battery itself—people of color weren't allowed so close to the water—but they found a bench set back from the shore. They sat so they could look at each other, and she let her knees touch his. He smiled at her daring.

As she ran her spoon around the little cup to get the last of her ice, he leaned close. "Is it good?"

She leaned close to meet him. "Yes," she said, smiling.

He kissed her, a prolonged kiss, and she met him, her lips parting a little. Their first kiss had been a question: Do you care for me? Do you desire me?

This kiss was different. It was an answer. He was hers. Now she knew that he would belong to her forever, and she to him.

He let her go and said softly, "We are sworn."

She said, "We are."

He smiled, a boyish joy mixed with a newly adult gravity. "You taste of lemon," he said. "Tart and sweet together."

&OCR&

THEY GREW SLYER IN FINDING places to be alone together. Charleston was full of narrow alleys behind the grand houses where Thomas Bennett's customers lived. In the alley behind a house on Ladson Street, they discovered a sequestered spot. He touched her cheek. "I wish I could court you properly," he said. "Sit with you in the parlor, both of us on the settee, and no one to frown or disapprove if I took your hand or even stole a kiss."

She tried to tease. "You can come to Tradd Street and sit under Sophy's watchful eye while she keeps all of us in order, even my mother."

"Oh, Caro," he said, caressing her face. "I love you."

She kissed his palm. "I love you."

He put his arms around her and pulled her close. She could feel his heart beating against her breast. She could feel him through her skirt, seat of love calling to the seat of love. His embrace warmed her and dizzied her, making her hungry for the other joys that a man and a woman might give each other.

And in the wet heat of Charleston's summer, she was suddenly cold. She knew full well that love could make a baby, which wouldn't be his and wouldn't be hers. Their child would belong to Lawrence Jarvie.

She pulled away and he let her go.

He touched her cheek. She met his eyes. "It isn't right," she said. At the worried expression on his face, she said, "Not us. But this."

He nodded.

Her voice caught in her throat. "I wish we could marry."

He caught her by the hand. "I want to marry you."

As though all the difficulties could be swept away. She thought, *We are sworn.*

"If I asked?"

"Ask," she said fiercely.

He caressed her cheek. "Will you marry me?"

She raised her eyes to his. She let her eyes fill. "Yes,"
she said.

⁎

AFTER THE NEXT SUNDAY DINNER, when everyone was
replete and drowsy, Danny slipped into the alley behind
his uncle's house, and Caro followed him there.

"I haven't spoken to my mother yet," he said. "But I
will."

"And my mother," she said, her heart heavy.

"Caro," he said. She heard a ghostly voice echo: *Cara*.
"We love each other. They can't take that from us."

He leaned close, and his lips had just touched hers
when an angry voice startled them apart.

Uncle Thomas cried, "What is this?" He pulled Danny away by the shoulders, as though he were handling a
randy dog. "What in God's name is this?"

Separated, they stared at their feet and said nothing.

"Danny!" Thomas said, putting all his reprimand into
it.

Danny raised his head. "I love Caro, Uncle Thomas,"
he said.

"Love! The way a puppy loves. A pup's foolishness."

"No, it isn't like that." He gazed at Thomas, plucking
the string of his uncle's affection. "I want to honor her. I
want to marry her."

Thomas let Danny go. "Good God!" he said, in a groan of dismay. "Go inside. I'll speak to you later. And to your mother."

Danny turned a regretful face toward his uncle and then toward Caro. His shoulders slumped as he walked into the yard.

Thomas turned to Caro. "As for you!"

She was suddenly sick with fear.

He said, "I'm very angry with you. I promised my sister that this would be a business connection and nothing more. You've betrayed my trust in you."

She couldn't speak. She shook her head.

"You can't come to the house anymore," he said. "Not as a member of the family, since you haven't behaved as one. If you want to attend the church service, that's your business, but you won't be welcome to join us."

She knew the rest. She would never work for him again. The three dollars, the difference between slavery in comfort and abject slavery, would be gone.

He said, "I won't disturb our business arrangement. That was always for Kitty, not for you. But I'll keep a close eye on you." He glanced in the direction of the house. "And on him, too. How far has it gone? What has he done?"

Thinking of the handclasps and the kisses, she whispered, "He's been the gentleman with me."

He reached for her arm and held it roughly, as he had mishandled Danny. "Do you swear it?"

"Yes," she whispered again. She lifted her eyes to her uncle's. "On my father's memory, I swear it."

He let go her arm. "Go," he said. "Go home." His voice was sharp, and it tore a wound in her. "A matter of business," he said. "That's all the connection you must have with us. A matter of business."

℘℘

CARO TOOK HER TIME RETURNING to Tradd Street. She wanted to brace herself. Sophy was sure to pry and nag her to tell her mother what had happened. She needed to be ready for her mother's anger. She wished that she could go to the Battery and lean against the stone wall that overlooked the water of the harbor. But not even a free person of color was free enough for that. She, even less so.

But Sophy was out and her mother was asleep. Relieved, Caro sat at the pine table, too unhappy to sew or read. Chloe twined around her ankles, and she swept the animal into her lap. She buried her face in Chloe's coat and listened to the rumbling purr. It gave her no comfort.

She set the cat on the floor and crept into the shack. Her mother's eyes fluttered open. "Caro?" she asked, in a drowsy voice.

"I'm going to rest for a bit, Mama," she said. "The heat."

Her mother didn't reply, and Caro lay on the bed without taking off her boots.

"Caro?" Her mother's voice was still drowsy.

"Yes, Mama?"

"Take off your dress and hang it up."

Despite her pain, she nearly laughed. She knew how much her mother hated the sight of a girl in a wrinkled dress. "I didn't want to bother you, but I will, Mama."

ഗ‌ാ

THE NEXT MORNING, CARO sat in the kitchen, listless about taking up her sewing again. The shirt in her hands reminded her of Thomas. She heard his words and, worse still, his angry tone every time she touched the cloth. Sophy sat opposite her, her eyes a little bleary. She said, "Sunday bring us hock yesterday, and I drink too much."

Ordinarily she would have sassed Sophy, saying, "Don't you know that a lady never drinks more than three glasses at supper?" But today she couldn't find Miss Sass's voice.

The bell at the gate jangled and Sophy rose. "Probably for you, with all them callers you get," she said.

It was Danny. His elegant suit made him look paler and contrasted with the dark shadows under his eyes. He had been sleepless last night, as she had.

Sophy took them both in and said, "You look a sight, both of you. What happen?"

Caro wished she could say, *Hush. It isn't any of your business.*

But Danny was ahead of her. He said to Sophy, "I've come to speak to Mrs. Jarvie."

"Oh my," Sophy said. "It come to that."

Caro couldn't contain herself. "You don't know," she said. "You don't know a thing!"

Sophy said, "It ain't a secret that you like young Danny and that he like you. And it ain't a secret that his mama hate that you like each other. Is there more?"

Caro began to protest, but Danny put his hand on her arm. "Yes, there is, Miss Sophy," he said, and he explained how his uncle had found them together and how angry he had been.

Sophy said, "Do it occur to you that he act like this because he love you? And he love both his sisters, your mama"—she glanced at Danny—"and yours, too?" She nodded to Caro. "He caught right in the middle, like a fly in a spider's web. What else can he do but get mad and pull you apart?"

"Sophy, he meant everything he said to me," Caro said.

"What a man say when he mad and what he think later at his leisure, that ain't the same thing."

Danny said, "He's still angry at me. I know he is."

"Did he whup you?"

"He didn't have to. He let my mother take off a layer of skin with her tongue."

Sophy's eyes gleamed. She said, "Everyone can be got round. I know it." She took them both in. "You mighty charming, both of you, when you ain't hurt and mad. And smart, too. Think about it. How to get round them, the ones who so hurt and mad because they love you."

Danny sighed. "I've come to speak to your mother," he said to Caro.

"I haven't told her yet," she said, letting misery flood her.

He reached for her hand and clasped it hard, for courage. "We'll tell her together," he said.

❧☙

CARO LED DANNY THROUGH THE yard. She had never taken him to the shack. "Oh, Caro," Danny whispered. "Is this where you live?"

She saw it afresh through his eyes. The oiled paper. The weathered boards. The door that didn't lock. She hesitated, then tapped on the door. "Mama?" she called.

"What is it, Caro?" Her mother's voice was throaty, as though she'd been asleep.

"I've brought you a visitor."

"Not Maria I hope." She sounded louder. Stronger.

"No, Mama." Caro pushed open the door.

It was too hot in the little house, and the fragrance of the garden was punctuated by the smell from the midden. Danny's eyes took in the rope beds, the rickety furniture, the tin plates and cups that they never used, since they ate in the kitchen with Sophy. As much as she trusted Danny, at this moment she burned with shame that he saw this.

Her mother sat on the rope bed, and Caro pulled the chairs close to the bed, as though it were a settee where her mother could hold court.

Danny settled carefully on the chair. He said, "Mrs. Jarvie, it's good of you to receive me."

Kitty said, "That depends on your purpose here."

He held himself very still. He let the fatigue and the worry show in his face, but his voice was level and calm. "I've come because I love your daughter."

"As I feared," Kitty said.

"My mother isn't glad of it, either."

"It doesn't surprise me."

Danny continued to hold himself very straight. "I love her," he said, his eyes unwavering on her mother's face. "I love her as my father loved my mother. As Caro's father loved you."

Kitty met his gaze with her own. "Yes, exactly like. Because you can't marry her."

"No, ma'am. I can, and I intend to."

"Over your mother's objections? And your uncle's?"

"I'm well aware of their feelings," Danny said. He clasped Caro's hand in both of his. "I want to honor your daughter. To cherish her forever. Until death do us part."

Caro thought of her mother pleading with Maria. Reminding her that love was greater than wealth. That love had freed her.

Kitty turned her head away and began to cough, a hoarse, racking sound. The cough grabbed her and squeezed her and shook her until she was weak and trembling.

Caro had never heard Kitty cough like that. She fell to her knees beside her mother's bedside and reached for her mother's hands. Full of guilt and fear, she said, "Mama, shall we call for the doctor?"

Kitty waved Caro away. "He'll tell me I have a weak chest. I've always known that. What good would it do?"

As Danny watched, Caro entreated her mother. "What if you're really sick? You could die!"

Kitty's gaze swept over Danny, who had just promised to love Caro as long as he lived. She said, "We are all going to die. We just don't know when."

"Mama, no," Caro pleaded.

Caro saw her mother's face flicker. For a moment, she was Mrs. Jarvie again, the beloved companion to James Jarvie, a lady dressed in silk with diamonds flashing on her earlobes. She said to Danny, "Tell your mother that I will call on her. That Caro and I will both call on her."

Then it was gone, and she was thin and haggard and ailing, a slave helpless to take care of herself or protect her daughter.

෯෬

As before, Maria greeted them at the door; as before, she offered them no refreshment. Kitty sat quietly on the settee, her posture dignified, and she said to her half sister, "You want to hurt and insult my daughter. I won't allow it."

"She—"

"She charmed your son, and why shouldn't she?" Kitty said, her eyes very bright in her flushed face. "Look at her." Caro felt Maria's eyes on her, and she mimicked her mother's posture, with the straight back and grace of a lady.

Kitty found her old voice, the voice of the mistress of the house. "Gently raised and educated and fair of skin. And lovely into the bargain. Of course your son fell in love with her." Kitty gazed at her half sister. "Doesn't she deserve a young man like him?"

Maria spat out the words. "She is a slave."

"Ah, Mimi, we were both slaves once. Don't you recall? Someone was kind enough to free you, and someone else was kind enough to treat me as though I were free. How can you blame her, when freedom is so much a matter of chance?"

She began to cough. She strained to stop it, and when she caught her breath again, Maria said, without kindness, "I heard that you weren't well."

"I'm not," her mother said. "I worry a great deal about Caro. What will happen to her after I'm gone?"

Caro wanted to cry out, *Mama, don't speak of it.*

But Kitty continued to pin Maria with a level gaze, and she said, "Who will protect Caro and maintain her?"

"Not my son," Maria said.

Kitty said, "After I die, she will be in the hands of Lawrence Jarvie. Who was bid to treat her as a member of the family."

"I can't help that," Maria said.

"No, you can't," Kitty said. "But you can help her, as the only family she will have, you and Thomas."

"She can't marry my son."

"I can't help that," Kitty said, mocking her half sister. "But don't insult her. Don't hurt her. Don't cast her away. When God takes my soul, I want to know that someone cherishes her." She rose. "Let's go, Caro."

Maria's face looked pinched and ashen, as though she had eaten something that disagreed badly with her. In a voice no less gruff than her greeting, she said, "Wait here. I'll summon a hansom for you."

🙜🙝

"You quiet," Sophy said to Caro several days later, as they worked together in the kitchen. "It ain't like you."

Caro shook her head.

Sophy said, "My man Sunday come tonight. Sunday come on Saturday!" It was a small joke, but it was Sophy's way to cheer her. "Eat with us. You and your mama."

To her surprise, Kitty agreed to join them in the kitchen.

Sunday Desmond came with a bottle under his arm. Pleased, Sophy said, "You working again."

He set the bottle on the table. "Busy. That fuss about hiring out, it blow over like I thought it would. Busy all the time now." He hugged Sophy, and she folded into his embrace.

She bends with him, when she's so jagged with everyone else. Love is a strange thing, Caro thought miserably, watching the joy that these two work-worn slaves had in each other.

When Sunday released Sophy, he hugged Caro, enfolding her, too, a fatherly embrace without any threat in it. He had told her that she put him in mind of his oldest daughter, whom he hadn't seen since she was sold away to Mississippi.

He said politely to Kitty, "Miss Catherine, you look peaked."

"I've had a little cough," her mother said.

"I hope you better soon."

"I hope so, too."

He said softly to Caro, "You look a little peaked yourself. No sass in you today, Miss Sass."

"I'm fine," Caro said.

"She in love," Sophy offered.

"Sophy, don't tell," Caro said, irritated.

Sunday teased a little. "And it don't go right."

Caro sat at the kitchen table and propped her chin in her heads. She felt too weary to tell the story to Sunday.

Sunday opened the bottle and poured a glass for Caro and another for Kitty. They drank their wine from thick glass tumblers, not crystal glasses, but that didn't change the taste any. He lifted his glass and said to Caro, "If he jilt you, if he love another, he a fool."

Sophy said, "Her young man's family against it."

"Why?" Sunday asked, offended on Caro's behalf. "Is they rich? Or high-rumped?"

"Both," Sophy said. "His mama a Bennett, and his daddy was a rich Israelite."

"Sophy, please," her mother said.

"What? We love Caro, Sunday and I, and we unhappy that her heart break."

Caro said angrily, "He's free. And I'm not."

"Is that all?" Sunday asked.

"*Is that all*," Miss Sass replied. "His mama would rather die than see her son married to a slave."

Sunday looked puzzled. "But it happen all the time," he said. "Free husband, slave wife."

"Why would a free man marry a woman who's a slave? Why would he let his children be born into slavery?" Caro said.

"My friend Lewis," Sunday said. "My neighbor."

"The drayman," Caro said. "Mama, he drove us from the wharf. Do you recall?"

Kitty shook her head.

Sunday said, "He a free man. Not grand, but he make a good living as a drayman. He fall in love with a slave woman and wouldn't have no other. He go to her massa, and he ask to buy her."

Now Caro was puzzled. "To be his slave?"

"No. To be his wife. In law, he own her, but in life, he protect her and keep her so that no one can sell her away from him. On paper, she a slave, but she able to live like a free woman."

Kitty asked, "And her master agreed?"

"He softhearted. He say yes, and he let her go for less than she worth. Glad for her happiness."

Caro wondered if Lawrence Jarvie had a soft spot for anyone. Kitty asked, "Are there children?"

"Four children. In law, they his slaves too, but he love them and cherish them while he protect them."

Caro said slowly, "And they all live as though they're free."

"Yes, they do." Sunday raised his glass. "Have a happy life together." He drank.

Free husband, slave wife. A husband the master to keep his wife in freedom. Danny couldn't afford to buy her, even if Lawrence Jarvie sold her cheap. But someone else might. And there was yet someone else who might advise her. Whether her mother liked it or not, she would write to Benjamin Pereira.

☙❧

When the reply came from Pereira, she showed it to her mother, who shook her head. "What can he do for us?"

"How will we know unless we ask?" She took her mother's hand. "We'll see him together."

"And Danny?"

"I'll write to him."

She sent Danny a note, admonishing the little messenger boy to give it to young Mr. Pereira, not to Mr. Bennett who owned the shop, adding a dime to fortify his memory. She wrote to Danny to tell him that she had arranged a visit to Mr. Pereira, the lawyer, to ask about the legalities relating to their ability to marry and hoped that Danny would accompany her.

The messenger boy returned so swiftly that she

despaired of what had happened. But he said, "Don't have a note. Do have word."

"From Mr. Pereira? Not from anyone else?"

The boy regarded her with a contemptuous expression. "I ain't a fool. Pereira. Young, fair-skinned, got eyes too light for a black man. Hand to him direct and as soon as he see it, he look at me and say, 'Yes.' That's all. 'Yes.'"

On the day of their appointment, Kitty dressed carefully to meet with the man who had been James Jarvie's best friend and had been so cordial to her at the Jarvie dinner table. Once dressed, her hand stole to her earlobe, feeling for the missing earbob as though it were a lost limb. She held out her arm to Caro. "Shall we?"

"Let's find a hansom."

"It isn't far."

"And you aren't well."

"I'll bankrupt you," Kitty said.

Caro shook her head. It gave her a pang to be the one who worried and took care. "Of course not," she said.

As Caro sat in the hansom with her mother, she breathed in the familiar smell of summer in Charleston, floral perfume and rot in the streets, and brushed away the mosquitoes that whined around her face. It was fever season again in Charleston. Emily hadn't visited for weeks; she had escaped to the pines.

Caro's heart ached. Her whole body ached, as though she were her mother's age and not well herself.

Caro still hadn't spoken to Danny, and she worried that he might have changed his mind. Had Uncle Thomas learned something? Or worse still, wormed it from him? Despite the yes, she let herself think of everything that might go wrong. His mother, scourging him again with her anger. Thomas, keeping him a prisoner in the tailoring room. Danny's own heart, eroded by the family's antagonism and opposition.

They waited in the pleasant anteroom. Caro sat on the edge of the comfortable armchair, too wrought up to accept the servant's offer of refreshment. Pereira's servant was a light-skinned young man, as well-dressed as a lawyer, and for a sickening moment Caro wondered if he was Benjamin Pereira's son.

But they had waited only ten minutes—she knew because the cased clock in the corner ticked away the minutes as well as showing them—when the door opened with a fair amount of force, and Danny burst in. He was soberly dressed in a wool suit that had glazed his face with sweat in the August heat. He greeted Kitty, but all his attention was for Caro. Panting a little, he said, "I've deceived Uncle Thomas to be here."

Caro rose and held out her hands. "But you came."

"Of course I came." He clasped her hands. "What is our business here?"

She said, "I thought that Mr. Pereira might have some advice for us."

He glanced at her mother. "You thought more than that."

Benjamin Pereira was his uncle, too, even though no one admitted to it. "Perhaps he can help us," she said.

"You're not planning on trying to get round Mr. Pereira!"

She recalled the dinners of her girlhood, when Benjamin Pereira would tease her and encourage her and ask her what she read. When he would smile at her mother, a look she now understood as one of longing. "I might. And you might, too."

He shook his head and let go of her hands. "What if it isn't a matter for the law?"

She thought of the look on Pereira's face as he tried to interpret her father's will to Lawrence Jarvie. She said, "Then it might be a matter of family feeling. Of conscience."

The servant ushered them into Pereira's office, and Benjamin Pereira's pleasant expression, his lawyer's look, faded away at the sight of her mother. "Oh, Kitty," he said, in a tone shadowed by his grief for James Jarvie and his unspoken affection for the woman who had been mistress of her father's house. He could see how diminished Kitty had become, and he took a deep breath to compose himself for the matter at hand.

Kitty said, "Caro and Danny have business with you, Ben, but I'm the only family she has, and I'm here to help her."

Pereira's smile for Caro and Danny was less fraught. Friendly. He invited them to sit.

Pereira's office was very like her father's study, except that the armchairs were upholstered in leather rather than velvet. Behind the expanse of mahogany desk were shelves full of books bound in leather the color of dried blood, so well used that the gold had rubbed from their spines. The smell of the books was intensified by the smell of the chairs, and her memory of the next-to-the-last time she had sat in her father's study, to hear Mr. Pereira read her father's will, came over her in a wave of nausea.

"So," Pereira said. "Caro, you wrote to me, but you didn't tell me much. What brings you to see me?"

As though they had rehearsed it, Danny took her hand and said earnestly, "Mr. Pereira, Caro and I have fallen in love. We wish to marry."

"And if things were going smoothly, you'd be calling on a minister, not on me," Pereira said. "What is the difficulty?"

Danny said, "My mother is dead set against it. And my uncle Thomas as well."

Pereira asked Kitty, "And you?"

Kitty tried to speak, but she had to stifle a cough.

Alarmed, Pereira asked, "Do you need a glass of water?"

Kitty shook her head.

"I can make a guess here," Pereira said. "About the opposition. But you'd best tell me."

Caro said, "It's because I'm not free."

"I thought so." He leaned back in his chair, disengaging himself. He said, "How can I help you?"

Caro asked, "What is the law governing marriages between slaves and free persons of color?"

Pereira sighed and leaned forward again. He said, "The law is quite clear. An enslaved person can't legally enter into a marriage. These church ceremonies, which many slaves arrange, aren't legally binding. And I remind you that the legal status of any children follows the legal status of the mother. The children of an enslaved woman inherit their mother's chattel status."

Caro shifted in her chair. "Yes, I know," she said. "What of the status of the free person?"

Pereira gave her a look heavy with distress. "I hardly need to remind you of that, Caro," he said.

"Does it make any difference if the free person is a man of color?"

"No, it does not. The marriage isn't legally binding, and the children are slaves."

Danny's hand was hot and sweaty in her own. She clutched it tightly. She said, "What if a free man of color buys a slave woman, then marries her? What does the law say about that?"

Pereira glanced at Kitty and looked away. In his driest voice, he said, "Slavery is a very different chattel relationship than marriage in the eyes of the law. But a man who owns his wife as a slave can protect her. He can keep his marriage intact, and if there are children, he can keep his family intact."

Kitty asked fiercely, "Will he allow her to live as though she were free?"

"That's outside the realm of the law. But if he has bought her because he loves her and cherishes her, because he wants to protect her and maintain her, he's likely to treat the law as a formality."

Danny couldn't contain himself. The words burst out. "Mr. Pereira, I can't buy Caro. I can't afford it. But my uncle Thomas can."

"If he'll see to it," Caro said. She turned to her mother. "Do you think he might?"

"Let Danny ask him," Kitty said.

Danny leaned forward, an imploring stance, and Caro saw, for the first time, his resemblance to the Pereiras. "Mr. Pereira, might you help us? To speak with my uncle and my mother to help them see to it?"

Caro saw the lawyer war with the uncle. The uncle spoke. "You want me to make a case for you."

Trembling, Danny said, "Yes. To persuade them to give Caro her freedom."

Pereira regarded his brother's son with a rueful affection. "Danny, you try me," he said. "It's never a legal matter, is it?" He shifted his glance to Caro, then to Kitty, where his gaze lingered. "Yes, I'll speak to your mother and your uncle."

Caro fumbled for the reticule she kept in her pocket. "Mr. Pereira, we must owe you something for your advice," she said.

He waved away her words. "No," he said, his voice betraying his emotion. He glanced at Kitty. "For James. For his memory. A matter of family feeling."

∞⊗

Sophy grumbled to Caro when the bell at the gate rang. "Another one of them callers of yours." But she came back with only an envelope in her hand. "A little messenger boy again. Look hopeful, wait for a tip. Tell him he don't get paid twice. Hah!" She handed Caro the envelope.

She recognized the copperplate hand even before she opened it. It was from Benjamin Pereira, Esq., and it told her that the meeting with the Bennetts had been arranged.

When she told her mother, Kitty said, "I'm going with you."

Caro said, "I thought you didn't want to see Thomas. I thought you were ashamed."

"This is not for me," her mother said quietly. "It's for you."

ℬℭ

BENJAMIN PEREIRA HADN'T summoned them to his office. Instead, he had come to Thomas's house on Queen Street. As her mother stood beside her, Caro rang the bell at the gate with an odd sense of detachment.

Thomas himself answered the door. "Kitty," he murmured.

For a moment her mother was a lady again. "Isn't it usual, Thomas? For a girl's mother to smooth the way when she's old enough to be married?"

Thomas shook his head. "So many years," he said. "I still remember you as a little girl."

"I remember it, too. How you held my hand to take me to church." She extended her fingers to her half brother, the veins prominent with age, and Caro saw their past shimmer in the air between them, blurring all the pain of the present.

"Come in, both of you," he said. "We're in the dining room."

To Caro, it seemed like years since she had been banned from this house instead of a few weeks. She was surprised to see that it looked the same. The mahogany table, set so brilliantly with china and crystal on Sunday, was bare save for a pair of silver candlesticks. Thomas headed the table, as he headed the household; to his right sat Maria, and next to her, Danny. Pereira was to Thomas's left. Kitty and Caro sat next to Pereira. Caro had never been so close to the head of this table before. Maria nodded at her half sister without greeting her.

Maria was the one to break the silence. She said, "Don't lawyer us, Mr. Pereira. We all know why we're here. You want to talk Thomas into buying Caro so Danny can marry her."

Caro wondered if Mr. Pereira had already spoken to her and to Thomas. Had they made up their minds?

"I'm not here to lawyer, as you say it, Mrs. Bennett."

Maria fixed him with a gaze that would quail a lesser man. "Mrs. Pereira," she said, insisting on their connection. "We call ourselves Pereira since Jacob died."

"Mrs. Pereira," he said, acknowledging the connection. "This isn't strictly a legal matter but a family one."

Caro thought of the words in her father's will: *Treat them with kindness…as members of the family.*

Pereira said, "James Jarvie was my friend, and I knew his intentions for his daughter. He yearned to free her, and knowing that he could not, he wanted her to live as free a life as possible. He entrusted her to his brother in that hope. It was a hope proven false, as all of you know."

Maria said impatiently, "We all know her father spoiled her for slavery by educating her. What difference does it make now? She's still a slave."

"Mrs. Pereira, her father raised her gently and educated her because he cherished her. He gave her the life of a lady because he wanted the best for her. Would you punish her for that? For her father's love for her?"

His eyes rested on Maria, who didn't blink or look away but also didn't reply. "Mrs. Pereira, I think you can understand why a father, or a mother, would love a child in that way and would hope against hope for the best possible life for that child," he said quietly.

Maria said, "What of Danny? His education and his future? Marrying her won't help him."

"What of his happiness?" Pereira asked, his voice even quieter.

The question fell into the silence like a stone slipping into a pond. Pereira let it ripple outward, and he disturbed it. "I know something about sons and about filial duty," he said. "My own son, with every advantage, has disappointed me."

Caro knew, as everyone in the room knew, that Pereira's son William was a drinker and a gambler who had fathered more than one slave child. Caro thought, *He must love Danny very much to lay himself bare like this.*

"But your son, Mrs. Pereira, is a steadfast young man. He loves this young woman, and his only thought is to protect and maintain her, in the most honorable way, through marriage." Pereira said, "Don't hurt him. Don't estrange him. Don't lose him. Think of his happiness, Mrs. Pereira."

Caro thought, *He speaks to her as his brother's widow. As his sister-in-law.*

Maria said, "I won't let him give up his education."

Thomas spoke for the first time. "Maria, they're very young to be married, but not to be engaged. If this love is steadfast, it will endure through an engagement and his education. If they are dedicated enough, they will be able to wait."

Maria addressed Caro. "Can I trust you? To be steadfast?"

Thomas said, "Maria, when her father died, she was dealt a terrible blow. What has she done? She's become resourceful. She makes a living. She helps her mother, and she saves her money. I know that she is."

Kitty clasped Caro's hand under the table. She said, "She is more than that. She is my light and my support and my life."

Tears rose to Caro's eyes.

Maria addressed Caro. "Will you promise it? To be steadfast toward my son?"

Caro felt her mother's hand tighten around her own. She met Maria's gaze. "I will love him forever," she said.

Family feeling roiled through the room: between brother and sister, between uncle and nephew, between aunt and niece. Under the sharp words, beneath the silences, were the bonds of love, as delicate as a spider's web and as painful as shackles.

Pereira, his voice soft and silken, said, "Mrs. Pereira? Will you help them?"

Maria cleared her throat as though she were choking. She said, "Thomas, go to Mr. Jarvie. See what kind of arrangement he's willing to make." She shot a look at Mr. Pereira. "Go with him, for the love of God. He'll listen to you."

ഇരു

When they returned to Tradd Street, Caro told her mother that she intended to accompany her uncle and Mr. Pereira when they made their case before Lawrence Jarvie. Kitty put a hand on her arm. "I'll go with you."

Caro felt a wave of sickness. She had feared for months that Lawrence Jarvie might sell her. Now she was going to see him to beg him to do so. "Mama, no. Mr. Jarvie tolerates me. But he detests you."

"I don't do this for him. I do it for you."

"Then let me go alone. It will be better for both of us."

Kitty's smile was rueful. "Ah, Caro, it isn't right that you take care of me now," she said.

Caro rested her hand on her mother's. "We take care of each other," she said, even though it was a lie.

℘

WHEN CARO STOPPED AT THOMAS'S shop, he didn't order Danny into the back. He let them greet each other. As she handed over the finished shirts, she said to Thomas, "When you and Mr. Pereira call on Mr. Jarvie, I want to go with you."

Thomas said, "Caro, no."

"He won't spare me, whether I'm in the room or not."

"Caro, it isn't right."

Miss Sass blazed forth. "What? For me to intrude on a matter of business or for the merchandise to listen to the transaction?"

Thomas said, "Caro, you know it won't be pleasant."

When the two of them appeared at Benjamin Pereira's office, he objected, too. She said, "Would my father have wanted me to know?"

"I doubt it," Pereira said.

One uncle said wryly to the other, "Don't argue with her."

℘

AT THE JARVIE HOUSE, AMBROSE let them in, looking askance at both Thomas and Caro, even though Benjamin Pereira insisted that they had accompanied him on a matter of business with Mr. Jarvie. It was painful to come through the front door today and equally painful to be ushered into the room where she had been terrified with the certainty that Lawrence Jarvie planned to sell her.

Lawrence looked up from the ledger on the desk, frowning. He asked Pereira, "What is this?"

"As I wrote to you, sir. Thomas Bennett, who is Caroline's uncle, has come here on a matter of business. Caroline is here as well, since the matter concerns her."

He glanced at Thomas. "What business matter? The man is my tailor. I settle my account every month."

Danny had told Caro that he did not.

"May we sit?" Pereira asked.

"Suit yourself." As the men sat, Lawrence said, "Not the girl. She stands by the door."

Like a servant.

Lawrence said, "What's the business, Pereira? Is there any difficulty with the will? I thought the will was settled."

"The will is settled," Pereira said. "There's no worry about that. Mr. Jarvie, if you patronize Thomas Bennett, you know that he's a free man of color, well-to-do and well respected among persons of color in Charleston. He is also kin to both Catherine and Caroline. He is Catherine's half brother, and Caroline's uncle."

"I see," Lawrence said impatiently.

"Since your brother's death, Thomas Bennett has taken an interest in Caroline. He has taken on the attitude of a father toward her. He is concerned with her welfare and her prospects in life."

Lawrence said, "Pereira, get to the point and tell me why I should care that my slaves have kin or not."

"Thomas Bennett would like to do everything he can to protect and maintain Caroline. He would like to act as her guardian." Before Lawrence could say, "Stop lawyering," Pereira said, "He would like to buy Caroline from you."

"Buy her? Can he?"

"He's a free man. There's no barrier to it."

Lawrence said, "I hadn't thought to sell. It seems contrary to the intention of the will."

"The will asked you to treat her with kindness," Pereira said. "It might be a kindness to allow her to live within the bosom of her nearest kin."

Lawrence said, "What a slippery pettifogger you are."

"Thomas Bennett would like to help the girl," Pereira said, his tone unperturbed. "As would I."

"That isn't my concern," said Lawrence.

Caro felt fear prickle on her neck.

"Would you consider it, sir?" Pereira asked.

Lawrence let his eyes rest on Caro. It reminded her of the stare of a Guardsman, a man charged with sending disobedient slaves to the Work House. He said, "I don't need to consider. I can give you the terms now."

"Please do."

"I won't sell her alone. I'll sell her and her mother together."

Thomas nodded at Pereira, who said, "Thomas Bennett is amenable to that."

"I want five thousand dollars for the pair of them."

Thomas drew in his breath.

Pereira said, "That's quite a sum, Mr. Jarvie. Considerably more than they would command in the market."

"They aren't for sale on the market. They're for sale in this room. Five thousand dollars for the two of them."

Thomas spoke. The words were for Lawrence, but he turned to Pereira. "I don't have that much money to hand. Could we write a note?"

"I want the cash. I won't take a note," Lawrence said.

Pereira said, "Mr. Jarvie, it's customary to allow a note."

"It's at my discretion. Five thousand dollars, in cash."

She had been stupid to be so blithe. It hurt to be the merchandise, and it hurt even more to listen to the transaction.

Thomas had turned ashen. "I can't manage that," he said.

"Then I won't sell her." He returned to the ledger. "Good day, Mr. Pereira."

ℴℹ

WHEN THEY RETURNED TO THE shop, Danny, who stood behind the counter, looked up, his face full of hope. At the sight of the two of them, gray and silent, he said, "He said no."

"He said yes, for five thousand dollars," Caro said.

Danny, who knew how well his uncle's business did, who knew what his mother's house was worth, who knew what she had paid for her slaves, said, "That's madness!"

Thomas straightened a bolt of cloth on the counter that needed no straightening. Danny reached for Caro's hand. "Uncle, excuse us," he said, as he led her out the back and into the alley.

Without a word, he held out his arms, and she pressed herself against him as he sheltered her. Her voice hoarse, she said, "He doesn't want me. But he wants to keep me. He'll never sell me."

"There must be a way," he whispered.

She shook her head, grieving as she had grieved for the loss of her father.

Chapter 11: The Abolitionist

In Sumter County, as the air cooled and the frost approached, Camilla Aiken called on Emily. In the privacy of the back parlor, while Susan rested upstairs, Camilla flung herself onto the settee, crumpling her skirt and Emily's. She said, "Mr. Ellison likes you a lot. Do you like him?"

Emily had kept to her subterfuge all season. She conversed with John Ellison at dinners and suppers, danced with him at parties and balls, and allowed him to call on her every Tuesday before noon. She had never encouraged him to believe that her interest was more than polite. She knew what the gossips would say. Camilla had just said it.

She said, "He's been kind to me."

Camilla pressed so close that both of their crinolines crackled. "Do you think he'll ask for you?"

Emily laughed. "Perhaps," she said. "After he's weighed every bale of cotton and counted every bushel of corn. And bought another dozen hands and another pair of hunters for his stable. After all that, he might think of it."

"A country wedding," Camilla said. "A white satin dress, and everyone in the county in church, and the best slave fiddlers in South Carolina! Such fun, Emily!"

"Let Jane have her glory first," Emily said. "And then you. I'm in no hurry."

"How nonchalant you are. Do you have another beau hidden somewhere? Will you surprise us?"

Camilla rattled her. Joshua now addressed his letters to "Dearest Emily" and closed them "With affection." Sandwiched between was the business they shared: praise for the last piece and payment as well, quotations from the readers who liked "A Southern Voice" and wondered about the truth behind the nom de plume, and inquiries after her reading and comments on his own. He had gotten bolder and bolder in his recommendations. She hadn't dared to ask a Charleston bookseller for Walt Whitman's chapbook, *Leaves of Grass*, said to be scandalous.

"Marriage is like a conspiracy for you," Emily said, smiling. "You look for it everywhere."

On the day before she and Susan planned to return to Charleston, John Ellison called on her. He chatted politely with Susan for a while—about corn and cotton, which came easily to him—and asked her, "Ma'am, will you excuse us? May I speak to Miss Emily in private?"

"Of course," Susan said, smiling, her skirts rustling as she left them with each other.

John Ellison pulled up his chair. He said, "Miss Emily, I ain't grand, and I probably won't say this as smooth as you'd like to hear. But I care about you a lot, and I believe you like me, too. I've been a widower for nearly two years, and I'm ready to marry again. Will you do me the honor? Say yes and be my wife?"

The subterfuge had worked better than she thought.

She blushed—it wasn't coquetry; she was genuinely surprised—and she said, "It's an honor to be asked, Mr. Ellison. But I'm not quite ready yet." She gestured to her dress. "Despite this."

He took her hand in his roughened fingers. "You take your time," he said. "I can wait."

She let her hand rest in his. "Thank you, Mr. Ellison. Will you do me a favor?"

"Of course, Miss Emily."

"Don't let my mother or father know you asked. Not yet, until I'm sure."

He patted her hand. "I never did want to press you."

She would be sorry to disappoint him. He might actually regret a refusal, once he had accounted for every bale and bushel, every hog and horse and hand. "Thank you, Mr. Ellison."

෫෬

IT WAS OCTOBER, PAST THE FROST, when Emily and her family finally abandoned the pines to return to the city. Emily sat at the breakfast table with her father and stepmother. Her father barricaded himself behind the newspaper, rustling the pages, until her stepmother asked, "Lawrence, whatever is in that paper to aggravate you so?"

Her father said, "It's nothing for a lady to know about."

"Then it's politics," her stepmother said, her tone aggrieved.

Emily knew, as her father did not, that her stepmother had already begun to calculate the effort of a wedding and a trousseau and weigh it against the effort of the Charleston season, when her father would go to the expense of entertaining the men who would support his candidacy for the Assembly.

Her father shut the paper and tossed it onto the table. He looked tired and pinched, as though his head ached all the time. Untangling Uncle James's estate had burdened and aged him. His temper was short. Usually courteous to a servant, he had raised his voice to Ambrose, the most amiable of servants.

Susan asked, "Lawrence, do you have the headache again?"

"It's nothing," he said, but he pressed his fingers to his temple.

"I'll make you up a dose of laudanum."

"Laudanum? Do you think I'm a lady invalid? I have business to transact today." He took up the paper again, shielding himself with it.

Emily was fiercely curious to know what had aggravated her father. After breakfast, when the table had been cleared, she went in search of the newspaper. Likely her father had left for his office on Broad Street, and the study was empty. She put her head into the room to look.

As she stepped into the room, Ambrose startled her. "Miss Emily, what do you look for?"

"The newspaper, Ambrose. This morning's *Mercury*."

"I set it on your daddy's desk," he said, gliding into the room, finding it for her. "Right here, Miss Emily."

"Thank you, Ambrose."

And he knew to leave her to read the paper that young ladies shouldn't see.

She scanned the pages, looking for something that would upset a South Carolina planter. She found it on the second page. A "disturbance" at Harper's Ferry in Virginia. An "uprising" of "negroes and infuriated abolitionists" that required the "infantry and artillery" to quell. A "miserable" business, the work of "insurgents."

What her father would call "an insurrection."

"Emily!" Her father strode into the room. "What are you looking at?"

She dropped the paper as though it burned her fingers. "Nothing, Papa. I was just straightening your desk."

"Give that to me," he said, as if the act of reading it had been an insurrection, too.

"I thought there might be a poem. Sometimes there is."

"I saw no poem."

Her ability to lie suddenly failed her. She met her father's eyes. "I wanted to know what upset you so at breakfast," she said. "I saw it. I read about the"—she groped for the word—"events in Virginia."

He repeated the words of the breakfast table. "That's nothing to concern a lady."

"Papa, if there were"—she hesitated again—"an insurrection here, surely a lady would be affected as much as a gentleman. Why shouldn't she know beforehand, if the worst came to pass?"

"You've never seen an insurrection," he said. "You don't know what it's like." He shook his head. "I was only a boy during the Vesey rebellion, but I saw how it marked my father, and he passed all his feeling about it to me."

"The cheval de frise," she murmured.

"We thought—we believed—that the Negroes would rise up to murder us," he said, his face grave with the inherited memory. "We have long memories in Charleston. Your mother's family fled San Domingo during their insurrection." He looked past her at something that was not in the room. "The scenes of horror…the murders… the bloodshed…" He returned to the present and met her eyes. "We have never forgotten it, and it haunts us to this day. All of us who live in Charleston."

"But it's past now," she said.

"Ah, Emily," he said, his voice softening. In a rare gesture of affection, he stroked her cheek. "I'd much rather worry about your trousseau," he said. "I hear from your stepmother that Mr. Ellison of Sumter County has taken a liking to you over the summer. Do you like him, too?"

"I don't know," she stammered.

"He's an upcountry man. Not a man of Charleston. But very sound."

"He is, Papa."

"Leave politics to those who need to know," he said. "Let's get you happily settled, as a girl should be."

"Yes, Papa," she said.

He patted her cheek, as though she were still a little girl.

As she left the study, she thought of her real defiance. Now that she had returned to Charleston, so had Joshua's letters, which again went into Caro's hands for safekeeping. Emily left the house, her sketchbook in her pocket, to ask Caro if she had a letter for her. She felt more than a twinge of guilt about Caro, whom she hadn't seen in the weeks since she had been home.

Had there been so many Guardsmen on the street last spring? They seemed to be everywhere in their greatcoats and their military hats, billy clubs tucked under their arms. Black people, usually so easy and voluble on the street, fell silent and dropped their eyes as a Guardsman walked by. They seemed to shrink into themselves.

At the corner of Broad Street was a familiar sight, the market woman who sold flowers from a basket balanced on her head. Emily knew her market song as she knew Sophy's. As a Guardsman approached her, she fell silent. He was a short man, made taller by the cap he wore. He grasped his club firmly as he called to her, "You! Let me see your badge!"

The badge glinted on the woman's chest, pinned there like an amulet. Last spring, Emily recalled, few slaves wore their badges so prominently. The woman lifted the badge for the Guardsman to examine, and he bent close to peer at it. *Awfully close*, Emily thought. But the woman stood quietly without drawing back or flinching.

"It looks all right," the Guardsman said gruffly. Still standing too close, he said, "You watch yourself."

"Yes, suh," she said, touching the badge with her fingers as though it would protect her from another Guardsman's scrutiny.

Emily pulled out her sketchbook and began to sketch the Guard. He noticed and strode over to her. "What are you doing?"

She said politely, "Taking your portrait, sir."

"Why? You ain't one of those abolitionists, are you? Sketching for a paper up North?"

The half-truth startled her so much that she tore the page from the book and handed it to him. "No, just taking a likeness. It's yours, sir. Perhaps your wife would like it."

He refused the proffered page. "I ain't married," he said. He tapped the club in his palm.

Emily began to tremble with anger as well as fear. "Sir, you forget yourself," she said, as she walked away.

℘℘

She was still unsettled when she arrived at Tradd Street. She found Caro in the kitchen, her sewing in her lap. She rose when Emily entered.

"Caro, don't," Emily said. "Not for me."

Caro sat. Her face had a grayish cast, and her eyes were red-rimmed. At the familiar signs of grief, Emily felt a flash of alarm. "Oh, Caro, what is it? Is your mother ill?"

"No, Miss Emily," Caro said, her voice hoarse and low.

She laid her hand on Caro's arm. "What's happened?"

"It's nothing."

"Don't fib to me. I can see how downcast you are." She addressed Sophy. "Do you know?"

Sophy said nothing.

"Caro, shall we talk in the yard?"

"If you wish."

"Yes, I do." She was ashamed of the note of command in her voice. Surely Christian charity was needed here if friendship failed them.

They went into the yard to stand under the live oak. It was too cold to linger outdoors, but Emily tried again, softening her voice. "Please, Caro."

Caro lifted shadowed eyes to Emily's. She said, "Danny Pereira asked me to marry him."

How stupid of me, Emily thought. *She's heartbroken.* "Did you refuse him?"

Caro laughed, a mirthless sound. "His family refused me," she said.

"But why? How could you possibly not suit him?"

"I don't suit a free man of color," she said.

"I don't understand."

"A slave can't suit a free man of color," Caro said bitterly.

Emily reached for Caro's hand, but Caro pulled away. "But you can marry, can't you? I thought Negroes could marry. The hands on my father's place are always getting married."

"Oh, I can marry," Caro said, still bitter. "If I don't mind seeing my children born into slavery or being sold away from my husband. That's no matter, is it?"

Emily stared at the cousin who had suddenly become a slave again. Upset, she stammered, "I never thought. I never knew."

"There are many things you don't know, Miss Emily," Caro said, her tone angry, intending to hurt.

"What can I do?"

"Nothing," Caro said, and she turned away.

Emily felt wounded. She would not show it. She said, "I came to ask if there's a letter."

Caro took the letter from her pocket. "This is yours, Miss Emily," she said, in a mockery of servility.

She should put it in her pocket to read later. But she was so eager for Joshua that she tore it open. The bank draft tumbled into her hand, and so did the clipping from the newspaper, Cincinnati's *Penny Press*. She scanned it. It was a very different version of the "events in Virginia" than she had read in the Charleston paper. She held out the newsprint with a trembling hand. "You should read this," she said.

Caro glanced at the page. "I've heard about it," she said, her voice matter-of-fact.

"Is it a rebellion?" Emily asked. "An insurrection?"

"Do you think I'd be crazy enough to tell you?" Caro flared.

Suddenly, Caro, the bookish planter's daughter who had become her friend, did not trust her cousin. Emily asked, "Caro, what's happened to make you so angry with me?"

Caro turned her face away. It didn't hide the tears that slipped down her cheeks. "Leave me alone," she said.

ぷひ

EMILY WALKED SWIFTLY THROUGH the yard and ran into the kitchen, letting the door slam behind her. Sophy, who stirred a pot of rice, looked up at the sound. She sighed. "Did she sass you, Miss Emily?"

Emily felt the tears rise. "What happened to her, Sophy? Why wouldn't the Pereiras allow it?"

"She didn't say?"

"No."

"Don't tell her I told you."

"I promise I won't." How strange that she would swear like that to a slave.

"Her uncle go to your daddy to ask to buy her."

"If her uncle owned her, she'd still be a slave. I don't understand, Sophy."

"Her uncle her flesh and blood. Do you think he sell her away? Or take her children from her?"

"He would own her to protect her?"

"Yes, Miss Emily," Sophy said, as though she were a stupid child who had finally said something intelligent.

"Own your kin! Your flesh and blood!"

Sophy was silent, and Emily heard what she had said.

Joshua's letter seemed to smolder in her pocket. She asked Sophy, "What did my father say?"

"He refuse it."

"Why?"

Sophy shook her head and said, "Better for you if you don't let your daddy know that you know." She turned back to the pot of rice.

Outside the gate, Emily pulled her bonnet tightly around her face to hide the storm of guilt and fury that no lady should feel.

∞∝

EMILY WAITED UNTIL SHE COULD keep her temper. She would gain nothing by raising her voice to her father. Christian charity, she reminded herself, even though her heart burned with a sinner's rage. She found her father in his study, writing a letter. "Papa, may I speak to you?"

He laid down his pen and smiled a little. "Is it about your trousseau? You know that's a trouble I would welcome."

"No, Papa, it's not that," she said, sitting in the chair before the desk and carefully arranging her hoops to fit its confines. "It's about the girl Caroline."

"Yes? Why does she concern you?"

"I heard that her uncle came to you to ask to buy her. To act as her guardian and to protect her. And that you refused him."

"Who told you?"

"Papa, does it matter?"

"Are the servants gossiping?"

"No, Papa."

"Well, you heard wrong," her father said, his affection about her marriage prospects gone from his voice. "I didn't refuse him. I quoted him a price. He refused to pay it."

"Why, Papa? Why would you say no? Caroline wanted to marry. The sale would have allowed it. Why would you stand in her way?"

"My brother left her to me," he said. "He never intended for me to sell her."

"I heard the will, too," Emily said. "Perhaps I heard it differently."

"Emily, it's not wrong to treat servants with kindness. But they need a firm hand. Especially now."

"The events in Virginia," she said bitterly.

"They think of insurrection."

"Does Caro think of insurrection? I think not."

"It's not your business to say," he said.

"Why not sell her to her uncle and let her marry? Live quietly out of your sight?" She pressed him, even though she should not. "Let her marry and be happy. What any father might wish for his daughter."

"Your uncle made his intention very clear," her father said. "To keep them in this family. Not to sell them. It's not for you to question the will or how I discharge my duties."

She sat very still, struggling with the words, knowing they were insurrectionary, no matter how quiet her tone. "Is that how you understand family feeling?" she asked.

"That's not for you to question," he said.

She cried, "We can own them and sell them, fear them and loathe them. And call it right and good!"

"A firm hand," he said. "A father's duty, too." He picked up his pen, a sign that he was finished with her.

℥ↄଊ

EMILY GRABBED HER SKETCHBOOK and left the house without a word to Ambrose. She was suddenly sick of Charleston, where the fragrance of azalea covered the stink of manure and mud, where fever lurked in the flames of the crape myrtle blooms, where grand houses were locked and fenced and guarded with iron spikes, and where men like her father honored the ghost of fiery secessionist John Calhoun and reviled the ghost of the murderous insurrectionist, Denmark Vesey.

She walked without knowing where she wanted to go, but she found herself outside the Slave Mart, just built earlier this year. She had driven and walked past it, the gray stone building in Gothic style, but she had never been inside. Her father, who was still careful with his money despite his inheritance, bought his slaves in the Low Country from other planters rather than in Charleston.

Women bought slaves all the time, but they didn't

attend the auctions. For that, they relied on their agents or male relatives. The man at the gate regarded Emily with surprise. "Miss, do you have business here?"

Act the lady. She smiled politely. "I live in Sumter County, and I was curious to see it," she fibbed.

The interior of the Slave Mart was as plain as a warehouse, a large, bare room filled with folding wooden chairs. An iron stove sent out a feeble heat. At the front of the room stood the auctioneer's dais and beside it, a block for the merchandise. The buyers milled together, and among them, she was the only lady. Some of the men smoked and others made notes, reminding themselves of the lots they wanted to bid on and for how much. Uneasy to be surrounded by so many men, Emily found a chair and sat.

To the right of the auction block, on a wooden bench, sat a girl who waited for sale, her hands clasped tightly in her lap. Under her dazzling apron, the sleeves of her dress were intricately ruched. Was she always so well-dressed? With a jolt, Emily recalled attending a horse auction in Colleton County with her father. She had pointed out a pretty little pony. Her father had said, "Can't you see? He's been brushed to look his best. To know his real condition, you'd have to look at his hooves and his teeth."

Gold hoops glinted in the young woman's ears. She was darker-skinned than Caro, without Caro's melting beauty, but there was something of Caro in the way she

held her head and looked so clearly about her. She didn't
smile. Emily examined her with a feeling of foreboding.
Those earrings marked her.

Next to her sat an older woman with a bright-red
scarf wrapped around her head. Beneath it, her face was
dark, shadowed, haggard. Despite her crisp dress and
neat apron, she looked weary and ill. She glanced at the
young woman, her face full of worry. She reminded Emily of Catherine. Was she the girl's mother?

Emily drew her sketchbook from her pocket and
began to draw. A man asked, "What are you sketching?"
as he leaned over her shoulder.

"I'm just taking a likeness."

Another man joined him, watching her as though
seeing a lady make a sketch was a spectacle.

"Miss Emily!" It was young Mr. Herriot, who had
seen her standing in King Street to sketch the Herriot
house. "You'd best put that away."

"Why?" she asked pleasantly. "Who would mind that
a lady is sketching?"

A short, slender man, in his shirtsleeves despite the
chill in the air, pushed through the crowd. He said roughly, "What do you think you're doing?"

"Who are you, sir?"

"This is my auction house. We don't want anyone
drawing in here. We've thrown out artists before."

Emily closed her sketchbook. "I'm not an artist," she
said, in the same pleasant tone. "We all learned to sketch

at Madame Devereaux's school. For our own pleasure."
She glanced at Mr. Herriot.

"Put that away," the auctioneer demanded.

"And if I did not?"

The auctioneer grabbed her roughly by the arm. "Out
you go," he said.

At this violence, Mr. Herriot said, "Don't bother her,
sir."

"She's a troublemaker."

"She's just a foolish girl. Leave her alone."

"She has to go," the auctioneer said roughly. He pulled
her to her feet, and the sketchbook fell to the floor.

"I'll escort her out," Mr. Herriot said.

"My sketchbook," Emily said faintly. "May I have it?"

The auctioneer glared at her, but Mr. Herriot bent to
retrieve it. He took her arm—his touch was gentle, but
the flesh smarted—and led her outside, where he scolded
her as he handed her the sketchbook. "What possessed
you to do such a thing, Miss Jarvie?"

She was silent. She had done wrong, and she knew it.

"And to sketch it! I'm sure you don't know but there
have been incidents elsewhere—illustrations sent to the
northern papers."

She raised her eyes to Mr. Herriot's, but she thought
of Joshua.

"Go home, Miss Jarvie, and leave these matters to
wiser heads," said Mr. Herriot, who wore a fop's tall hat.

On the sidewalk, she lifted her eyes to the inscription

over the gate: *The Mart*. As though the commerce within was as ordinary and as harmless as selling a bucket of oysters. She thought of the young woman on the auction block, her price run up by the fancy of a man like Mr. Herriot, and she hugged her sketchbook against the pain in her chest.

✄✁✄

JOHN BROWN WAS SENTENCED ON the second of November and hanged a month later. Emily defied her father and read every account of the trial and execution that she could find. The *Mercury* called John Brown a "diabolical incendiary" whose intent had been to "incite the slaves to rise and cut the throats of their white masters."

She wished that Joshua would send her the accounts from the northern papers. She had written to him but had heard nothing, and his silence worried her.

On a cold day in mid-December, Ambrose announced a visitor. Even though it couldn't be Joshua, Emily's heart pounded in anticipation. It was Camilla, chaperoned by an elderly aunt. Susan offered to entertain the aunt. She said, "You girls sit in the back parlor. I'm sure you have plenty to gossip about."

Camilla plopped herself down on the settee in the back parlor, saying, "We came before the season this year, to see the modistes. Jane's trousseau!" She snorted. "At least I'll get a new dress or two out of it."

Of course she would. Emily let her chatter about

dresses, the season, and people they knew in Sumter County. Sumter County seemed very far away, as did John Ellison. Emily's head ached with the burden of polite interest.

"Cousin Joshua came to Sumter County for the holiday," Camilla said.

Her headache vanished. Her heart leaped at the news. "Did you see him?"

Camilla leaned close, even though her voice didn't drop below a stage whisper. "No, but there was such a scandal!"

"Why? What happened?"

"Joshua Aiken's family has disowned him!"

Emily felt a shock throughout her body, as if she'd been hit by lightning. "Why? What has he done?"

"Oh, he came to visit and told his father that he hated slavery so much that he was ashamed to be a South Carolina man. And his father told him that if he felt that way, he was no longer worthy to be one. They had a fight! They nearly came to blows! Old Mr. Aiken told Joshua that he no longer considered his son an Aiken, and if he came back to Sumter County, Mr. Aiken would shoot him."

"My goodness," Emily said, shaking. "It's bad enough what the papers say. Now they've had an irrepressible conflict of their own."

"Emily, don't tell me you read the papers! All that horrid stuff! A lady isn't supposed to."

"Camilla, it must be exhausting to pretend you're a ninny when you aren't."

Camilla laughed. "A lady who's a ninny can do things that a clever girl can't," she said, her eyes gleaming.

❧❦

ON THE DAY AFTER CHRISTMAS, Ambrose found her in the back parlor to tell her that she had a visitor at the side door.

"Ambrose, who is it?"

Ambrose said softly, "Wanted to surprise you."

"Don't tease me."

Ambrose smiled as softly as he spoke. "Wouldn't dream of it, miss."

For a wild moment she wondered if Joshua had come to see her surreptitiously in Charleston and waited by the back door like a servant. But it was Caro, wrapped in a shawl, the blue paisley had been Emily's first gift of Christian charity.

She reached for Caro's hands, but Caro shook her head.

"I know you're still angry with me," Emily said.

Caro sighed. "Sophy has been schooling me. She reminds me all the time that it's dangerous to be angry."

"Yes, it is," Emily said. "Caro, it's Christmas. Might we have a moment of peace?"

Caro struggled with herself, friend and cousin warring with the slave. She met Emily's eyes. "Yes, we shall."

As she asked anyone, Emily inquired, "Did you have a happy Christmas?"

"We did our best. Sophy tried very hard to cheer us. A canvasback duck, and a whole bucket of oysters, and hoppin' john for luck next year."

"Better luck next year." Emily held out her hand again, and this time Caro took it. Her fingers were cold. Emily asked, "Are you warm enough at Tradd Street?"

"We're staying in the kitchen. We're all right."

"Caro, why did you come here? You know you shouldn't."

She reached into her pocket. "A note from Mr. Aiken. He wrote directly to me, too, and asked that I give this to you right away."

Emily took the envelope from Caro's cold fingers and pressed them in her own. "Thank you, Caro." She dropped her voice to a whisper. "I'll come to see you after the New Year. Better luck, I hope."

Caro let go of her hand and nodded. Then she slipped away. When had she learned to move with a slave's stealth?

⁊⃝ℭ

JOSHUA HAD NAMED A SPOT on the Battery, quiet in the cold air of December. The day was unusually bright for winter in Charleston, with a lemony sunlight that belied the cold of the air. He leaned against the fence that looked onto the water, so absorbed in the current that she had to tap him on the shoulder to greet him.

He turned, and the wary look on his face disturbed her. There were shadows under his bright brown eyes. He smiled with his lips, not the rest of his face, saying only, "Emily."

"Joshua." She reached for his hands, and they stood like that, hands clasped, eyes meeting. "I heard about your quarrel with your father."

"There's no mending it, Emily. I've been disowned, and I can never return to South Carolina."

"I know." She pressed his hands in her own. "Was it about Harpers Ferry? And its aftermath?"

"That started it. I told him—I told the whole family—that I hate slavery with every fiber of my being and was ashamed to be associated with a place that allows it and profits from it."

"You're an abolitionist," she said.

With great resolution, he said, "Yes, I am."

When she didn't reply, he said, "If you want to break with me, too…if you want to throw me over…"

She continued to clasp his hands. She wished that she dared embrace him. "Of course not," she whispered.

"It will make no end of trouble for you."

"Come with me," she said. "There's someone you should meet."

She led him to the house on Tradd Street, to the address he had written on so many envelopes but which he had never seen. She stood at the gate and rang the bell to take him past a puzzled Sophy, down the driveway, and into the yard.

Caro bent over the washtub, her arms in hot soapy water, her apron splashed with suds over her oldest dress. At the sight of Emily, she straightened and wiped her hands.

Emily said, "Caro, there's someone I want you to meet." She took a deep breath. "This is my friend, my dearest friend, my beloved friend, Mr. Joshua Aiken." She turned to Joshua. "Joshua, this is my cousin, Miss Caroline Jarvie."

Chapter 12: The Badge of Servitude

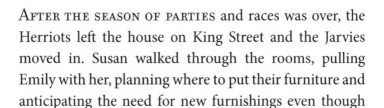

AFTER THE SEASON OF PARTIES and races was over, the Herriots left the house on King Street and the Jarvies moved in. Susan walked through the rooms, pulling Emily with her, planning where to put their furniture and anticipating the need for new furnishings even though the most recent ones hadn't been paid for yet.

In the back parlor, Susan put her hands on her hips and surveyed the room. "It's a much bigger house," she said. "I don't know how we'll manage."

Only a few days later, as they sat together at breakfast, her stepmother told her father that that they needed more servants.

He rattled the newspaper and said irritably, "We have three hundred Negro slaves on three plantations. Certainly some of them would suit you."

"I don't want a field hand. We're people of fashion now. I want servants to suit."

Emily had already heard her stepmother say the same thing about a new dining room table and a settee.

Her father said, "I know what you want. You want

a pretty, light-skinned parlor maid and a tall, handsome coachman."

Susan said happily, "You see!"

"What I see very plainly is how much they'll cost me. A thousand dollars each! On top of what we've already spent on the house. And the season."

Susan pouted. "What does it matter? Another expense?"

Lawrence rattled the newspaper again. "Another debt," he retorted. "I won't do it."

"How do you expect me to manage?"

He laid the newspaper down. "There is a servant who might do," he said. "That girl from James's place."

They know her name, Emily thought, *and they won't even speak it.*

Susan drew in her breath. "Lawrence, don't even suggest such a thing."

He picked up the paper again. "Then you'll have to do without," he said, his voice muffled by the barrier of newsprint.

☙❧

AT THE END OF APRIL, CARO told Sophy that she was going out. Sophy said, "It worry me that you don't have a badge."

"The Guard has never bothered me."

"Don't you know? The town full of them Democrats come here for their convention." Sunday, keen on politics, had mentioned it on his last visit. "Sunday tell me the Guard out in force, looking for black people to arrest. Show them visitors how South Carolina feel about slavery."

Caro shrugged. "Don't worry about me."

Sophy and Sunday had been right: there were more Guardsmen on the street today than usual. She was careful to keep her eyes down and do nothing that would bring notice, much less offense, and she arrived at the post office without difficulty. She collected Emily's letter from Joshua Aiken, and when she turned, she met Danny. "Walk with me," he said.

"Why? What can you say to me?"

"Please, Caro," he pleaded, and as she snapped out the door and onto the sidewalk, he followed her so abjectly that she let him. He asked stiffly, "How are you?"

"I do fine," she said, her voice sharp. *If he says one thing about loving me and taking care of me*, she thought, *I'll slap him, right here on the street.*

"We miss you at the service and at the dinners, too."

She had absorbed her mother's bitterness and had not attended the church or sat at the Bennett family table since her uncle's failure to buy her. She said, "That's too bad."

He reached for her arm, not very gently. "Caro, you talk like you hate me."

She shook her head. She hated her life, and she hated that she wanted to tell Danny so. He fell silent and walked alongside her without speaking.

When they reached the corner of Tradd Street, they both stopped. She knew he was struggling to find something to say to comfort her. She shook her head again, and he left her without a word.

She was so absorbed in her emotion that the Guardsman startled her. He demanded, "Where's your badge?"

She had enough wit to say in her best Low Country accent, "Oh, suh, my missus sent me out in such a hurry that I leave it behind. Don't have it with me."

"I don't believe you," he said, tapping his club in his hand. "You hire out, and you don't have one."

She had seen the arrests over and over, but she had let herself feel safe. She said, "Oh, no, suh. Hire out? My missus send me to do the wash for a friend of hers. Don't know about hiring out."

"I'm taking you to the Work House," he said. He grabbed her by the arm, clamping his hand so tightly that she felt the skin bruise.

She said, "Suh, please, don't take me to the Work House." She raised her voice, hoping that her distress would summon help. "Not the Work House."

The Guardsman said, "If you don't shut your mouth, I'll beat you senseless and drag you there." Without waiting for a reply, he tightened his grip and began to tow her to the Work House, an impromptu coffle held together by pain and threat.

Caro had rarely walked past the Work House, tucked away on Magazine Street. Flanked by stone turrets, every window barred, it presented a forbidding face to the street. She had never entered it and had never expected that she would be dragged inside to be treated like a criminal.

Inside, the Guardsman shoved her onto a hard wooden bench, where she was eyed by a man who stood behind a tall wood counter, as though this were a shop and not a jail. The bench was full. She jostled the others who already sat there, black and brown, some clearly free people of color, some listless, and others seething with quiet fury.

A little barefoot boy, his pants and shirt ragged, sidled up to her. "Does you have money?"

She was supposed to be a slave who never had a coin in her pocket. She dropped her voice very low. "What business is it of yours?"

His reply came easily. "For money, I take a message to someone."

He must make good pocket money with errands like these, Caro thought.

She reached into her pocket and put the coin in the little palm that was creased like an old man's. "Go to King Street and ask for Miss Emily Jarvie. Tell her that Caroline is at the Work House. Tell her to go to Mr. Benjamin Pereira."

The boy held out his hand again, and she slipped him another coin.

∞∞

WHEN EMILY HEARD THE MESSAGE, she threw on her bonnet. Her father had put himself forward as a delegate to the Democratic convention—he said that it would help him in his campaign this summer for the Assembly—and her stepmother was on one of her pleasurable and interminable visits to the merchants who sold furnishings for the home. She was free to fly to Mr. Pereira's office.

Panting for breath, she fell into the chair he kept for visitors and said, "Caro's at the Work House. She's been arrested for not having a badge."

Pereira flushed. "Why hasn't your father bought her one?"

"I don't know." She knotted her hands in her lap. "What can we do?"

"We'll get her a badge, one way or another," he said, his voice urgent. "I think we can persuade them to allow us that. Otherwise, the fine is twenty dollars."

"Twenty dollars! That's hardly a trifle." She thought of her father opening a bill from the city of Charleston for twenty dollars. "What does the badge cost?"

"For a house servant, two dollars a year. And a little extra for the Guard to look the other way."

Trembling, Emily said, "Let me stop at the bank."

"No, my dear. We won't waste our time going to the bank." He opened his desk drawer, pulled out his wallet, and put some bills into an envelope, which he handed to her. "We need to tell them a tale."

The Southern Voice knew how to spin a tale. She raised her head and said, "I believe I have one."

At the door of the Work House, Emily stared at the forbidding arch and the barred windows. "Oh, Caro," she whispered. Pereira held out his arm to escort her inside.

The Guardsman behind the desk spoke with scorn. "What is your business here?"

Emily stepped forward and rested her gloved hands on the wood of the counter, where so many others had rested their hands and elbows. She thought, *My father is a wealthy man, a planter.* The Southern Voice found the sugar to hide the poison of her anger. "Oh, sir," she said to the Guardsman. "There's a slave of ours here. But it's all a misunderstanding. The girl is my father's servant."

"Where is your father? Why isn't he here?"

"He's engaged in attending the political convention. I've come with Mr. Pereira, who is his lawyer. I believe we can straighten this matter out." She was shaking.

"Well, hurry it up," the Guardsman said.

Tell a tale, she thought. "Sir, the girl just came up to Charleston from Colleton County, and we haven't bought her a badge yet. I'm so sorry, sir. We'll make it right." She smiled, holding out the envelope clenched in her fist. She said, "For your trouble, sir."

He pocketed the money. He said, "We'll bring her out. What's her name?"

"Caroline. Caro."

"All right." He stared at her, then at Pereira. "And make sure she keeps it about her when she walks the streets."

"Sir? Will you give us the badge today?"

He stared at her again. "We have them made up," he said. "We'll send it out when it's ready."

When Caro emerged into the waiting room, Emily

fought off the desire to embrace her and reached for her hand instead. Caro shook her head.

Pereira cleared his throat, and all three of them left the waiting room to leave through the stone arch.

Emily said, "I'm so angry I can't contain myself."

"You?" Caro said. Her face was an ashen mask. "Why would any of this anger you?"

"Oh, Caro!"

Caro said, very low, "Think of me." She turned away, her walk swift and angry.

ഇൻരു

TWO WEEKS LATER, EMILY SAT with Susan in the back parlor. It was warm for May. Usually, by this time of year, they were well into their preparations for their visit to the pines. This year, her father insisted on staying in Charleston over the summer, telling them both that he would need to speak to voters at every frolic and every gathering until the election in November. Her stepmother grumbled. Her father said, "I thought you were deep in your business of refurbishing the house."

"Oh, I am," she said.

"Well, don't stint on it," he said.

"Oh, I won't."

Now Emily agreed as Susan asked her if the back parlor would look better with a new settee. She smoothed her skirt and ached for the privacy of her room, where she could write for *Hearth and Home* at her desk. Ambrose tapped on the door. He bore a silver tray. "The morning's mail, ma'am," he said, as he set the tray on the side table.

Susan nodded without looking up, and Ambrose backed from the room.

Susan opened the mail, piece by piece, using the letter opener with the efficiency that a soldier brought to a sword. She smiled as she opened a small, creamy envelope, the sign of an invitation. At the sight of the heavy envelope made of coarse paper, she looked puzzled. "The city of Charleston? What do they want? Whatever could this be, Emily?"

"Isn't it addressed to Papa?"

"Well, it is, but it can't be anything shameful, could it?" She slit open the envelope and the contents fell into her lap. She picked up the metal lozenge and let it rest in her palm. She laughed. "Oh, he meant it to be a surprise," she said happily. "Another servant! What a peculiar man he is. Trying to make me happy in secret." She rose. "I can't wait to thank him!"

Emily trailed after her into the study.

Her father sat at his desk, the ledger before him, his forehead furrowed.

"Is it the estate again?" Susan asked, her tone gentle.

He put down his pen and sighed. "What else?"

"More trouble?"

"Always. Why have you interrupted me, my dear?"

Susan held up the badge. "To thank you! Oh, Lawrence, another servant, just as I wished! When are you going to the Slave Mart? I'll go with you."

"Susan, whatever is this about?"

"Isn't that why you bought another badge? To please me?"

Now he frowned. "I renewed the old ones at the end of last year," he said. "I never bought another one."

Susan's face fell.

Her father said, "It must be a mistake. I can't imagine how it happened."

Trembling, Emily said, "I bought it."

"You!" her father exclaimed.

"When you were at the convention. The Guard picked up Caro and wanted to arrest her for not having a badge. Mr. Pereira and I straightened the matter out. I paid for a badge for her."

Her father's gaze was so intense that it unsettled her. A courtroom gaze. "Why would you do such a thing?"

"Papa, Mr. Pereira told me that the city would fine us twenty dollars for a slave without a badge. I hoped to spare you the expense."

"Why didn't he ask me about it?"

Emily flushed. "And leave Caro in the Work House? It hardly seems right, Papa."

Her father drew in a sharp breath. "Why was she running free in the streets of Charleston? No wonder she was arrested."

"Papa, she needs to walk from Tradd Street to King Street to deliver the laundry that you've commissioned her to wash. That's hardly 'running free.'"

Her father said, "I'm tired of it. She's our servant,

and she should be under our control." His gaze rested on Susan. "You'll have your wish, my dear. We'll bring her into the house, where we can govern her with a firm hand." He nodded at Emily.

"But I don't want her," Susan said. "I won't have her in the house!"

Her father looked pleased, as though he had resolved a thorny difficulty. "Haven't you always told me that you can command any servant, my dear? Here's your chance. She'll be yours to command."

EMILY WAITED UNTIL SHE WAS calm enough to reason with her father. She slipped into the study at the end of the day, when he allowed himself a little whiskey. She found him in his wing chair, the glass on the little table at his elbow, his eyes closed.

He looks so tired, she thought, feeling a flash of affection for him, despite all the distance between them. "Papa?" she asked. "May I sit with you for a little?"

"You have an argument to make, don't you, miss?"

"Not an argument, Papa. Just a notion, as the servants say."

"When they try to get round me. What is it, Emily?"

"It's about the girl. The servant, Caroline."

"Yes, Emily? What is your notion?"

"If you really want to bring her into the house as a servant"—she swallowed hard because she was about to defy her father, no matter how sweet her tone—"would you consider giving her to me as a maidservant? I like her, Papa. It would be easy for me to command her."

To protect her and treat her with Christian charity.

His ease was gone. He was burdened again, and stern along with it. "No, I can't," he said.

"Oh, Papa," she said, making herself sound girlish. "Why ever not?"

He sighed. "Emily, when you have a house of your own, you can order it however you like. But this isn't your house to order. It's your mother's and mine, and you'll need to let us decide how to treat our servants."

"Papa, please. Remember the will."

Her father sat up straight in his chair. He was a slight man, but his anger made him seem taller. "Emily, they are not members of the family. There's no reason for you to defend them."

She remembered Joshua's voice, low and choked and full of pain for the life he had cast off. Now she choked, too. "Christian charity," she whispered.

"It starts with charity," he said. "Where does it end up? With insolence. With disobedience. With rebellion."

She thought of the iron spikes on the fence out front, the cheval de frise that would tear the flesh of any would-be insurrectionist to shreds. She said softly, "She's a servant in our charge. Not a criminal or a conspirator."

"A firm hand," he reminded her. "Emily, I've made up my mind to bring her into the house, and your mother will decide how to make use of her. That's enough."

"It is not!" she said.

"Leave it alone," he said.

She rose. She cried, "I can't! My conscience torments me!"

He rose too. He seemed to tower over her. He said, "I won't have you going to Tradd Street to warn her. If she disobeys me, if she runs away, I'll punish her. I'll hire a slavecatcher to find her. I can sell her, the will be damned."

❧❧

AFTER BREAKFAST, WHEN SHE AND her stepmother had settled in the parlor, Susan said to Emily, "I'm going to the upholsterer's today. He says he has something pretty for the new dining room chairs."

Emily nodded.

"Come with me," Susan cajoled.

"I have some letters to write," Emily said. A half-truth. She owed *Hearth and Home* a thousand words.

"We have the carriage today!" Susan said, full of cheer.

"It's all right, Mother. I'm not as fond of upholstery as you are."

"Goodness, Emily, what will you do when you have to choose your own? Let the upholsterer choose for you? Come with me. You look peaked. The air will do you good."

Emily sat in the carriage in silence. Susan tried again to cheer her. Her tone was sweet. "What is it, chick?" she said, using the endearment of Emily's childhood.

Emily couldn't tell her. She thought of Caro all the time, and she felt too worried and too unhappy to try to lie.

The upholsterer's shop reminded her of Thomas Bennett's, even though his counter was marble instead of mahogany. The upholsterer himself was a light-complected man of color, well-dressed and well-spoken. He said to Susan, "I'm pleased to see you, ma'am. I have some lovely silks to show you."

"I can't wait to see them," Susan said, her face alight.

He disappeared into the back and reemerged with an armload of bolts of cloth. He laid them on the counter. "What catches your eye, ma'am?"

"Oh, that one," Susan said, pointing to a figured pattern in bright-red silk.

"It's very striking, ma'am." He unfurled it and let her stroke it.

"So nice," she said.

He unrolled another bolt, a subtler pattern in blue and cream stripe. "This is very handsome, too," he said. "Mrs. Manigault was here yesterday, and she admired it."

"Did she take it?"

"Yes, ma'am, she did, for all her new parlor chairs."

Susan rested her hand on the red silk. He said, "Ma'am, the red is very fine-looking. But I believe you might tire of it."

Susan looked from the bright pattern to the subtle one. She wavered. "Emily, what do you think?"

I have no opinion, Emily thought. But the upholsterer's eyes were upon her, and for his sake, she said, "The blue and cream is very elegant."

Even in her distress, Emily saw the faintest smile on

the light-complected face. He had not raised his voice or contradicted either of them. But he had guided her step-mother toward the tasteful thing without slighting her own taste. How well he got round his customers. Emily envied his tact.

Susan smiled. "You're right, Emily," she said. "We'll be as elegant as Mrs. Manigault." She turned to the uphol-sterer. "The blue and cream. For a dozen chairs. How soon can you have it ready?"

SO CR

AS SHE DID EVERY WEEK, CARO trudged into the kitchen of the house on King Street and set the clean wash on the wash table. Her arms ached. She had never learned Sophy's Low Country trick of carrying the load on her head. She asked Dulcie, who kneaded bread on the table reserved for cooking and eating, "Where's Bel?"

Dulcie didn't raise her head. She slapped the dough with her palms, making a sound like a blow on human flesh. "Must be in the house. She be back in a moment."

Caro leaned against the wash table's edge. She had no desire to wait. She wanted next week's dirty wash, and she wanted her money.

The door slammed, and Bel clattered into the kitchen. Dulcie said irritably, "How many times I tell you about slamming the door?"

Bel's apron was dazzling in its whiteness. She said to Caro, "Marse Lawrence want you. You come with me."

Caro tried to sound light, but she felt a sweat of fear trickle down her sides. "What is it?"

"Do I know?" Bel said, and she tugged on the side door so hard that it complained on its hinges.

At the library, she pulled Caro into the room and said, "Marse."

Lawrence sat at the desk. He wiped his pen and blotted the page. He looked up and said, "You can go, Bel," in a voice without praise in it.

She had not seen him since he had refused to sell her. Caro was alone with her father's brother. With her master. With the man commanded to treat her according to his conscience.

He said, "I've decided what I'll do with you."

This man still commanded her. Had he changed his mind? He could still sell her. Her fear swelled in her chest.

He said, "Mrs. Jarvie needs another servant. You'll stay in the house and work for us."

"Stay here?"

"Yes. Go to Cressy. You'll work under her."

"Sir—"

"You'll remember to call me 'master,'" he reminded her, in a cold tone that was worse than anger.

She swallowed. "Master," she said, making no effort to soften it with the Low Country slur. "My mother. She needs me. How will she manage?"

He said, "That's not my worry."

"She isn't well. Let me stay with her, to help her."

"Sickly, is she? I don't need a servant who's sickly."

"Please," she pleaded.

Lawrence said, "Bel will take you to the kitchen. Cressy will acquaint you with your new duties."

To be in this house, under Cressy's hand. To be truly a slave to Susan and Lawrence Jarvie. After all her efforts to live as though she were free, it had come to this. She went weak in the knees. "And if I won't?" she asked, knowing that sass in this house was insolence and rebellion.

He rose. "I'm a fair man, but I punish those who deserve it," he said. "And for those who remain insolent, there's the Work House."

She didn't bother to back out of the room. She bolted, out the side door, past Ambrose, down the driveway, to the gate, hoping that it had been left unlocked after she arrived.

It had not.

Ambrose came hurrying after her, too fast for dignity. He caught her arm, already bruised by Bel's grip, but his touch was gentle. "Don't run like this. It go worse for you."

"To bring me into the house! To make a slave of me!"

Ambrose shook his head, a father's rebuke. "You is a slave. Did you forget?"

"Ambrose. You were kind to me once. You were a friend to me once. Open the gate and let me go."

His face creased with sadness, he said, "Oh, Caro. Oh, sugar. I can't."

∞ભ

BEL RETRIEVED HER. SHE GRABBED Caro roughly by the arm and kept her grip as they made their awkward way through the yard and into the kitchen, where Cressy sat at the table. At the sight of Caro, she rose. "I knew you'd try to run away."

"My mother. I must tell my mother."

Cressy laughed, a mirthless sound. "Oh, she find out soon enough," she said. She said to Bel, "Take her upstairs and get her dressed. Leave her there until I come for her."

Bel dragged her up the narrow stairs to the second floor where the house servants slept. Through the narrow hallway, which smelled of the smoke and grease from the kitchen. Bel unlatched a door and pushed Caro inside. The room's only window was darkened with dirt. Within stood a pine chair and a rope bed with a ragged blanket. It was just like the room where she and her mother had spent their first dreadful weeks in Charleston.

On the blanket was a pile of cloth. Bel released Caro and said, "You take off that dress you wear and put that on."

"I will not," Caro said, her voice shaking.

Bel slapped her hard across the face. She said, "You do like I tell you, or I tell Cressy, and she tell Missus. And she punish you worse than that. She have a switch."

"And if I refuse?"

"Marse send you to the Work House," Bel gloated.

Caro hesitated.

Bel said, "You hurry or I tell Cressy."

Caro raised her eyes to Bel's. Bel's expression was

pure malice. Caro saw the joy in talebearing in it and the further joy in punishment. She said, "What have they promised you to spy on me and bully me?"

Bel slapped her again on the spot that was already raw. "Take off what you got on. Your boots, too. And give it all to me."

Caro thought, *She wants my good boots. And she'll rub her big feet raw in them.* She said, "God help your soul, Bel."

Bel laughed. "You, talking about God! You godless! Never prayed in your life!"

Caro undressed as though she didn't care that Bel watched. *Look all you like,* Caro thought. *You'll never be taller, or slenderer, or lighter of skin. Being cruel to me won't help you with that.*

The dress was gray cotton, new and whole and clean, and the apron was bright white and freshly starched. The shoes were rough but serviceable. They were too big, thankfully. Sophy had shown her how to wrap her feet in rags to make ill-fitting shoes fit better.

When she was dressed, Bel said, "Fold up your things nice before you give them to me."

Caro obeyed.

As Bel took the dress and the boots that had been Sophy's gift, Caro asked, "Don't I get a badge, as the other servants do?"

"No," Bel said, unable to disguise her pleasure in it.

"How will I be able to leave the house?"

"You won't," Bel said. With Caro's clothes in her arms,

she left the room, pulling the door tightly shut behind her.

Caro heard the key turning in the lock. She went to the door to discover that it locked from outside. She sat on the bed, her hands knotted in her lap, to wait for whatever Cressy had planned for her.

⊱⊰

SUSAN HAD FIBBED TO EMILY. After the upholsterer, they visited the carpet merchant and the home furnisher, where Susan looked at mirrors for the foyer until Emily said, "Mother, my back aches. I have to sit down."

"Are you all right?"

"Just tired."

"Only a little longer, Emily," Susan said, as she surveyed the mirrors again, badgering the clerk to measure each one until Emily thought she would burst into tears with boredom and fatigue.

When she was satisfied, Susan took Emily by the arm. "You do look tired, chick."

I'm not a little girl, Emily thought. She sank into the carriage with relief and said nothing on the way back to King Street.

When they returned, Susan leaned forward to call to Henry, "Bring us around the front." She said to Emily, "I want to look at the spot where the mirror should hang. I'm still not sure about the mirror."

Since it was unusual for them to use the front door, Susan had to rap as though they were visitors. They waited, and Susan said impatiently, "You see why we need a proper servant to open the door."

Emily nodded wearily.

The door was opened by a tall, slender figure in the neat gray and dazzling apron of a parlor maid. Under the white kerchief was an ivory-skinned face. A face much too sad to be an obedient slave's. A very familiar face.

Caroline's face.

Emily cried out, "Mother, what have you done?"

∽〇〇∼

EMILY KNEW TO WAIT UNTIL late afternoon, after dinner, when aristocratic Charleston slept and slave Charleston labored. She slipped into the kitchen, where Dulcie washed the dinner dishes. "Where is she?" Emily asked. "Where is Caro?"

Dulcie shook her head.

"Tell me, Dulcie," Emily pleaded.

"Don't make it worse, Miss Emily," Dulcie whispered.

Emily ran from the kitchen. She bolted down the driveway and out the gate. It was too hot to hurry, and by the time she arrived at Tradd Street, she was sweating and panting as no lady should.

Sophy ran to the gate. "I thought you was Caro. Where is she?"

"At King Street."

"He take her?"

The will be damned. "To keep her in the house."

Sophy sagged in relief. "She work in the house? That ain't the worst news I ever heard."

Emily said, "Where they can mistreat her, and punish her, and send her to the Work House."

Sophy said grimly, "Come with me."

Kitty sat at the kitchen table, her cheeks even more hollow than usual, her eyes even more shadowed. At the sight of Emily, she sprang up. "Where is she? How is she?"

"My father has taken her into the house as a servant. He won't let her leave."

"Why didn't he tell me?"

"As though he would," Emily cried out.

Kitty's eyes were fever-bright. "Why didn't you tell me?"

Emily wanted to burst into tears. "He threatened to sell her if I warned you," she said.

"I'll go to him! I'll speak to him. I'll get her back."

Sophy put her hand on Kitty's arm. "Kitty, wait," she said.

Kitty shrugged off Sophy's touch. She said to Emily, "Now. We'll go now."

Sophy entreated her. "We sit down, we talk, we think of something. How to get round him. Don't rush off in a frenzy. It don't go well for you."

Kitty said, "I don't care much for myself. But I'd do anything for Caro."

Emily held out her arm. "Lean on me."

Sophy watched. Emily flushed under Sophy's scrutiny. In a world arranged differently, Kitty would be her aunt.

They hastened down the driveway, Kitty and Emily together, and at the gate, Kitty halted, her hand over her chest, her breath coming in short rasps. "Give me a moment," she said, trying to regain her strength.

"You aren't well."

She breathed more deeply and stood up straight. "It doesn't matter," she said.

ഇരൽ

AT KING STREET, KITTY SAID to Ambrose, "Tell Mr. Lawrence Jarvie that I'm here to see him." When Ambrose hesitated, Kitty said, "Go on. Do it!" Ambrose shook his head, but he obeyed his former mistress. In a moment he returned and ushered both of them into the study.

Lawrence looked up from his desk. At the sight of Kitty his tone was irate. "What is this? Why are you here?"

Without raising her voice, Kitty said, "I've come for my daughter. Where is she?"

"Emily, take this woman away, or I'll have Ambrose throw her out."

"How could you do this? Take her without asking me?"

"You? What do I owe you?"

Kitty said, "James didn't want this for her. You know that."

"James left her in my care," Lawrence said acidly. "And you as well, if you recall."

Kitty stood very still. Her voice was calm and cold. "You defile his memory by doing this," she said.

Her father flushed, as he had when the will was read. "Get out," he said to Kitty.

"Not without my daughter."

"Get out, or I'll have the Guard throw you out."

From the corner of her eye, Emily saw the movement of a shadow. A gray shadow.

"Caro!" Kitty cried. "Caro, is that you?"

Lawrence rose. Full of fury, he said, "Get out now."

A muffled cry came from the hallway where the gray shadow waited.

Kitty flew at him. He lunged forward to seize her hands. She pulled them away and slapped his face as hard as she could.

He clutched her wrist and said icily, "Strike your master, will you? You'll go to the Work House for that."

Kitty sagged in his grasp. In disgust, he let her go as she bent double with a wracking cough.

"Ambrose!" Lawrence called into the hallway.

Emily darted between the two of them, trying to shield Kitty. She put her arm around the stricken woman's shoulders.

"You get out of this," her father said.

Emily said, "Papa, not the Work House. Can't you see that she's ill?"

Lawrence yanked Emily by the hand so hard that she felt it in her shoulder and said, "That's enough." He called, "Ambrose!"

Ambrose appeared in the doorway. "Yes, Massa?"

"Take this woman away, Ambrose. Send for the Guard. Have them take her to the Work House."

Ambrose's pleasant face went gray. "Massa, please," he said quietly.

"Do you defy me, too?"

"No, Massa," Ambrose said.

"Then do as I say."

Ambrose reached for Kitty, who was now sobbing as well as coughing. Between coughs, she pleaded, "Caro. Oh, Caro."

From the hallway, Caro watched, her eyes wide, her hand over her mouth, and Emily felt their shared anguish resonate between them.

Chapter 13: The Purloined Letter

As she sat at her desk, Emily held Joshua's latest letter in her hand, reading the Cincinnati address as though it were a talisman. She hefted the letter, knowing that he had enclosed a clipping as well as a bank draft. His own words would give her hope, but she wanted to prolong her anticipation.

Caro was in the house, and she had been enslaved in a way that brought tears to Emily's eyes. Slavery's worst was no longer far away, in the Work House and the Slave Mart. It was in this house, too. It was incised in the flesh of a work-worn, heartbroken girl and engraved in the soul of a planter's daughter who could do nothing for her.

Emily sliced open the letter and unfolded the pages. *Hearth and Home* patronized a bank that adorned its notes with its own imposing building on one side and Lady Liberty on the other. Emily was fiercely glad of the freedom in the inscription: *Six dollars payable to Emily Jarvie*. She had more than a hundred dollars in the Bank of Charleston now, all of it gained by her own hand.

Joshua hadn't sent her a clipping of her own piece from *Hearth and Home*; instead he had enclosed the front page of the *Liberator*, William Garrison's great jeremiad against slavery. Charleston had a particular hatred for the *Liberator*. She had heard her father reminisce about the day in 1835, a generation ago, when Charleston's postmaster censored the *Liberator* by removing it from the post and making a bonfire of the issues in the street.

A page from the *Liberator* was an incendiary thing. She flushed, proud of Joshua's zeal and angry that he would take such a risk.

Confined to the house and the yard, Caro could no longer fetch the letters. Emily had asked Sophy to retrieve them from the post office. The first time that Emily came to ask for a letter, Sophy didn't unlock the gate. The ironwork was open and lacy, and Emily realized—she had never seen it before—that it was adorned with the symbol of welcome, the pineapple. Emily asked, "Sophy, is there a letter?"

Sophy shook her head. She asked, "How is Caro?"

"We don't speak. My mother forbids it." Tears rose to her eyes. "But she looks dreadful."

"What about her mama? Any word?"

"Just that she went to the Work House." The tears trickled from her eyes, and she wiped them, in the most unladylike fashion, with her gloved fist.

Sophy said nothing. To Emily, her silence seemed to speak. *Ain't you ashamed? Don't it burn your soul? You have to answer for it.*

Now the gentle tap on the door, and the low voice, brought her back to her room and her desk. "Miss Emily?"

Emily swept the letter into her lap as Lydia stepped into the doorway. "Yes, Lydia?"

"Come to fetch your mending, miss."

She forced a benevolent tone. "Later, Lydia."

"Yes, miss."

"Close the door after you."

"Yes, miss." She closed it softly. Lydia did everything softly.

Emily's heart stopped pounding. She recovered the letter from her lap and smoothed the pages that held the words Joshua had written.

He wrote as he spoke. Even on the page, the words had a northern cadence, a swiftness that no southerner could muster. It had been dreadfully cold in Ohio, he said, with snow that lingered on the streets. He was glad of his heavy wool coat. He wrote about the business of *Hearth and Home*. Circulation had increased, and they had several new advertisers, which pleased his publisher. *We may catch up to* Godey's *yet*, he wrote, and Emily heard the joke in his rueful tone. A cat had strayed into his boardinghouse, to his landlady's dismay, and now every boarder, no matter how hard-bitten, fussed over Puss; there was no thought of the cat's removal to the alley. He told her what he had been reading: Walt Whitman's poems, *Leaves of Grass*. He wrote, *I doubt that a bookseller would order it for a southern girl. It's thought of as scandalous, even in freethinking Ohio.*

As she read, she thought of how she yearned for the life he wrote about—the snow, the cat by the boarding-house hearth, the business of literature, the booksellers who would sell any book to anyone. On the page, Ohio seemed more tangible than Charleston, and Charleston, for all the vigor of its beauty and its ugliness, seemed like the dream.

She shook her head. She was too much the writer. She was hearing voices and seeing ghosts.

She read:

My dearest Emily, I think every day of the promise we made to each other on the Battery, and I swear to be steadfast in it. I miss you greatly. Someday we will be free to speak the truth and stand beside each other. I yearn to take your hands, and I long to kiss your lips. I remain, as always, with greatest affection, your Joshua.

With a start, she thought, *He writes as though we're engaged.* The thought spread a sanguine warmth through her body. She caressed the page as though it were a man's bearded cheek. Smiling, she folded everything decorous-ly together and put it back into the envelope.

"Emily?" her stepmother called.

She stuffed the letter in her pocket, and not a moment too soon because Susan was prone to open the door with-out asking. When her stepmother hurried into the room, Emily was innocently seated at her desk, her pen poised over a sheet of letter paper.

Susan was smiling. "Emily, put that away. You have a visitor."

Emily looked up, letting herself smile brightly in return. "Don't tease me, Mother. Who is it?"

"It's Mr. Ellison, come from Sumter County."

Since her return to Charleston last fall, Emily had written several polite notes to Mr. Ellison. She had always reminded him that she hadn't forgotten his proposal but wasn't yet ready to reply.

She hoped, with all her soul, that he was still kind enough not to press her.

He rose at the sight of her and turned his ruddy face, the clean-shaven skin a little chapped from the air of the upcountry, toward her. She was always surprised by the color of his eyes, a cerulean beauty in his otherwise plain face. He grinned as he pressed her hand.

She settled on the sofa, one of her stepmother's stylish new things, upholstered in a slippery satin, and Susan sat beside her. Even on this big piece of furniture, their skirts, enlarged by hoops, touched each other.

Emily asked, "Mr. Ellison, what brings you to Charleston?"

"Oh, some business," he said. Then he grinned. "And the races," he said, happy at the thought of horses. "Even though it ain't the season for them."

"Of course. Since you're a horseman. Are you racing your own? Your black beauty?"

Her stepmother smiled as she listened to the arch tone and the familiarity.

"No," he said. "I don't want to risk her racing. But I don't mind taking a flutter on another man's nags."

"Gambling, Mr. Ellison?"

"That's what the races are for, ain't they, Miss Emily? A little wagering, a little drinking, and maybe, if I'm lucky afterward, a little dancing, too." As during the season. "Will you dance with me again, Miss Emily?"

Was it disloyal to flirt with John Ellison when her heart was so full of Joshua Aiken? It was absurdly easy, as though she were in a theatrical, as she had been as a girl at Madame Devereaux's. "If I have the chance? Of course I will, Mr. Ellison."

"And that other matter, Miss Emily? The one we discussed last summer? Have you had enough time to think it over?"

"Just a little longer."

He leaned forward, smiling, but she felt faint at the pressure in it. "Don't make a man wait forever, Miss Emily. That ain't right, either."

Her stepmother said, "Mr. Ellison, is this what I think it is?"

"Miss Susan, last summer I asked Emily to be my wife."

Susan said, "Emily, you never said a word!"

"I wanted to give it the most careful consideration, Mother. I asked him to allow me—"

"You've been as good as engaged for months, and you've never said a thing."

John Ellison's patience had run out, and the pressure felt like a vise on either side of her head. "Mother, please, don't misunderstand me. Don't misunderstand us."

Grinning again, Ellison said, "Miss Susan, if you

could help her to see to say yes, I'd be the happiest man in South Carolina."

Susan said, "My husband should know about this." She shot Emily a chiding glance. "But I doubt he'd say no to it."

"When you talk to him, let him know that I hope to make her the happiest woman in South Carolina," Ellison said.

Emily stared down at her lap. Entrapped by her own subterfuge! She raised her head and stammered, "Mother, please. Surely it depends on me? Surely it can hold a bit? It's too important a decision to hurry."

Susan took Emily's hand and pressed it, too hard. "Don't disappoint us, Emily," she said, her voice as unforgiving as her hands.

ಬಂದ

MONDAY WAS WASH DAY, AND Caro stood over the wash table, sorting the soiled laundry as Sophy had taught her: cottons in one pile, woolens in another, white cloth and colored cloth separate. Susan Jarvie had taken Caro into the house for her looks, but Cressy was the taskmistress who meted out her work and cuffed and threatened her if she wasn't satisfied. Cressy took a dim view of keeping a pretty face to open the door when the floors needed sweeping, the rooms needed dusting, the hearths needed cleaning and blacking, the carpets needed beating, and the silver needed polishing. She set Caro to work in the kitchen, and she relegated the wash to Caro, too.

Caro sighed as she checked every garment with pockets. Sophy had told her that you never knew what might
be lurking in a pocket. The ink on a letter could ruin a
whole washtub of white cottons.

Bel sat at the kitchen table, peeling potatoes. Dulcie
was at the City Market, and the two of them were alone
in the kitchen.

Caro worked slowly. She had little enthusiasm for this
task now that she was no longer paid for it. It was strange
that the promise of money would make it possible to
bear something otherwise so distasteful. She reached for
a plain cotton dress that belonged to Emily. In the pocket,
she felt the thick paper of the envelope and slipped the
letter into her own pocket.

Bel, who had one eye on her potatoes and the other
on Caro, saw her do it. "What was that?"

"A letter that belongs to Miss Emily."

Bel held out her hand. "Give it to me."

Trying to keep her temper, Caro said, "Let me give
it to Lydia, and she can take it up to Miss Emily's room."

"I take it."

"Why?" Caro asked. "What do you want with it?"

"Give it to me," Bel said, her temper rising. "Hand it
over, Miss High and Mighty."

Caro turned to face Bel. "What does it matter to you?
The letter belongs to Miss Emily."

"Then why do it matter who give it to her? Won't be
you."

Caro remembered the day that her mother had chastised Bel and threatened her with a swift return to a scullery maid's work on the place on St. Helena Island. "And why should it be you? What would you do with it? You can't read."

"Miss Sass," Bel sneered, and she raised her hand to slap.

Caro grabbed Bel's wrist. "Don't you slap me," she said. "I know I'm a nigger and a slave, but so are you."

Bel wrenched free and rushed her, hands outstretched, in a gesture that could choke Caro or blind her, depending on how she used her fingers. Caro grappled with her to keep Bel's hands away from her face.

"I tell Massa on you," Bel panted.

"Try it, damn you."

"He send you to the Work House."

The door opened, and they sprang apart. Susan Jarvie stood in the doorway and said, "What is this?"

Bel straightened her apron and said sulkily, "Carrie steal something of Miss Emily's."

Caro addressed Susan, her eyes properly cast down. "Missus, I do the wash, and I find a letter of Miss Emily's in her dress pocket. Take it to give to Lydia for her."

Bel said, "She steal it to keep it."

"Bel, why would she want a letter?" Susan held out her hand to Caro. "Give it to me. I'll take it to her."

Caro curled her fingers around the letter with the Ohio address on it. In her most pliable voice, she said,

"Missus, I spare you the trouble. Give it to Lydia to lay on her desk."

"Nonsense. Hand it to me."

Caro tried to think of another honeyed fib to keep the letter from Susan Jarvie's hands. *Help me, Lord,* she thought. *Inspire me.* But her mind felt dull and blank.

Susan said impatiently, "I don't have time for your insolence. Just give it to me and be done with it."

"I tell you she stole it," Bel said.

Susan said to Bel, "You hold your tongue." To Caro, she said, "Give me the letter, or I'll take the switch to you."

"Missus—"

Susan grabbed her by the ear and twisted her earlobe, an astonishing pain. Tears rose to Caro's eyes. Susan said, "Is that bad enough? Or do you want the switch? Or the Work House, where they know how to punish a disobedient servant?"

Where Mama and I can suffer and die together. The tears rolled down her cheeks. Caro reached into her pocket and held out the envelope. When Caro spoke, the words came out as a sob. "Missus, stop, please."

Susan wrenched the letter from her hand. She turned it over to read the return address. She said, "It's from that man in Ohio who wanted us to subscribe to his magazine. I told Emily to write to him and refuse." She glanced at Caro. "Why would you make such a fuss about it? Do you really know how to read?"

"What do it say?" Bel asked.

Susan pulled the contents from the envelope. Emily had read many of Joshua's letters to Caro. *My dearest Emily*, he would write, *with deepest affection from your Joshua*. And God knows what words of devotion and rebellion he had written in between.

Susan's face darkened as she realized what the envelope contained. She stuffed the papers into it. Susan asked Caro, "Did you read this?"

Trembling, sick to her stomach, Caro stared at her shoes as she mumbled, "No, Missus."

"Did you know about this?"

"No, Missus."

"I'll find out who's lying," Susan said. "And believe me, you'll be punished for it."

Caro knew to expect the slap, the locked door, the switch, and the Work House. She could not imagine what Susan and Lawrence Jarvie had in store for Emily.

෨෬

IT WAS AMBROSE WHO SUMMONED Emily to the study. "Your daddy and your mama want to talk to you."

"Did they tell you why?"

"No, miss." He hesitated, and as though he recalled every time that she had shown him a courtesy, he warned her, "They mighty mad about something."

When she entered the study, her father sat barricaded behind his desk, and her stepmother stood beside him, her hand on his shoulder. Her father's color was high, as it had been on the day he heard the will, and her stepmother had a pitiless look, as though her switch were close at hand.

On the desk lay an envelope. Her father picked it up with two fingers, as though it disgusted him, and asked, "What is this?"

Her father pulled the contents from the envelope and let them spill onto his desk. He raised the bank draft, holding it so that she could see Lady Liberty. "What in God's name is this, Emily? Who is paying you?"

That she could answer. "I wrote a story for a magazine called *Hearth and Home* in Ohio," she said. "The editor is paying me for it."

Susan said, "You let them print your name? For everyone to see?"

"I used a nom de plume. No one saw my name."

"Your name is on the draft!" her father said.

"Only to pay me," she said. "The readers don't know who I am."

"What have you written?" her father asked. His color was unnaturally high. "Was it sedition? Was it filth?"

Shocked, she said, "Of course not, Papa. It's a magazine for ladies, like *Godey's*." She gathered her strength. "I wrote about life in Charleston and South Carolina. Tales to amuse a lady who doesn't know us. The City Market. The races. A summer barbecue in the pines. It was all perfectly innocent."

"Did you write about the peculiar institution?" It was odd to hear the politician's circumlocution. But of course, he was a politician now.

"No, Papa. The magazine is about dress and house-hold management. They avoid any controversy. I only mentioned it in passing, as anyone would when visiting Charleston."

Her father crumpled the bank draft in his hand, and she winced, thinking of all the effort that it had taken her to write last month's pieces. He growled at her, "How dare you, a lady of Charleston, put your name in print, even if you disguise it. And how dare you shame us by earning money, as though you are deprived in any way." He flung the crumpled draft on the floor. Through her distress, she wondered if the bank would take a draft so badly damaged.

He said, "You are to stop writing for money, do you hear me? You are never to put your name in print again. A lady's name appears in print twice in her life—when she is married and when she dies. Is that clear to you?"

"Yes, Papa," she whispered.

Susan leaned over to ruffle the pages of the letter. "And this, Emily," she said, in the voice she used before she brought down the switch on a slave's back.

Emily said, "Mr. Aiken is the editor of *Hearth and Home*. He's become a friend, and sometimes he writes in a familiar tone. Perhaps I should have discouraged it, but I thought there was no harm in it since I never meet him."

"Don't lie to us," Susan said. "I know who Joshua Aiken is. He's a distant cousin of mine, and he's embarrassed his family more than once. Studying up north in Boston.

And then refusing to come home. Living in Ohio and soiling his hands by making a living."

Emily said softly, "Is it so wrong to be enterprising? Since he won't inherit until his father dies? He occupies himself in making a living."

"He occupies himself in more than that," Susan said. "Evidently he's occupied himself by courting you. He writes as though the two of you are engaged. What have you promised him?" She picked up the letter, without any haste, and held it daintily between her fingers. "What have you given him?"

The promise on the Battery. The truth. A life together, steadfast. "He misunderstood me," Emily whispered.

Susan said, "I doubt it. When a man writes to a girl like that, it's because she's encouraged him. What have you done, Emily? You promised John Ellison, too."

Susan tore the letter in two and tore the halves in two again. Emily stifled a cry at the ripping sound. Susan said, "You're a liar. A cheat. Will you be a jilt, too?"

There was yet another piece of paper on her father's desk. He pushed it toward her with his knuckles, not wanting to touch it with his fingers. The *Liberator*'s masthead entreated her that "thou shalt love thy neighbor," and reminded her that "we come to break the bonds of the oppressors." In the central medallion, John Brown, in a Christlike pose, gave succor to a chained, kneeling slave and scourged a man who looked like a South Carolina planter's son. To the left was a scene of an auction where "slaves, horses and other cattle are sold," and to the

334

right, a scene of black people jubilantly pointing to a gate labeled Emancipation.

Her father said, "This is sedition, Emily. This is filth. Why has Joshua Aiken sent this to you?"

All the lies fell away. Instead, she said, "Papa, why do you bother to ask? I think you know."

"I do know," her father said, with a look she had never seen him give a white person before. "His family has cut him off. His father disowned him. Do you know why?"

Emily was silent because she knew, too.

"Because he despises slavery and despises the South for holding slaves. He is a traitor to his family, to South Carolina, and to the South that gave him birth. And you take money from such a man! You make promises to him! You hope to marry him!"

Susan said, "You'll break it off. You'll write to him to tell him so, and after that you'll never write to him again."

Emily remained silent.

Susan continued, "You'll stop foxing with Mr. Ellison. You'll say yes, and you'll set a date for the wedding. If decency allowed it, I'd have you married next week."

Jane Aiken, honorably engaged to a man with three hundred slaves, had taken a year to arrange her wedding. Emily Jarvie, entrapped into marriage against her will, might manage a reprieve of a few months.

☙❧

A WEEK LATER, SUSAN BUNDLED Emily onto the train to Stateburg. When Emily asked why they were going to the pines when they had planned to stay in Charleston while her father campaigned, Susan's face turned flinty. "We'll start making arrangements for your wedding," she said.

In a place where her stepmother, her sister, and her future husband could keep an eye on her.

Emily sat uneasily on the cushioned bench of the first-class car. Susan sat opposite her, her expression icy. Beside her sat Lydia, who made herself small to give her mistress, in her expansive hoops, enough room on the bench.

Emily stared out the window, recalling the trips she had taken when she looked forward to the cool piney air of Sumter County. Now she felt so burdened that it was hard to take a breath of the air that smelled of coal smoke, oil, and pine.

At the house in Sumter County, Lydia unpacked her trunk. Lingering, Lydia offered to brush her hair. Everything about Lydia was soft: her voice, her step, her hands. Lydia's touch eased the tight feeling in her temples. When Lydia laid down the brush, Emily said, "Thank you, Lydia."

Still standing behind her, Lydia asked, "Miss, is it true that you're engaged to be married?"

"Yes, it is. Why do you ask?" Emily tried to smile. "Do you doubt what you hear?"

Lydia rested her hands on Emily's shoulders. A soft touch. "You look so sad, miss."

"Just tired, Lydia. It's been so sudden."

"Yes, miss."

Emily turned to look at her servant and saw the beauty in her face, her lidded eyes, her high cheekbones, her sienna lips. "Do you have a sweetheart, Lydia?"

"Oh, miss!"

"It's all right. I won't tell anyone."

Lydia ducked her head. "I do," she said, her soft smile saying more than words could.

Emily smiled too, even though the tears rose to her eyes. "I'm glad for you," she said.

ॐ

THE NEXT MORNING, AFTER breakfast, Emily sat leadenly in the parlor. Despite Lydia's ministration, her head ached this morning, and her chest felt wrapped in iron bands. The Aikens would find her, she knew. The thought of Camilla's chatter made her feel even worse.

But the Camilla who came to see her was unfamiliar. She was gaunt, and her face was pale and shadowed. Her fashionable dress didn't disguise her bones. She wore a scarf over her head, wrapped as the women of the Low Country wrapped theirs. "I look a sight," she said.

"You're changed," Emily said politely.

"It's kind of you to put it like that. I was ill. I had yellow fever in the spring, and I nearly died of it."

"Yellow fever? In the upcountry?"

"I went into Charleston for a week. Didn't mind the night air. When I came home, I burned with fever, and Jane tells me that my eyes looked like hardboiled eggs." She gestured toward her head. "My hair fell out. Thank goodness my servant knows how to hide it until it grows back." She laughed a little, a ghost of her former self. "Jane won't want a bald sister at her wedding."

"I'm glad you're well."

"Mama tells me to thank the Lord because most white people die of it."

"Don't joke, Camilla. If God spared you, He had a reason."

Camilla settled next to Emily, as she had in happier moments, and said, "Now what's this I hear? That you're engaged to John Ellison?"

Her bitterness spilled out like water from an over-filled bucket. "He asked for me. I asked him to wait. And then he told the tale in front of my stepmother, and she thought I'd been hiding an engagement."

"You don't care a fig for him. You never have, Emily."

"How do you know?"

"I heard something else," said Camilla, this odd ghost of Camilla, who had once had glossy blonde curls and a rounded feminine body and the wicked, knowing tongue of a woman twice her age. "I heard that my cousin Joshua wrote you a love letter."

"Camilla, if I tell you the truth, do you swear you'll keep it a secret?"

"I believe I already know the truth," Camilla said, a smile lighting her drawn face.

Emily seized Camilla's hands. "Then help me. Help me spread the tale of the engagement, and the wedding, and my affections."

Camilla raised her eyes to Emily's. Camilla's recovery had left a lively blue iris in a sea of bright white. Camilla said, "While the truth lies elsewhere."

"Yes."

Camilla laughed, a reminder of her previous self. "So that's why God spared me," she said.

&)(3

JOHN ELLISON INVITED HER, AS THE fiancée who would be a bride, to his house for a dinner. He asked if she wanted to see the horses and led her to the stable, where he stroked the black mare's neck and murmured sweetly to her. Emily recalled Camilla's sharpness about Ellison's preference for horses.

As though he'd read her thought, he gave the horse a final pat and turned to the woman. He put his hand on her waist, a touch as gentle as the one for the mare. He met her eyes—the beauty of his eyes surprised her afresh—and asked, "Now that we're engaged, may I kiss you?"

She didn't reply, letting him think the reason was maidenly modesty. She cast down her eyes. He surprised her. He came closer, leaned forward, and kissed her decorously on the cheek. His lips were chapped and rough. He said gently, "I won't press you on that, either."

"Thank you," she said.

He took her hand. "Let's go see the little 'uns before they have their dinner," he said.

As before, they found the children in the yard,

playing while their nurse watched them. Johnny had found a toad and was deeply absorbed in making it leap. "Look, Daddy," he said, prodding the creature. "Look at how good he jumps."

Ellison laughed. "Practice on that toad, and when you're old enough, I'll give you a pony to teach how to jump," he said.

Amelia, the crawler, was now old enough to walk and talk as well. "Daddy, who that?" she asked.

Ellison laughed and tousled the little girl's hair. "That's Miss Emily Jarvie," he said. "She's going to be your mama. Would you like that?"

The little girl glanced at her nurse. "Polly's my mauma," she said, matter-of-factly, as though everyone knew it, and her father was too stupid to know.

Emily tried to think of these children as orphans who might need a mother. Her spirit failed her as she contemplated the boy who had mastered a toad and a girl who would grow like a cornstalk, whether she had a mother or only a black nurse.

Polly's baby, which had been a suckling infant on her last visit, had learned to walk, and he staggered the few steps to his mother, where he clutched her skirt and pulled himself upright. Ellison laughed. "That's a fine little pickaninny," he said proudly. "Ain't he sturdy?"

The little mulatto boy had grown into a resemblance with his father. Emily took in the nurse and her child, took in Ellison's offhand pride in a slave's increase, and the admonitions of the *Liberator* echoed in her head.

Love thy neighbor. That was easy. It was akin to the Christian charity that she had always tried to practice. *Break the bonds of oppression.*

Emily thought of being married to a man who treated her with his rough upcountry notion of honor while using a slave for his comfort and his increase. No doubt the little pickaninny would have brothers and sisters. They would be blood kin to her own children, her own increase, and she would be expected to pretend that she was blind to the connection and treat them as slaves.

She thought of Joshua. She thought of Caro. *I cannot,* said an inner voice. *I cannot.*

PART 3

Confederates in Slavery

1860

Chapter 14: Slaves Have No Mothers

As DULCIE PASSED CARO IN the kitchen after midday dinner, she whispered, "In the yard. Word of your mama."

Fear clutched at Caro's chest. Since her mother had been taken away, there had been no word. Why would a prison send word of a prisoner? Caro had labored in the house in a daze of worry and fear burdened by forcing herself to look pleasant whenever she heard Cressy's or Missus's footsteps.

She had been a privileged slave, protected and petted by her father. She had become a lucky slave, free by the whim of a master who didn't care what she did as long as she lived out of his sight. Now she was truly a slave, and she knew what it meant to be imprisoned in body and soul.

No wonder the Vesey uprising had been fomented by men who were half free. Overworked maids were too oppressed even to think of rebellion.

She met Dulcie in the yard's hiding place behind the shed in the still heat of midafternoon. Dulcie's pleasant face was creased with worry and wet with sweat. "Sophy come this morning. Your mama come back from the Work House."

"How is she?"

Dulcie wiped her face with her apron. "Sophy say she ain't at all well."

Caro grabbed Dulcie's arm and forgot to keep her voice low. Wild with worry, she cried, "I'll go to her, if I have to run away."

Dulcie remembered to whisper. To remind her, too. "No, Caro. I tell Miss Emily. I have a notion how she help you."

Emily had returned from the pines a few days ago. On that day, Emily had drifted past her, as pale as in her days of mourning. She didn't speak or look up. But she touched Caro's hand, the faintest, ghostly touch, invisible to her stepmother, who watched her as closely as Cressy watched Caro.

That afternoon, Cressy sent her to beat the dust out of the parlor carpet. It was a noxious task, since the dust went into the nose and throat, making her cough. As her mother coughed. *Oh, Mama*, Caro thought, staring at the pattern in the bright, new Turkish carpet.

"Caro." It was Emily.

Caro looked up from her task but didn't let go of the carpet or the carpet beater. "Yes?" she whispered.

"Come with me." A low, urgent whisper. But not a command.

"If Cressy sees me…"

Emily reached for her hand. "Leave that to me," she said.

"I'm filthy," Caro said ruefully.

Emily took her hand. "I don't care," she said.

As they walked toward the kitchen, Caro asked, "Is it true you're engaged now?"

Emily nodded.

"Not to Joshua Aiken."

"No."

Caro coughed. "So that's the prison they found for you," she said.

They found Cressy sitting in the kitchen, drinking a cup of coffee. At the sight of Emily, she pushed the cup away and rose. "Yes, Miss Emily? Something the matter?"

Emily took on an imperious tone. "Cressy, I have an errand to run, and I need Caro to go with me."

Cressy looked at Caro, whose apron was streaked with dust, and aimed her words at Caro, too. "Miss Emily, she busy this afternoon."

"Surely you can spare her." She sounded like any young miss, contemptuous of a servant.

Cressy drew herself up. She repeated, "She have her duties."

Emily's tone turned icy. "Who is the mistress here?"

Cressy was unperturbed. "Miss Emily, your mama don't want to hear that Carrie shirk her duties in the house."

Emily's voice became even icier. "I'm sure that my

mother doesn't want to hear that you've been insolent to me."

Cressy's expression changed from surprise to resentment. She looked sullen. With bad grace, she said to Caro, "You go on and do what Miss Emily ask you."

In the yard, Emily took Caro's arm and whispered, "Now we'll go to see your mother."

ഇര

IT WAS DISTURBING TO RETURN to Tradd Street. She had missed it so much. But she was too worried for a homecoming.

At the gate, Sophy put her arms around Caro and embraced her for a long time.

Caro asked, "How is she?"

"Bad."

Caro's eyes filled with tears, and she blinked them away. She hastened to the shack, trailed by Emily. She pushed open the door, calling, "Mama?"

Kitty struggled to rise from the rope bed. Her eyes had dark circles, and her lips were cracked. Caro ran to her mother and gathered her into her arms. "Mama," she cried, clinging to Kitty.

Kitty had been thin before her arrest, but now she was so gaunt that Caro could feel every bone in her spine. Kitty drew back to caress Caro's face. "Caro, beloved," she said. "You're so thin. What have they done to you?"

If she hadn't been so upset, she would have laughed. "Mama, don't worry about me. We need to take care of you." Caro laced her fingers through her mother's. Kitty's hand was papery skin over bone.

Kitty began to cough. A wracking cough, that she couldn't stop. "The cloth—" she gasped, gesturing toward the table. Caro handed it to her. Kitty pressed the cloth to her mouth, and it reddened with blood. Caro watched, speechless, as Kitty wiped her mouth.

She said gently, "Mama, you must rest. Sophy will nurse you and help you get better." Caro caressed her mother's cheek. The skin of her face felt papery, too.

Her mother kissed Caro's palm. "My darling girl," she whispered.

Caro's eyes filled. She remembered how her father had said that, calling them both his darling girls.

She turned to see Emily lingering on the threshold, a look of dismay on her face. She pushed past Emily to run into the yard, her worry turned to dread. She caught hold of Sophy and gasped, "She coughs blood now."

Sophy nodded. "She mighty sick."

"Sophy, will she die?"

"I don't know. Only God know."

Caro buried her face in her hands. Sophy pulled on her arm. She said, "Come into the kitchen to cry so she don't hear you."

She didn't hear Emily close the kitchen door. She didn't look up as Emily sat down. When Emily put a hand on her arm, she shook it away.

Emily said, "She needs a doctor."

Caro raised her head. Emily's face was pinched and waxy, the look of grief that she doffed as easily as a black dress.

"I don't know how I'll manage it. My father would know, even before the bill came."

"Mr. Pereira," Caro said, her voice choked. "Ask him for help."

❧❧

EMILY BULLIED CRESSY—THERE was no other word for it, and Caro delighted to watch it—into letting Caro accompany her on another errand. At Tradd Street, they met Benjamin Pereira and the doctor in the kitchen. The doctor was a very well-dressed young man, used to doctoring planter families. Caro wondered how Pereira had persuaded him to attend an ailing slave.

Sophy showed the way and Pereira followed her. At the sight of her mother, supine on the rope bed, her eyes closed, her hands resting on the coverlet, Pereira cried out, "Oh, Kitty!"

Hearing that plaint, Caro understood that he had always loved her mother as much as he loved her father.

Kitty opened her eyes. "Oh, Ben," she said.

For a moment Caro recalled the woman who presided over her father's house and beguiled his best friend at the dinner table.

"Don't get up," he said, sitting on the edge of the bed. He stroked her forehead. "We've brought the doctor to see you."

"As though it would do any good," she said, stifling a cough.

Pereira touched her cheek. "I'll let Dr. Cohen be the judge of that," he said, and he rose.

Dr. Cohen said, "Please, let me examine her."

"Of course," Pereira said. Caro saw how his eyes glistened with tears.

The doctor bent over Kitty, looked into her eyes, felt for her pulse, and listened to her cough. It took no effort to bring up blood. He wiped her mouth gently with the cloth and set it on the rickety table. "Please rest," he said to the sick woman. Glancing at Pereira, he nodded, and when he left, Pereira left with him. Caro followed, and so did Emily and Sophy.

Pereira said, "I must go." They all knew that he meant, "I can't bear it." He said to Dr. Cohen, his voice thick, "Send the bill to me."

Dr. Cohen inclined his head. After Pereira left, he spoke to the rest of them. "Where can we talk privately?"

Out of her earshot, he meant. Caro said, "The kitchen."

He settled uneasily in the pine chair at the great scarred table, not comfortable in the slaves' domain. Emily asked, "How is she?"

He asked Emily, "Are you her mistress now?"

"She's my father's servant."

"She has consumption. It's advanced. She's very ill."

"What can we do?" Emily asked fiercely.

"Keep her comfortable," the doctor said.

Sophy said, "I have a tea for the cough."

"Let her have it. There's no harm in it." He clenched his hand into a fist. "Why wasn't she seen to earlier? I could have helped her."

Emily said, "She was already ill when my father had her arrested and sent to the Work House."

"How long was she there?"

"For a month."

Dr. Cohen's face darkened. He said, "Damn the man for a brute. Doesn't he know any better than to abuse a servant like that?"

‽‽

After the doctor left, Caro and Emily returned to the shack. Kitty lay back on the bed, her shadowed eyes opening at the sound of their footsteps. Caro sat on the edge of the bed to take her hands.

Kitty said, "Don't lie to me, either of you. I know it's consumption." She coughed. "I know how bad it is."

Caro implored, "Mama, we'll nurse you. You'll get better."

Kitty turned to Caro to say, "I'm so sorry, Caro."

"Mama, there's nothing to be sorry for."

"Once I'm gone, who will take care of you?"

"Don't worry about that now, Mama." Caro pushed away the thought of being a slave who was also an orphan. She rose. "I'll come again tomorrow, Mama."

Kitty tried to speak, but she began to cough. Caro waited until the spasm passed, then she smoothed her mother's forehead.

Kitty shook her head. "Caro, there's something I want you to have."

"What is it?"

"It's under the bed, wrapped in a cloth."

Caro started to rise, but Emily said, "I'll look for it." She knelt on the dirt of the floor to search under the bed. She scrabbled a little to pull out a small bundle of black silk.

Kitty said, "Give it to me." She unwrapped it, and the ivory gleamed in the shack's dim light. She pressed it to her cheek and handed it to Caro.

In the portrait her father smiled at her, and the sight of his face, forever young, forever sunny, brought back all the grief of his death. "Mama, I can't take this from you."

"I won't need it anymore. I want you to have it."

"Please, Mama. Not yet."

"It's for you now," Kitty said, and she closed her eyes.

෨෬

ON THE WAY BACK TO THE HOUSE on King Street, Emily said to Caro, "Let me take the portrait. For safekeeping."

"No," Caro said, feeling the weight of the little portrait in her pocket.

"I don't want anyone to think you took it. That's why I offer. Not because I want to wrest it from you."

"No."

෨෬

CARO HAD ALWAYS SUSPECTED THAT Bel rifled her room, and now she knew for sure. Bel found the portrait and tattled to Cressy, and Cressy grabbed her by the arm to pull her into the study, where the tribunal of master and mistress awaited her.

They looked alike in their anger, their eyes bright, their cheeks flushed. Their fear of rebellion was a kind of fever, and she had roused it in them.

Susan held the portrait between her fingers as though it had been dipped in filth. She said to Caro, "You stole this."

Caro kept her head down and her voice low. "No, Missus."

Lawrence said, "Don't compound the theft with a lie. We know that you stole it."

She shook her head. "No, Massa," she whispered.

"Why else would it be in your hands?"

A low voice came from the doorway. "Because I gave it to her!" Emily marched into the room. "Leave Caro alone, Papa, Mother."

"Why are you here? This has nothing to do with you." Her father's voice shook with anger.

"Yes, it does. I took it," Emily said.

"Why would you lie to protect her?"

"It's not a lie. I took it, and I gave it to her."

"For God's sake, Emily!" her stepmother cried. "Why?"

"I thought she might want something to remember her father by," Emily said. "After Robert died…"

"Don't lie to me, Emily. I know she stole it." That was Susan.

"You yourself gave it to me. I thought it was mine to use as I wished. I gave it to Caro. Did I steal it?"

Her father said, "Don't defend her. I know why you speak for her. It's the influence of that Joshua Aiken, a man who has betrayed everything you should hold dear. Are you lying for him, too?"

"Papa, you know that I wrote to him to break it off and that he no longer writes to me."

"I wonder, since you have such a talent for duplicity."

"Not in this."

He said to Caro. "I can send you to the Work House, as I sent your mother."

Caro flinched. Emily said, "Catherine's stint in the Work House made her very ill, Papa."

Her father's expression of anger was suddenly suffused with shame. Did he regret mistreating a servant so? He sharpened his tone. "I've told you before, Emily. It's not my concern or yours. Keeping the servants and this house in order are my concern." He glowered at Emily. "Take the portrait and keep it out of her hands. Her thieving hands."

He ordered Caro, "Go back to the kitchen."

Caro murmured, "Yes, Massa," as she backed from the room.

Lawrence turned his ire on Emily. "The sooner you're married to Ellison, the better," he said. "Have you fixed on a date yet?"

"Not yet." Emily swallowed hard. "Papa, Jane Aiken had a year to assemble her trousseau and plan her wedding party. Give me the courtesy of a long engagement, too."

"I never heard a report of Jane Aiken defying her family. It doesn't take a year to sew some bedsheets and a dress or plan a wedding breakfast. Stop dawdling, Emily."

৪০৫৪

CRESSY TOOK CARO HER ROOM above the kitchen and locked her in. In her prison, she had nothing to do. No floor to sweep, no carpet to beat, no silver to polish, no petticoat to wash. Without taking off her shoes, she lay on the bed, curled into a ball, and slept.

The sound of the key in the lock woke her. It was late in the afternoon, still light, still hot. Cressy said, "Well, they decide what to do with you."

Caro said nothing.

"You stand up and show me respect when I talk to you."

Caro rose.

"I don't know why they don't sell you. You lucky. They leave you to me. So I put you under Bel, and you do anything she ask you."

Caro dropped her eyes, as she would for Missus Susan.

"You don't wear that good dress anymore. You do rough work, you wear a rough dress."

The ragged dress and the coarse shoes again.

"You do it now." She tossed the ragged bundle onto the floor and waited.

Caro said wearily, "Cressy, please, leave me to dress in private."

Cressy slapped her cheek. "No sass," she said. As Caro reached for the buttons on the gray livery she had always hated, she thought of Sophy's affectionate tease in her nickname, and she steeled herself not to cry.

഼ഌ

BEL DELIGHTED IN GIVING HER the dirtiest and smelliest jobs—cleaning the ashes, emptying and washing the chamber pots, blacking the stove. She often came to watch as Caro worked, her arms crossed, her mouth set in a smirk, mimicking Cressy's stance and expression. The work exhausted her, and her worry for her mother kept her awake at night. Caro started from sleep every hour, in terror that her mother had died in the night and that she had not been there to hold her hand and say goodbye to her.

Today Caro knelt on the kitchen floor and poured sand into the big iron pot that was crusted with the remains of dinner's gumbo. She felt dizzy. She had been too wrought up to eat, and she had slept fitfully in her stifling room. She sat back on her heels to steady herself. She thought of the days when she had willingly helped Sophy, sharing in the cooking and the scouring, and had never minded it. Now, forced into the kitchen's worst task by a gloating Bel, she bent her head, lowered her hand into the pot, and scrubbed.

Bel came to inspect the pot. "That ain't clean," she said.

"I know. I'm not finished yet."

"You clean it good," Bel said.

"I know."

Bel reached for her shoulder and dug her hand into it. "Don't you sass me," she said.

Caro thought of the day that Kitty had chastised Bel for her insolence. She rose.

Bel's hand flew out for a slap. Caro stepped aside to dodge it. "I'll tell Cressy. She'll tell Missus," Bel panted. "She punish you."

Dulcie, who had been kneading bread on the kitchen table, left the dough. She grabbed Bel by the hand. "You leave her alone."

"Cressy tell me to keep an eye on her."

"No, you leave her be."

"She lazy. Don't do her work right." Bel added, "Look sullen all the time, too."

"Her mama dying!" Dulcie grabbed Bel by the arm. "How would you feel, if your mama was dying?"

Caro looked up to see a peculiar expression on Bel's face. It was very like pain. "I was sold away from my mama when I was a little thing," she said, her voice sullen. "My mama might be dying right now. I wouldn't know." She shook off Dulcie's grip and clomped away.

Dulcie said, "You look a sight, sugar. You want something to eat?"

Caro shook her head. "I don't feel like eating," she said, sitting back on her heels. "Dulcie, what if she dies, and I don't know?"

Dulcie bent down to whisper in Caro's ear. "Sophy promise me that she come if your mama start to fail. And I tell you the moment I know."

₭⋊

SHE BEGAN TO DREAM ABOUT Sophy's message, and the nightmare woke her nightly in a sweat of fear. She thought about her mother all the time, and everything seemed like a waking dream: the endless, dirty tasks; the meals she was too tired to eat; Cressy's angry mask; and Bel's smirk. When Dulcie caught her sleeve to whisper to her, "In the yard," she didn't take it in at first.

Dulcie said, "Sophy here. It's nigh, she say. You come soon."

Caro began to untie her apron. She had become so thin that she had to wrap the strings around her middle twice. "Now, Dulcie. I'll go now."

Dulcie said, "No, don't run away. We manage it, Ambrose and I. We let you slip away near dark." She added, "I tell Miss Emily, too."

"No," Caro said.

"She want to help."

Caro shook her head. "She can't," she said.

That evening, after supper but before curfew, Dulcie tugged on her sleeve. They walked down the driveway, where Ambrose waited at the gate. Ambrose said to Caro, "You go. We manage it with Marse and Missus."

Dulcie took off the badge that she wore on a string beneath her dress. "You take this," she said.

Caro slipped it over her head and pressed her fingers to it. It was warm from Dulcie's skin.

Dulcie hugged Caro. "I'm so sad for you," she whispered.

Ambrose said, "You do what you got to do. And take care." He embraced Caro, too.

Caro walked swiftly into the street. It was high summer, when all the fragrant flowers of Charleston were at their peak. Magnolia, azalea, and camellia all perfumed the warm evening air, and the crape myrtles were blazoned with red blooms. Caro thought of the August heat that had accompanied her father's sickness. She remembered sitting at his bedside as he failed, the air scented with flowers, lavender water, and the sweat of fever. She shivered and pushed the memory away.

Once at Tradd Street, she asked Sophy, "How is she?"

"Still with us."

"How long?"

Sophy took her hand. "Not long."

The light in the shack was dim. A single candle flickered; as the sun set, it barely made a dent in the darkness. It was hot, even with the door ajar to catch an evening breeze. The smell of her father's sickroom, sweat and lavender water, was intertwined with the fragrance of magnolia and the reek from the midden.

Kitty lay motionless on the bed, her eyes closed, her hands crossed over her chest, and Caro was suddenly terrified that she had come too late. Kitty's eyes flickered open. "Caro," she said, her voice faint.

"Mama, I'm here," Caro said, and she clasped her mother's hand, feeling the papery skin over bone. Sophy had pulled both chairs up to the bed and Caro sat.

"My darling girl," Kitty said, her voice almost too faint to hear.

She struggled not to cry. The dying needed attention. Tears could wait.

Sophy sat next to Caro, a lavender-scented cloth in her hand. She bathed Kitty's forehead with it. Caro thought of the night two years before, when she and her mother had sat with her father, anointing him with lavender water and fretting whenever the ice melted and the water warmed.

Sophy stroked Kitty's hand and spoke gently to her. "We here, Caro and I," she said. "We stay with you."

Kitty nodded, an imperceptible movement. She struggled to speak. "I'm so sorry, Caro," she whispered.

Caro bent to kiss her mother's cheek. "Mama, no," she whispered back.

The sun set, and the shack darkened except for the flame of the single flickering candle. Her mother's face fell into deep shadow, the light-brown skin ashen in the darkness, the closed eyes hollow, the mouth sunken.

Caro remembered it too well, sitting at her father's bedside, unable to look away, certain that each breath would be the last. Kitty's breathing became slow and uneven. But her chest continued to rise and fall.

Caro sat unmoving in the hard pine chair. She remembered the ache of sitting and watching and waiting as her father failed.

Kitty's breathing became erratic, and when it halted, Caro thought, *This is the last.* But her mother kept breathing.

It was too hard to watch every moment, and Caro let herself look away. She asked Sophy, "How will I bury her?"

Sophy said, "We worry about that when we have to."

She and Sophy sat together throughout the night. Just before dawn, as the birds of Charleston began to wake and to sing, Kitty's breaths slowed even more. Caro listened in an agony of her own, not knowing if there would be another breath.

And as the sun began to rise, as the light began to turn the oilpaper windows to their daytime color, the dying woman rasped. And stopped. And rasped again. And stopped.

And then there was silence, and both Caro and Sophy knew that Kitty was gone.

Caro rose to cradle her mother's hand in her own. Life seeped from the dead woman quickly; even though her hand was still warm, her face was the waxen color of death. Caro wept.

Sophy washed the dead woman's face for the last time with lavender water and straightened the coverlet over her. She clasped Caro's hand. "I come back later to lay her out proper," she said.

They stood in the yard as the sun rose. Sophy said, "You'd best go back before they miss you."

Caro remembered Sophy telling her about her husband's death, how Lawrence Jarvie gave her only a few hours to mourn, enough time for a funeral service and a burial. *I'll have less than that*, she thought.

Sophy didn't embrace her or let her weep. She said, "You save your grief for later. Now ain't the time."

☙∞❧

WHEN CARO RETURNED TO KING Street, she found Cressy waiting for her in the yard. Her face creased, her arms folded, Cressy said, "You been out all night."

Caro felt too tired to reply. She nodded.

"Massa and missus both furious."

Because you told them, Caro thought. Her head ached.

Cressy said, "They want to see you now."

Dulcie opened the kitchen door and wiped her hands on her apron. "I go with you," she said. The three of them walked together through the side door, where Ambrose met them. He said to Cressy, "I go with you, too." When Cressy pushed Caro into the study, Dulcie and Ambrose followed and came to stand beside her, their quiet presence bolstering her.

Lawrence said, "I asked for Caro. She ran off last night without my permission. Why are the rest of you here?"

Dulcie said, "Marse, we know she was away last night, but we come to tell you why."

"It's of no concern. She was gone last night, after the curfew, and she didn't come back until this morning."

Ambrose said, "Marse, you been good to us, and we grateful to you for it. We done our best to be good servants to you. Please, Marse. Let Dulcie and me speak."

Someone with a light step and a rustling skirt came into the room. Even before Lawrence said, "Not you, too," Caro knew that it was Emily.

Dulcie said, "Massa, I excuse Caro to go last night. And Ambrose open the gate for her."

"All of you! Defying me!"

"Please, Massa," Dulcie said. "It weren't to let her run away. Her mother fail last night. She go there to sit with her, close her eyes, say her goodbye."

"She broke the law."

Ambrose said, "Massa, please, she a good girl who do the right thing for her mama. Massa, you been kind to us. Treated us right. Can't complain of a thing. But it trouble me, it trouble Dulcie too, that you think to rebuke a girl who love her mama and take care of her in her last hours."

"A runaway, whom you abetted—"

Emily said quietly, "No, Papa. A loving daughter who acted out of kindness. As we should, as we would with any of our servants, to let her lay her mother to rest."

"Christian charity," Lawrence mocked her.

"Not even that, Papa. Common decency."

Lawrence stared at Caro. "What do you have to say for yourself?"

She was too tired to force herself to speak in the slave's diction. "Master, please let me lay my mother to rest."

"To run away again!"

"No, master. Not to run away. With your permission, to arrange for the funeral and attend it."

Emily broke the silence. "As we would for any servant, Papa."

"I won't pay for it."

Caro said, "With your permission, I'll go to my uncle Thomas to ask for his help in arranging the funeral. He's her brother."

At the mention of Thomas, his mouth tightened. "I don't care about your mother's relatives, or if she has any relatives, or if you do," he said, even though he knew full well who her relatives were. "And don't think about running off again. I'll have the Guard hunt you down to bring you back, and you'll go right to the Work House. Do you understand me?"

Caro bent her head. "Yes, master."

ℰℛℭℛ

NOT AN HOUR LATER, CARO WALKED down the driveway, accompanied by Ambrose, to go to Thomas Bennett's shop on Queen Street. She had heard Ambrose cajole Lawrence into it, insisting that he would keep an eye on her. But as they shut the gate behind him, Ambrose held out his arm and said, "Lean on me, Miss Caro. You look done in."

The worry that kept her awake last night and the fear she had felt in Lawrence Jarvie's presence had worn off, and she felt fatigue hit her like a flash of lightning. She had no stomach for the task of seeing Thomas and asking for his help. She thought, *I am an orphan now*. She pushed the thought away. No time to grieve, not until the funeral, and maybe not even after that.

On Queen Street, outside Thomas's shop, stood a familiar figure. "I didn't want Papa to know," Emily said. "But I had to be here, too."

Caro was so tired that all she could do was to nod. Emily opened the door, and their odd caravan—the mourner, the rebellious daughter, and the faithful servant—filed in to stand before the mahogany counter. Thomas Bennett stood behind it, writing. He looked up and laid down the pen, careful to prevent a blot.

Then he allowed himself the emotion of grief. "Kitty?"

Caro said hoarsely, "She died last night."

"Come around the back. All of you."

In the yard, out of his customers' or employees' sight, he put his arms around Caro and stroked her hair. Releasing her, he said, "Poor Kitty. God rest her soul."

"The funeral," Caro said, her voice as thick as if she'd caught a cold. Or if she'd been weeping for hours. It was too hard to speak in complete sentences. "To honor her. To lay her to rest."

"There are difficulties."

"You loved her. Help me, Uncle Thomas."

Emily said, "Mr. Bennett, if there's anything I can do to help…"

"No, thank you, Miss Jarvie," Thomas said, dismissing

her. "This is a family matter." In a softer tone, Thomas said to Caro, "Let me talk to Maria. We'll make some arrangement. Where is she?"

"Tradd Street," Caro said. "Ask Sophy. She can help." She sagged against Ambrose, who braced her with his strong shoulder. She asked, "Is Danny here?"

"No," Thomas said. "He's not."

"Tell him," Caro said.

Thomas said, "Of course."

₭)℞

IN DEATH, KITTY WOULD NOT REST beside free people of color. Thomas found a plot in the Black Fellowship Society cemetery and persuaded Reverend Girardeau of Zion Presbyterian to preside at the service for the unchurched Kitty. Thomas also found a mourning dress for Caro. It must have belonged to Anna or Charlotte because it was too short and too wide for her tall, slender frame. It didn't matter. For the few hours that she would wear it—for the few hours that she would publicly grieve for her mother and be counted as a mourner—it would suffice.

On a weekday morning, the church was empty save for the Bennetts and Pereiras, and they sat in the front pews to hear the reverend lead the service. Caro scarcely heard the words of prayer. She was in a fog again, as she had been when her father died, and the only thought that penetrated it was that she was now alone in the world.

Afterward, she stood at her mother's graveside and listened to the clods hit the coffin. She thought of a life in which she would be a slave by her master's whim. A life in which she would never be able to marry the man she loved or call her children her own. A life in which the only freedom was here, in death.

After the service, after the words at the graveside, Danny tugged on her sleeve. He said, "My mother is having the funeral meal. Come with us."

"I should go." Back to the King Street house, back to the kitchen, back to servitude, where her mourning would be over, while her grief ate away at her heart.

"Stay with us."

"No," she said, and she walked away. Emily caught up with her. Caro stared at her cousin and said, "Let me go."

Emily caught her hand. "Caro."

Caro raised her eyes to her cousin's. "I can't go back," she said.

They both knew what she meant.

"Tradd Street," Caro said, her voice hoarse with fatigue.

Emily nodded. "Sophy."

"If you come with me..." Emily took Caro's arm. "Mistress and maid, going on an errand together. Who will know any different?"

"You'd do this."

Emily said, "We don't run. We walk slowly, like we're going to the market and have all the time in the world."

Caro nodded.

It was torment to stroll. Caro's muscles twitched with the urge to run, and she felt Emily's arm tremble with the effort of pretending to be nonchalant.

They passed through the crowd on the sidewalk, slaves and free people of color going about their business. No one gave them more than the passing glance necessary to prevent a collision on the crowded sidewalk.

When they turned onto Tradd Street, which was less traversed than King, they both breathed a sigh of relief. Emily gripped Caro's hand, and they forced themselves to continue their leisurely pace.

At the gate, ringing for Sophy, Emily abandoned her calm and shifted from one foot to another in a fever of impatience. "Sophy," she whispered. "Hurry!"

When Sophy arrived at the gate, she took in the two of them: their urgent air, their black dresses. Emily said, "I can't stay. Help Caro."

Sophy said, "Help her how? Help her run away?"

"God help all of us, Sophy," Emily said and turned on her heel.

As she walked away, Caro heard her stifle a sob.

Sophy glared at Caro, but she opened the gate. "Come in," she said.

Caro slipped into the driveway. Sophy clanged the gate shut. "You in a proper mess," she said.

"And if I went to the Work House? Then how would I be?"

"You a runaway. He come after you, try to find you."

"Not if you help me."

Sophy said sharply, "Not if he sell me, too."

Caro grabbed Sophy's hands. "I need to hide. Not

here." She grabbed Sophy's arm. "I'll go tonight. Just let me stay here until tonight."

Sophy fell silent. Looked away. Pondered. Finally she said, "You do that, you get caught. I get a message to Sunday. He know what to do."

"Does he help people who run away?"

Sophy said fiercely, "Hush. You go upstairs and stay quiet. Lay low."

Sophy hid her in the smallest room above the kitchen, unused as a bedroom. It was empty, save for a chair. Sophy brought her a dress—her own dress, the everyday calico. "You put this on. They look for a girl in a black dress." Sophy left her to dress and returned with a bundle.

"What's this, Sophy?"

"Your good dress that Danny give you. And that book Miss Emily give you."

"Where am I going, Sophy?"

As she closed the door, Sophy said, "You hush and wait."

෨෬

LATER THAT AFTERNOON, CARO heard the clatter of wheels and the clop of hooves in the driveway. A carriage? Surely not. Sophy ran up the stairs. "Come down and stay in the kitchen until I tell you it all right."

Caro heard a deep voice outside the door. "Hear you need me to make a delivery, Miss Sophy," he said.

"Up to the Neck."

"Where's the parcel?"

Sophy opened the kitchen door and beckoned to Caro, who followed her. Outside, a deep-bottomed wagon, hitched to a sturdy brown horse, had been parked. It was Sunday's friend Lewis. He said, "I take my wagon home to the Neck." He gestured toward the wagon, where a piece of canvas covered the wagon bed. "Won't be easy, lying on them boards, but it ain't far." He held out his hands to Caro. "Let me boost you up."

With his help, she clambered into the wagon. The wagon bed was full of bricks, but he had made a space for her, a narrow aisle. "Lie down," he said. She lay on the wooden slats of the wagon bed—he was right, it wasn't easy—and wriggled to fit among the boards. The air was thick with brick dust. He covered the wagon bed with the canvas. "You all right?" he asked.

"Yes."

"Now you lay still and stay quiet."

Not far, he had said. It was a half hour on foot to Calhoun Street, the border between Charleston and Charleston Neck. It would be swifter by wagon.

He slapped the reins, and the horse moved forward, making the wagon creak and groan. She listened as the horse's hooves clopped on the cobblestone of the driveway. She felt the wagon lurch as they turned onto the street.

It was dark under the canvas, and she sweated in the hot air trapped beneath the heavy cloth. She could hear the sounds of the street—other draft horses and wagons, the swifter pace of carriage horses, and the higher squeal of carriage wheels—and the sounds of the sidewalk, where people milled, talked, shouted, and laughed. A chestnut seller, a man with a sweet tenor voice, sang about his wares.

Were there Guardsmen on the street? In the heat, she felt a shiver of fear. Were they looking for her? Would they stop the wagon, rip off the canvas, cry in triumph at finding her, and drag her away to the Work House?

She listened to the unhurried pace of Mose's hooves, and it galled her as much as the stroll to Tradd Street. Her thoughts spoke to her in Sophy's voice. "We fool them if we look like we go about our business. We ain't usually in a hurry, and we ain't in a hurry today, either."

She closed her eyes, trying to will herself into patience. Every plodding step of the horse, every groaning turn of the wheel, took her closer to the Neck.

The wagon stopped. Why? They were still far from the Neck. She lay motionless, her heart racing. So close, she thought. So close.

Lewis yelled, "Move on! Move them horses of yours!"

Another voice—a black man's, loud and jocular—yelled back. "They can't fly! Have to wait for them carriages to clear out!"

She could have wept with relief. An ordinary stoppage, since wagons and carriages battled for space on the road. But she kept in her tears. She remained silent. She felt cramped and wished she could roll over. Stay still, Lewis had cautioned her. She closed her eyes and let herself feel all the pain in her head and the soreness in her limbs. She was so tired. But the equal discomfort of the wagon bed and fear kept her awake.

Where were they? It was a torment to hear but not see. The clop of the hooves. The groan of the wheels. *Dear Lord*, she thought. *I hope you'll hear a plea from a godless girl.*

Lewis called out to his horse. "Mose, you lazy old thing, pick up them hooves of yours. We cross Calhoun Street, and we nearly home."

Across the street that had once been Border Street, the demarcation between Charleston proper and Charleston Neck. The Neck, where the Guard was rarely seen. The Neck, where no one checked for a badge. The Neck, where slave and free lived side by side, on the same street, in the same family.

Lewis said to the horse, "Mighty close now! Almost home, and you rest in your stable and get your dinner." She felt the fear and tension ease. Mighty close.

The wagon halted, jolting everything in the wagon bed, including Caro herself. She got a bruise or two from the bricks as they shifted. She didn't care.

Lewis pulled on the canvas. Pulled it back. Let in the light.

He said, "Girl child, is you all right?"

She sat up and winced. He held out his hands. He lifted her as though she were a feather pillow and set her down lightly on the street. He led her to a small wooden house, the clapboards freshly painted white, the door a bright, welcoming blue. He tapped on the door, and Sunday answered it. Lewis said, "Parcel got delivered safe."

Sunday took Caro by the hand and drew her into the house. Inside, he wrapped her in a rough, fatherly embrace. He said, "We shelter you."

Chapter 15: You Must Be Mad

AFTER SHE LEFT CARO AT Tradd Street, Emily lingered. She walked down to the Battery, where she leaned against the fence to gaze into the harbor. She untied her bonnet and let the breeze flow over her face. The air smelled of salt and rot. From this spot, where she and Joshua had confided in each other, she could see the flags of Fort Sumter flapping in the wind off the sea and beyond them, the steamships that arrived every day in Charleston harbor.

For her father and stepmother, Emily had made a show of writing to Joshua to end the connection, but she had also asked Sophy to retrieve his letters from the post office. Emily read them at the kitchen table at Tradd Street, and she wrote her replies there, too. Sophy couldn't read, but she knew about Joshua, and she shook her head as she handed Emily the envelopes. *Joshua, beloved*, she thought, watching a steamship that had left the harbor for the sea. A steamship ticket north cost fifteen dollars, she knew, since in happier days, her father had occasionally traveled north. She was unlikely to travel anywhere. When she rode the train to Stateburg, a journey safe and familiar on both ends, her stepmother insisted that she have an escort, even if it was only her maid. No unmarried girl could walk into the steamship agency, put her money on the counter, and buy a ticket to travel alone to places north.

Emily sighed, retied the strings of her bonnet, and steadied herself to walk back to King Street.

₧₧

BY THE NEXT MORNING, CARO had not returned, and the house was in an uproar. Her father was so angry that he didn't summon the servants to his study. He went to the kitchen to question them. She found Ambrose in the hallway, obviously upset, and when she asked him what had happened, he said, "Nothing to tell you, Miss Emily."

"Is it about Caro?"

He didn't reply. So he had lied to her father, and now he was protecting her, too.

She walked into the kitchen and found Dulcie covering her face with her hands, making no attempt to muffle her sobs. She put her hand on Dulcie's shoulder. "Whatever is the matter, Dulcie?"

Dulcie looked up. Her eyes were red-rimmed, and her face was puffy. She said, "Your daddy in a temper."

She moved her hand to embrace Dulcie around the shoulders. "What was it?"

"He come into the kitchen, all mad, and he ask me where Caro is. I tell him I don't know. He say she run off. I tell him I didn't know that, either. He say that I lying, and when I say, 'No, Massa, I really don't know,' he slap me and tell me that I tell him the truth or he take me down to the Slave Mart and sell me. And my littlest gal, the one who help me in the kitchen, she bust out crying, and he slap her, too."

"He did not!"

"He do. And Bel, she watch with a mean look on her face, like she glad we all in trouble. And she say to him, 'Miss Emily, Massa. You ask Miss Emily.'" Dulcie used her apron to wipe her eyes. "He get even madder. Stomp back to the house." She began to cry again. "Miss Emily, do he mean it? Will he sell me?"

Emily hugged Dulcie with a reassurance she didn't feel. "I hope not," she said.

She returned to the house, trembling, to be greeted by her stepmother's frosty tone. "Your father wants you."

"Is it about Caro?"

"Don't ask. Just go."

Emily tapped on the door. Her father called, "Emily? Is that you?" His tone was even frostier than Susan's. As she crossed the threshold, she braced herself.

Her father was very angry, but it was the coldest fury she had ever seen. "Where's that slave girl?"

A soft voice turneth away wrath, Emily thought. A Christian thought, like charity or loving kindness. "I don't know, Papa."

"Oh, I believe you do."

"No, Papa," she said softly.

"She's run away. Did you help her?"

She thought of the enforced stroll to Tradd Street and felt a sickening fear. Had anyone seen them? "Of course not, Papa."

"My slaves lie to me and so do you."

"No, Papa."

"You can spare me a lot of trouble and a lot of embarrassment if you tell me where she is."

Emily was silent.

"If you continue to lie to me, I'll have to find someone who can make inquiries. Don't lie to me, Emily. Tell me where to find her."

"And what will you do when you find her?" Emily gazed at her father. "Will you beat her half to death? Or will you sell her? Or both?"

He rose from the chair behind the desk, as though he were facing an opponent in court. He said, "Are you aware of the punishment for helping a slave to escape?"

"No, Papa."

"In South Carolina, abetting a fugitive slave is a crime. The punishment is hanging."

She shivered under the cold look, the look of justice without mercy. As sweetly as she could, she said, "Papa, surely you don't want to see me hanged." She added, "My name would be in the papers!"

He laughed, a dry, bitter sound. "No," he said. "There are better ways to punish a wayward girl."

She stumbled from the room. If anyone discovered the truth—that she had abetted Caro as far as Tradd Street—then she was as much in rebellion as any slave.

She was in league with the forces of insurrection. She was guilty of a crime that shared a punishment with John Brown's.

Susan ran down the staircase, her hooped skirt brushing against the walls. "Emily!" she said, her voice full of regret.

Now Emily raised her eyes in alarm. She said, "Does he mean it?"

Susan took her hands. "He's very angry," she said.

Emily whispered, "I've never seen him like that."

"You can put an end to all of this, Emily. Tell Mr. Ellison that you've settled on a date for the wedding. Your father will forgive you."

Emily's mind raced. "Mother, please. Give me enough time for an engagement." She pleaded, "Don't you want me to have a full trousseau? A lovely wedding dress? A beautiful wedding ceremony at St. Michael's, with all our kin and friends around us? A proper wedding journey, as everyone welcomes us as a married couple? Would you deny me the glory of it and yourself the pleasure of it?"

"I'll invite Mr. Ellison to visit us in Charleston, and we'll get this settled." Susan squeezed her hands. She said, "Please, Emily. Before it tears this family asunder."

∞℃℞

A FEW DAYS LATER, THEY SAT at the breakfast table, and her father spoke to her stepmother as though she herself wasn't there to hear. "I don't want her to leave the house unless she's chaperoned."

"Goodness, Lawrence, do you think she's going to run away, too?"

"It's not a laughing matter."

"Is there any news about the slave?"

Her father flushed. "Don't press me," he said. "I'll handle it quietly."

"Quietly! Too quietly. You haven't done a thing."

"Susan, it's a family matter. I don't want it talked about. It's an embarrassment, especially now."

Emily thought, *A proslavery man, sworn to secession, who can't even command his own servant.*

Susan said, "Find someone to make an inquiry. Someone who will keep it quiet."

"I'll handle it. Don't press me."

℘ℭ

AND A FEW DAYS LATER, as Emily walked past her father's study, she caught a glimpse of the stranger who sat companionably with him in the wing chairs before the hearth. He wasn't a planter or a lawyer. He had sleek, dark hair, and when he turned his head, she saw the whiskers that curled around his cheeks. He wore a frock coat in a checked pattern, which even her stepmother would have thought flashy. He gripped a pair of yellow kid gloves in his hand. Was he a new overseer? He held himself with too much confidence for a hired man.

She didn't linger. Her father would notice, and he would chastise her, too. He was still angry with her. She stepped quietly into the back parlor, where her step-mother looked up from the letter she was reading.

She asked, "Mother? Who is that man in Papa's study?"

"What man?"

"The one in the checked frock coat."

"I don't know. Probably another overseer. Your uncle's place is still a bother. The last overseer didn't last long."

Her father hadn't put an advertisement in the *Mercury* about a runaway slave. Inquiries, he had said. The man in the frock coat could do more than make inquiries. He was likely a slave catcher, and Emily was sick with the thought.

♏☒

Her stepmother, who knew her moods well, tried to distract her. She took Emily to visit the dry goods shops to look for satin lengths for a dress and lace for a veil. The dry goods merchant, a middle-aged man in a well-cut waistcoat, smiled and said to her, "I wish you happiness, Miss Jarvie."

There were many visits to Susan's friends. She pro-pelled Emily firmly by the elbow into the carriage and into one overdecorated parlor after another, hoping that the pressure of gossip in Charleston would accomplish the same task as in Sumter County: to shame Emily into her promise to marry John Ellison.

Emily was never alone, to the point where her head ached, and she found it difficult to breathe. After breakfast, she and Susan sat in the parlor as Susan opened her letters and consulted her daybook, reminding herself who might be at home today.

Emily said, "Mother, may I take a little exercise by myself this morning? Just down to the City Market to get a little air."

Her stepmother sighed. "Your father is wrong to try to keep you cooped up," she said. "All right. Take Peggy with you."

"Doesn't Dulcie need her?"

"Dulcie can spare her. If your father asks, I can tell him you weren't alone."

She set out with Peggy, who carried a basket over her arm. When they turned the corner, Emily said, "Peggy, will you help me?"

Emily knew that Peggy shared her mother's regard for "young miss." "Yes, miss."

"Will you go to the market and wait for me there?"

She said, "I surely will, Miss Emily."

Emily put her head down, as though she were on a trek, and walked swiftly to the house on Tradd Street, where Sophy met her at the gate without unlocking it. Sophy whispered, "You can't come here. If your daddy find out, it dangerous."

Emily also dropped her voice to a whisper. "I think he's hired someone to find her."

Sophy was silent.

"Where is she, Sophy? Do you know?"

Sophy looked at her with a slave's blank expression. "Can't say, miss."

Slaves said that to mean "Don't ask me to tell you." Emily reached through the ironwork for Sophy's hand, hating the sudden distance between them. Sophy stepped away. She said, "Don't make it worse, Miss Emily."

ℰ︎℣

Emily dreaded John Ellison's visit to Charleston. It had become more and more difficult to remind him not to press her when she wrote to him. To see him face to face was a different sort of difficulty. She hoped that he wouldn't try to clasp her around the waist or kiss her. She carried Joshua's image in her mind all the time, recalling his haggard and resolute look as he told her that his family had disowned him. The prospect of looking into John Ellison's self-satisfied face, and worse yet, of receiving a kiss from the lips that boasted of getting his slave Polly with "increase," dismayed and disgusted her.

She missed Caro badly—not the starved and beaten slave who served under Bel's whim, but the clever girl who had earned a living by her own hand and who met Emily's opinions about literature with her own. *Miss Sass*, Emily thought. Sophy's nickname brought tears to her eyes. *Where are you, Caro?* she thought. *Have you truly run away? Will he find you?*

On the day that Ellison had been invited to share midday dinner, Susan laid out Emily's showiest summer dress for daytime, the one with the gauzy sleeves that let the flesh of her arms peek through, and admonished Lydia, "You make her look pretty for that man she's going to marry."

"Yes, Missus," Lydia said.

Lydia fell silent as she helped Emily into her corset and her hoops. Emily didn't speak, either. She raised her arms in silence to let Lydia ease the dress over her head and do up the little buttons in the back. Lydia was the one to break the silence. "Miss, you look sadder all the time," she said, in her soft voice.

"I'm not ready to get married," she said.

Lydia knelt to smooth the fabric of the skirt over the hoops. She rose. Emily reached for her hand. "What do you think, Lydia?"

Lydia shook her head. She said, "I think you look pretty, Miss Emily."

Ellison waited in the parlor, where her mother and father had joined him. He had taken his ease to stretch out on the sofa. He shifted to give her a place to sit beside him. She was glad of her hoops. If he moved closer to her, he would feel the spring of the hoop, not her flesh.

He clasped her hands. "Emily, it's good to see you. It ain't enough to write a note."

Susan smiled as she said, "Mr. Ellison, you know you're always welcome to visit us in Charleston."

"That's kindly of you, Miss Susan." He smiled at Emily. "But a man wants to know he'll get a warm welcome from a girl before he uproots himself."

Emily did her best to smile warmly in return.

Ellison reached into his pocket, and at the sight of the little blue velvet box, Emily's heart sank. "I brought you something," he said, opening the box. Nestled within was a rose gold ring, its sapphire heart captured by golden prongs that looked like claws. He said proudly, "So we're properly engaged." He held it toward her. "Try it on. I guessed at the size. You can always have it done over if it don't fit."

Emily hesitated. Ellison removed the ring from the box and took her hand. He was a little clumsy, and he forced the ring onto her finger. "It do fit," he said, pleased, but he was wrong. It was too tight.

He said, "Don't a man get a kiss? Now that the world knows we're engaged?"

She said, "It's a lovely ring." She kissed his cheek.

"You don't get off so easy," he said, smiling, and he kissed her on the lips, with a little too much vigor for the parlor, as her stepmother looked on.

Emily tried to sound lighthearted. "Mr. Ellison, you take advantage."

He reached for her beringed hand. "Call me John," he said. "Seeing as I'm nearly your husband."

"Not yet," she said, smiling to take the sting of her words away.

Still holding her hand, he said, "Emily, I came to get that settled. It's wearing me to wait."

Trembling, Emily glanced at her stepmother. "It can't be done overnight," she said. "Mother, tell him about the arrangements." She tried to look arch. "Even the upcountry girls take a year to get married!"

"Something plain would suit me just fine," Ellison said. "A year! That's hardship."

Her father walked into the parlor. "Hardship?" he said. "What's a hardship?"

Ellison appealed to her father. "I've just given your daughter a ring, and she tells me that she needs a year to get her flimflams together for the wedding."

Her father said sharply, "Emily, we've talked about this more than once. We can give you a perfectly fine wedding much sooner than that."

Susan said, "Not in a month, Lawrence."

"How long?" her father said impatiently, addressing her stepmother and not Emily.

"We could do it in three months," Susan said.

Emily was trembling very badly. She said, "You talk about me as though you're planning to sell a bushel of rice."

Susan said, "Of course not. Just getting you settled."

Her father said, "Emily, we've discussed this more than once. Your mother and I have been patient with you. We've indulged you. No more. You'll settle on a date."

"And if I don't?"

Her father reminded her, "We've talked about that, too."

Ellison said, "Sir, let me." To Emily, he said, "It's time for you to make me happy. I'm asking you. Settle on a date, and we can make whatever arrangements you like. But don't put it off any longer."

Emily jerked her hand from Ellison's and rose from the sofa. "You said you wouldn't press me," she said, her voice trembling. "You promised you would never press me."

"We're past that," Ellison said.

Her father said, "He's about to be your husband, Emily."

"No!" Emily cried, and when the tears rose to her eyes, she allowed them. She was in a haze of anger and upset. She wanted to wrench the ring from her finger. She wanted to fling it at John Ellison's feet. "You promised!" she said to Ellison, starting to sob. "You lied to me!"

Ellison reached for her hand, but she turned away. Weeping, not caring that her stepmother saw, that her father saw, that the man she dreaded marrying saw, she ran from the room and up the stairs, letting her feet thud heavily, most unladylike, on the steps.

ഇരുൻ

AFTER HER OUTBURST, EMILY expected that her father might order her locked in her room, and her stepmother might send her bread and water to eat, in the hope of starving her into submission. But they did not. Emily recognized the nature of the silence, heavy and ominous, like the ache in the air before a storm. Her parents had gone quiet like this before when they had reprimanded, scolded, slapped, and switched an obdurate slave with no result. This was their time to brood over the punishment to come next.

A week after Emily had fled from John Ellison in tears, Ambrose showed her into the study, where her father and a stranger stood before the hearth in conversation. The early afternoon air was thick and warm, and the smell of whiskey suffused it, a manly perfume. The stranger was taller than her father and broader in the shoulders. He wore his hair long in the manner of a Virginia man, and the face he turned to Emily was softened by courtesy. His eyes were the same color as a turkey vulture's: a light, translucent brown.

Her father said, "Emily, this is Dr. Powell."

"How do you do, sir," Emily said. She wondered who his people were and how her father knew him. She had never met a Powell, either in Charleston or in up-country.

Her father said, "I've asked him to take a look at you."

"But I'm not ill," Emily said politely.

"Dr. Powell is a specialist in nervous diseases," her father said.

Puzzled, Emily said, "But I'm not nervous, either."

"Let me be the judge of that," Dr. Powell said, smiling to soften his words.

Her father said, "I'll leave you with him."

"No one to chaperone, Papa?"

"He's a medical man, not a suitor. You can trust him," her father said, and he departed, leaving the door slightly ajar.

Dr. Powell gestured toward the chairs that faced the hearth, where no fire was laid in the summer's heat. He was at ease, as though he were in his own house, or wherever he saw his patients. "Shall we sit?" he asked.

Emily sat, arranging her skirt. The pretense of a social visit gave her comfort. "Dr. Powell, what is this about?"

"Your mother and father are concerned about you. They tell me you haven't been yourself. Subject to fits of weeping."

"There are girls who cry over everything—a sentimental novel, a sick pet, a tiff with a friend. Surely that isn't a sign of illness? Or nerves?"

"These ailments are very stealthy, especially in young women," he said, smiling again.

She thought, *Some women must find him charming.* But his smile bothered her. His teeth were very white, and the smile showed the canines, which were surprisingly pointed.

Emily folded her hands in her lap to hide that they were trembling. "My father said that you were here to take a look at me," she said. "How do I look?"

"Miss Jarvie, he meant for me to examine you, and in my capability, that means to talk to you as well."

"Then by all means, talk to me."

He settled into his chair. "Miss Jarvie, your father tells me that you have been writing for publication. How did that come about?"

"A friend of the family is the editor of a magazine for ladies. He asked me to pen something, and I put my hand to it."

"You kept it from your mother and father."

"It was a lark. Why trouble them with it?"

"You have put yourself forward, into the public eye, in a most unladylike way. Why would you do that?"

Emily heard Madame Devereaux's voice echo in her head. "Many ladies write for publication," she said. "Did my father tell you that I never let my name be published? I wanted to spare him any embarrassment."

"But you earned money by it, and you continued with it."

"The editor paid me for my efforts. Should I have refused the money?"

He frowned. Any girl who was easily intimidated, who wanted his good will, might be upset at that dark expression. "Your father provides for you, as your husband will provide for you once you marry," he said. "Why would a Charleston girl of good family soil her hands with the filth of the marketplace?"

Emily said, "I'm well acquainted with many a young man of good family who makes a living as a lawyer or a broker. I've never seen them refuse a fee or a commission, and they never think of money justly earned as filthy."

"But you're not a young man, whose place is in the world. You're a young girl, whose delicacy and purity should be sheltered at home, in the bosom of your family."

Emily thought of Camilla, who was as calculating as any broker or factor. "Dr. Powell, perhaps you have seen a *young girl* engaged in finding a husband? It's quite a worldly business."

"That's a most unladylike attitude for a maiden, Miss Jarvie."

"But I'm not a maiden, Dr. Powell. I was engaged once, and my beloved died. Now, it seems, I'm engaged again."

"But you're reluctant to make arrangements for your wedding."

"Marriage is a very serious business, Dr. Powell. Even the most innocent maiden is aware of that. Shouldn't it be undertaken with a great deal of judgment?"

He leaned forward. "Do you think that your judgment is better than your mother's? Or your father's?"

She felt very tired. "Doesn't love enter into the decision to marry, as well as duty? I'd hope that my parents would allow me that much judgment."

"You exercise your own judgment quite a bit, Miss Jarvie."

"Oh yes," she said. "Every day, I decide which dress to wear. And when to leave the house for a bit of fresh air. I can even go to the dry goods merchant and pick out my own handkerchiefs."

"Much more than that, Miss Jarvie." His voice was pleasant, as though they were discussing an upcoming ball. "You refuse to marry the man your father has chosen for you, but you correspond with your lover, who has beguiled you with the immorality of opposition to slavery."

In an equally pleasant tone, Emily said, "Oh, Dr. Powell, it's no such thing. He writes to me about the business of the magazine, and in friendship, he tells me about his life in Ohio."

"You're lying to me, Miss Jarvie."

"A gentleman doesn't tell a lady she's lying."

"I know you're lying."

"How?"

He pulled the packet from the pocket of his frock coat. "Because of these."

Joshua's letters, bound with a black ribbon, the ones she thought she had hidden in her room. "You've read them? Who gave them to you?"

"Your father. After he read them."

She felt a fury so intense that it made her temples throb. It made her dumbstruck.

He said, "He is a traitor. A Carolina man! He is unhinged. A man who admired John Brown and grieved when he was hanged! And you are not a whit different. Caught up in his lunacy."

She controlled herself, even though her hands were trembling. "Dr. Powell, surely a strong political opinion isn't a sign of madness? Judge Pettigru, an esteemed man of Charleston, has called support of secession a form of madness. Would you send every secessionist in South Carolina to the asylum?"

"A headstrong delusion may be a sign of madness, Miss Jarvie. I understand that you think of one of the kitchen maids as your cousin. Carrie, I believe her name is."

"She's called Caroline," Emily said.

"Do you think of her as your cousin?"

"She's my uncle's daughter. Isn't that the definition of a cousin?"

"You think of a Negro slave as your cousin?"

"Whatever her color, she's still my uncle's daughter."

"Why did you help her escape?"

Emily was stunned into silence.

He held up the bundle of letters. Still pleasant, he smiled, as though he might ask her to dance. "If you would burn these, I'd take it as a sign of your health," he said.

Joshua's letters, as dear to her as Joshua himself. "And if I don't?" she asked.

"I'll insist that your father allow me to take you to the asylum in Columbia where I can examine you fully."

"And what will happen then?"

He said, "If you're ill, you'll remain there until you're well."

"When would that be, Dr. Powell?"

"When your father and I deem it."

He was a madhouse doctor, and he was sure that she was mad. She rose. "There's no fire in the house, not in the summer, but there's one in the kitchen. Come with me."

They walked through the yard and into the kitchen, where Dulcie and her children were at work. "What is it, Miss Emily?" Dulcie asked.

"May I put something on the kitchen fire, Dulcie?"

Dulcie looked puzzled. "Yes, miss, but why?"

Emily said, "Don't worry, Dulcie." She approached the great hearth, where the fire always burned, and she dropped the letters into the flames, with no show of fury. She watched as the pages flamed, twisted, and blackened into ash. As she watched, as Dr. Powell watched her, she recalled Caro's words: *So that's the prison they found for you.*

Chapter 16: We Are All Slaves Now

WHEN CARO WOKE, SHE DID not remember where she was. The sheet beneath her was soft, worn cotton, as was the quilted coverlet over her. The pillow under her head rustled with feathers, not straw. The last of the night's cool breeze whispered from the windows, but the rising sun had turned the room's white walls the color of the palest honey.

She threw back the quilt and sat up. The bruises on her legs had turned an ugly color, blue ringed with a sickly yellow. She touched her discolored skin, and it all returned to her, her mother's funeral and her own flight in a wagon full of bricks.

She was in Sunday Desmond's house in the Neck. She was an orphan, and she was a runaway.

Outside, the Neck stirred and woke. A sleepy-sounding woman called, "Jackie, you take up that pail and go to the pump. I need water." A baby wailed, and a girl's exasperated voice said, "Can't you hush!" Hens cackled, benefiting from an unseen hand casting crumbs. A man's deep voice roused a horse: "Mose, get on. We got work to do." The smell of the Neck, a place less well tended than the rest of Charleston, wafted into the room, the reek of backyard privies and middens mingling with the smell of coffee, bread, and bacon. As everywhere in Charleston, the smell of flowers in bloom—the strong fragrance of magnolia, azalea, and camellia—struggled against the stink and failed to overwhelm it.

Last night, too tired to care, she had flung her dress over the back of the bedside chair and fallen into bed. This morning, it was neatly folded. On the wash table, the ewer and basin had been set, along with a cloth and a sliver of soap. Someone—was it Sunday, or did someone else live here, someone used to folding and tending?— had done this for her while she remained asleep.

She splashed her face, glad that the wash table had no mirror. She put on her dress and slipped into her shoes. She descended the steep steps.

The house was hushed. Empty. She walked into the kitchen—in a house this small, the kitchen was indoors— where a pot of coffee warmed on the stove. She held her hand near the firebox. The fire had been banked.

If the house was supposed to be empty, feeding the fire would draw attention. She would let it go out.

On the kitchen table sat a loaf of bread covered with a cloth; a dish of butter, also covered; and a jar of preserves. The table was set with a thick china plate and a thick china cup. She hadn't eaten since the funeral meal, and the smell of coffee was suddenly savory. She poured a cup and cut herself a slice of bread, spreading it with butter and jam. But when the meal was before her, her throat closed, and she couldn't eat. She bent her head, as Sophy did when she said grace, but all that came to her lips was, "Mama." And a scalding rush of tears.

She could hear Sophy's voice. "She gone, but you got to eat. Don't want you to fade away, too."

Caro picked up the bread and forced herself to eat. Despite the jam, it tasted of the tears she had wept into it. It tasted of salt.

When she finished, she left the cup and plate on the table. She looked for a bucket of water to wash the dishes but saw none. The nearest water was probably at the neighborhood pump, and someone in hiding had no business walking through the neighborhood to fetch water.

Outside, the Neck went to work. Women emerged from their houses with bundles balanced on their heads, wash or sewing. Men in coarse cotton shirts and nankeen trousers strode toward King Street to walk south to Charleston proper. Horse-drawn carts rumbled down King Street, draymen calling to their horses to encourage them and to each other, to get out of the way. On Line Street, just below her window, a handcart rolled down the cobblestones, and a man sang out, "Sweet as sugar! Strawberries, blueberries, blackberries! The blacker the berry, the sweeter the juice!"

She wandered from the kitchen into the parlor, careful not to stand at the window. Last night she had been too tired and terrified to notice anything in the house.

Today, in sunlight, she took its measure. The furniture—sofa and chairs—was secondhand, worn with a century of use, but it had been well tended. A faint smell of beeswax lingered. A little shelf had been fitted into the room's darkest corner.

The top shelf sported two miniature Staffordshire china dogs, kin to Sophy's shepherdess, but the middle shelf held books. Caro read the spines. The King James Bible. The *Plays of Shakespeare*. Sir Walter Scott's *Ivanhoe*. Frederick Douglass's *Narrative of My Life*.

She had never read Mr. Douglass's autobiography, and she took Douglass's volume from the shelf and cradled it in her hands.

She sat in one of the armchairs—the one least visible from the window—and opened the volume to Douglass's portrait, dignified and leonine. He had been a slave and a fugitive before he became an eminent man.

She stared back at him as the flagrancy of her escape washed over her. She wondered if Lawrence Jarvie had published a runaway notice in the *Mercury*. Would he send the Guard for her? Or would he keep the shame of her flight quiet?

At the sound of footsteps outside, footsteps hesitating on the sidewalk before the house, she froze. But when she dared to peek out the window, she saw only a stout woman who had halted to adjust the great bundle of laundry that she carried on her head. Her burden secure, she resumed her walk down the street, her heavy shoes echoing on the pavement.

Caro bent her head again, tears welling in her eyes, and as the grief returned, as vivid as sickness, she closed the book.

Book in hand, she fled upstairs to the room she had slept in, with its white walls and white sheets. She slumped onto the edge of the bed as exhaustion swamped her. She lay back on the bed and closed her eyes. She kicked off her shoes and let the book fall beside her. As the morning light flooded the room, Caro crawled under the covers and pulled them over her head to block out the day.

The night that her mother died, Caro had taken Sophy's advice to heart and put mourning aside until later. At the funeral, she had been stony, and as she fled her servitude in the Jarvie house, she had been too frightened to weep. Now she felt grief deluge her. "Mama," she whispered, and the tears came in ragged sobs that tore at her chest. She buried her face in the pillow to muffle the noise. She thought of her mother, her face waxy in death, her beauty consumed by her cough, her dignity taken away by slavery. She recalled the lovely mother she had known before her father died, her earbobs sparkling in her ears, her silk dress rustling around her ankles, her smile quick and sweet when Caro's father caressed her cheek or spoke to her with love.

Papa. She had never grieved properly for him, either. She had been too busy trying to take care of her mother. She thought of the expression that his portrait had captured forever. The portrait was lost to her, too. She pressed her face into the pillow, curling herself around the pain in her chest and belly, feeling no relief as she sobbed. *Dear God,* she thought, unable to call it prayer. *Help me. Let me follow them, both of them, so I'll be with them once more.*

When she had wept her eyes and throat raw, she fell asleep, and her body unclenched like an opening fist. In broad daylight, as Line Street washed and sewed and carted and built, Caroline Jarvie slept.

୧୦୯ର

THE SOUND OF THE KNOCK ON the door woke her. It was still daylight, and the sounds of the street had not abated since the morning. Neither had the day's heat. She sat up, a little dazed with sleep, and smoothed her hair. She stood up and smoothed her wrinkled dress. Yawning, she descended the stairs.

The knock sounded again, and it woke her to fear. Who wanted her?

She crept into the front room, where she could see out the window without revealing herself. Her heart pounding, she peered around the curtain.

A stranger stood on the steps. She was a dark-skinned woman wearing an apron and a white kerchief that made her skin look darker. She carried a cast iron pot, holding it with both hands.

Caro put her hand to her chest to steady herself. She opened the door. "Who are you?"

Surprised, the woman asked, "Didn't Mr. Desmond tell you I'd stop here?"

Caro leaned against the doorframe. "No. Who are you?"

"Friend to Mr. Desmond. Mrs. Evie Harris. I live next door."

"What are you doing here?"

She lifted the pot, and the smell of hoppin' john wafted from it. "Brought him some supper. Ain't unusual, unless he tell me he stay in Charleston with his friend Miss Sophy." She shook her head. "Didn't mean to startle you. Thought he'd tell you I'd be here."

Caro stepped into the foyer. Mrs. Harris was taller than she had appeared. Her expression was unruffled. Caro said, "What did he say about me?"

"That you need a place to stay after your mama pass on."

Caro felt stupid with sleep and fear. "Anything else?"

As Caro hesitated, Mrs. Harris said, "Didn't mean to give you a scare, girl child." She sighed. "Mr. Desmond's friend, the man who make the delivery yesterday, he board with me."

"I thought the Guard had come for me."

Mrs. Harris's eyes glinted. "The Guard don't come up to the Neck. We take care of ourselves up here." She raised the pot again. "Let me put this in the oven, keep it warm for your supper."

෨෬

AFTER MRS. HARRIS LEFT, Caro's fear blossomed. She tried to sit in the front room and couldn't. She was afraid to pace and show herself before the window. She ran up the stairs and forced herself to sit on the bed. She couldn't. She ended up in the rocking chair in the front room, as far from the window as possible, too wrought up to read, waiting.

At the sound of the key in the lock, she sprang up, not thinking whether she could be seen, and rushed toward the door. Her voice ragged, she said, "Mrs. Harris came. I didn't know to expect her." She pressed her hand to her chest again. "Scared me half to death!"

He shut the door. "Caro, sugar, didn't mean to frighten you. Left you a note about Mrs. Harris. You didn't see it?"

"No."

"Thought I left it on the table," he said, his face creased with concern.

She had missed it in her grief this morning. Trembling, she said, "I thought the Guard had come for me!"

"We get away from the window," he said gently and took her by the hand. He settled her at the table. Still holding her by the hand, he said, "You right to be wary."

"Mrs. Harris told me the Guard won't come up here to look for me."

"That true. The Neck ain't their beat. They don't come here."

"But I'm not safe up here."

"I bring you something to show you." He handed her a copy of today's *Mercury*.

She took it with trembling fingers. "The notice. The runaway notice. You saw it."

"No. No notice."

"How can that be? Lawrence Jarvie wants me back."

Sunday said, "He don't want to advertise it. Big man, run for Assembly, all hot about secesh. Do he want Charleston to know that he can't keep his own servant in the house? No notice."

"But he'll send someone to look for me. Someone to do it quietly."

"Maybe," Sunday said.

"No, certainly."

"If he do, we don't make it easy for him, up in the Neck. The Neck home to all kinds of people who should be elsewhere. Some of them should be in massa's house, and some of them should be in the Work House. We make the Neck a refuge for them, like the swamp a refuge down in the Low Country."

She searched the seamed face and thought of yesterday's promise: *We shelter you.* She said, "You've done this before."

"Yes, I have," he said. "Lewis and Evie, they help me."

"The others," she asked. "Did they get away? Are they all right?"

"Hush," he said.

It reminded her of Sophy, who told her to be quiet when she had something to conceal. Sophy had never given anything away when Caro pressed her. Sunday wouldn't, either.

He let go of her hand. "What you say we eat some of

Mrs. Harris's good hoppin' john? We put some meat on your bones, build you up."

Despite Sunday's reassurance, Caro felt despair wash over her. "What am I going to do?"

"After supper, we talk about how you lay low," he said.

ℰ⃝

Emily knew that her father had browbeaten every slave in the house, demanding that they give Caro up, and he had been furious when they insisted, pleading and weeping, that they didn't know where she was. He had even been rough with Ambrose, whom he liked so much. She wondered if he had threatened to sell Ambrose, too.

But her father hadn't put a notice in either newspaper, the *Mercury* or the *Courier*, the easiest way to announce a flight and find a runaway. He would consider it a private family matter, nothing to advertise in public. If he planned to find Caro, he would do it quietly.

A slave who ran away had to act in secret. Anyone who sought a fugitive, who was under suspicion herself, had to be secretive, too.

Since Dr. Powell's visit, Emily had been as tractable as a servant. She had kept her eyes cast down, and her voice pitched low. She never left the house unless it was to accompany her stepmother on an errand or a call. She had hidden away her diary and ceased to write in it. She spent no time in her room unless it was to dress or to sleep. Every moment of her life, save for using the chamber pot or dreaming, was visible to her father and her stepmother.

On a warm morning several weeks after Caro's disappearance, Emily sat with her stepmother in the back parlor. As Susan ripped open her letters, Emily opened the latest issue of *Godey's Lady's Book* and let it rest in her lap. When Susan looked up from her letters, Emily said softly, "Mother, may I ask a favor of you?"

"What is it, Emily?" Her stepmother had become less curt with her as she had become more and more docile.

"May I go for a walk in the morning, before the air is so hot? A constitutional, for exercise."

Susan sighed, the sound of a mistress beleaguered by bad behavior in the yard and the kitchen. "I promised your father I'd keep an eye on you," she said.

"I know. But I've done everything you've asked of me. I've broken with Mr. Aiken." She let her hands rest on the pages of *Godey's*. "I burned all his letters. I've agreed to the wedding. Just a few minutes of fresh air. Please, Mother."

Susan looked down at her letters, the envelopes ripped ragged from her zeal to open them. She said, "Take Peggy with you."

"You know as well as I do that Dulcie needs her in the kitchen. But if you insist, I will."

Emily saw the old affection flicker in her stepmother's face. "You aren't a prisoner," she said. "All right. A few minutes by yourself to take some exercise."

Emily rose and took her stepmother's hands. "Thank you."

Susan pressed her hands, and a shadow of worry passed over her face. "I'll speak to your father. I'll manage him."

Emily asked Ambrose to unlock the gate, and she strode onto the pavement of King Street. She breathed in the azalea fragrance and welcomed the damp kiss of the breeze on her face. In a plain skirt and stout shoes, she delighted in taking a long stride, and to confuse anyone who might be watching her, she made her way to the Battery.

How could she find the spot where she and Joshua had stood when the railing looked the same wherever it had been erected? The wind skated over the water, bringing the smell of salt and fish and rot. She remembered the promise that Joshua had made to her, and hers to him. His voice, his expression, and the touch of his fingers were hers forever, even though the letters were ash.

She straightened her shoulders and turned to find Tradd Street.

Sophy came to the gate. Her face gave her away before she spoke. She whispered, "Go away, Miss Emily."

She didn't speak. She dropped her eyes. Emily reached through the gate to touch her arm, and she drew back.

"Sophy," Emily said softly. "Did my father come here?"

Sophy shook her head.

"Or was it his agent? A man in a checked coat?"

Sophy didn't reply.

"What did he say? What did he do?"

Sophy cast her eyes down and didn't reply.

"He threatened you, didn't he?"

Sophy remained silent.

"What was it? Was it the Work House?" And suddenly she knew. "Or was it that my father would sell you?"

Startled, Sophy raised her eyes. But when she spoke it was so softly that Emily could barely hear her. "Can't say, miss."

Emily reached through the ironwork, hoping to touch Sophy's arm or even to take her hand, but Sophy pulled away. Emily bent close and whispered, "Sophy, please. Tell me. Where is she?"

Sophy raised her head and let Emily see her fear for Caro. She whispered, "I don't know a thing, Miss Emily, and you shouldn't, either."

She couldn't stay. It was one thing to risk her own punishment; that was hers to choose and hers to bear. But she could not jeopardize Sophy. Just as softly, she whispered back, "Take care, Sophy."

❧❦

EMILY TURNED AND WALKED slowly to Queen Street. She hoped that Thomas Bennett kept a workman's hours there rather than a planter's. His door was locked, but he was within. He unlocked the door and said to her, "Miss Jarvie. I'm not open for business yet."

"I'm sorry to trouble you. May I speak to you for a moment?"

"Are you here on your father's account?" His tone cooled.

"My father doesn't know I'm here. Has my father's agent been to see you?"

"His slave catcher? Yes, he has. He demanded that I tell him where Caro was, and when I told him I didn't now, he threatened to have me arrested."

"Arrested? Whatever for?"

"Miss Jarvie, have you looked around you? The Guardsmen patrol the streets day and night. They arrest anyone they please, brown or black, slave or free. Yesterday, outside my door, I saw a man arrested for not doffing his hat to a Guardsman."

"Why?"

He said bitterly, "Why not? It seems that a man of color can offer insult by walking down the street and minding his own business."

"I'm sorry," she whispered.

Thomas Bennett's voice became icy. "I couldn't help your father's *agent*, and I'm afraid I can't help you, either, Miss Jarvie. I have no idea where Caroline is, and no threat will alter my ignorance."

"Is your nephew here?"

Thomas Bennett said, "Please leave him alone, Miss Jarvie."

She was wrong to think that a free person of color in

Charleston would not be in jeopardy. "I'm sorry to have troubled you," she said.

Thomas Bennett swiftly shut the door and locked it again.

❧❧

CARO ADJUSTED TO THE ODDITY of her new circumstances. If Sunday was out, she obeyed him and stayed quiet in the house, not moving much, not lighting the fire. She settled in the armchair in the parlor and tried to read Mr. Douglass's life story. His early life—the loss of his grandmother, then his mother—refreshed her own grief, which wearied her so much that she climbed the stairs to lie down. She lay on her bed, too exhausted to move or plan.

I can't stay here, she thought. *But I don't know where else I might go.* Douglass's journey as a fugitive seemed impossible to her.

She missed Sophy and worried about her. Sunday was cagey about Sophy, as he was about everything outside her hiding place. But one day he came home with a bundle made from an old sheet, which he handed to Caro.

"What is it?" she asked.

"It's from Sophy."

"You saw her? How is she?"

"She all right. She give me this for you. Open it."

Caro laid the bundle on the dining room table and untied the knot. "Oh, my shawl!" she said, shaking it out, pleased through her worry. "And my best dress!" Her eyes stung as she remembered the day that Danny had brought her Uncle Thomas's gift. The yellow roses seemed to glow in the light of the dining room. "And my boots! I hope she didn't buy me another pair."

Sunday forced a smile. "No, she said to tell you special that they your own. Dulcie take them away from Bel, since her feet too fat for them, and Dulcie give them back to Sophy for you."

Sunday said, "And there's something else, too." He reached into his pocket and withdrew another bundle, the size of a man's handkerchief.

"What's that?"

"Your money that you had under your bed. Sophy guard it for you, and now she want you to have it."

"But there's so much less of it."

Sunday nodded. "I take all them little coins you have, them nickels and dimes, and I go to the bank and ask for ten-dollar silver coins instead." He hefted the handkerchief. "Easier to hide."

"Why, Sunday?"

His good cheer faded.

She pressed him. "What else did Sophy tell you?"

"You right, Miss Caroline."

She grabbed his arm. "What is it?"

"Mr. Jarvie hire someone to search for you."

Caro stared at the money in the handkerchief. She thought, *Easier to flee with.*

ΩΩ

ALONE IN THE HOUSE, CARO SMOOTHED the gray windowpane dress with its yellow roses and pagoda sleeves and slipped it over her head. She struggled to reach the back buttons by herself, thinking sadly of the times that Sophy or her mother had buttoned them for her. She sat on the edge of the bed to put on the boots. Those buttons were easy to reach, and once they were done, she admired the sight of her feet, glad that they were daintier than Bel's.

Even though she had no mirror, she took pleasure in the pattern of the cloth across her lap. She thought of the day that Danny had brought her this dress, and the day that he had blushed and stammered to see her in it. She had worn this dress on the day he kissed her, and the sight of the roses brought back every pleasure of that day: the acrobats, the marching band, and even the peculiar food. How odd that recalling the taste of pickled cabbage would make her feel so glad.

The dress reminded her of the life she had lived before Lawrence Jarvie had reclaimed her as a slave and hastened her mother's death with a stay in the Work House. She smoothed the pattern of gray squares and yellow roses and let them summon the self that had taken pride in the money she earned "with her own hand." Who had fallen in love with a free man of color and had felt like his equal. Who had believed that her beloved could marry her and that nothing would keep them apart.

She remembered what it had felt like to be free.

She had always prided herself on being her father's daughter, the clever girl who could translate from the Latin and take apart an argument the way that a good cook could dismember a chicken. She had tried for weeks to read the life of Frederick Douglass to teach herself to feel free. With an ache in her heart, she realized that she was her mother's daughter, too, half a slave and half a lady.

For the first time since her father died, for the first time since her mother died, she knew that they would always be with her. They would remain close to her in spirit, urging her toward a life of freedom. Part of freedom was being able to read Cicero, who had hated tyranny. And part of freedom was standing tall in a dress with pagoda sleeves. She let the tears fall, and for the first time since her mother's death, the agony was laced with a sadness that twined together the bitter and the sweet.

∞ Q

Sunday, who wanted to reassure her, was obviously worried. He brushed it off when she asked him what bothered him. But one afternoon, when she lay on her bed in a doze, he returned early, accompanied by his friend Lewis. Their voices drifted up the stairs to her bedroom, rousing her.

Sunday said, "It blow over, like it always do."

"Never seen it like this," Lewis said, his deep voice resonant even at a low volume.

Alarmed, she sat up and dispensed without making herself look presentable. If there was trouble, it didn't matter whether her hair was mussed and her dress wrinkled. She ran down the stairs and found them at the dining room table.

"What's wrong?" she asked, her heart pounding.

"Miss Caro, did we wake you?" Sunday asked in apology.

"I was awake. What's the matter, Sunday? What's happening?"

Sunday said, "Some trouble in Charleston. Nothing to worry you here, Caro."

Lewis glanced at Sunday. Caro said, "I'm not a child. I'm not a fool. I'm in trouble myself. I think I should know."

"The Guard arrest some people. That business about the badges again," Sunday said.

Lewis said, "Some! They act like they gone mad. Arrest dozens of people a day. Slave. Free. For not having badges. For not paying capitation tax that free colored people pay. For not taking off they hats in respect or for sassing the Guardsman in the street. Jail and Work House must be full to bursting."

She said, "Is it about hiring out, like last time?"

Sunday said, "That start it. But it about more than that now."

"No black man or woman safe," Lewis said. "Not just anyone who live out or hire out. Free men, like me." He pressed his hands against the edge of the table.

"A Guardsman come up to me and demand to see my badge. When I tell him I free, he threaten to arrest me. He tell me I better get a badge." He looked disgusted. "Free man, born of a free mama, and to walk down the street in Charleston, I need to find a white man to say he my master and buy a badge for me, and then I wear it around my neck!"

Sunday tried to soothe. "We see it before. It pass, like it always do."

Lewis glared at him. "I hear that free colored people rush to City Hall to buy badges for themselves. Hope that having a badge mean that the Guard let them alone."

Caro thought of the proud, educated, well-to-do families like the Bennetts and the Pereiras. Had they joined the panicked throng at City Hall? Or were they sure enough, and angry enough, to refuse to act like slaves?

Caro stared at her hands. She said, "I can't stay here, Sunday."

Sunday tried to compose himself. "You all right up here in the Neck. You know the Guard don't come up here. We cluster around you, keep you safe."

Caro asked, "What about you? Are you safe?"

◈

BEFORE CARO DISAPPEARED, IT HAD been easy for Emily to find Danny Pereira. Now it was not. Not at the shop, where his uncle was so bitter toward the Jarvies, and not at Tradd Street, where Sophy had so much reason to be silent. Where did he live? She doubted that she would be allowed into his mother's house, but she might walk down the street in the hope of meeting him by chance.

Benjamin Pereira would know. But she hesitated, fearful that Pereira, for all his cordiality toward her, would retract his promise of confidentiality. Her father could not know that she sought Danny's whereabouts, the key to Caro's.

The city directory. The anonymous pages of the city directory. The Pereiras, free people of color, were likely to pay for a listing. If her father had a city directory, she didn't want to be found consulting it in his library. She would go to the post office, where they might have a copy, and they could assist her if they did not.

That morning, later than usual—the post office opened later in the day than the City Market—she told Ambrose that she was out for her daily exercise, and she walked to the handsome building on Broad Street that had once been the customs house. In the post office she was overwhelmed with longing for Joshua, since their love affair had always been epistolary. What an odd thing, to feel a rush of love at the thought of a stamp and the sight of the postmaster's window where the letters where handed over.

As she turned to ask the clerk about the city directory, she saw Danny Pereira. He stood a few feet away, a sheaf of envelopes in his hand, a look of weariness smirching his handsome face.

She approached him and said quietly, "May I talk to you?"

"I have nothing to say to you, Miss Jarvie."

"For a moment. Not more."

"After what your family has done to mine, I don't wish to speak to you at all."

She said, "I'm very sorry that my father threatened your uncle."

"That was bad enough," he said. "But it was much worse of him to take away his custom and to tell his friends to do the same."

"I had no idea," she said.

"Our business has dwindled to nothing." He brandished the letters in his hand. "We'll never collect on these debts. And at such a moment! When feeling against free men of color is running so high."

"I'm sorry," she said.

"When we close up shop and move to Canada, you can regret it all you like."

He sounds just like Joshua, she thought. "It's shameful," she said.

He began to turn away.

"Danny," she said, her voice very low. "Have you seen her?"

His face crumpled, and for all his elegance, for all his polish, he looked like a little boy trying not to cry. "I can't tell you," he said.

"Do you know where she is?"

He didn't reply. He turned his back to her, a rudeness even if he were white, but she forgave him. She knew that he was ashamed for her to see the tears trickling down his face.

☙❧

SUNDAY DIDN'T COME HOME AT his usual time. Caro tried to reassure herself the way he would reassure her. He was late working on a job. Perhaps he had gone to see Sophy and decided to stay with her. But the evening lengthened, and the sun went down, and the hour of curfew approached. The Neck had no curfew, as it had no interference from the Guard. But anyone who walked home across Calhoun Street had to worry about the curfew.

She knew she wouldn't be able to sleep. She didn't dare to light a candle to reveal her own presence in the house. She sat in the front room, far from the window, in the dark, straining for the sound of Sunday's footsteps on the porch, for the sound of a key in the lock, for the sound of his hand on the doorknob.

At the sound of a knock on the door, she thought, *He's been caught, and now they've come for me.*

But it was Mrs. Harris. Caro opened the door, and Mrs. Harris hurried inside. She said, "Mr. Desmond don't come home yet."

Caro said, "I thought he might be with Sophy."

She looked grim. "No, he tell you if he intend that because he don't want you to worry."

They stood together in the darkened house, both of them thinking the worst, neither of them willing to say it.

"I sit with you," Mrs. Harris said, in a tone that brooked no contradiction, and they sat in the front room on the edge of their chairs, listening for the sounds of Sunday's return. Neither spoke. Caro clenched her hands in her lap. She had never been so afraid, not even when she thought Lawrence Jarvie would sell her.

If Lawrence Jarvie's man caught her, he would do worse than sell her.

When the key turned in the lock, she stared at the door in terror. The door opened, and Sunday quickly came into the house. He was hatless and his shirt was torn. His cheek was bruised and puffy from a blow.

"Sunday!" Caro sobbed, throwing her arms around him.

He said, "Caro, sugar, be gentle, they bruise me about the ribs." Caro let go.

Mrs. Harris cried, "What happen to you?"

"The Guard arrest me."

"Why? What for?" Caro cried.

"Say my badge ain't right. Don't listen to reason about it. Beat me with they damned clubs and drag me off to the Work House."

Caro stared at Sunday in horror.

"Lewis, he was right. The place full to bursting. My massa come to bail me out, and he mighty mad. Not at me. At the Guard. Tell them they crazy to bother decent black folks going about they business."

"You've always said it will blow over."

"Never seen it like this. Heard talk of secesh all my life, and never paid it much mind. Now I do. All of South Carolina itching for a fight. Smell it in the air, like a thunderstorm coming."

"Sunday, I can't stay here. I have to go."

Sunday was angry about his mistreatment, but he raised his voice to her. "Where you go? How you get there? You think they sell a runaway a ticket on a steamer?"

She thought of Douglass's flight. "Somehow, Sunday."

He glared at her. "You stay put. You lay low. I promise you I shelter you, and I do it."

᪥᪣

SEVERAL DAYS LATER, AS CARO SAT in the parlor, her copy of Douglass's book facedown in her lap, her eyes closing in the heat of late afternoon, she was startled wide awake by the knock on the door. She retreated to her vantage point in the parlor to see who it was.

Danny Pereira stood on the front steps.

She ran to the door. Opening it, she whispered, "Come in, and quickly." He hastened inside.

"How did you find me?" she asked, still breathless with fear.

He looked haggard, as Sunday did these days. No longer blithe, he looked older. He looked like a grown man. He said, "Sophy told me."

"Does anyone else know where I am?"

He shook his head. "I haven't told anyone else."

"Why did you come here?"

The grown man's mask cracked and fell away. He looked as hurt as a boy. "Because I couldn't bear it any longer. Not seeing you."

She stared at him, remembering what it felt like to love him, trying to push it away. She said, "Come into the parlor. We'll sit where no one can see us from the street."

She sat in her usual chair and gestured to him to take the chair opposite. For a moment, it was as though he had come to call.

Awkwardly, he asked, "Are you all right?"

She laughed, a bitter sound. "No one beats me or starves me," she said. "But I worry every moment about seeing the runaway notice and hearing the slave catcher's knock on the door." She wondered if he knew about the slave catcher, but he said nothing. "And you? How are you?"

"Haven't you heard?" he asked.

"About the trouble? The harassment and the arrests? Of course I have." She added bitterly, "Sunday Desmond was arrested."

"About the badges?"

She thought, *He's free, and all he can worry about is the shame of wearing a badge stamped with the word* slave. "Sunday tells me that free people of color rush to buy badges for protection." She glanced at his shirt front. The fine Sea Island cotton was badly wrinkled in the heat. "I don't see you wearing one."

419

"No." He rubbed the sweat from his face with his sleeve. "As though it would help us."

Alarmed, she asked, "Why? What's happened? Who's been arrested?"

"Uncle Thomas's business is ruined. No one will patronize a free man of color. Or pay him, either."

"What will you do?"

"I don't know. I can't make a living in Charleston. I can't even walk down the street. I dread that I'll be arrested next. My mother dreads it, too."

She stared at him in shock. "Surely Mr. Pereira would help you, if you asked."

"No one will help us. Our white friends have deserted us. They don't care if we wear badges, or go to the Work House, or end up at the Slave Mart." His tone was cold and bitter. "We're black. That's all that matters. They think that every black man should be a slave."

She laughed, sounding bitter, too. "You could go into hiding, like me."

He looked up. Today his eyes were so dark that they were nearly black, the iris shading into the pupil. "We're thinking of leaving. Leaving Charleston and leaving South Carolina."

"Where would you go?"

"North."

Douglass's path. She leaned forward. "Take me with you."

He held her gaze but didn't reply.

"If we went north together, I'd be free," she said, her

voice eager. "We could get married. Nothing could stand in the way."

"Caro," he said, a low groan.

"Honorably married, as we hoped for."

He looked away.

She said, "Do you remember? Telling me that nothing would keep us apart? That there must be a way for us to be together?"

"As though I could forget," he said, a sound like a sob.

"This is the way." She reached for his hand. "Danny, look at me." Those odd eyes, black with worry and hurt. "In my heart, I've always been your wife," she whispered.

He closed his hand over hers, and at the familiar feeling of the needle-pricked fingers, warmth seeped through her body.

He whispered back, "I know."

"Let me be your wife. Take me with you."

He rose and pulled her toward him. He kissed her, his lips still soft, his breath still sweet, and in his embrace, she set aside her worry and her fear. She pressed herself against him, feeling his desire against her belly, letting him feel her desire in return. She whispered, "Let me be your wife now."

He kissed her cheek and released her. With a sigh, he said, "Not like this. With honor, once you're free."

They stood with hands clasped. Very softly, he said, "I'll come back."

"Soon."

He let go of her hands. "Soon."

At the door, she found a voice that had gone into hiding with her. It was the voice of Miss Sass. "Don't get arrested," Miss Sass teased.

Despite all his worry, he knew it was a tease and laughed as she closed the door behind him.

ℰℭ

EMILY SAT IN THE BACK PARLOR with her stepmother, the picture of quiet, but she seethed with worry. In a city where any person of color could be arrested and sold into slavery, Caro was lost, and Emily had no way to find her.

Should she go back to Sophy, despite the danger for Sophy? Should she retrace her steps to Thomas Bennett? If she found Danny Pereira, would he tell her? Perhaps she should throw caution to the wind and visit Benjamin Pereira.

Perhaps she should hire her own slave catcher to find Caro so that she could find her to help her flee.

She laughed, an unladylike snort. Susan asked her, "What was that about?"

"Something I read this morning."

"What was it?"

"In the *Mercury*. If I find it, I'll show you."

Susan said, "There's nothing entertaining in the *Mercury*. Is something bothering you?"

She said, "I'm really getting married. A touch of nerves." She smiled at her stepmother, the demure girl's smile. "Nothing to bring the doctor for."

Susan rose and enfolded her in an embrace. "It's all

right, Emily. All brides have nerves. He loves you, and he'll make it easy for you."

The thought of her wedding night with John Ellison made her nerves shiver. She stayed in Susan's embrace long enough to reassure her stepmother. She said, "I believe I need some air. I'm going out for a bit of exercise."

"In this heat?" Susan asked.

"It won't be cool again until October, Mother."

"Emily, don't worry about getting married." Susan reached out to touch Emily's cheek. She searched Emily's face. "You do love him, don't you?"

Emily covered her stepmother's hand with her own. "When you married my father, did you love him?" she said softly.

Susan let her hand slip away. She looked thoughtful and said nothing.

Outside, it was worse than hot. It was chokingly hot. After a few paces, her face was beaded with sweat, and by the end of the block, she felt sweat trickle down her sides and soak into her corset.

She had no destination in mind, but she wandered toward Queen Street. She wondered if Thomas Bennett's shop was shuttered and if he or his nephew still came there. Queen Street, home to many shops that catered to planters and their families, was not busy at this time of day. The shops that were open were drowsy in the late afternoon heat.

She stopped before the familiar glass window, still emblazoned with *T. Bennett, Tailor* and peered inside.

No customer graced the elegant front room; no one sat at the dainty table or leaned on the mahogany counter. But behind the counter sat Danny Pereira, sealing a letter.

She pushed open the door, and at the sound of the bell, he looked up. "Miss Jarvie," he said, in an icy tone that echoed his uncle's.

"Are you open for business?"

"Not for long. What is it, Miss Jarvie?"

"Danny, please."

He laid the letter on the counter. "I don't know if I can help you."

"Where is she, Danny?"

He was silent.

"Tell me. I want to find her before the slave catcher does."

He said, "Why should I trust you? To find her yourself and not to tell your father's slave catcher?"

She leaned against the counter, dizzy in the heat. She said fiercely, "Because she is my cousin. And because I love her. If you have any love for her, let me find her and help her."

He looked up. Met her eyes. She had never looked so intently into a black man's eyes. He said, "I can't."

∞CR

CARO HAD BEEN WILD WITH impatience since Danny's visit.

Sunday said, "Settle down. You make me dizzy." She couldn't.

When Sunday was gone, she put on her good dress and her lady's boots and hefted the silver bound in the handkerchief. She could pay her own way, whether they took the train or the steamer.

Soon, he had said.

The knock on the door came in the afternoon's hush, when Line Street was at its quietest, working people away at their work, women and children at home resting in the heat. Line Street enlivened after six o'clock, when men and women came home from their work laden with eggs and greens and, if they were lucky, shrimp for dinner. Not even the trouble in Charleston had broken the rhythm of the day on Line Street.

It was Danny, and she flew to the door let him in. He looked worse than before, his eyes dark-circled with lack of sleep. He wore no frock coat in this heat, only his sweaty shirt, and his hair was disheveled as though he had been running his hands through it.

"What's wrong?" she asked.

He said, "The Guard came—"

"For you?"

"For our neighbors down the street. Free, like us. Last night. Dragged them down to the Work House."

"Why?"

His voice rose and his cheeks flushed. "Do you need to ask?"

"How are they?"

"In jail. And if no one bails them out, they go to auction."

Caro felt dizzy. She had never thought that the crisis would come to this. She had always believed that people like the Pereiras and the Bennetts, with their wealth and their reputation, would stay safe. Would stay free.

Danny said, "We're leaving."

"When?"

"As soon as we can buy a steamer ticket."

She reached for his hands. "I can be ready in a moment. I have so little to pack."

His hands remained at his sides. He said dully, "Caro, we can't take you with us."

"Why not?"

In despair, he said, "We can scarcely get out ourselves. We spent the day trying to find an agency that would sell us tickets. They think that every colored person is a fugitive."

"But you're not," she said.

"We can't risk taking a fugitive slave with us. We'd be found out and arrested. And all of us would go into the Work House. We'd all be slaves together."

"But you have papers to prove you're free. And I could hide somehow."

"I have my mother to take care of. My brothers. We can't risk it. We can't take you with us."

She reached out her arms and cried, "Don't you love me?"

He blanched. He said, "God help me. I do."

As he left, she stood with her arms still outstretched, too stunned to lock the door behind him.

❧❦

CARO TOLD SUNDAY THAT SHE didn't feel well and that she didn't want any supper. She lay on the bed in her white-walled room, still hot early in the evening. She was too shocked to cry.

What a fool she had been to hope that Danny Pereira would free her.

No one would free her—not her father, not her uncle, not her cousin Emily, not her cousin Danny. The bonds of servitude wrapped tighter and tighter around her.

If she stayed where she was, Lawrence Jarvie would find her. He would send her to the Work House. He would likely sell her. She would join a coffle bound for the cotton fields of Mississippi or Louisiana, where slavery was a prison of heavy labor and punishment until death stole a slave away.

Or she would end up in a different kind of prison, the subject of a white man's fancy, whether in Charleston or Natchez or New Orleans. Her mother's fate, without the guarantee of her father's affection.

She was alone in the world, with no one to help her and no one to stop her.

❧❦

AMBROSE PASSED EMILY IN THE hallway and bent to whisper to her, "I have something for you."

"What is it?"

Since her father had threatened him, Ambrose had become secretive. He slipped it into her hand. "Come this morning."

The envelope was blank. The paper inside had no date, no salutation, and no signature. It bore only an address.

She tore the paper into tiny, undecipherable pieces and handed them to Ambrose. "Would you burn that trash for me?"

"Yes, miss."

Do nothing unusual, she thought. Asking Henry for the carriage was unusual for her, as was taking a hired carriage. A walk was not. She told her stepmother that she would linger after her walk today to stop on Queen Street. "I need a new pair of gloves," she fibbed.

Susan said only, "Well, wear your bonnet and carry a parasol against the sun, or you'll get a headache."

She took Meeting Street, which ran due north, keeping her pace leisurely. It was more heavily traveled than King Street, and she would be less noticeable in the crowd. She had never gone past Calhoun Street on foot. North of Calhoun Street, the sight of a white woman on foot was not unusual. The women of the Neck, white as well as black, traveled that way.

She wished that she had brought her sketchbook. Whatever she observed, she thought of Joshua and how she would tell him about it.

She realized that the slave catcher might follow her. She scanned the crowd for the curling whiskers, the top hat, the frock coat. She turned to look behind her. She saw no one she knew, no one she could identify. Should she muddy the trail? Walk out of her way? She scanned the crowd again, and a stranger stared at her for her rudeness.

Emily wiped her face with her handkerchief and turned from Meeting Street onto Line Street.

Before the house she hesitated. She glanced up and down the street, but it was quiet, save for a couple of little boys who carried a pail of water. She mounted the steps and knocked on the door.

She waited, but no one answered. Had she gotten the address wrong? Or was Caro already gone? She began to feel a gnawing fear.

The door was unlocked by a cautious hand and opened only a little to admit a cautious eye.

An uncautious gasp floated through the opening.

"May I come in?" Emily asked.

The door opened, and Caro beckoned her inside. She locked the door and stared Emily up and down. "Why are you here?" she asked.

Caro looked less gaunt, but her eyes were reddened, and her cheeks were drawn. *Still grieving*, Emily thought, remembering James Jarvie's beautiful, stricken daughter in her fine black silk.

Emily said, "Because I've missed you."

"Missed me?" Caro said, her tone derisive.

Emily heard how foolish it sounded.

"Would you miss me if I went to the Work House?

Would you miss me if I were bound into a coffle for Mississippi?"

"I was in terror that I wouldn't find you before my father did."

"Will he find me?"

"Not if I can help it."

"I don't think you can," Caro said quietly. This wasn't Miss Sass. However quiet, this was defiance. Caro said, "Do you know what's happening to the colored people of Charleston?"

"Yes, I do," Emily said, her tone as quiet as Caro's.

"The Pereiras are gone," Caro said. "Afraid for their freedom."

"He didn't take you with him," Emily said.

"No, he did not."

"I'm so sorry, Caro."

Caro said, "Don't be." But the shell cracked a little as the choked note came into her voice.

"What does it matter?" Emily asked, defiance seeping into her voice, too. "A love lost? A love affair broken? For either of us?"

Caro took a deep breath. She asked, "Would you like a glass of water?"

The house was small enough that Emily could hear the clink of the glass, the gurgle of the water from the pitcher, and the stifled sob. Caro returned with the glass, and Emily drank deeply, with no ladylike pretense, and set the glass down. "I'm getting married," she said.

"I heard. To a Mr. Ellison of Sumter County. A cotton planter. How many slaves does he have, Emily?"

"One would be too many." Emily brushed her cheeks with her hands, ashamed of the way her eyes were misting. "My father brought a madhouse doctor from the asylum in Columbia to declare me mad unless I agreed to marry Mr. Ellison." She stared at her hands, which were clenched in her lap. "I can't bear it. I can't do it. And I don't know how I can escape it."

Caro leaned forward. "I do."

"How?"

Caro reached for Emily's hands. "Two fugitives together," she said.

Chapter 17: The Northern Star

Do nothing unusual, Emily reminded herself, as she left the house to visit Benjamin Pereira at his office. She certainly could go to the Bank of Charleston and withdraw any sum of her money. But they had never seen her before, and if anyone asked, they would remember her.

"Miss Jarvie," Pereira said, sending his light-complected office boy to bring a cup of tea and some sesame wafers. "What can I do for you?"

Emily had dressed carefully for this visit in a new dress of blue flowers on a white background. The sleeves were ornate enough to make a dressmaker mad. The dressmaker had trimmed the new bonnet with a matching ribbon in the same azure color. She said, "Mr. Pereira, I've done a foolish thing, and I need your help."

He laughed. "Surely you haven't struck someone in a drunken brawl or contracted a debt of honor. What it could it possibly be, Miss Jarvie?"

"I've run up such a bill at my dressmaker's," she said, lifting her arm prettily to let him see the fussy sleeve. "More than my father allows me."

"I don't think your papa would begrudge you a few dollars at the dressmaker's."

"But I'm getting ready for my wedding, Mr. Pereira, and there's been quite an expense already for the trousseau. I hate to ask him for more. So extravagant!" She disliked the tone in her voice, the one that Camilla Aiken used to fool her suitors into thinking she was a ninny.

"How much is this extravagance, Miss Jarvie?"

"I shudder to think of it. Nearly two hundred dollars."

He laughed again. "Compared to a gambling debt, it's a bargain," he said.

"Don't laugh at me, Mr. Pereira. I feel awful about it."

"How can I help you?"

"If you could help me withdraw my money from the bank—discreetly, so my father doesn't find out—I'd be in your debt, Mr. Pereira."

"I see," said Benjamin Pereira. "Would you like a draft in your dressmaker's name?"

"Oh no," Emily said. "My dressmaker prefers cash. In coin, and it might as well be in large denominations, since it will go right from my hands to hers."

"That's no difficulty, Miss Jarvie."

"Thank you so much, Mr. Pereira."

Two days later, summoned by his note to her, she returned. He handed her a small canvas bag. "I withdrew all but a few dollars for you, to keep the account open," he said.

She hefted the bag. The coins made a dull chime. "How much was it, in all?"

"Two hundred dollars. That's a lot of dressmaking, Miss Jarvie."

"I know." She made a rueful face. "I've learned my lesson. I'll never be so extravagant again."

Pereira regarded her with his keen azure eyes. He said, "Miss Jarvie, I believe you're foxing me, as my daughter likes to say."

Emily kept up her pretense. "Why would I?"

He dropped his voice. "If you told me what this is really about, I might be able to help you more," he said.

She replied, "If I don't tell you, you can say that you didn't know."

𝕤𝕠𝕔𝕢

When Caro told Sunday of her intention to leave, he said, "It too dangerous."

She said, "And to stay? What of that?"

Mrs. Harris, who had briefly been a servant to a woman who put on amateur theatricals, said to Caro, "You need to disguise your looks. Dress different. Talk different."

Caro fell silent, as though she were taking in this piece of advice. She dropped her head, hunched her shoulders, and let her hands hang loosely by her sides. She shuffled her feet and took the smallest of steps, as though her joints hurt. When she stood up again, she said, in the heaviest Gullah Low Country accent, "Like dat? Like my rheumatiz bodder me somet'ing awful? Just like dat?"

Mrs. Harris laughed. "Yes, like dat," she said. "You do better not to talk at all. Not to call attention." She gave Caro an appraising look.

Caro said, "Stop that. You aren't selling me."

"No. Figuring how to rough you up, hide that pretty light face of yours."

"Smear me with dirt?"

"Coffee," Mrs. Harris said. "Put the grounds on your face, soak your hands in the brew."

Caro began to laugh. "Coffee to make me black!"

They experimented, and while Caro would never be dark brown, the coffee turned her from ivory to tan. Mrs. Harris said, "That help you a lot. Not so pretty."

Sunday looked askance at their efforts. "Never saw a light-skinned woman turn herself dark," he said.

Her face was covered with coffee grounds, Caro said, "You know it isn't for beauty's sake, Sunday."

"You all wrought up," he said. "Giddy. Got to calm down. Otherwise you act wrong, someone notice, you get found out."

Caro sobered. She asked Sunday, "Can I say goodbye to Sophy before I go?"

"Wouldn't let you go without it," he said, his voice full of regret.

§∞CR

IN THE SECRECY OF HER ROOM, Emily slipped the money into her reticule: a half dozen silver coins from her hoard of twenty. Cabin passage on a steamer was fifteen dollars and a servant's ticket ten, but she had never forgotten the lesson of the Work House, where the right silver coin helped a Guardsman to look the other way.

She strolled to the agency office on East Bay Street, close by the docks where the great ships arrived and departed. The smell of the sea was strong on East Bay, briny and rotten. She pushed open the agency office door.

At the counter stood a man of color, well-dressed in a frock coat and a beaver hat. Behind him huddled his wife, light-skinned and bonneted. A half-grown girl in a white lawn dress pressed close to her; a little boy clung to her skirt; another child, in the long dress of a baby, hid its face against her shoulder.

The well-dressed man, whose fist was curled on the counter, said to the agent, "Sir, it's urgent. We must have passage on the next steamer to Philadelphia!"

In an agitated tone, the agent said, "I can't sell you a ticket unless you can prove to me that you're free."

"Sir, we're well-known as free persons of color. I have no such papers."

"Then I can't sell you a ticket."

The man struck the counter with his fist. "Sir, I implore you! We have the money. What will it cost us?"

The agent said, "If you can't act civil, I'll have you thrown out."

The half-grown girl began to cry, and the little boy joined her. The bonneted woman, whose arms were burdened by the baby, began to sob, too.

The agent said, "Get out of here, all of you. I can't have you bawling in the office."

As they left, Emily asked the ticket agent, "Why won't you sell them a ticket?"

He glared at her. "Do you know how much trouble I've had with fugitives running away?"

Emily leaned against the counter to control her trembling. She said, "I've come here to buy a ticket for the next steamer leaving for Philadelphia."

"Just you?"

"And my maidservant."

"How do I know she ain't a fugitive?"

Emily forced herself to laugh. Camilla Aiken's laugh. "I never heard of slaves having to prove they were slaves," she said. "You'll have to take my word for it."

"It's on my head if I sell a ticket to a runaway. Do you have anything better than your word?"

Emily opened her reticule and slid one of the shiny ten-dollar coins onto the counter. "Does that help?"

He glanced at the coin and made no move to take it. She pulled another coin from her reticule and laid it on the counter so that the reverse, the figure of Lady Liberty, was visible. He swept both coins from the counter and put them into his pocket. He said, "Do you want her in the servants' quarters or will she berth with you?"

"With me."

"That will be the full fare. Fifteen dollars each."

Shaking, Emily exchanged the coins for the two slips

of pasteboard. Still shaking, she slipped them into her reticule. As though he had been courteous to her, she smiled and said, "Thank you, sir."

୫ଓ୯୫

SUNDAY BROUGHT WORD OF THE departure date, and very early in the morning, before sunrise, Lewis drove his wagon into the side yard. Inside, shielded from view, Caro stood with Sunday. He said, "Time for you to go."

She clasped his hands. "Thank you, Sunday. You kept your promise. You sheltered me."

He enfolded her in a rough, fatherly grip. "Miss Caro. Miss Sass." He stroked her hair as though she were a child. He whispered, "You stay safe. You get free." When he let her go, his eyes were wet with tears.

She pressed her hand to her own eyes as she ran down the stairs toward the wagon. Lewis lifted her up. She wedged herself and her bundle into the wagon bed, which was full of boards today, a plausible delivery. The smell of the wood was pleasant, even if the boards made for a narrow berth.

"Let's go, Mose!" Lewis called to the horse, and the wagon began to move slowly south, to Charleston.

This time she knew not to panic in the canvas-induced dusk deepened by the predawn darkness. She rested her head on the bundle that held her good dress and shawl and patted the smaller bundle, the coins tightly tied together to keep them from making a sound in her pocket. She felt oddly calm. *I may be godless*, she thought, addressing her thoughts to Sophy as though she were in the wagon, *but it's in God's hands now, not mine.*

By the time the gate at the Tradd Street house whined and opened, Caro was so relaxed that she had begun to doze. The jolt of the wagon woke her. She heard Sophy's voice scolding Lewis in her worry. "You brought that delivery?" As the canvas was peeled away, her calm deserted her, and she sat up with a start.

Lewis extended his hand to help her from the wagon, but she clambered out by herself. Sophy embraced her and held her at arm's length, scrutinizing the disguise.

"How do I look?" Caro asked. "Less like myself?"

"Pull your scarf down low and wear your shawl high up. And keep your head down, too. Don't let anyone look you in the face."

Caro nodded. "Is Emily here?"

"She in the kitchen."

"How is she?"

Sophy's eyes glittered. "Scared," she said. "She should be. And so should you."

"Not anymore," Caro said.

"Don't be a fool."

"I'm not."

Sophy took her hand and led her to the kitchen.

"Sophy, what is it? This isn't like you."

"I'm scared for you."

Emily sat at the kitchen table dressed in a plain gray dress. She started to her feet when she saw Caro. At her side was a carpetbag, the kind that genteel travelers without much money carried. Caro said, "Is that my old dress?"

"I'm pretending to be a widow who isn't rich. Am I all right?"

Caro nodded. "What are you calling yourself?"

"Mrs. Morris."

"What am I called?"

"You're my servant Annie. You don't mind? I thought it was a name that no one would remark on."

Caro pulled her kerchief so low that it covered her eyebrows. She dropped her head and murmured in her Low Country accent, "I be like a shadow, missus. No one see me at all."

Emily's laugh was a little ragged with nerves. "Don't overdo it," she said. She took a deep breath, but it didn't help her. She asked Caro, "Aren't you afraid?"

Caro reached for Emily's hand. "Courage," she said.

Emily squeezed Caro's hand and looked into her eyes. She breathed deeply again. "Courage," she said.

"How will we go?" Caro asked.

"I'll hire a carriage. It's safer."

Caro said, "I have money. Do you have yours?"

Emily nodded. "I brought something else," she said. "What is it?"

Emily pulled a small velvet bag from her pocket. She opened it and let the earbobs spill into her palm. "Your mother's earrings," she said. "The ones my stepmother took from her."

Caro closed her eyes against the memory.

Emily said, "They belong to you."

Caro opened her eyes but didn't reply. Emily pressed them into her hand. "Take them," she said.

Caro stared at the diamonds, bright in the early morning darkness. She curled her hand into a fist, and she put her fist into her pocket.

ಬಂ

THE CARRIAGE LET THEM OFF at Adger's Wharf just as the sun was beginning to rise. When the driver handed them out, a muscular black man asked them, "Does you have a trunk, ma'am? I carry it for you."

Caro said, careful to use her Low Country accent, "I help missus."

The man looked askance at the carpetbag, as though he had never seen a white lady travel with so little. Emily, playing the lady, took Caro's arm. "Come along, Annie," she said, pretending to be severe. "The agent told us to be there early."

Along the dock, Caro whispered, "Should have tried to manage a trunk."

Emily whispered back in irritation, "A trunk? How would I have smuggled a trunk from King Street?"

Caro began to feel afraid. *What else have we done wrong?* she thought.

They hesitated on the dock. Emily stared at their boat, the *James Adger*, named after the family that had also named the wharf. In dismay, she said to Caro, "I thought it would be bigger. I thought we could disappear on it."

"How many passengers?"

"I don't know."

As they waited, the crowd grew: white families, surrounded by trunks and servants; groups of white men, with neither. Caro saw no well-dressed people of color. She wondered if the Pereiras had gotten to Philadelphia safely.

Emily scanned the faces. She whispered to Caro, "What if I see someone I know?"

Caro whispered back, "Do you?"

"No. They're all strangers."

Caro ached with impatience to board the ship and disappear into their cabin. She hoped that they could stay there. She felt more and more exposed as they waited.

A man in a dark-blue frock coat made his way through the crowd to stand on the gangway. He raised his voice. "Ready to board," he said. "Have your tickets out."

The passengers formed a ragged line, the servants carrying the trunks, and the sound of friendly chatter rose from the crowd. Emily pulled the tickets from her reticule and held them tightly in her gloved hand. She was pale and obviously nervous.

The woman behind them laid a hand on Emily's arm. Gray hair escaped from her bonnet. Age had crinkled the skin around her eyes, but she looked as though smiling had deepened the lines around her mouth. "What's the matter, my dear?" she asked Emily, in a Yankee accent.

"I've never taken a steamboat before."

"It's as safe as a carriage. There's nothing to worry about. Are you alone?"

"With my servant."

The friendly woman said, "It's all right. Two days, and you'll be in Philadelphia." She added, "I'm sure I'll see you in the ladies' cabin." Once her ticket had been handed over, she walked the gangway onto the boat.

Caro wished she could give Emily the advice that everyone had given her: *Keep your head down. Don't show off.*

The clerk said to Emily, "Tickets, ma'am."

Emily handed him the tickets. He said, "There's a space on the deck for your servant." He glanced at Caro, and her heart constricted in her chest.

Emily said, "I'd rather have her stay with me."

Caro dropped her eyes and wished she could pull her shawl over her face so that he would have nothing to remember if anyone asked. He asked Emily, "Do you have a trunk?"

"No, sir."

Caro thought in silent fury, *Why didn't you get Sophy to help you find a trunk? We're the only lady passengers on the boat without one! He'll remember that!*

But all the clerk said was, "Ma'am, if there's anything you need, for your convenience or your comfort, let me know. You can send any of the cabin boys for me."

Emily stepped carefully onto the gangway, and Caro followed her. Still raging, Caro reminded herself to keep her mouth shut and her head down.

ॐ

THE CABIN WAS SMALL AND SQUARE, most of the room taken up with the bed. The room also contained a dresser and two armchairs. Everything was plain. Emily set down the carpetbag. She said, "I thought it would be grander than this."

Caro sat wearily in one of the armchairs. "It doesn't need to be grand," she said, dropping her accent.

Emily hissed, "Keep your disguise!"

"Here? Who will know?"

Emily gestured toward the window, which could be fully opened to let in the sea air. "Anyone could hear us."

Irked, Caro made a point of her accent. She thought of Sophy, and Sophy's advice, as well as her diction, came out of her mouth. "Well, you stay in disguise, too, Missus Morris. Might be smart to lay low. Stay right here and not call attention to yourself instead of setting down to dinner and getting friendly with the first person who act kind to you."

Emily said fiercely, "If we stay in our cabin, they'll notice. We go out, we hide in plain sight."

"I won't."

"Yes, you will. I'm going to midday dinner, and so should you. Wherever the servants eat their dinner."

Caro stared at Emily, a new worry frothing up in her. "What happen, *Missus Morris*, when your family notice that you gone?"

Emily clenched her skirt in her hands hard enough to wrinkle the heavy cotton of her traveling dress. "I tell a tale. And I pray I tell it well enough that whoever asks will believe me."

Caro grabbed Emily's wrist. She was too upset to keep her accent. She said, "Then we spin that tale together, and neither of us goes anywhere until we can tell it as though it's the truth."

∞∞

BY MIDDAY, THE STEAMER HAD reached the open water of the sea, and with the movement of the ship, Emily had begun to feel peculiar, slightly nauseated and slightly dizzy. She opened the cabin door, which opened to a hallway that led to the salon. The smell of food, meat and potatoes fried in grease, made her feel even queasier. She hoped there would be a clear soup to eat.

One end of the salon had been set up as a sitting room, with sofas and chairs arranged for conversation, and the other, as a dining room, with several tables, each big enough to seat a party of eight. The furniture here, like the furniture in the cabin, was plain. The tablecloths were linen, but the fabric was coarse.

At one of the tables, the friendly woman from the ticket line was already seated. Her pleasant face broke into a smile at the sight of Emily. "Please, sit with me," she said.

Emily sat and they made their acquaintance. Her name was Mrs. Reynolds, and she was from West Chester in Chester County, Pennsylvania. She had been visiting a friend who had recently married a man of Charleston. Emily admitted that she had grown up in Charleston but had married a man from Kershaw County, who had left her a widow in straightened circumstances. She was going to stay with a distant cousin in Philadelphia, a Carolina girl married to a Yankee.

Mrs. Reynolds said, "I hope you don't hold it against her."

The lies pressed on Emily's chest, and her queasiness grew worse. "Of course not," she said, smiling.

A family with two children, a boy and a girl, also joined them. They were Pennsylvanians on their way home, and when they discovered that Mrs. Reynolds was a near neighbor, they asked after her acquaintance. It was a relief to Emily. Waiters brought soup, which had grown cold in its journey from the kitchen. To her surprise, the waiters were white men. Just after the soup arrived, a dapper whiskered gentleman in a frock coat, the color too loud for gentility, claimed the chair next to Emily's.

"Excuse me," he said.

The accent made her heart sink. She knew that voice, with its upcountry accent.

But he didn't blink an eye when the introductions were made. He told her that his name was Mr. McHenry and that he was a broker in Orangeburg County, but he had kin up North, and he liked to see them several times a year.

She went along with his fiction. "What do you broker, Mr. McHenry? Are you in cotton?"

"Mostly cotton, but I buy and sell whatever comes to hand," he said. "Livestock and corn, if that's all I can get."

She accepted his lies, as he accepted hers.

How had he found her? And unbidden came the memory of the ticket office, where the coins glittered on the counter. And what did he plan? She pushed that thought away.

As the rest of the meal appeared on the table, she felt too nauseated even to attempt it. She stayed at the table until the pie and the custard had been eaten, and she excused herself and rose. She walked slowly to the promenade, where she could lean against the railing and look at the sky and the sea. She was sure that fresh air would make her feel better.

Mrs. Reynolds followed her to stand beside her. She said, "You don't look well, dear."

Emily felt so ill that she couldn't reply. To her shame, the illness overwhelmed her, and she managed to cast the little she had eaten at dinner over the railing.

Mrs. Reynolds said, "It's all right, dear. You're seasick. You go into your cabin to lie down. May I help you?"

Emily nodded. Her face flaming, her eyes tearing, she took Mrs. Reynolds's arm.

℘℘

CARO PULLED HER KERCHIEF low on her forehead and regarded her hands with dismay. The coffee was already wearing off. Perhaps she could wear Emily's gloves. Or keep her hands in her pockets.

The servants ate at a table on the deck that was placed awkwardly near the kitchen. The smell of the food—and the refuse—interrupted the servants' meal, as did the waiters, who carried tray after tray of food past them to the salon above.

The meal was simple but generous, black-eyed peas without rice, cooked with salt pork and too much grease. Even the greens were overcooked and swimming in fat. Caro took a piece of cornbread and ate it plain.

"Is that all you eat?" asked an older woman, a mauma from the Low Country by her speech.

"Not hungry."

"You never been on a boat before?"

"Not on the open sea."

"Where you bound?"

"Missus has kin in Philadelphia."

The woman leaned forward and dropped her voice, despite the noise from the kitchen and the rattling roar of the steam engine. "I hear that colored people in Charleston run to freedom in Philadelphia," she said.

Caro dropped her eyes and shook her head. "Wouldn't know," she said, as stony as Sophy.

"I hear that a colored family get put off the boat. Say they free, but the captain think they runaways."

Caro felt as though she would choke. She said, "Haven't got any idea." She cursed Emily's foolishness. They would stay in the cabin for the rest of the journey if she had anything to say about it.

❧❦

WHEN SHE RETURNED TO THE CABIN, she found Emily lying on the bed, her shoes off, her hand over her eyes.

"Is you all right?" Caro said, remembering the pretense.

Emily groaned. "Seasick."

"Set up and let me help you."

Emily groaned again. Caro sat on the bed and dropped her voice to a whisper. "What's the matter, Emily?"

Emily didn't bother to lower her voice. "Sick as can be, and I'm not getting up until I feel better."

❧❦

BY EVENING, EMILY HADN'T IMPROVED, and although Caro hated to see her so ill, she was relieved that supper in the salon was out of the question. "I'll tell them that you're sick and that you want supper in your cabin," she told Emily firmly. Even though Emily groaned, she did not refuse.

Caro made her way to the kitchen, where one of the waiters, used to seasick passengers, assured her that it was no trouble to assemble a tray. He was a white man with a Yankee accent, and as she waited at the table reserved for the servants at their meals, Caro wondered what it would be like to be addressed politely by white people day in and day out.

The waiter returned with the tray, the plate covered with a metal dome. He gave her more than a passing glance as he handed it to her, and suddenly Caro hated that anyone would look at her because he might recall her.

She walked carefully down the passageway and up the stairs to the cabin deck, not used to the ungainly tray. As she reached the promenade, she heard footsteps behind her. A man's steps, judging from the tread of the boots.

Don't be a fool, she told herself. Anyone might walk along here. But she was wary.

When she turned to take the passageway to the cabin, the footsteps followed.

She thought, *His cabin is along here somewhere. It's nothing.*

But when she stopped before their cabin, the footsteps stopped as well. Unable to open the door with the tray in her hands, she had to set the tray on the floor. As she straightened, she turned her head.

He lounged against the wall a few feet away, taking his ease as though he were about to light a cigar. He watched as she opened the door and picked up the tray. In the room, she set the tray on the dresser.

As she shut the door, he was still there, watching, as though making a note of the cabin.

Shaking, she brought the tray to Emily, who sat up and said, "Is that toast? I believe I could eat a piece of toast."

Caro fell into the armchair that she had pulled close to the bed. "Someone followed me when I brought up the tray."

"Followed you?"

"A man in a frock coat."

"Dapper-looking? Dark whiskers?"

Caro nodded.

Emily stared at the toast in her hand. "I met him in the salon. He says he's a broker from Orangeburg County, but I know better."

Caro said, "He's the slave catcher."

Emily's hand trembled so badly that she had to set her toast down. "Yes," she said.

SO)CR

THEIR CABIN WAS SITUATED TO show them the setting sun, and as the last glow of dusk entered the room, so did the air, a pure smell of salt this far from the coast. Emily rose to stand at the window. "I feel better, breathing the air," she said, but she clutched the windowsill as though she were still dizzy.

The knock on the door alarmed them both. Emily turned, but Caro said, "I go," disguising her voice for whomever it might be. She asked through the door, "Who is it?"

"Ship's doctor," said a muffled voice.

"Didn't send for the doctor," Caro said.

"Mrs. Reynolds asked me to inquire."

Emily asked weakly, "Mrs. Reynolds? Is she there?"

"She sent me," said the voice.

But Caro opened the door to a dapper man in a frock coat whose whiskers curled darkly around his face.

He didn't grab her wrist to manacle her. Instead, in a pleasant tone, he asked, "Is your missus here?"

He was subtler than she realized. He had been quiet all those months in Charleston, and he would be quiet now.

Caro looked down, acutely aware of the way that her coffee-ground dye had faded since this morning. She would be subtle in return. "Sir, she ain't feeling well."

"It's very important that I speak with her. Please tell her that Mr. McHenry is here to see her."

He wanted Emily, too. And he was reluctant to use force to capture a lady. Caro turned to say to Emily, "Missus, there's a Mr. McHenry to see you, and he insist on it, even though I tell him you ain't well."

Emily braced herself against the wall beside the window. She raised her head. "It's all right. I'll see him." She took the few paces toward the door.

Mr. McHenry stood outside in the passageway. "May I come in, ma'am?" he asked. Still that low, pleasant, honeyed voice.

"Sir, this is a lady's private room."

"This is private business, ma'am. I don't wish to discuss it in the passageway."

Emily hesitated. She said, "You may come in but only if I leave the door ajar."

He stepped into the room without replying and stood as though he belonged there. Caro's stomach tightened, as though she had caught Emily's queasiness.

He gave Caro a long, appraising gaze, the professional look of a dealer in enslaved flesh. He said to Emily, "Your servant is very like a runaway advertised in the Charleston papers."

Emily laughed, as though he had offered her a beau's pleasantry. She said, "That can't be. She's been with me for years. I've always known her whereabouts."

Mr. McHenry appraised Caro again. She felt sick with fear, as she had before Lawrence Jarvie. She thought, *He came alone, and quietly, because he knew Emily was ill and thought I was unlikely to fight.*

If she screamed, if she resisted, if she fled, he would call a hullabaloo, and she would be in shackles in minutes, bound for auction, and Emily would be arrested, bound for jail and trial in Charleston.

Caro slipped her hand into her pocket and drew out the little velvet bag. She handed it to Emily.

Smiling, Emily asked, "Do you have a wife, Mr. McHenry?"

"I do, but what does that matter here?"

Emily opened the bag and let the earbobs spill into her palm. Even in the low light of sunset, the diamonds flashed and the gold gleamed. "Perhaps she would like these," she said.

He looked at the earbobs. "Do you know what they're worth?"

Emily smiled. "They were a gift from my mother. I never thought about it."

His gaze went from the earbobs to Caro, who stood mute, her eyes cast down. "They're worth as much as that slave of yours."

Still smiling, Emily said, "I had no idea." She closed her fingers over them and extended her hand to McHenry. "Take them. I'm sure your wife will like them."

He opened his hand for the earbobs and let them rest there. The diamonds sparkled and the gold gleamed. "I reckon she will," he said, closing his hand over the jewels.

He slipped the earbobs in his pocket, and Caro was suddenly sick with fear again. Would he pull out a pistol? Would he raise the alarm? But he removed his hand and said, "I've been very much mistaken." As he left, he doffed his hat to Emily. "A good evening to you, Mrs. Morris," he said, as Emily closed the door.

☙◊❧

THEY SPENT THAT NIGHT IN FEAR, starting awake and waking each other, thinking that they heard a tap on the door. They remained in their cabin the next day, too worried to care that they hadn't eaten.

When the knock on the door came, it was Mrs. Reynolds. She asked Caro, "Are you all right?"

"Yes, ma'am," Caro said, her head down. The coffee had worn off, and she was her usual ivory color.

Mrs. Reynolds entered the cabin. She asked, "Mrs. Morris? How are you?"

Emily, who was tired and hungry and the worse for wear, sat up in bed. She said, "A little better but not well enough to walk about."

"Should I ask the clerk to bring you something?"

"No, Mrs. Reynolds. I'm all right."

Mrs. Reynolds said, "I saw that man at your door last night. The broker. Did he trouble you?"

"No, Mrs. Reynolds. He thought he knew me from Charleston, but he was wrong."

"Was he inebriated?"

Emily was trembling. "No, just forward."

"He won't trouble you again."

For a wild moment Caro thought, *He's fallen overboard, or he's been arrested.*

"Since the boat docked at Baltimore, I haven't seen him."

Still trembling, Emily said, "So he's gone."

"Yes, dear."

Emily lay back on her pillow. "I believe I'll rest for a while," she said. "I may want supper later."

Mrs. Reynolds patted her arm. "You do that, dear."

They stayed in the cabin until the ship was well past Baltimore. The sea, which had been a grayish blue, was now gray with a tinge of green, and the birds that swooped over the water were unfamiliar.

They stood close together at the window, watching as the birds followed the ship, diving toward the water in its wake. Caro thought, *Everything will be different in the North, even the birds.* She thought of the hiss of the turkey vultures and for a moment felt a twinge of regret that she might never see them again.

છ્ઉિ

THEY DISEMBARKED IN PHILADELPHIA in midmorning to a late summer day that held a whisper of the autumn to come. The dock in Philadelphia was a crowded place, much more heavily traveled than Charleston, and everyone in the crowd seemed to be in a hurry. Emily paused and beside her, so did Caro, trying to get her bearings as people jostled her in their rush to get wherever they hoped to go.

"How will Mr. Aiken find us?" Caro asked Emily.

Emily stood still. All the journey's weariness showed in her face. "He'll find us," she said, and she began to walk the wharf.

A man came through the crowd, breasting it as though he were swimming the ocean, so intent on his search that people stood aside to let him pass. His frock coat was unbuttoned, and his bright-red cravat, which was about to come undone, streamed behind him as he hurried. When he came close enough, his bearded face blossomed into a grin of delight, and he held out his hands to Emily. He clasped them. "Emily, dearest Emily," he said.

"Joshua, beloved," she said, her eyes brimming.

He embraced Emily so tightly that he lifted her in the air and kissed her with such vigor that her bonnet slipped from her head to fall onto her shoulders. They held each other like that, cleaving together, without speaking.

When he released Emily, he straightened his cravat and composed himself. He turned to Caro. Holding out his hand, he said, "Miss Caroline Jarvie. I am overjoyed to see you, too."

"The feeling is mutual, Mr. Aiken."

At Joshua's elbow stood a short woman in a plain black dress, her brown face welcoming above the white collar that was her only adornment. He said, "This is Mrs. Williamson, a good friend, who is also a good friend to those who travel north. She can help you."

Mrs. Williamson smiled and laid her hand on Caro's arm in a caress as tender as a mother's. "Come with me," she said. "I'll take you home."

"Where is that?" Caro asked.

Mrs. Williamson smiled. "Oberlin, Ohio," she said.

Historical Note

This novel is based on a now-forgotten aspect of antebellum Charleston's history: the status of people of color, free and slave, and their fate during the reenslavement crisis of the summer of 1860 on the eve of the Civil War.

Free Persons of Color

Visitors to antebellum Charleston were struck by the sheer presence of so many black people on the streets of the city comporting themselves with dignity and confidence as though they were free. They did not know so many of them were truly and legally free. Charleston was unique in the antebellum South in having a substantial community of free persons of color, or FPCs, as they were designated in the city directory and the census. Most FPCs had either been manumitted by their masters or allowed to buy their freedom. Many of them were their masters' children and were given special assistance by doting or guilty fathers.

One of the foremost FPCs in antebellum Charleston was a man named Anthony Weston. He had begun life as the slave of Plowden Weston, a wealthy planter. Plowden Weston freed "Toney," as he was then known, and acknowledged him as a son in his will. Anthony Weston became prosperous as a millwright; by 1860, his estate was worth $40,000.

The FPCs of Charleston considered themselves an elite separate from the enslaved and the dark of skin. They practiced skilled trades—the free black Westons were well-known as tailors and dressmakers. They accumulated property, owning houses and land. They owned slaves. While some of them owned their own kin—

Maria Weston, a free woman who owned her husband, was a notable example—others used their slaves as servants and capital assets, just as white slave owners did.

The FPCs of Charleston prided themselves on their education, cultivation, and refinement. Like the white planter families who were their relations, they educated their children, sending girls and boys alike to academies for free black scholars. The young men of the FPC community joined debating societies—the Clionian Debating Society was the best known—where the topics of debate echoed the curriculum of Charleston College. They amused themselves as the planter families did, at parties, picnics, and balls, where they mingled with each other and arranged marriages within their small circle.

They consciously set themselves apart from the black and the slave. They founded the Brown Fellowship Society, a beneficent organization that provided for their burials, and even in death, they insisted on lying beside their peers. Slaves were buried in the adjacent but separate Black Fellowship Society cemetery. While they were not admitted as citizens in South Carolina—they could not vote or serve on juries, and they were levied with a capitation tax—the FPCs were keen in their sentiment that they were different from, and better than, persons who were slaves.

Nominal Slaves

In addition to the FPCs, Charleston was home to a much larger group of persons of color who were slaves according to a strict legal definition but who lived with varying degrees of freedom.

Beginning in the early nineteenth century, the state of South Carolina made freeing a slave increasingly difficult. By 1820, badly shaken by the "uprising" organized by Denmark Vesey, the South Carolina Assembly enacted legislation that insisted that all petitions for manumission be approved by the entire body. In the forty years between the Vesey uprising and the outbreak of the Civil War, only one such petition was approved: it was for the man who had informed on Vesey himself. The old practice of freeing a slave in a will became legally impossible.

The status of Lydia Weston, whose master died in 1821, was the result of South Carolina's draconian approach to manumission. She was no relation to Plowden Weston, but he made provision to free her because she had nursed him through a long illness. However, her legal status did not deter her from living as though she were free. She paid the capitation tax levied on FPCs. By 1840, she had accumulated property, including two slaves; the slaves were gone by 1850, but the property remained in the family throughout the nineteenth century.

A much larger group of Charleston slaves were unambiguously enslaved, but they were allowed a day-to-day freedom unthinkable on a plantation in the countryside. They were usually slaves with a skilled trade: men who were carpenters or masons or women who were dressmakers or laundresses. They were allowed to make their own contracts for work ("hiring out") and their own living arrangements ("living out"). Their owners took half of their wages and allowed them the flexibility to live and work as they pleased. They were identified—and protected—by wearing badges that proclaimed their status as skilled slave workers. The system of hiring and living out worked greatly to a skilled slave's advantage—it provided a day-to-day freedom that made life very different from that of a plantation hand or a house servant.

Being allowed freedom was very much a matter of a master's whim, and it was fragile. Slaves who changed hands—or whose owners changed their minds—could find their lives altered overnight. This was the case with Nancy Weston, who was likely related to the white Westons. She was housekeeper and companion to Henry Grimke, brother to Angelina and Sarah Grimke, South Carolina's most famous apostates on slavery. After Grimke's wife died, Nancy Weston became his de facto wife, bearing him three children. Henry Grimke died suddenly and bequeathed Nancy Weston and her children to his son, Montague, asking him that he treat them with kindness "as members of the family."

Montague left the care of Nancy and her family to his older sisters; they brought Nancy and her family to Charleston, built her a little house in Charleston Neck, and sent her sewing and washing to eke out a living. The Weston-Grimke family lived out of Montague Grimke's sight until he remarried, and his new wife insisted on new servants. He brought Nancy's older sons, Archibald and Francis Grimke, into his house as slaves, where they rebelled and ran away despite all his efforts to contain and punish them.

The Reenslavement Crisis

The reenslavement crisis of 1860, which conflated the status—and the fate—of free persons of color and slaves, had its catalyst in two events that white South Carolinians considered incendiary. One was the uprising at Harpers Ferry. Proslavery advocates saw it as a rebellion no different from the Vesey plot. The historical memory of Vesey—and of the rebellion in Saint Domingue, which had sent so many Huguenots to South Carolina as exiles—was exacerbated by the present-day possibility of insurgence fomented by northern abolitionists.

461

The fear John Brown aroused was not allayed by the presidential election of 1860. Proslavery feeling ran so high that white Charlestonians began to feel that no person of color should be free. Charleston was the site of the 1860 Democratic convention, which could not resolve the issue of slavery and ended without a presidential endorsement. During the convention, the Charleston militia was out in force, arresting black people regardless of their status.

Over the summer of 1860, the situation only became worse, and in August of 1860, the arrest rate soared. The old distinction between FPCs and other persons of color disappeared. Abuse and arrest could come to black or brown, slave or free. The FPCs of Charleston had learned how to live as anomalies in a South sharply defined by race. By August of 1860, there was no more middle ground.

For the FPCs of Charleston, the events of August 1860 had the same effect as Kristallnacht had on Germany's Jews in 1938. Their illusions about being different and protected were shattered. They gave up hope for a future in South Carolina. While FPCs had begun to leave Charleston in 1850, when the Fugitive Slave Act was passed, they fled Charleston after the events of August 1860.

Lydia Weston and her family left for Ohio, where they remained until the Civil War was over. Archibald and Francis Grimke, still enslaved, spent the Civil War as they had spent the years before it: rebelling and running away.

Further Reading

Johnson, Michael P. and James L. Roark. 2001. *No Chariot Let Down: Charleston's Free People on the Eve of the Civil War.* Chapel Hill, North Carolina: University of North Carolina Press.

Johnson, Michael P. 1986. *Black Masters: A Free Family of Color in the Old South.* New York: W. W. Norton.

Myers, Amrita Chakrabarti. 2014. *Forging Freedom: Black Women and the Pursuit of Liberty in Antebellum Charleston.* Chapel Hill, North Carolina: University of North Carolina Press.

Perry, Mark. 2002. *Lift Up Thy Voice: The Sarah and Angelina Grimké Family's Journey from Slaveholders to Civil Rights Leaders.* New York: Penguin.

Wikramanayake, Marina. 1973. *A World in Shadow: The Free Black in Antebellum South Carolina.* Chapel Hill, North Carolina: University of South Carolina Press.

If You Enjoyed This Book

Discover the Novels

I've written a number of books that share a theme: stories of white and black, slave and free, often connected by kinship, in the decades on either side of the Civil War. Visit my website for more information about my other books at https://www.sabrawaldfogel.com/books/.

The Low Country Series

The first book in the series: *Charleston's Daughter*. A Charleston belle with slavery on her conscience. A slave with rebellion in her heart. In South Carolina in 1858, no friendship could be more dangerous. As South Carolina hurtles toward secession, will their bond destroy their lives—or set them both free? Find out at mybook.to/CharlestonsDaughter.

The second book in the series: *Union's Daughter*. A renegade planter's daughter who abhors her past. A fugitive slave who fights for freedom. Will their battle for emancipation leave them casualties of war? Find out at https://www.sabrawaldfogel.com/books/unions-daughter.

The Georgia Series

The first book in the series: *Sister of Mine*. Slavery made them kin. Can the Civil War make them sisters? Find out at http://mybook.to/SisterofMine.

The second book in the series: *Let Me Fly*. The Civil War is over, but it isn't. For two women, one black, one white, a new fight is just beginning. Find out at mybook.to/LetMeFly.

Join the Inner Circle of Readers

Want to stay in touch? Get the first look at new books: covers, back stories, and prepublication sneak peeks. And as a thank-you, I'll send you a copy of my story, *Yemaya*. When a slaving ship meets an avenging African mermaid...what happens? Find out at https://www.sabrawaldfogel.com/sign-up/!

Leave a Review

Please let other readers know about this book by leaving a brief review at Amazon, Amazon UK, or Goodreads. Just a few lines will help other readers find the book and make an informed decision about it. It's the electronic version of telling your friends or your book club (although that's great too). Thank you so much!

Author Biography

Sabra Waldfogel grew up far from the South in Minneapolis, Minnesota. She studied history at Harvard University and got a PhD in American history from the University of Minnesota. Since then, she has been fascinated by the drama of slavery and freedom in the decades before and after the Civil War.

Her first novel, *Sister of Mine*, published by Lake Union, was named the winner of the 2017 Audio Publishers Association Audie Award for fiction. The sequel, *Let Me Fly*, was published in 2018.